DARK TAPESTRY

DARK TAPESTRY

First published 2000

ISBN 1-56871-179-4

Printed in Israel

About the Author

Ruthie Pearlman is the bestselling author of *Working It Out, Getting it Right, Making it Last,* and *Daniel My Son*. She lives in Golders Green, London, where she works from home as an Internet Web site designer, prenatal teacher, and lactation consultant. She has seven children, four of whom are married, and fifteen grandchildren. She has only recently returned to her first love, fiction writing, after almost ten years.

I dedicate this novel
to my newest young couple,
my daughter Tavya and her husband, Dov Harris,
who got engaged and married while I was working
on this book.

Tavya never failed to encourage me to forget the past
and go back to writing Jewish fiction after my long
hiatus since Daniel My Son.

Acknowledgments

Firstly, I want to thank Targum Press for giving me back my faith in myself as an author after my long absence. Representatives from Targum came to see me in our Jerusalem house asking me to write for them a full two years before I actually managed to break down the stone wall I had built up around my writing.

Thank you, Mikey Wulwick of the Jewish bookstore Torah Treasures in London. When I struggled to overcome my own inner writer's block and almost gave up, he encouraged me and pointed me in the direction of Targum.

Whilst writing the book I had help from various sources. The Golders Green Police Station problem-solving department was infinitely patient and helpful to me with my questions about police procedure.

Several Internet guru friends of mine were a useful source of high-tech information. Thank you, Christopher Sharp, Chris Needham, and Harry Broomhall for the hacking lessons!

I did my research on forensic science on the Internet.

I must thank my daughter Avigayil Hool from Bnei Brak who read the novel-in-progress while she was staying with us for Pesach 5759. Her constructive critique resulted in a much stronger ending to the book.

And last but not least, my husband, Joseph, who, when he finally found time to do his nitpicking act on *Dark Tapestry*, found many inconsistencies and anomalies despite being "nailbitingly" (his words) gripped. Thanks, Joseph, as always.

PROLOGUE

The morning Josh Hardman disappeared could not have come at a worse time for Ilana and Don Hardman. But then again, when is it ever a good time for one's firstborn son to disappear?

Especially when that firstborn son is also the last-born son.

And just eight years old.

DAY ONE

CHAPTER ONE

It was a surprisingly warm Sunday morning in May for North West London, the kind of morning that made Ilana want to throw caution to the wind, forget about work, and go out into the garden to plant the new and tender bedding plants she had been nurturing indoors in pots for the past few weeks. Logic told her it was too early for planting, but the desire to grow green and living things was strong in her on that fateful morning.

Ilana Hardman rose at seven as usual, showered, dressed recklessly (after a quick peek and sniff out the window at the unseasonable summery morning) in her first cotton shirt of the year and a long, flowing skirt, slipped her feet into mules, and padded into her son's room to wake him for cheder.

The bed was empty, but Ilana didn't panic. Don sometimes woke him early and took him to shul for the seven o'clock minyan. It was strange, though, because Don knew Josh hadn't gone to bed early enough. Shrugging and yawning, she went back to her room to finish getting ready for the day. The day which would change her life forever, so innocent and beautiful though it looked now.

Downstairs Ilana sipped coffee and read the news. The Hardmans subscribed to a serious paper, but even that had its fill of murder and mayhem to catch new readership and retain the interest of the existing one. She read the paper, sipped her coffee, and *tut-tutted* quietly from the insulation of her safe little world. Terrible things like she was reading in the paper didn't happen to families like hers, nice *frum* families from Golders Green. She took her time about her breakfast, enjoying the streaming sunshine through the window. Work could wait awhile.

Treacherous, treacherous Time. Dark tapestry of Time, why just show the sunny side when your darkness is there, waiting?

She glanced at her watch. Seven-forty. Don should be back from shul soon. It was time to prepare some breakfast for her menfolk and make Josh's sandwiches for school. Then she would get ready for work. Even though it was Sunday, she went into the office whenever she could to catch up on backlog.

Ilana worked for Don's small Web designer company, designing and preparing Web pages for uploading to the company server, using HTML and CGI scripts, and working with graphic designers and computer techies who handled the parts of the job at which she was less competent. She loved the work, loved being near Don all day and yet not too much in his pocket as their coworkers' presence served to dilute the closeness.

The front door opened. It was Maria, her Filipino cleaner, faithful after many years, loyal and dutiful.

"Morning, Ilana!"

Ilana greeted her cheerfully. There was no point in trying

to make Maria address her more formally; Maria was at least fifteen years her senior. She had been her mother's cleaner, willingly and lovingly passed on to Ilana eight years ago when Josh was born in anticipation of many babies filling this large sunny Golders Green house. "Your need is greater than mine, darling," Sarah Grossberg had said. But as it turned out, this wasn't true. Her mother still had Ilana's younger siblings at home while Josh remained an only child. The youngest were twelve-year-old twin girls, but her mother had generously given up Maria on condition that the loyal Filipino found her a replacement.

"Where's Josh?" Maria asked.

"Gone to shul with my husband," replied Ilana. Maria's knowledge of Jewish terminology, customs, and laws bettered that of many Jews.

"I see your husband coming home as I arrive in my car. Josh not with him," Maria offered airily and, taking the vacuum cleaner out, went upstairs.

The first vacuum is created by uncertainty. It settles gently, like powdered snow. There is no real sense of fear, not quite yet, not quite now. Things are still okay. Only a small shiver, a tiny tremor, a comforting knowledge that many explanations can still be found.

Ilana folded the newspaper and finished her breakfast. The sandwich for Josh's lunch was made and wrapped. A glance at the wall clock showed it was 7:50 A.M.

The door opened again, and she saw her tall, handsome husband striding past the kitchen door to put his tefillin away in his study. She looked at the empty space behind him for Josh.

"Hi," he said as he came into the kitchen, then stopped and looked around. "Where's Josh?" His words, not hers. A tremor, a mini-earthquake, caused her to shudder.

"I thought he was with you." Her voice was shrill, loud in the empty, childless kitchen. "I thought you took him to shul!" She jumped up. "Where is he?"

Don looked concerned. "Are you sure he isn't in bed and you didn't notice? Or maybe he fell out and is underneath?"

Both parents took the stairs two at a time. They stood in the small single room which echoed its nothingness.

Don peered under the bed. Ilana patted and patted again the racing car cover. Fearful, she opened her son's wardrobe to see if he might have become trapped inside. Don looked out of the window at the ground outside.

"Oh, no," Ilana said. "Don't say it."

"He's not there," Don said.

Small relief, quickly extinguished. The couple raced around the house, opening closets, peering into hiding places, possible traps, the freezer, the roof space, all the while calling Josh's name. Maria stood with the vacuum cleaner, keeping it silent in case Josh should reply. She kept repeating inanely, "I told Ilana, I see you coming home from shul and Josh not with you." Ilana wished she would be quiet.

"Maybe a friend? Maybe he went over to Moishie or David or..." Don spoke with a desperate calmness that did not reach his eyes.

Ilana began calling the boys Josh had painstakingly entered into the electronic personal organizer he had received for his birthday present. It was a long shot. Josh was only eight years old. An only child, still clingy and dependent, he never went anywhere without telling his parents.

None of Josh's friends had seen him since Shabbos afternoon the day before except David, who had played with him after *minchah* until both boys were called in to go to bed.

Each mother expressed concern and offered comfort. "I'm sure he'll be fine. Probably just gone somewhere like the kosher store to buy nosh. My Yossie has started doing that before school. They get *so* independent at *such* a young age, don't they?"

Ilana murmured, "Yes, they do," thinking, Josh never goes anywhere alone and certainly not to the store.

At nine the Hardmans called the police.

CHAPTER TWO

North West London's Orthodox community, a neighborhood of homes, shops, shuls, schools, and other communal facilities, extended its tentacles south, touching Hampstead, almost to the famous untamed parkland known as the Heath. In the north it joined with Hendon, its dividing seam the busy North Circular Road. Comprising a hotchpotch of between-the-wars detached houses, similarly dated semidetached homes, apartment buildings, and some newly built or renovated luxury homes, Golders Green was home to a multiethnic community. A large percentage of Kenyan Asians, an influx from the reign of Idi Amin, mixed smoothly with Japanese, Indians, and Pakistanis to create the main non-Jewish element in the suburb.

The Asian community did not pose any antisemitic threat that could be observed, save for a possibly underhand attempt to put local Jewish food stores out of business by opening up a large kosher supermarket of its own. Local rabbis tried to discourage their flock from frequenting this store, but were not always successful in achieving a blanket boycott.

Jewish grocers continued to ply their trade and thrive side by side with the infiltrators, the latter mainly attracting the slightly left-wing and out-of-area Jews who liked to take advantage of the price cutting war.

It seemed to Ilana Hardman that only a few short years ago there wasn't even a pizza parlor in the neighborhood, never mind a coffee shop and a choice of other eateries. Now pizza parlors abounded, both in Golders Green and neighboring Hendon. Kosher food stores seemed to be opening almost daily. To Ilana Hardman, Golders Green was London's Boro Park. Her American visitors who came to see how the British managed to survive in such "primitive" surroundings just laughed indulgently and longed for home. Rather than another Boro Park, they thought, North West London had just clawed its way out of the primeval slime.

Clothing stores that catered to the Orthodox dress code did not exist in North West London, aside from those enterprising few who sold American, Canadian, and Israeli imports from their own homes. It was not unknown for a British bride and her family, if they had the means, to shop transatlantic.

Ilana was an attractive, slender woman in her late twenties, sincerely Orthodox but not chassidic. Her interest in worldly things such as the Internet, which gave her and her husband, Don, their livelihood, set her up as marginally "modern," whatever that term had come to mean. She wore shoulder-length straight wigs on weekdays and sometimes a curly one on Shabbos in a smoothly mixed brown-red color. Her eyes, which were blue, were slightly shortsighted, but she would blushingly admit to vanity and wore her glasses only when doing close work on a computer.

The Hardman home, centrally placed for shops, the underground — London's subway system — shuls, and schools, was a mid-war, rambling detached affair, large but not luxuriously appointed, with a disappointingly small but neatly maintained garden. Ilana loved to garden. She loved feeling at one with nature as she dug her bare hands into the warm soil, tenderly placing plants within its welcoming environment. Maybe her love of growing things was partly due to the fact that her dream of having a large family so far hadn't come to fruition. Unusual in her community, Ilana was the mother of only one child, a son called Josh.

Josh Hardman had been born on a warm spring morning like this one, eight years previously; in fact, his birthday had just been. Don had never forgotten the enraptured look on his wife's face when she first held Josh. Nor had he ever forgotten the magical moment when he had first gazed on the face of his newborn son. The miracle of birth, renewed with each baby born to the world, seemed untainted by repetition. It could never be sullied by familiarity. It was utterly incredible, superbly wonderful, and Don cast his eyes heavenward and sent a prayer of thanks as he made the customary *berachah* on the birth of a son. If he had known that the coming years would not bring him subsequent children, his prayers and blessings would have been even more heartfelt.

Being the parents of an only child is only slightly harder than being that child. In the attempt not to spoil or overprotect, it is easy to allow the pendulum to swing the other way and be too harsh or deny those privileges a child from a larger family might enjoy without thought. However, Don and Ilana Hardman had done their research. They had consulted local *rabbanim* for spiritual guidance. And they had downloaded articles from Web sites devoted to the subject of only children and the pitfalls of raising them.

"More children may yet come," one rabbi recently told

Don. "Keep davening. Eight years is not forever. In the meantime, though, you're doing a great job."

It was true. Josh was blossoming. At eight he exhibited none of the classic only-child syndromes such as spoiled and demanding behavior, ultra-sensitivity, or inability to bond with his peers. He was popular, well adjusted, polite to adults, and definitely "one of the lads" with his peers. His dark hair and vivid blue eyes had taken the best of both parents' features and combined it in a good-looking package.

"If you're only going to have one," Ilana's mother, Sarah Grossberg, herself the parent of a large, rambunctious family, had pronounced, "at least you got it right the first time. Josh is perfect."

Ilana put this overeffusive gushing of praise down to typical Jewish mother syndrome and took it with a large pinch of salt, but deep down she was pleased and partially agreed with her mother. Josh was as near perfect a child as she could have hoped and prayed for.

"Except for his teeth," she had said laughingly to Don. "Josh will need orthodontics when he gets older. His second set of teeth are coming in a bit crooked."

Don had smiled. "I'm sure it won't spoil his *shidduch* chances, but don't worry, they'll get sorted at the right time."

As Ilana phoned the police with trembling hands, the memories welled up and tears fell. Now she wondered if she ever would have to deal with braces and *shidduchim*.

☼ ☼ ☼

"Missing kid down Golders Green," the desk sergeant reported to the backroom boys. "Probably nothing. Kid's only been missing an hour and a half. Panicky parents."

Detective Inspector Colin Sommers looked up. "Hour and a half missing or an hour and a half since they noticed he was missing?"

"Huh?" said the desk sergeant.

"There is a difference, Potter. Kid could have been missing all night for all you know. For all they know. How old?"

"Eight."

"Eight. Crumbs. Too old for the parents to keep popping in, checking to see if he's still breathing, too young for him to be staying out all night keeping the parents up. Hmm. Eight is an age I don't like when they go missing. Put the call through, Potter."

"Yes, sir. Oh, and, sir, it *is* a boy. How clever of you to work that out." A sardonic grin as the desk sergeant put through the call.

A tremulous woman's voice, obviously fighting for control, told the story to D.I. Sommers. No, she didn't know exactly when her son went missing. She was asleep. So was he, as far as she knew. When she awoke, he was gone. Yes, the window was open; it was a warm spring night. No, he wasn't the sort of child who went anywhere without telling his parents. He was a bit of a mummy's boy. This last bit sent the woman over the edge. She started sobbing.

"Look, Mrs. Hardman, it's probably okay. Most cases are. Mostly they turn up within an hour or so. They've just gone on some jaunt or other. Remember, even if he hasn't so far done anything like this, there's always a first time, and the first time is when they scare you half to death. Then you yell at them for frightening you and cuddle them till they can't breathe and threaten them if they ever do it again. That's what usually happens."

A little teary laugh on the other end of the line, a hiccuping sob, wanting so much to be convinced.

"What's your name, Officer?"

"I'm Detective Inspector Colin Sommers, Mrs. Hardman."

"Detective Inspector Colin Sommers, you are being very nice, supportive, and encouraging. But let me ask you this: what if this isn't like 'most cases'? What then? What then?"

"We'll deal with that if and when. Don't worry. We have plenty of resources to help us."

"So you'll be able to find him?"

"Should do." One way or the other, he added silently to himself.

"He's only a baby." She started crying again. "I don't even know what clothes he was wearing. Maybe he was taken in his pajamas."

"You can have a look round his room, his closets, see what's missing. That will be useful for us, to know what he might be wearing. But try not to disturb things more than necessary, and don't clean up whatever you do. Okay?"

"Okay." Then she added, "What about those children who vanish and are never found?"

"Most are found," D.I. Sommers said. "Don't even think about him not being found."

"I can't understand how we didn't hear anything. His bedroom's right next to mine."

"Heavy sleeper, are you?"

"No, but Don, my husband, snores so I sometimes wear earplugs." Treacherous earplugs, my baby calling for me in the night and I could not hear.

"Well, there you are then. Listen. We'll be round shortly. In the meantime, don't touch anything in the room if you can avoid it. It might destroy vital evidence. Get ready an up-to-date photograph and try to work out what he was last wearing and when he was last seen."

"I know when he was last seen! I put him to bed myself!"

"We'll be round shortly."

The connection was severed. Ilana looked at Don, then at her hand, which was shaking.

"They're coming round soon."

"Good."

At the police station, Colin Sommers wondered if he should go to the Hardmans' himself or send Detective Sergeant White. As Detective Inspector, the job really fell to him. But as a fallen Jew, the thought of going back to Golders Green, to that tightly knit ghetto he had fought so hard to escape, the thought of getting involved again, of being sucked in by all that religious stuff, well, he wasn't very keen. No, not keen at all.

On the other hand, it was rare for an Orthodox Jewish kid to go missing like this. Especially at eight. Eight was a funny age and not funny ha ha. Funny peculiar. The whole thing was peculiar, and Colin Sommers didn't like it one bit. It had a bad smell to it.

Detective Inspector Sommers decided to brace himself for the inevitable and go to the Hardmans'. He reckoned he could withstand the influences of his past. He was long gone from that kind of thing. Nothing could touch him now.

CHAPTER THREE

Detective Inspector Sommers had avoided going to the Orthodox neighborhood for over ten years. He had moved to a nonreligious area to the north of Golders Green, where no Jews lived since there was no community to serve them. He had applied for a transfer to the local constabulary even further out, in rural Halford Village, but the Golders Green branch had put the spokes in. His immediate superior, Detective Chief Inspector Roger Willis, had called him into his office one day and told him outright that he would oppose the transfer request.

"But why, Roger?"

"We need you here, lad. You're the youngest D.I. we've ever had and probably the best, and you'd be totally wasted in Halford Village. For heaven's sake, man, the nearest you'll get to a serious crime out there is some old biddy's cat going missing."

"Maybe I want a peaceful life," Colin had protested. "And anyway, if Agatha Christie is to be believed, the most heinous murders happen in little rural English villages."

"Well, for a start, Agatha Christie talked a lot of rubbish most of the time, and anyway, Goldbergs Green" — he deliberately used the misnomer, making Colin wince — "is hardly the hotbed of London's criminal fraternity, is it. We haven't had a good murder here since that chemist did away with his brother- in-law by slipping powdered cyanide into his instant coffee."

Despite himself, Colin grinned. He had read about the case in the archives.

"Thing is, lad, we need you. And they don't."

So Colin had stayed, but he'd made jolly sure he avoided going into the ghetto that made up his past if at all possible. Though the police station served that area, it also served other, less religious neighborhoods in North West London, and to these neighborhoods Colin was content to divert his attention, giving the Golders Green patch to Sergeant Peter White. Colin was happy to give White the benefit of his experience when cultural or religious matters came up, although he always spoke as if he had never been part of the culture himself. He instructed White on not ringing doorbells on Saturdays ("They'll probably have the timer on, and it won't ring — better just knock"), on not telephoning on Saturdays or Jewish holidays or expecting the Orthodox Jewish residents to phone the station then. When White asked him how he knew so much about Jewish culture, Sommers would always answer, "Used to live next door to some when I was little. Used to go round their place to play."

Colin Sommers never admitted to anyone in the police force that he was Jewish. It was not something he wanted to think about, not something he was particularly proud of, and he had noticed some undercurrents of antisemitism among his colleagues, especially when discussing the wealthier

Golders Green inhabitants.

"Huge great big houses they got, some of them. I been inside. Furnishings like you wouldn't believe. Something out of a magazine. Kitchens bigger than my whole flat. And they come whining to us when the third of their silver candlesticks gets nicked. Diddums."

"Crime is crime," Sommers defended. "If it's a wino or the Queen. Still a crime."

Deep down he felt half guilty and half angry at his people for their overt displays of wealth. Words rang in his ears, words from his youth, words he tried — and failed — to forget.

"You Jews think you're so much better than the rest of us."

"No, we don't!" he had protested defensively.

"Yes, you do. Otherwise, why won't you marry non-Jews? And why do you live in such posh houses and have so much money?"

"Not all of us have money. And anyway, we give a lot of charity," he had responded lamely, but the other had snorted derisively. For him the case was proven and closed.

Colin had never forgotten that exchange and his total helplessness at replying to it. Maybe they did think themselves better than anyone else. Maybe this was all the more reason for cutting himself off from them. He reasoned his own doubts away, and he was comforted.

Detective Inspector Sommers was only twenty-six years old, young to have achieved that level of promotion, a prodigy. His peers in police academy had called him a swot; his senior officers and teachers had called him a fast learner and a dedicated and gifted student. His mother had once described him as her "genius," but he firmly pushed that out of his head. Anything that reminded him of his roots had been given a large dose of weed killer. Besides, it wasn't true. He knew he wasn't a genius or even gifted. He was a methodical and ploddingly determined student, determined to do well and achieve. Most of his fellow students did the minimum to get by; he went the full route.

Now Colin lived a totally secular life. His girlfriend, Lucy, wasn't Jewish, and he had never shared with her the secrets of his past. They spent their free time, which wasn't much, together. Lucy was a journalist on the local newspaper and was given to interesting stretches of imagination when interviewing her "victims," who were generally local wannabe celebrities. Her latest piece had been about an elderly man who had self-published his memoirs. He had been told at a writing circle he attended weekly, where he bored the other members reading out a chapter each session, that memoirs were only fascinating if they referred to someone famous, and that his, about a nondescript sort of life, coming of age in World War II, would be of little interest. Undaunted, he carried on and used his life savings to publish the book himself. As a result, he had no distributor, so he carted suitcases of the masterpiece around with him wherever he went and accosted total strangers with heavy sales talk until they either fled in panic or bought a copy just to shut him up.

Finding herself in agreement with the general public about the book itself, Lucy took the human interest angle and made a fascinating study of an old man who was determined to be a writer against all odds. The old man was a great character; his inability to write did not detract from his endearing nature and eccentric ways. The book was almost incidental to the piece itself, but Lucy knew that a bit of publicity in the right places never came amiss, so she gave it the best write-up she could while staying precariously just this side of the truth.

Lucy was a sharp, intelligent, and extremely talented journalist, probably wasted on the local rag. But she liked it because it gave her a certain amount of freedom of expression and also freedom from the dog-eat-dog world she knew she would encounter in the higher echelons of the national press. She would have probably been at her best doing an investigative piece into a murder or miscarriage of justice, but those were thin on the ground in Golders Green, and she had only been on the editorial staff a year, having moved up to those giddy heights from the slush pool of copy typists who eked their lives out entering data into computers.

For Lucy Colin had invented a past, one he liked better than his own, and this was the past he'd shared with her. Aside from his distaste for getting drunk on his night off, he displayed not a single inherent Jewish characteristic. He was working on the drinking; it seemed both churlish and prudish to keep refusing to join in the off-duty revelry down at the pub. He might yet conquer this final Jewish inhibition.

He drove toward the Hardmans' slowly, driving unwillingly into his own past. In the back seat of the car was a forensic man called Joe Willers who was expert in collecting and analyzing evidence. Joe never said much, which normally suited Colin just fine. Right now, though, he needed to be distracted from his disturbing thoughts. Looking at the familiar yet alien streets, his mind drifted inexorably into memories that made him intensely uncomfortable. The men in the street, black-hatted, dark-suited, and bearded; the women, long-skirted, bewigged, some elegant, some frumpy, all modestly attired. And children. Preschoolers, toddlers, babies everywhere. In the nonreligious or non-Jewish neighborhoods, there weren't nearly so many kids, thought Colin. He supposed the Hardmans also had a houseful of screaming kids. Probably had to do a role call to find out one was missing. He gave a cynical sneer as he drove slowly through Golders Green.

The Hardmans' house surprised him. It was on the large side, granted, but it had none of the trappings of luxury. Unencumbered by large metal security fences, tall hedges, or long paths, it stood on a corner, exposed, its front door opening almost directly onto the pavement. A simple, tidy but unmanicured garden could be viewed through an old side gate. The only sign that children lived there was a small bicycle lying on its side on the lawn. In the front, neatly pruned rosebushes burgeoned upward, ready for their summer's blooming.

Stepping the few inches from pavement to front door, Colin Sommers rang the bell. His inner mind registered the mezuzah. His conscious mind refused to acknowledge it. Joe stood reverently a few paces behind him, whistling quietly to himself.

The door was opened at once by a red-eyed and tearful woman, young, wearing a cotton T-shirt and long skirt, her hair — no, her wig — was shoulder length and slightly mussed.

"Detective Sommers?" she asked. When he nodded, her relief was palpable, as if his very presence was proof of the end of the nightmare being in sight. She looked at Joe.

"This is Sergeant Willers. He's our forensic man." Again the woman looked pathetically grateful when she saw Joe's steel briefcase with its hidden mysteries, which were, to her eyes, just waiting to solve everything at one stroke.

If only that were true, he thought ruefully as they stepped into a decidedly nonglamorous hallway and living room. Well furnished and comfortable, yes. Functional, certainly. But luxurious, expensive, glamorous, certainly not. The two men sat

down as bidden on a battered-looking leather sofa.

A tall, dark-haired man came into the room, handsome, wearing glasses and a short dark beard, neatly trimmed. Colin stood up again, not an easy feat from that soft, squishy sofa. Joe remained seated, staring into space, as if manners were not part of his brief.

"Don Hardman. How do you do?" An accent. Where from? The United States? Canada? They shook hands. Colin introduced Joe and sat down again. Don took a dining-room chair, turning it from the table to face them. The wife did likewise, twisting a bunch of sodden tissues in her lap with white-knuckled fingers.

"I know the last thing you want to do at this moment is fill in a form," Colin began, "but it's policy, and it helps us with details we might otherwise forget, like a full description, any distinguishing marks, whether he wore glasses or not, a watch. We'll also want to know who saw him last, what clothes he was last wearing, and, of course, a recent photograph if you have one. I can help you fill it in if you don't feel capable."

"Yes, please," Ilana said. "I don't think I could write a straight word at the moment."

As Colin helped the Hardmans fill in the lengthy missing persons form, his cynicism disappeared. This was an only child, much loved and much wanted.

Colin finished filling in the form and looked it over. "In cases like these, we have to start from the assumption that the child has gone missing voluntarily," he said.

Ilana's eyes blazed. "But he wouldn't! He has never gone anywhere on his own. He's just a baby!"

"Yes," Colin said patiently, "but we cannot assume foul play unless there is proof of it. Have you checked with his school? With his friends to see if he is there?"

"I have phoned all the friends I can think of," Ilana said, getting increasingly frustrated with his unwillingness to take her seriously. "I didn't call the school because it hadn't started when he went missing, so no one would have been there."

"All right, then. Let's take a look at his room."

They all trooped upstairs. "At this point, we are just looking, not touching. I hope nothing has been touched or cleaned up in here. Valuable clues could be destroyed or evidence spoiled."

"No, no. As soon as we realized he was missing we told Maria to stop vacuuming. We haven't done any cleaning or anything. Then you told us not to touch anything, so we didn't even go into the room."

"Well, let's take a look."

They stood in the emptiness of Josh's bedroom, listening to the absence of a child. The room was not only empty, it was like a vacuum, sucking things into itself, a black hole. Colin shivered involuntarily.

Joe looked at the open window. "This been open all night, has it?"

These were the first words they had heard him utter, and they all jumped. His voice had a grinding, hoarse quality, as if someone had run his vocal chords over a cheese grater.

"Yes, it was a lovely, warm night, and Josh doesn't like it when it's stuffy."

Joe took a pencil out of his pocket and gently pushed at the window. It swung slowly on a hinge.

Ilana put a hand to her wig distractedly and pushed at it. "I don't think I left it open so wide. I always leave it fastened on the second hole, in case he might..." Her voice trailed off.

Colin and Joe looked at her.

"Mrs. Hardman, with all due respect" — Colin was using a highhanded tone he hated, but he didn't seem able to stop himself — "this window has no bars. What is to prevent a child from falling out?"

"He's a sensible child, Detective Inspector," Don said firmly. "He knows about safety, and he's not a toddler anymore that we need to put up bars on the windows. And it is exactly because he's a sensible boy that we do not for one minute imagine that he has gone off willingly without telling us."

Colin hmmed. Joe, meanwhile, was engaged in a close examination of the windowsill and surrounding area.

"Can you work out what he was wearing when he was last seen?" Colin asked.

Ilana looked in drawers and cupboards which Colin obligingly opened with a pen.

"Hard to say, but I don't see anything missing besides the pajamas he wore last night."

"What did they look like?" came Joe's voice from the window.

"Red and black with Batman on the front."

Joe was looking at the catch on the window. Out of his pocket he took a pair of tweezers and a clear plastic evidence bag. He tweezed something and bagged it.

"Did it rain last night?" he asked no one in particular.

"I think I heard it rain about half past three," Colin said. "I was awakened by the patter against my blinds. Didn't last long, though."

"There's mud on the windowsill. Just a bit. Looks like someone's tried to clean up."

"We'll have to check this. Could be your son was mucking about with muddy shoes last night."

"It didn't rain till half past three, you said," Ilana protested.

"It might've earlier, too. I can't remember. Has to be checked."

Maria popped her head round the door.

"Wasn't me clean up," she said. "I didn't touch nothing, not even the washing."

"Washing? Was there any in the room?" Colin's head came up sharply.

"He always leave his socks. I always telling him to tidy up," Maria informed the policemen.

"Where's it now?"

"I leave it like you say. " She looked affronted at this slight on her cleaning abilities. "There." She pointed to a spot on the floor by the bed.

"Bag it, Joe," Colin said. Joe took out a larger plastic bag from his capacious pocket and put the socks in, using his pencil and tweezers.

"Have you phoned around all your family and friends? Anyone to whom Josh might possibly have gone?"

"Well, I didn't call my family. I didn't want to...to worry them."

"What family do you have, Mrs. Hardman?"

"My parents. They still have four unmarried children at home, and I have a married sister, but she lives in Israel."

Colin looked at Don.

"My family are all in the States," he said. Colin tried to place the twang. He had never been very good at accents.

"New York, sir?"

"No, my family is from a small middle American town in Iowa. Not a very big Jewish community there." He grinned. "Not every American Jew comes from New York, Detective."

Colin had the good grace to look sheepish. He cleared his throat and turned to Ilana. "Don't you think it's possible your son has gone to his grandmother or some relative?"

"Highly unlikely. My mother lives across a busy main road which he knows he isn't allowed to cross. Anyway, she'd call me and say, 'Is Josh meant to be here?' She has such a busy household of her own, and with me having only the one, it's only fair that she doesn't quite see why she should have my child there all the time as well. There's no one really his age there. My youngest sisters are twelve. Girls, of course. Well, sisters are, usually." A smile crossed her face and lit the ravaged expression for an instant.

"Worth crossing off your list, though?" asked Colin. He had seen enough of this before, well-meaning people who didn't want to trouble their families so they didn't phone them, and that's where the missing child had been all the time.

Ilana shot Don a panicked look.

"They'll have to know sooner or later," he said kindly.

Silently Ilana handed her husband the cordless phone she had been carrying around with her, just in case her son rang.

Did the presence of her family around her, silently supportive but unable to offer any tangible hope, make things better or worse? The dashing of that last trace of hope that maybe Josh had been at her mother's had engulfed her in despair. That, together with her mother's anguish joined with her own to make one, larger anguish which threatened to swallow the world. They sat downstairs, waiting for Joe to finish up with his steel box, tweezers, pencil, and whatever secrets they held. Sarah Grossberg sat with her arms around her daughter, but after a while Ilana couldn't bear it, couldn't bear the closeness, the smothering, and got up. "Anyone for coffee?"

"I'll help you," said her mother, jumping up.

"I'd rather go alone, thanks."

In the kitchen, she leaned her head against the cool of the refrigerator. On any other day, at this time... A glance at the overhead clock. Eleven o'clock. Only eleven? It seemed like forever since she went into Josh's room and found him gone. She should be busy at work, happily involved in her safe, cocooned little world. How long had he been missing? What time had that dark, secret someone stealthily removed the future from her life?

Voices from the living room. "Darling, the forensic man is finished."

Ilana brought mugs of coffee into the living room on a tray, along with a plate of cookies, semblances of normality.

"Did you find anything else?" Ilana asked Joe.

"Bits and bobs. You know how it is," Joe said with maddening vagueness. It was obviously an inside thing, nothing he would tell her directly, only Colin when she was safely out of earshot.

Colin caught the angry look on Ilana's face and said reassuringly, "We need to analyze samples back at the lab. We can't tell here and now if anything is relevant. We bag everything. Nine-tenths of it gets trashed at the end."

"What can I do?" she cried. "I can't just sit here and do nothing."

"There is very little anyone can do until we know more. I'll send one of my officers round to the school to speak to his classmates, find out if he had spoken to anyone about leaving home or if he seemed unhappy..."

"I'd know if he was," Ilana broke in, distressed.

"Sometimes kids tell their friends things they wouldn't dream of telling us oldies," Colin said, lumping his own generation together with Don and Ilana to let them feel he understood. "Meanwhile, does he keep a diary or a notebook, somewhere he might have made notes about his day, what he intended to do, that sort of thing?"

Ilana's face flooded with color. She had no idea if he kept a diary; he had certainly never spoken to her of it. She realized maybe she didn't know her own son as well as she thought she did. Colin saw her consternation.

"Don't worry. You might look around his room a bit, see if you can find a notebook or diary. But wear surgical gloves, if you have any, or use a pair of tweezers to pick things up with."

"I have some surgical gloves," Ilana said. "They're useful for gardening sometimes, when handling seeds and small plants."

"That's good, then. Use those."

Don looked at Ilana. "We have a computer at home. You can work from here and e-mail the pages in to the office if you like. I'd better go in."

"That's a good idea," Ilana said. Perhaps it would take her mind off Josh for a little while.

"I'll be along then," Colin said. "I'll be in constant touch, don't you worry. We won't rest till we find him."

"Thank you," said Ilana in a small, dead voice. Then she cried out, as if her effort at containing her despair had just given out, "There must be something else I can do!"

"There is," Colin said, and even as he uttered the words, he had no idea why he was saying them. "You can pray."

CHAPTER FOUR

Ten years ago, he wasn't called Colin. His name was Chaim. Chaim Sommers at sixteen was a handsome young man, rather marred by a surly, rebellious expression. Overlong blond hair flopped into his blue eyes, but he wore *payos* behind his ears, a black yarmulke, and a chip on his shoulder a mile high.

His parents, Rifka and Moshe Sommers, were typical Golders Green parents, if there was such a thing — devoutly Orthodox, middle class, British born. They had four other children, two younger, two older, all conventional, all toeing the line. Chaim thoroughly disapproved of his parents having so many children. His two brothers went to the local *chareidi* boys' primary school, where the most outrageous thing they did was to be cheeky to the teacher or not do their homework. His two sisters were in seminary in Gateshead, one a year ahead of the other, both thoroughly caught up in the spirit of the learning and the ambience.

"Chaim in the middle," his mother used to refer to him fondly, mussing his hair.

"Go to the barber," his father would yell at him angrily. "How can you put on tefillin with hair that long?"

"I can. See?" Defiantly he put on a Native American–style headband to keep the recalcitrant locks out of his face. Moshe's face was like thunder. Rifka turned hers away and sent up a silent prayer for guidance.

"Look on the bright side," Rifka's friends counseled her. "At least he puts on tefillin. He goes to minyan. He has a *chavrusa*. He does well in his studies, doesn't he?"

"Yes, he's a very bright boy. Probably my brightest," Rifka admitted.

"So he wears a headband. So he wears jeans instead of dark trousers. Is it the end of the world?"

"No," Rifka said slowly. "But why does he do these things if not to make a statement? A statement that he doesn't belong? Doesn't want to conform?"

To this her friends had no answer.

Chaim Sommers was popular among his peers. The slightly off-the-wall kids often are — they represent danger, excitement, a challenge to the status quo. He was always up for a dare, always the first in line for a prank at school and frequently defiant at home, too. Despite all this, he did go to shul, he did have a *chavrusa* every night, and he did take his *limudei kodesh* studies seriously.

"But," Moshe said to Rifka late one night when they had some rare privacy, "I've heard him discussing *Chumash, Nach,* Talmudic issues, and to be honest it frightens me."

"Why?" she asked, puzzled. "He seems to discuss them like a real scholar. I've heard him, too."

Moshe jabbed a finger into the air. "Exactly! Like a scholar. But not a Torah scholar. He learns Torah like a secular Bible scholar. He learns it like a piece of academic literature to be dissected, analyzed, and discussed in abstract terms. He doesn't learn Torah as if he believes. And that's what's so frightening. I've seen Bible scholars discussing whether or not Genesis can be taken at face value or if it is all allegory, that sort of thing. They nearly always come to the conclusion that it's mere allegory. He reminds me of that."

Rifka said in a small voice, "Surely not." She was a loving Jewish mother, after all, and this was very unpleasant to contemplate.

"He has an excellent brain, an analytical mind. Remember when he was small, how he used to take our clocks apart to see how they worked? We didn't always get them to work again, but we didn't mind. We wanted to encourage his inquiring mind."

"It is good, isn't it?" Rifka said doubtfully.

Moshe sighed. "Yes and no. We can't dissect God to see how He works, Rifka. Some things you just have to take on board without question."

Rifka was quiet for a moment. "You think that's what he's doing? Trying to dissect God?"

Moshe looked at her, his expression somber. "I hope to the bottom of my heart that I'm wrong."

One night, Chaim came home late and wouldn't tell his parents where he had been.

"Gimme some space, for heaven's sake," he snapped, then went up to his room and slammed the door.

Rifka stared up at the landing, trying to think of all the legitimate places her son might have been and why he wouldn't tell his parents.

Chaim didn't put his light on, welcoming the anonymity of the dark. He lay on top of his bed, fully clothed, smoking a cigarette. He didn't think his parents knew he smoked. He was always careful to leave the window open and air the room. In truth, he severely underestimated their astuteness. They couldn't mistake the smell of tobacco that clung to his clothes, his furnishings, his hair. Smoking, however, was the least of his problems right now. Young though he was, he was far from the only one in his class who smoked.

He thought about the night's events. He had been to a youth club that was rather more secular than religious in nature. He had been slowly drawn into attending this club by a boy he knew slightly who attended a non-Jewish school. The boy, Ben, had enraptured Chaim with his love of rock music and his ideas of fun. Chaim, both repelled and fascinated at the idea of this other world and the elusive attractions it held, had finally brushed aside the last of his inhibitions and guilt and gone there with Ben.

The club was dark, with strobe lighting and blaring music to which several dazed-looking youngsters were dancing apathetically. Chaim felt out of place with his yarmulke and *payos*, though the latter were tucked neatly out of sight. He stood around, drinking Coke and feeling awkward, watching, with part horror, part excitement, what was going on. Several times he reached up to touch his yarmulke and wondered if he dared slip it into his pocket. But this move was, as yet, beyond his capabilities.

Ben sauntered over and asked him how he was getting along.

"Oh, it's getting pretty late," Chaim said uncomfortably. "Maybe I'd better go."

"Lighten up, will ya?" Ben said crossly. "Here. Have some of this." He held out a can of beer.

Even in the semi-darkness Chaim could see Ben looked

different from the guy he had arrived with. He's drunk, he realized, and suddenly he was repelled. He roughly clenched his fists.

"Nah. S'okay," he said, and turned away.

"I knew it was a mistake, bringing you. You're a wimp. You want to go? So go! Back to your *frummy frummy* home, won't ya," Ben sneered, and walked off.

Chaim, stunned at the viciousness of this attack, blushed in the darkness. He knew he was being "uncool," but he didn't really like the idea of looking as out of it as Ben had. If he left now, Ben would have achieved a victory. Maybe in ten minutes I'll go, he said to himself.

He tapped his feet to the music, trying to blend in. Maybe he wasn't cut out for this. So what was he cut out for? It seemed like he didn't belong anywhere. He felt out of place in his home society and equally out of place here. Adrift, miserable, he slid his back down the wall until he was sitting on the floor. He looked at his watch, waiting for when he could legitimately slip away without handing Ben victory on a platter. Well, he thought, the way Ben looks right now, I doubt he'd notice if I left.

Someone slid down the wall next to him, a young man, older than himself by at least four years, his hair long and curly, with a goatee, looking rather like young William Shakespeare must have looked. Piercing blue eyes observed him curiously for a moment.

"Hiya." Then, to Chaim's horror, he yanked at Chaim's *payos*, exposing them.

"Are these *payos* I see before me?" he asked in a dreamy voice with a mock Shakespearean accent mixed with an American Midwestern drawl.

"Yeah," Chaim said sheepishly.

"Hey, and a *kappel,* too! I caught me a live one. I've always wanted to meet one, to talk to him, to find out what he really believes."

"Maybe I'm not your best example," Chaim said. "I'm kinda confused myself, to be honest."

"Perfect. The strong believers are boring. There's no chink you can get in through. I like 'em confused. It leaves me room to maneuver. Let's see if we can unconfuse you with a dose of my very own homespun philosophy. See? I even have the sandals." He wiggled his toes, showing his open sandals.

He offered Chaim beer. Chaim said no again, but this was a much weaker refusal. The young man grinned. The hook was baited, the line cast, and the fish was reeling in. "It's only five percent alcohol," he said. "Like lemonade."

Chaim was thirsty, so he accepted the can of beer and gulped at it. It was semisweet and refreshing. He finished it in three gulps. Then, somehow, there was another in his hand.

There followed an important philosophical discussion. Afterward, Chaim could not recall why it had seemed so vital, of such world-shattering significance. It was just that at the time nothing else seemed to matter except sharing deep thoughts with this Shakespeare look-alike. He even called him Shakespeare, and the young man didn't object.

"Call me Shake," he told Chaim seriously, then, after a pause, added, "Maybe I'm a reincarnation of William Shakespeare. I really like his plays, man. They speak to me, y'know? At school all my friends thought them mega-boring, but I found them deep, you know?"

Somewhere in Chaim's increasingly befuddled brain was the awareness that the beer was getting to him. If he had had the presence of mind to examine the beer cans he'd have seen that the alcohol content was fifteen percent, not five. Nevertheless, this guy seemed to make a lot of sense. All the niggly things that bothered him about his religion which, unlike any other, had undergone no change in the past five thousand years — all his deep-seated feelings came to the surface in the face of Shake's arguments. Even though a part of his brain spoke with his father's voice and said to him, "Son, there's an answer for all your doubts if only you'd let it in," right now he didn't want to let it in. It suited him just fine if that old answer stayed right outside the door in the cold.

Shake's long, curly hair and goatee had taken on the misty blurry quality of a Biblical prophet as portrayed by Hollywood. "Be free, man," Shake said. "It's the only way to be. Follow your own heart, not some old guy's ideas of what you should be doing, some old guy who's been dead for thousands of years. What can he know about the way we live today?"

"Nothing," giggled Chaim, taking another deep gulp of beer. "He didn't even have Space Invaders!"

The idea of playing Space Invaders on an ancient Biblical computer made Chaim and Shake totally lose control, and they rolled around the floor, giggling helplessly. The room spun and whirled. The strobe lighting made Chaim's brain curdle. The heavy metal music pounded in his skull. He began to feel nauseous and swallowed hard.

"Be free, man, be free."

"Glad you've lightened up. Pleased you came?" Ben's face came briefly into focus.

"Yeah," Chaim managed, trying to control the upsurge of nausea. He looked at Ben's figure, which seemed to be floating like a balloon.

Shake elbowed him in the ribs painfully. "Free from all that binds you down, man," he told Chaim in a slurry voice.

"Yeah," Chaim agreed, feeling the beginnings of an awful

headache but choosing to ignore it for now.

The pair rolled and giggled and felt so free, man, so very free. And they had decided on Very Important Matters, indeed. Yes, indeed, they had.

After a few moments, Chaim's newfound freedom manifested itself in a dive to a quiet corner in a room where he freely, and rather painfully, threw up. He knelt on the floor, trying to recapture the elusive magic that Shake had spun. He could not remember ever having felt this dreadful, even when he had the flu. The sour taste of the alcohol made him retch again and again.

Eventually he staggered to a sink, washed his face thoroughly, and looked at his reflection in the mirror hanging above it. A bleary-eyed stranger gazed back, a stranger with wild, tousled hair and red eyes in a pale face. He excused himself from the party, saying he had an early class the next day, and went home alone.

Lying on his bed now, the effects of the evening beginning to wear off, Chaim found it hard to remember all those important matters he and Shake had discussed, earth-shattering though they had undoubtedly been at the time. He was left feeling headachey, sick, irritable, and bereft, as if there was something he needed that was being withheld from him. This he largely attributed to the archaic practices of his environment, where people followed a religion that had been out of date for millennia. He thought of Ben and Shake and the youth club, which seemed to be dedicated to the pursuit of enjoyment and hedonism, and he smiled despite the beginnings of a nasty hangover. Somewhere inside him the words floated like golden feathers on a summer breeze. "Be free, man. Be free."

He drifted to sleep fully clothed, until the smell of smoldering bedclothes brought Rifka running in. She batted out the flames and woke her recalcitrant son, her fear for him overcoming most of her anger, but not all. He gazed groggily and uncomprehendingly at her as she stood at his bedside and yelled at him.

"You could have been killed! Bad enough to be smoking at all, but smoking in bed..." She hurled the cigarette out of the window. "Burn the house down, would you?" She switched the bedroom light on to make sure she hadn't missed any stray sparks. She patted and batted and pulled his bedclothes off the bed just to be on the safe side, ranting at him. All the while, Chaim lay there, watching her passively, stupefied, blank.

Rifka stopped in mid-rant and stared at him.

"I smell alcohol. Have you been drinking, Chaim?" she said sharply.

"Of course not. What do you take me for?" Chaim said. Well, it wasn't really a lie.

"I wish I knew, Chaim Sommers," Rifka said sadly. "I honestly wish I knew."

"Why don't you just get off my case?" Chaim muttered and turned over on the scorched under sheet so his back faced his mother. Rifka stared at his humped back, wondering whether to go around to the other side of the bed and force him to gaze at her. But she knew it would be fruitless. He was too large and strong for her to use force, and he would only turn away again or, God forbid, turn abusive. It would not be the first time that her beloved son had turned on her, face purple with suppressed rage, fists raised as if to strike her, although that ultimate act of aggression he had not yet reached. Rifka knew part of his aggression stemmed from his stage in life. He seemed uncomfortable in his own skin, unhappy, confused, and Rifka loved him but knew not how to help him.

To walk out now and leave the matter unresolved, would that not be an act of apathy unworthy of a Jewish mother? Was giving him his "space" tantamount to not caring enough?

Torn asunder by guilt and quandary, she stood there until at last he said, "Go on, say it, why don't you." Cruelly he mimicked her higher pitched voice. "Are you drunk, Chaim?" and turned to face her at last. Eye to eye, mother and son gazed at each other. His eyes were bloodshot and his face had a greenish tinge, as if he'd been sick. She knew.

"If you tell Dad, I'll...I'll..."

"You'll what, Chaim? What?"

He was not used to his mother like this, and it stopped him in his tracks for a moment. Rifka Sommers was usually an easily manipulated softie of a mother, desperately unhappy at what she thought was happening to her son but unable to put her foot down about it. It was his father's rages he feared the most.

He used the one weapon left in his armory, the one weapon he knew would wound her mortally.

Speaking slowly, deliberately, all the while looking straight at her, he said, "If you tell Dad, I'll leave home, and you'll not see me again as long as you live."

A deep intake of breath told him his barb had met its mark.

"But it's so wrong, Chaim. It can lead to worse things..." Her voice trailed off. Her knowledge of those "worse things" was confined to dark rumors and hearsay. She knew she was on shaky ground.

He snorted again. "Mother." He only called her "Mother" when he was at his most contemptuous. "It was just a few beers. That's it. And it was only the once. Some guy gave me some at the club."

"Club? What club? Not Pirchim, I'll bet."

He laughed scornfully. "Pirchim?" He spat the word out as if it disgusted him. "No, not Pirchim. Chevrat No'ar, actually. Ben invited me along."

"Chevrat No'ar? But isn't that..."

"Mixed? Not so *frum*? Yes to both."

"Your father would have a heart attack if he knew you'd gone there."

"Which is," Chaim said lazily as he sat up, "exactly why we aren't going to tell him. Now, do you mind? I'd like some privacy while I get undressed."

Rifka left his room without a word.

Guiltily she stuffed the burned bedclothes into a black garbage bag to dispose of them before Moshe smelled the scorching. Why am I doing this? she asked herself. Why am I being party to a deception I have no wish to condone? Why am I hiding my son's misdemeanors from his father? Why?

Even as she asked the questions, she knew the answers.

Because he's my son, and I don't want to lose him. I want to hang on to him at all costs, whatever the price I have to pay. Would it be better to tell Moshe all and risk Chaim leaving home? No. I must try to work things out myself.

Downstairs, in the study, Moshe sat over a Gemara. He looked up when Rifka came in.

"Chaim okay? You were up there a long time."

"He's okay. We had a little talk, that's all." The less I say, the fewer the lies.

Moshe raised an eyebrow. He knew if his wife and their son had a "little talk" it would hardly be about the weather.

"Talk? What about?"

Rifka smiled enigmatically. "Oh, just things." She knew Moshe would deduce wrongly but did not choose to enlighten him. She smiled at him and left the room, carrying the black garbage bag casually, swinging it.

She'd almost made it out when Moshe sniffed. "I smell something burning."

Her heart thumped. She turned to face him. "I burned some toast. Sorry!"

Do white lies count? I'm sorry, Hashem. I'm so sorry for telling lies. But I dare not tell the truth.

As it turned out, her lies were in vain. The next morning Chaim Sommers came downstairs with a backpack on. He was wearing jeans, sneakers, and a T-shirt.

"I'm sorry, Dad, Mum. I can't live this lie anymore."

Rifka stood like a stone. Moshe gazed at his son, openmouthed.

"What lie? What are you talking about, son?"

"I have to leave home for a while to sort my head out. I am having a lot of problems. I can't deal with them under this roof. Please try to understand."

"No, I don't understand," Moshe said, desperately trying to hold on to reality. He indicated the chair opposite him at the kitchen table. "Please. Sit down. Explain."

Chaim, standing, looked desperately uncomfortable. "I'm sorry, Dad, I can't. Just try to accept that I love you both, but I can't stay here."

"Where will you go? What will you do?" Rifka cried out.

"Ben said I can doss down at his place till I sort out what and where." Seeing their puzzled expressions, he added, "You don't know Ben. He goes to a *goyishe* school. I'll call you from there."

"You going to carry on going to school?" Moshe couldn't

believe he was having this conversation with his sixteen-year-old son. Sixteen! He was only a baby!

"No, well, not that school. I can legally leave school now. I've done my GCSEs. You'll get the results soon. I'll get a job, maybe. I dunno yet. Got to sort things. I'll be in touch. Really."

With that Chaim Sommers walked out of his family home, and out of his own life.

Staying at Ben's was strange for Chaim. Despite the confusion in his brain, he had been brought up Orthodox and to suddenly find himself living in a totally secular environment was akin to being dumped from a warm bath into a vat of icy water. Notwithstanding his negative attitude toward *frumkeit* when at home, when he was no longer pressured into it, he found himself clinging to it like to a comfort blanket. Ben watched in amazement as Chaim put on his tefillin each morning and davened assiduously. Sometimes he even went to minyan. Chaim never went to minyan when Moshe had pressured him to go. He chose a minyan where he was not well known — certainly he didn't go to his father's shul — but he went. He kept up his old *chavrusa*, having made him promise not to report back to his parents. He kept his own sterile kosher corner in Ben's kitchen, his own pots and pans. He found his *frumkeit* stronger now than it had been for many years.

During this period, he kept in constant touch with his parents, reassuring them that he was "sorting his head out" and would probably be home soon. Maybe, he thought, this is the answer. Take me away from having to do things, and then I want to do them.

He took a job waiting tables at a kosher eatery not far from Golders Green. The money was enough to pay for his food and board, but the hours were long and the work arduous. He longed for some time to himself. After he had saved up enough to tide him over for a few months, he quit the job.

"I'd like to look around for something that gives me a bit more time off, time to have fun," he told Ben.

"Good idea," Ben replied. They were sitting on the floor in Ben's living room, on giant cushions pushed up against the wall, smoking and drinking lite beer from cans. "Anyway," Ben continued, "I'm having a party here this weekend. Be a shame if you couldn't come because you were working."

"A party? What kind?"

Ben slid him a sly look. "The fun kind."

Shake was at the party. As soon as he saw Chaim, he cornered him and wasted no time in resuming work on his "new recruit." He chipped away at the battlements Chaim had built up around himself with fresh arguments and insidious reasoning that wriggled under Chaim's skin and fed, like parasites, slowly draining the lifeblood of Torah from him. The worst part was that this time, though he couldn't bear to get drunk again which would lower his resistance to the heresy Shake so ably spouted at him, to Chaim it still made an inordinate amount of sense.

By the end of the party, Chaim became Colin. That was the first step. A couple of days later, he began making excuses to his *chavrusa* and picking fights with him on the rare occasions they did still learn, until the *chavrusa* got the message. More steps followed, slowly, relentlessly. He stopped calling his parents. They tried to reach him at Ben's, but he was always "out." They came around looking for him and found Ben the gatekeeper refusing them entry, telling them their son was out.

"I don't believe you. Every time we call, every time we

come around, he's out!" Moshe shouted at Ben. "It's just not possible!"

Ben looked at Moshe sadly. "I'm sorry, Mr. Sommers. It's not my fault. Please don't yell at me. The truth is, he asked me not to let you speak to him. He's having a lot of problems at the moment, a lot of confusion. Maybe if you just gave him some space, he'd come around."

"Give him some space? That's all I've been hearing for the past couple of years. The boy can have all the space he wants. I've had it." Moshe began walking away, anger in every movement of his body, with Rifka alongside, crying and casting longing looks back at Ben. Ben stood helplessly at the open door, not wanting to close it until they were well out of sight. Colin, who had heard every word of this exchange, didn't want to talk about it. Ever.

After that he began sleeping late in the morning and missing minyan. Then he began to "forget" to put on his tefillin. Ben said nothing to encourage or discourage this metamorphosis, but secretly rejoiced when Colin started eating with him at the table instead of on his own in his little kosher corner. Then one day, after several fruitless weeks of looking around for a suitable job, Colin came home suffused with excitement.

"Guess where I've just been?"

Ben looked up from the television. "I couldn't begin to guess," he said dryly.

"I've been," he announced importantly, "to a recruitment drive for the police. And I've decided. I'm going to join up."

Ben looked at him, openmouthed. "Does that mean I'll have to watch my back from now on?"

Colin grinned. "And I've decided something else. I'm not

stopping at being a simple bobby on the beat. My parents always said that as a child I loved to dissect things, take things apart and see how they worked. I'm going to put my curious and analytical mind to good use. I'm going to be the best detective this town has ever seen."

DAY TWO

CHAPTER FIVE

Ilana had been so sure that Josh would turn up by nightfall, that it was just a daytime flash in the pan, a terrible, painful nightmare that would all be over by dark. Josh would come home, get scolded and cuddled, they would all cry and do a bit of yelling, and then it would be over. She could not even begin to contemplate the horror of darkness falling and Josh still gone. *No.* He would come home.

But he didn't come home. Don stayed with Ilana on Sunday to keep vigil, but after a sleepless night, morning arrived with no sign of Josh. Don had to go to work, and Ilana had to face the day alone. Now the new day was closing, and Ilana was desperately trying to hold herself together as the minutes ticked by and her son did not show.

She had spent the day psyching herself up to begin work on building a customer Web site on her home PC. It was an urgent job. The customers, a middle-sized corporation, were anxious not to be outstripped by the competition, all of whom had a Web presence, and had requested that the site be up and running as soon as possible.

The design itself needed her flair and imagination, and the coding needed her to have her head screwed on straight. After two disastrous attempts, viewed in her browser and despaired of, she gave up and sobbed piteously. It was hopeless. She was not only childless, but useless as well. She was purposeless, an empty shell, her essence sucked out. A small part of her prodded her to "have faith, daven, say *tehillim*; Hashem is the One who will help you," but at the moment she was incapable of responding to that small part of herself. She was going into shock.

At six Dr. Roston came, summoned by her mother. He took one look at her vacant expression and prescribed tranquilizers. Ilana swallowed two tablets obediently, not even asking what they were; they could have been cyanide for all she knew or cared.

Don walked in from work at that point and met the doctor in the hallway.

"Dr. Roston, what are you doing here? Is Ilana ill?"

"I'm concerned," the doctor admitted. "She's in denial. I've given her tranquilizers to help her deal with the shock."

Don felt like he'd been punched in the stomach. "Tranquilizers? Shock? Excuse me, I want to see my wife."

He walked past the doctor into the study, where Ilana sat vacantly at her terminal, her text editor blank. Not a word had been entered. When she saw him, Ilana got up from her desk.

"Hi, Don." She smiled, but her eyes were devoid of emotion. "I'm going to make Josh's supper. He's been out in the garden and very hungry. Maybe you'll run his bath?"

Don looked back at the doctor, who stood at the door of the study, an unreadable expression on his face. The look Don flashed him could have barbecued a steak.

"Will you please run Josh's bath?" Ilana repeated and

walked past him and the doctor into the kitchen.

"I can't play along with this charade!" hissed Don. "She has to be made aware of the situation!"

"Oh, she's aware of it, all right," the doctor assured him. "This is her way of coping right now, and if you try to enter that bubble of unreality she has built around herself, you had better do it extremely gently or you could do untold damage to her psyche. I gave her tranquilizers only to calm her a little. They aren't very strong and won't stop her perceiving reality if she is able to."

After Dr. Roston had left, leaving Don with a list of phone numbers where he could be reached, Don tentatively approached Ilana in the kitchen as she busily laid the table for three. She felt rather than saw him coming and, head averted, rushed across the kitchen to get some salad greens out of the big refrigerator. Don came up behind her and blocked her exit as she turned back.

"Don, let me pass."

"No."

She became agitated. "Don, please. Josh is hungry, and I have to prepare the salad." She flailed at him. Don reached out and caught her hands.

"Ilana, sit down. We have to talk."

"No time to talk. Have to get dinner ready. No time, no time."

Gently, firmly, he propelled her to the kitchen table. Pressure on her shoulders made her sit. She sat, eyes downcast, twisting her hands in her lap.

Don sat backward on another chair, facing her, his arms folded along the back.

"Ilana, look at me. Listen to me."

"No. Can't. Too much to do. No time, no time."

"Ilana. Look at me! Listen to me!"

The sharpness of his tone brought her head up like a whip. He looked into her empty, ravaged eyes and his heart bled.

"Josh is missing. But we hope and we pray, yes, we daven like crazy that soon he will be found safe and well. In the meantime, we have to keep our wits about us. Maybe someone will contact us for a ransom demand. We have to be alert and on top of things if that happens. I know that escaping into your own world helps you cope, but in the long run it's a false world, and you must confront the real one. Please, Ilana, try. For me. And for Josh."

Something flickered in her eyes, as if someone was switching on a light or opening a door. And as if that same someone had opened a floodgate, her eyes filled with tears that quickly overflowed.

"We'll never see him again," she whispered, tears flowing freely.

"You mustn't believe that. We will see him again, safe and well. We must daven."

"Maybe I don't have the *zechuyos,*" she said tremulously.

"Don't talk like that. Don't even think it. You're a good woman. Just have faith."

There was a long pause. Then, as tears overflowed again, Ilana lifted her devastated face to Don's.

"Why did you bring me out of that warm, safe place where I was hiding, Don? The place where at least I could pretend Josh was safe here with us? Why drag me into the real world, where all is dark and ugly and desolate?"

"That warm, safe place only looked warm and safe. It's a false safety and a dangerous one for you. You must be strong. You are strong, Ilana. Use that strength now as you have never used it before."

They maintained eye contact for a long moment. Then she nodded. She would be strong. For Josh.

Outside, it was growing dark. Unconsciously, Ilana was waiting for a ransom demand by telephone. Every time the phone rang, she ran as if trying to win a race in her eagerness to answer it. But it was usually her mother or her friends or well-meaning members of the community asking if she needed anything. To everyone she answered firmly in the negative. She did not need support or help from anyone. She was grateful they cared, but the phone calls were beginning to annoy. Every second she spent murmuring platitudes on the phone she was wondering if the kidnapper was at that very moment trying to get through. She would tell everyone, "Please, I really do appreciate you calling, but I must keep the line clear in case." Everyone knew what the "in case" was, and slowly the well-intended phone calls began to tail off.

Even her mother, who had spent the day at the Hardmans', was beginning to irritate, and Ilana had sent the protesting Sarah home. "I'll be in touch, Mum, really. I don't need people hanging around all day. It isn't helpful."

Well meaning though the rebuff was, Sarah was hurt. "If a mother can't help at a time like this..."

"You can't help. That's the whole point. No one can help except the police. And Hashem, Who is guiding them," Ilana had tried to explain while firmly propelling her mother doorward.

After speaking to the umpteenth well-meaning friend or relative on the phone, Ilana had put on the answering machine for two hours with the following message:

"Thank you for calling the Hardmans. We ask you please to understand that the family is undergoing much stress at the moment and that the phone lines need to be kept clear in case of developments. There is nothing we need from anyone, except to find our son, and for that reason we entreat you most politely and sincerely not to call unless you have news of that specific kind. Thank you."

It sounds so rude and ungrateful, Ilana said to herself, playing it back. She added another bit at the end and recorded it.

"Thank you for your tireless support and offers of help for which we are unendingly grateful. Davening and saying *tehillim* would be appreciated."

The good people of Golders Green took her up on this immediately, and Tehillim rotas were quickly set up. They took Ilana at her word, however, and once they had heard the message, they stopped calling.

"We can do more by staying out of her way and davening," they said. Once the phone had stayed silent for a few hours, Ilana had dared switch off the answering machine.

Don had not been pleased with this turn of events. "You need your friends. It's not right to drive them away."

"I can't cope with them now, Don. All I do is repeat the same old things to each one: no, there is no news; we are trying to keep the lines clear; no, there is nothing you can do to help except daven, thank you so much for calling. I can't take anymore, Don."

So now, as the evening turned into night, the house was silent, waiting for a little boy whose parents feared he might never come home.

☼ ☼ ☼

Colin had a team of constables lined up in front of him in the newly set up Josh Hardman incident room. Video display units all had a scanned picture of Josh on their screens, along with a sidebar listing all his statistics — height, weight, distinguishing marks, color of hair and eyes. Each officer had a printout of this picture and stats in his hand and was trying to look concerned and official, hiding his excitement. They were only human, and it had been a while since they had had a case like this in Golders Green. It made a change from the usual burglaries and petty muggings that were their bread and butter. Once in about six years they got a murder, but it had been quiet recently, nothing interesting to break the monotony. This was a case to get their collective teeth into, as it were, and they were champing at the bit.

The day before had been spent asking a few questions, doing a bit of tracking, but officially they couldn't open the investigation until the boy had been gone twenty-four hours. As soon as he could, Colin put together a task force and called a meeting.

"Now," Colin said, "first things first. The neighbors. I want every house in the street, and several streets around, door-to-door'd. Ask questions. Show a photo of the boy; you've all got a printout. Find out if they've got kids the same age, maybe go to the same school. Ask the kids if they've seen Josh anywhere. Above all, assume nothing. Sweet little old ladies are usually the worst." Here he grinned.

"But, sir, all the neighbors are Orthodox Jews, like the Hardmans." This from a young rookie at the end of the line.

Colin shot him a hard stare. "Your point being?"

The rookie swallowed. "Well, sir, ain't they all meant to be 'olier than thou? Good eggs and all that?"

"Plenty of rotten eggs in a basket," Colin said. "I repeat: assume nothing. A mean-looking chap might be innocence personified, and a sweet little old lady, well, as I said, they're the worst."

"In your experience, of course, of sweet little old lady ax

murderers," someone along the line murmured in a stage whisper.

"Of course, Simpson," Colin said. "Now get to work. This kid has been missing more than twenty-four hours. It's evening. Everyone should be at home. Check 'em out. And do your jobs well. Report anything. Get back to me on your mobiles and I'll come. In the meantime, I have some more questions to ask the Hardmans. Now on yer bikes."

Ilana and Don sat listlessly at the kitchen table. Supper, apathetically thrown together, lay untouched before them. Well, not totally untouched. They each poked the food around their plate. Friends and family had brought food in. All of it had gone into the freezer. Somehow the act of putting a meal together, however basic and however uneaten, was a small comfort, and Ilana needed that comfort.

The doorbell shattered the silence into a thousand ice crystals. They both jumped high, holding their hands to their pounding hearts.

"It's me. Detective Inspector Sommers. I need to ask you some more questions," said the voice through the door. Don opened it, ashen-faced.

"What's happened?" Colin said, alarmed.

"Nothing, nothing, you just startled us. Come in, please."

Colin stepped into the Hardman place carefully, as if afraid to step on something fragile, like their hopes. "I don't have any news for you yet," he began, and watched their faces fall. "But I do need some more information to help with our investigation."

"Of course. Sit down," Don said. Colin sat at the kitchen table, noting the almost full plates.

"I've disturbed your supper. I apologize," he said.

"Oh, please don't apologize, Inspector. We had no appetite anyway. We've been sitting here looking at the same congealed food for hours."

"That's no good. Gotta keep your strength up." Colin found himself voicing the same platitudes his mother used to spout at him many years ago.

Ilana smiled faintly but said nothing.

"What do you need from us?" Don asked, changing the subject.

"Firstly, I need something of Josh's, preferably something that has his smell strongly on it, if you get my meaning. Something your help didn't wash this morning. I know Joe took some socks, but they've been analyzed and I'd like something that hasn't passed through hands or microscopes. We have tracker dogs, and if they can pick up his scent, they might be able to trace where he went from here, at least till the trail turns cold. The scent will be stronger on something that's come straight from the house."

"Yes, of course." Ilana jumped up and ran upstairs to her son's room. "I'll get it at once!" she called down.

Don looked at Colin.

"I'm worried about her," he confessed. "She's slipping in and out of denial. I'm no shrink, but I see signs of post-traumatic stress disorder. She is finding it hard to focus on reality. She seems to find the safety of a dream world preferable."

"She'll need a lot of support," Colin said. "Try your best to keep her focused for now. If she wants to slip away every now and then, well, that's not the end of the world, so long as she comes back. It's when the periods away get longer than the periods she's with us, that's when you need to call in professional help."

"I don't think she should be in a dream world at all, to be frank," Don replied testily. "We have to find our son. I can't do this on my own, and if she's going to be spaced out most of the time, it will be much more difficult for me to cope."

"And what about her, sir? What about how difficult this is for her? Why not allow her some escape every now and then?"

Don colored. "I suppose I sound selfish."

Colin smiled thinly. "This is hard on both of you. You need to support each other and cope as best as you can in your own way."

Ilana entered the kitchen and handed Colin a plastic bag with an item of Josh's inside.

"Good," said Colin. "Excellent. Now, about Maria. How long has she been with you?"

"You suspect Maria? Oh, Inspector, no way. Maria was my mother's help for many years before she became mine. She's utterly loyal and dependable."

"Family of her own?"

"Yes, she has a husband and two sons."

"Husband works, does he?"

"Yes, as far as I know. He runs a private cab company."

"Hmm. Okay. I suppose her work permit's in order?"

Don coughed. "Look, Inspector, is this really necessary? You know how it is with these foreigners. They come over to make money. Maria's been wonderful. We have no reason to doubt her. Please don't start looking too hard under the wrong rocks. That's all I'm saying."

Colin tapped the side of his nose. "Understood. Don't worry, sir."

There was a small, embarrassed silence, then the policeman went on. "Now, sir, about your business. How many do you employ?"

"Oh, there are only twelve of us. It's very small."

"What kind of business is it and where are its offices?"

"It's an Internet design company called Intergraph, based in Camden Town. We design Web sites for corporate clients, doing our own graphic designs and running our own servers. We also lease Web space and offer e-mail services."

Colin nodded. He used computers extensively in his own work, accessing police databases and other networks.

"My wife works for me," Don went on unprompted. "She's a very good designer and she writes CGI scripts, too."

"Have your employees been with you long?"

Don thought. "They're not all employees. We are four partners. We've been together since the business's inception. My wife makes five. Then we have five guys on tech support. They work shifts. And there are two secretaries. The secretaries have been with us for years. The tech support guys, well, two are newish. The others have been with us for at least a year."

"Would you say any of the staff would have a reason to have a grudge against you?"

"None that I know of. We pay fairly and the hours are standard. I don't think I'm too horrible a boss." He smiled valiantly.

"He's a fine boss," Ilana confirmed. "The staff respect him. You can tell."

"I'll need to interview them if that's okay with you, sir," Colin said.

"Sure, that's fine. Here's my card. The address is on it."

Colin was at the door when he turned around. "Oh, one more thing before I leave."

"Yes?"

"I want no attempts at vigilante high jinks. You do not, repeat *not,* try and find your son yourself or badger people about him. Leave this to us now."

Don barked a short laugh. "He's our son, Inspector. Who better than we have the sixth sense that might help find him?"

Colin stepped slowly and deliberately forward. "Mr. Hardman, more damage has been done by well-meaning parents taking matters into their own hands than you can possibly imagine."

Ilana gave the policeman a stubborn look. "It's not only the sixth sense. Who better than we would have the motivation to want to continue looking for him long after you might consider the case closed?"

Colin closed his eyes for a moment, then opened them. "Mrs. Hardman, if you think for one minute that a missing eight-year-old kid doesn't bother me, you've got another think coming. You can rest assured I won't sleep nights until he is found."

"I wish I could believe you'd lose as much sleep as I will," Ilana said, and turned away. When she looked back, Colin had gone.

"That wasn't very helpful," Don remarked. "We want to have the cops on our side, not alienate them."

Ilana sighed. "I know. That was stupid of me. I'll call him and apologize. He left us his mobile number."

"Leave it." But she was already dialing. Her need to have as much right as possible in her life was strong. She spoke to Colin and humbly apologized. He was surprised. He was used to verbal abuse and this was mild; he had barely given it a thought. Strange people, these frummers. Real mixture.

Back at the incident room Colin gave Sergeant White the plastic bag Ilana had given him for the trackers. "Here. Give the dogs a sniff of this outside the Hardmans', then take them up to the kid's room and see where they go from there."

"Yeah. House-to-house proceeding normally. Nothing of much note yet. Most of the people round here know the kid. It's a kind of village really. Not like our other patches where you don't even know your next-door neighbor. Here they practically know what he had for breakfast. Most of the kids go to the same school. If they're boys anyway."

"There's a couple of alternative schools," Colin said, remembering.

"Yeah, but it seems a whole crowd of kids round here all go to that school. They all seem to like Josh. Real upset they are. Headmaster has ordered special prayers to be said."

"*Tehillim*," Colin said vaguely. White gave him a look.

"What's that?"

Colin recovered himself. "I remember hearing it from the neighbors' kids when I played with them. It means psalms. They say psalms as a prayer."

"I thought psalms were songs, not prayers," White said, shaking his head. "Well, so long as they think it helps."

"Yeah. So long as they think so. So nothing major in the house-to-house then?"

"No. One of the kids got a bit dramatic, fancies himself a future psychiatrist. Said Josh was acting disturbed for a couple of days before he disappeared. Other than that, nothing."

"Disturbed? How?"

"Dunno. Didn't take much notice, being as the Freud character was only eight."

"Assume nothing. Remember what I said? Which house was this? I want to speak to this kid myself. Even if it's a wild goose chase it's all we have for now."

White consulted his list. "Number 17, the street next to the Hardmans'."

White and Sommers went there together. The woman who answered the door was rather surprised to see the police there again. She was small and heavyset with a sweet round face devoid of makeup. Colin secretly thought her housecoat and scarf made her look frumpish; it reminded him of the way his mother had looked at her least glamorous. He had hated it then and still did. Why did women have to make themselves look so dowdy just because they were religious? he thought. Colin snorted. Don't these women care how they look?

"What's wrong, Inspector?" she asked White.

"Mrs. Brandt, Detective Inspector Sommers here would like to ask your young son some questions based on our earlier interview. Is he in?"

She looked flustered for a moment. "Come in. I'll see."

They followed her into a cluttered hallway scattered with toys and small sit-and-ride cars. Small children everywhere, it seemed to Colin. Bet she doesn't even know if he's in or out. Typical.

"Moishie!" she called. "Are you in your room?"

A clamor of voices, but not from Moishie apparently.

"He's out playing football," someone called from upstairs.

Colin sighed audibly. Mrs. Brandt looked even more flustered. Then, out of the blue, a small girl, looking no older than ten, appeared and gave the two policemen an angelic smile which they couldn't help but respond to with their own.

"I know where Moishie is. I'll find him for you, shall I?"

"Yes, please," said White. "We really need to talk to him."

The angelic smile flashed again, and she ran outside.

"Nice kid you got there," said White appreciatively.

Mrs. Brandt glowed with the compliment. "She's my best helper."

Colin tried his hardest not to roll his eyes. This house was a nightmare of mess, clutter, and kids. The woman obviously had far more than she could cope with, and if she was relying on a ten-year-old kid as her best helper, well. Says it all, really.

They stood around for a couple of moments. Then the woman, highly embarrassed, asked them into the living room to sit down.

The clutter there was only marginally less than in the hallway. Obviously there was no "best" room like in some non-Jewish homes he had been to. Kids allowed to run everywhere. She brushed an elaborate battle scene of toy soldiers off the sofa onto the floor and they sat.

"Cup of tea? Cold drink?"

"Tea would be nice," Colin said.

"Milk and two sugars for both of us," White confirmed.

At that moment the girl reappeared, younger brother in tow, a sulky expression on his face.

"He didn't like me taking him away from his football," she explained with a grin that lit up the room.

"Brachele, would you please make two teas for the policemen, milk and two sugars in each?"

Colin's mouth dropped open. A ten-year-old girl making tea?

"Sure, Mummy. Would you like one, too?"

"Oh, yes, please. You know how I like mine."

The girl disappeared. Moishie stood, looking longingly at the front door.

"The policemen want to ask you some more questions about Josh," Mrs. Brandt said.

"C'mere, lad," Colin said, trying his best not to sound patronizing. Moishie approached cautiously.

"Good football game out there, is it?"

The boy glowed. "Yeah, I scored two goals, and they need me."

"You'll be back out there in a jiffy. Just answer some questions about Josh, okay?"

"Okay. But I told him there," a pointed finger at White, "already."

"Yeah, I know you did. Just tell me again, okay? Now you told this nice policeman here that Josh had seemed a bit... strange the last few days before he disappeared. Can you explain that a little better for me? We policemen are a bit thick between the ears, you know."

"A little better?"

"Yeah. What do you mean by strange?"

"Well, Josh is a good friend of mine. We play a lot. Every break we're out playing football and stuff..."

"Yes," Colin said encouragingly.

"Well, the last couple of days he said he didn't really want to play. He said he was feeling a bit funny and wanted to sit down and watch instead."

"A bit funny? What do you mean? Ill?"

"I asked if he was ill and he said no. If he'd been ill, he'd have gone to the secretary's office and gone home maybe. But he said he wasn't ill, just felt a bit sad and didn't feel like football."

"And he usually did feel like football?"

"Yes, always. He was the second best footballer in the class."

Colin grinned. "The best being...?"

The boy had the good grace to blush. "Mummy says I'm not supposed to boast."

The two policemen smiled indulgently at him and his mother.

"So," the boy went on, assured of an appreciative audience now, "I asked him what he was sad about." He paused for dramatic effect. Little actor we have here, Colin thought.

"And he said, 'There's a man who keeps speaking to me when I'm out playing.' "

The two policemen froze in their tracks. Colin crouched down to Moishie's level and grasped his shoulders. "Now, lad, be very very sure of what you are saying."

The boy nodded solemnly.

"You are absolutely sure that Josh said a man kept speaking to him when he was out playing?"

Moishie nodded again.

"Did he mean in school or in the evenings or Sundays?"

Moishie considered. "Not in school. We have gates and a security guard, and his mummy comes to fetch him right after."

"The security at the school is pretty tight," put in his mother. "There's not much chance for anyone unauthorized to get in."

Colin nodded and gazed intently into Moishie's face. "So he meant at home, playing outside?"

"Yeah, I suppose."

"Did Josh say what the man had said to him to make him sad?"

Moishie thought hard. "Not exactly, " he said at last, "but he said it made him feel scared. And he never lied to me. So he must have been. Very scared."

DAY THREE

CHAPTER SIX

Ilana stood at her kitchen window, gazing out at a beautiful spring morning. The garden was burgeoning with new life; the flowers she had planted were firm and bright, like plastic, showing no signs of wither or droop. It had rained in the night, and everything looked washed clean under the new sun. Droplets of water sparkled off the crisp leaves, prisms of light captured in them as the sun danced. A robin, the first she had seen in ages, hopped delicately around the edge of the lawn, pecking politely at the rich earth for worms. It looked up and saw Ilana watching, put its head to one side and gave her the full blast of a button-bright eye. Despite her misery, Ilana couldn't help but smile. It was so contrived, so posed, so obviously for her benefit. Then she thought, How dare the world be so perfect this morning? How dare it go on as normal when my baby is missing?

Don had softly, gently, encouraged his wife to carry on as normal a life as possible, to get dressed as tastefully as possible, to keep her *sheitel* neatly combed and arranged, even though instincts screamed at her that nothing mattered anymore. Her whole psyche made her want to go around in an old housecoat, hair tucked under an old turban, no makeup. Why should she make herself look nice for a world that had turned on her, turned on itself, twisted and gnarled like the branches of some mutated tree? The safe, friendly world she knew and trusted had turned its other face to her, the back of a dark, sinister tapestry, showing her only a network of blackened and contorted threads in a meaningless pattern. A pattern she did not understand.

And so it was Don, caring Don, who tried to show her that she must fight the dark picture the world was trying to show her and see the truth underneath. The sunlit garden, the plastic-bright flowers, the robin, the dew on the grass, those were the things Hashem wanted her to see. Things of hope, of life, of the future. The right side of the tapestry.

Don sat with her for hours in the twilight last night, talking to her, making her see hope where she felt there was none, making her see how nothing that happened was without explanation and without reason, however unreasonable that seemed. While he spoke to her in the cool, lengthening evening, the light dim in the gathering dusk, she felt she could, perhaps, go on another day. In the darkening room, cool and breezy with the windows open and the curtains like maidens dancing in white, looking into his soft and serious dark eyes, hearing his gentle, kind words so full of Torah truths, she felt his strength and faith suffusing her whole being. She drank it in, wanting to drown in it, to hoard it like a camel for the lean dry hours ahead, the hours when he would be gone from her and she had to face the day alone. She felt like a battery, charged when he was around, speaking to her heart, and drained by the time he came home, needing that recharge once more.

During the draining hours, despite Don's admonition that she should carry on as normal, she could not do her work. She could not go into the office and create Web sites while her heart and soul were drifting someplace else. Her whole being longed for her child, cried out to hold him in her arms again, to hear his voice calling for her. The thought of him being in pain somewhere, lost and alone, was like a long sharp sword piercing her heart. Like one turns one's head away when an injection is about to be given, Ilana turned her mind away from the thought of what might be happening to Josh. She could not bear it. She allowed herself to think of only two possibilities: that he was well and safe somewhere, awaiting rescue, or that he was dead and had died without suffering. The in-between, that awful, yawning chasm colored red and full of agony, she did not allow herself to contemplate.

The phone rang. She glanced at it. It gave her no comfort, no pinprick of hope when her battery was discharged. It had never been the phone call she was waiting for, never a ransom demand, never a muffled voice saying, "I got the kid. Bring one million pounds," or something like that. None of that had happened. Nor the worst-case scenario either. Nothing.

She picked up the phone.

"Hi, darling," came Don's familiar voice, "how are you?"

"Fine."

Don heard the deadness in her voice. "Ilana, have you done any work? On the pages."

"No. Don, I can't."

He had given up saying how good it would be for her to immerse herself in some work. Now he tried a different tack.

"We need the pages, Ilana. The client is getting twitchy."

"Eli can do them," Ilana said.

"Eli is snowed under. We're all snowed under. We need your help. Please."

Ilana sighed. One hand held the phone as if for support, her other hand making aimless gestures at her wig.

"I...I...it's just so difficult...I...oh, all right. I'll make a good start on them this morning."

Don tried not to let his sigh of relief be audible down the wires.

"E-mail the pages to me as soon as you have done them. I told the client he'd have something to look at on the server by one today. Think you can manage that?"

"One?" Again the distracted gestures at loose strands. "I don't know. What time is it now?"

"It's ten. You have a good three hours and you're quick. Shouldn't take you more than two hours to get at least something for him to look at. The list of things to do to the site are on your desk. They've been there awhile. Let's hope Maria hasn't mistaken them for trash in the meantime and chucked them out."

"No, the list is still there. I see it every time I pass my desk." Passing her desk was as far as she'd gotten these past three days.

Don refrained from commenting. "So you'll e-mail me around noon with the stuff?"

"Yes, yes, yes. Leave me alone, Don." She hung up and stood there, trembling. From her vantage point in the kitchen she could see through to the study and the computer. It loomed menacingly.

Maria came into the kitchen, a purposeful look on her face and a bucket in her hand.

"Ilana, I wanna clean the kitchen. You gotta get out."

Well, that's telling me, Ilana thought with a faint smile.

Gathering up her things, she walked into the study as if to the guillotine. She sat down before the computer. The screen saver danced; it was an animated Torah and some mitzvah men, intended to teach Josh about *berachos*. Quickly she touched the mouse so the screen saver vanished and her familiar desktop appeared. With a few clicks, she turned off the screen saver.

She went into her text editor and brought up the relevant pages. As the browser loaded, she looked at the list of work to be done. Systematic, she told herself, be systematic. Just plow through the list, starting at A and working your way through to Z. Don't think. Just do it.

She forced herself to focus on the work, and it began to absorb her thoughts, to dissipate all intruders, to take over. Switching between the text editor, where she wrote the HTML, and the browser, where she viewed it, was comforting. The switching back and forth worked on her like a pendulum, soothing her, almost hypnotizing her. She loved seeing the Web pages take shape under her skilled hands. Making sure the tables were aligned, the graphics correctly sized and positioned, the frames pointing to the right target, all calmed her, gave her order in at least one part of her life while the rest was in chaos. She designed the background in Paintshop Pro, added some special effects in Photoshop, and saved it. She made it as pale as possible so as not to interfere with the text going on top and tried it out in her browser. It just needed a bit of adjustment.

She worked at it, not even stopping for a coffee even though she was parched. When she was satisfied with the pages, she sat back and realized her back was hurting. She cat-stretched in a few directions, hearing the bones crack, and it felt good. She stood up and stretched again, looking at the clock. It was half past twelve. The morning had not gone so fast for three days. She e-mailed the pages over to the office with all the graphics, feeling quite fulfilled. Once the pages had gone, just before she logged off, she saw an e-mail downloading. So absorbed was she in her work, she hadn't thought to check if she had any incoming mail. A message appeared on her screen. "You have new mail!" She clicked the OK icon and opened the letter.

It was a few brief lines. It had no header and no return address.

The devil can cite Scripture for his purpose,
An evil soul producing holy witness.
Josh is with me. More info will follow.
If you involve the police he will suffer.

It was signed, "Internet Fox."

CHAPTER SEVEN

Colin Sommers sat thoughtfully at his desk, tapping a pen against his teeth. *Tap tap tap*. Three days. Usually, in cases of missing kids, they were found within the first three days. On a jaunt usually, dead sometimes, but they were found. Now what did he have? One missing kid. One missing kid, some trace evidence taken from the house, and an untraceable e-mail message that was puzzling the living daylights out of him.

The trace evidence was stuff Joe had taken from the windowsill and carpet of Josh's bedroom. The fibers Joe had lifted from the windowsill turned out to be from a pair of red and black Batman pajamas. So it looked very likely that the kid had been lifted or dragged out of the window, catching his pajamas on the way out. There were some other fibers, which turned out to be from a dark sweatshirt or sweatpants. Josh did not own such a garment — he'd checked — so one could reasonably suppose it was from the abductor. The mud and dirt was, predictably, from their own front garden, but there was some fibrous, well-rotted plant material that did not seem to be from the Hardmans' garden. And there were some other trace elements that had been faithfully labeled and bagged but remained unidentifiable.

Colin was seriously considering calling in an expert. Someone who knew more than he did about deciphering the most flimsy of clues, a criminologist of some kind. Such people did nothing but study trace evidence. His men, good though they were, were like the general practitioners of crime detection. He needed a professor. Much as he hated admitting he was stumped, Colin was floundering in this case. He looked on the computer databases for expert criminologists, but no one immediately grabbed his attention.

Aside from that there was that mysterious e-mail. Ilana had called a few hours ago, frantic. He'd promised her he'd get on it right away and Jeff, the department computer whiz, said he'd work on it. Colin himself had absolutely no idea how an e-mail could be untraceable or anonymous. As far as he knew, before you could even send an e-mail, you had to fill in all your details, including a return address. Heck, you probably had to fill in your National Insurance number and foot measurements before the e-mail would send itself. And yet this mail had arrived, orphaned, origins unknown, and if you clicked the Reply icon there was a total blank in the sender's window.

How was this done? How was it possible?

Sighing, Colin felt about an inch high. He was in charge of a case that was going nowhere. All his efforts to solve it produced no answers.

Of course he submitted the photo of young Josh to all the local papers, and thanks to Lucy it was prominently displayed along with the caption "Have you seen this child?" So far this had garnered two dozen responses, with sightings of the boy in places as remote as Pinner and downtown London, known as the West End. Follow-ups had proved fruitless despite the ad stating quite distinctly the boy's eye and hair color; the boys spotted were nothing like the image of Josh.

The tracking dogs were a dead end. They had eagerly followed a trail leading out of the bedroom window, but the trail stopped dead at the curb and the dogs had stood, whining pathetically, unable to go any further. It seemed that the boy had been brought down some kind of ladder, pushed into a car, and taken away. The ladder was missing, but there were some holes in the earth outside the window that could have been made by a ladder. Joe had bagged the earth around the ladder holes, too. Another piece of trace evidence to be filed away, but nothing to compare it with.

Then there was the matter of the Hardmans and all the religious stuff he had so studiously avoided for the past ten years. He was finding it harder to sneer. His lifestyle was so different, and he had thought better. But now, seeing the life he had left contemptuously, he found there were elements he was missing. Small things, like the warmth of the Hardman home, despite the tragedy in it, the menorah and the Shabbos candlesticks in the glass-fronted cabinet. He recalled now his mother's delicious food, a meal always ready when he came home. Whatever Lucy was, she wasn't a cook. She was excellent at ordering takeout, and that was about it. Even in the midst of the Hardmans' crisis, more often than not he smelled good food cooking on the stove when he entered the house.

The more time he spent in Golders Green, in the homes so similar to his old home, the less antipathy he felt for it — and he hated himself for this weakness. Before the Hardmans, he had been comfortable with the life he had chosen, enjoyed his distance and coldness toward his roots. Now, thanks to this wretched case, he was once more thrown into the quagmire of his own past.

A knock on the door jolted him out of his reverie. Standing in the doorway was a forty-something man of imposing height and build wearing a black hat.

"The child," he said without introduction.

Colin leaned back in his chair, intrigued. "You have news of the child?"

"Unfortunately not," the man said, "but I do have some experience in searches."

Colin invited him to sit down. He introduced himself as Baruch Weiss, a friend of the Hardmans. When he got settled, Colin asked, "What experience?"

"A few years ago, a local child, a girl, went missing. It happened in North London, where I lived then. I was instrumental in organizing the search which ultimately found her."

"Alive?"

"Alive and well and in an Indian household. Apparently she had befriended the daughter of this Muslim family and had decided to abandon her own culture for a while and try Islam. By the time we found her she was glad to return to Judaism. She experienced little ill effects other than a deep sense of embarrassment about her escapade and a bad case of stomach upset from the unfamiliar spicy foods."

"Hmm. How old was this girl at the time?"

"Fifteen. She had a rather oppressive schoolteacher who preferred brain-bashing her into submission over her Jewish studies rather than imbibing her with enthusiasm by positive means. A gentle injection of Islam seemed like a good idea at the time for her, but as I said, she was thoroughly relieved to be rescued and brought home. The schoolteacher in question was reprimanded, the girl switched to a more inspiring mentor, and all was well."

Colin tapped his teeth with a fingernail. "And how was the search organized?"

"We spoke to her classmates, found out about the oppressive teacher. Her best friend told us the girl had expressed dissatisfaction with Judaism, that the teacher had put her off with her brainwashing ways. We investigated further and found that the girl had befriended an Indian girl from the neighborhood comprehensive school and was spending a great deal of time with her. After that, it was easy. We only needed to find out the identity of the Indian girl and follow the trail. But before we found that, we had teams of us going out looking for her all over North London day and night." Baruch paused, letting Colin take his measure. "I've done it before, Detective Inspector. I can do it again."

"This isn't a rebellious teenager, Mr. Weiss. This is a small child. He is unlikely to have been swayed by alien culture."

"I know. I heard on the Jewish grapevine that the Hardmans got some kind of e-mail from the person who claims he has Josh."

Colin didn't want to divulge classified information. "That's what you heard, is it?"

"News travels fast. So we play the game differently in this case. We look for the child, yes. But we also look for an abductor. If you are willing to divulge the contents of the e-mail, then we might have something to work on."

"Do you know anything about computers, Mr. Weiss?" Colin was still very cagey.

"Me? No. I confess to being computer illiterate and quite proud of it. I was born too late.

"But," Baruch said slowly, "I know someone who does. Avraham Pincus could figure out who sent that e-mail in no time."

"Abraham Pincus? Another Orthodox Jew?" Deliberately he mispronounced the name, converting it to the Anglicized version.

"An Orthodox Jew and a very clever one. What he doesn't know about computers isn't worth knowing. Well, I think so at least. Don Hardman himself would know Avi's qualifications, being in the business himself."

"Hmm," Colin said thoughtfully. "Well, I'll think about it. It's worth a try. Let me know where I can find him, and we'll check him out." Colin gave Baruch a sharp look. "We'll check you out, too, for that matter."

"Me? Why me?"

"Right now anyone could be a suspect, Mr. Weiss. Even you."

"Go right ahead, check me out. I'm no child abductor." Baruch sounded annoyed.

"We will. Have no worries."

"I'll have a word with Avi. But you're going to have to tell him about the e-mail."

"Information will be distributed on a strictly need-to-know basis," Colin said firmly.

Baruch stared at the detective, assessing. There was something strange about this policeman, something that didn't quite fit with the stereotypical British copper. Baruch found the man irritatingly confrontational, as if everything was a sort of battle. Even when he was being polite and the words were bland, the facial expressions and verbal intonations spoke of some hidden agenda that Baruch could not access.

He was reminded of a *shiur* he had attended on the subject of tapping the spiritual through the physical. The essence of the person behind the mask of his body could only be glimpsed through such avenues as speech, facial expressions, body language. He looked at Colin, trying to get a glimpse of the person behind the façade. He caught fleeting shadows of something dark and tortured. Very odd to see in a policeman, a man who investigated crime and brought criminals to justice. Why should he be tortured and agonized? Didn't make any sense. Baruch decided that for now there was no point in pursuing this line of thought. He shrugged it into a small corner of his mind.

"So shall we organize a search, Detective Inspector? I wouldn't want to tread on anyone's toes and do things behind your back, and we need your full cooperation."

"Look, Mr. Weiss, we can't have the general public gadding about Golders Green, poking their noses where they aren't wanted, without any control. They could upset all sorts of people and we'd get complaints. Any search done by the public would have to have the authority of the police, probably carry some documentation giving permission."

"Well, of course. No one's going to let us search their property unless we have some kind of authorization."

"Hmm. Well, I'll have to look into it," said Colin noncommittally. It was obvious the interview was over. Baruch stood up obediently and left the police station, again feeling that vague sense of discomfort at the essence of the man glimpsed behind the deceptive front.

Colin did not move from his chair. Baruch Weiss, with his sharp eyes, had unnerved him.

After Baruch left, he called Lucy to join him for an early dinner. They sat in the kitchen. The pile of cartons from a local Chinese restaurant sitting on the table spoke of Lucy's usual culinary expertise. Lucy's philosophy on domestic issues was "If someone else can cook it better, why do it yourself?"

She was bright and pretty and liked to look her best. She was short, only about five feet four, with dark curly hair worn collar length. She jingled with silver jewelry — large hoops in her ears, a dozen bangles on her wrists, rings on every finger. Silver was her color. Her makeup was silvery, too. She wore silver eyeshadow and touched the tips of her mascaraed eyelashes with silver to set off her dark, soulful eyes. She had even painted her nails the same color. It was as exotic and non-Jewish a look as one could wish to see.

She stared at Colin sitting across from her. There was something disturbing about him tonight, something she had not seen before in the set of his shoulders, the clenching of his fingers as he forked up his lo mein.

"Colin."

She had to repeat his name three times before he even acknowledged her.

"Hm?" he said finally, not looking at her.

"What's up? You're not yourself."

"Nothing."

This platitude, spoken so often and meaning so little, did nothing to placate her. She rose from her chair and began gathering the empty cartons together.

"Something's bothering you. I know you. Is it this case? The kid?"

With a sigh, he put down his fork and looked up at her. "Yeah," he answered, relieved. This was safe ground, something she understood.

"Shame when it's a kid involved, isn't it?" she agreed. "Any ideas yet?"

He sighed. "The pic in the paper has done no good. Aside from getting his mug shot plastered all over town, that is. Now we have this e-mail. Untraceable." Lucy was the only one outside the police he trusted with information like this. Sometimes he needed to talk about a case, and she was a good listener. Though she was a reporter, she never divulged what he told her in confidence.

"Hm. Well, I use e-mail and the Net extensively in my work, but I don't know how an e-mail can be untraceable."

"Nor do I. Practically have to give it your tooth imprint before it will work."

"Be interesting to find out, though," she said and grinned at him. Lucy liked a challenge.

"They got some Orthodox Jewish guy offering to organize a search party."

"That's rich." She laughed. "What do they know about search parties?"

To her surprise, he bridled. "Not as little as you think," he said irritably. "Apparently this guy's done it before, and successfully, so don't be so quick to condemn."

She held up both hands in a gesture of surrender. "Okay, okay. Sorry I spoke. Who rattled your cage today?"

"This case is getting to me. I don't like to think of that kid out there somewhere, possibly dead, maybe harmed, and frightened out of his wits. Sleep isn't coming easy at the moment."

"No, I imagine it isn't," she acceded and got up. "Well, at least you have to try. It's late. I'll be off. I'll throw all these empty cartons in your dustbin on the way out, shall I? Dustbin men call tomorrow."

"Yeah, okay," he said distractedly. She stood a moment, waiting for him to say good night. Then, with a slightly audible sigh, she left.

CHAPTER EIGHT

They gathered quietly, as if already in mourning. They came in ones and twos and threes, drifting in like smoke, silently, moving around the room as if to disturb the quiet would be to somehow disturb the aura around the missing child.

The people who gathered at the Weisses' were mostly men; somehow it wasn't women's work, searching for a child in strange places. One or two women had turned up, spoken to Baruch Weiss's wife, Malka, in the kitchen, and asked if they could do anything. Politically correct or not, Malka said with a wry smile, in this particular case the women's job was to hold up the men with creature comforts before they left and when they returned, and to take over any tasks the men would otherwise have done.

They understood perfectly. One undertook to supply great cauldrons of excellent homemade vegetable soup in thermoses. Another would make sandwiches, and a third would keep the home fires burning at the Weisses', the kettle always hot and plenty of tea, coffee, and cake on the ready.

In the main room, Baruch sat in his favorite armchair, leading the meeting.

"I've spoken to the detective in charge of the investigation," he began. "Colin Sommers, his name is. Seems a decent chap. I think he could use some help with that e-mail the Hardmans got. You've all heard about it by now."

They nodded. The Internet Fox. Just a name. And like a fox burrowed deep beneath the earth to make his home, he had chosen his lair deep within the wires and cables that connected the global network.

"I've been trying to get hold of Avraham Pincus, with no success. Does anyone know where he is?"

Chaim Karnovsky spoke up. "Avi Pincus is in Israel."

"Any idea when he's coming back?"

"He isn't. He lives there."

Baruch's brow wrinkled. "Can't be. I'm sure he was just here only a short while ago."

"He made aliyah a few months ago. He was probably here to finalize some details of his move. He lives in Jerusalem now."

"Oh, bother. "

Twenty-two-year-old Pinny Bloch spoke up with an ironic smile. "But that's the whole point of the Internet, Baruch. You don't need to be in the same place as someone else to work alongside him. Send him an e-mail and ask him what you want to know."

There was a small titter of laughter in the room. Baruch was again reminded of the *shiur*: "The cause of the problem can also be its salvation. The problem its own solution, the ordeal its own redemption." The speaker was talking about Egypt, but it seemed to fit rather nicely here, too. Want to know about e-mails? Send one to an expert to find out.

"If this abductor thinks he can outwit us because he is so computer literate that he can do clever things to fool us," added Pinny, "then we must use the very medium he is hiding in and turn it against him. We must find the cleverest hacker we know to chase the Internet Fox across the ether and capture him in the place it seems he feels most safe: cyberspace."

There was a murmur of assent.

"And, of course, find Josh," Pinny added.

"Do any of you know any other computer experts who live locally?" Baruch asked after the murmuring had died down. "What about Don? Surely he's got someone in his office who's an expert?"

"Actually, I just asked him about it in shul," called out Levi Kaplan, a good friend of Don's. "He said even if his staff is that good, he'd rather find someone on the outside. It's hard enough to come home to the reality of Josh missing; he doesn't want it to affect his work any more than it has. I think he's using work as a distraction, to help him deal with it."

Everyone murmured sympathetically.

"Besides, any of them could be a suspect," said Pinny.

"Okay. We contact Avi Pincus," said Baruch.

There was a pause.

"Does anyone know his e-mail address?"

Pinny said, "I'm going to suggest something. I think that it would possibly help us, and the police, to monitor things if all the e-mails are sent and received on one machine. That way, if the Hardmans do receive any more e-mails, at least they'll be going through the same server rather than all over the place. It's just an idea," he trailed off lamely.

All agreed that it was a good idea. The machine chosen was Don Hardman's home computer, the one on which the original e-mail had been received. All e-mails regarding this case, including the one to Avi Pincus, would be sent from that machine. Pinny volunteered to go over to the Hardmans that afternoon and send the e-mail to Avi.

☼ ☼ ☼

After Lucy left, Colin went to see Josh's friend, Moishie Brandt, the kid who possibly had firsthand information from Josh about the abductor. He went alone this time, for reasons he didn't take time to think about. He wanted to go into that home without White diluting the experience to see what feelings would wash over him.

He walked down the street slowly, absorbing the atmosphere, allowing it to soak through the pores of his skin. The days were getting longer, and it was still light out. He saw some children playing on bikes, all wearing yarmulkes, *payos* flying in the fresh spring breeze. He looked at their faces and saw in them the innocence of a childhood unsullied by twisted influences. Where he lived, kids as young as ten were smoking already, and some carried knives and heaven knows what else. Here, in this quiet street, the children played on their bikes and shouted and laughed and played like he remembered doing himself in his own childhood.

He stood still, watching them for a while. Small girls playing hopscotch. Hopscotch, for heaven's sake. When had he last seen girls playing hopscotch? Round his way, girls that age were already wearing makeup and high heels, tiny minature women looking ridiculous and world-weary by the age of ten, their childhood over, their future crammed into their present. These girls looked like what they were: children. Happy and innocent, wearing little girl clothes, not cutdowns of their mothers. Children with bows and bunches and ribbons and barettes and happy, laughing faces.

A mother came out of a nearby house and saw Colin

standing there, watching the children play. She gave him a peculiar look and a hard stare. He smiled at her reassuringly, thinking, Down where I live mums don't care enough what happens to their kids. They let them run wild, do what they like.

"Children, come inside" was the mother's response, running to her offspring and gathering them up.

Colin reached into his pocket and pulled out his ID. "I'm a police officer," he said, flipping open the identification.

The woman came forward cautiously and took the ID as if it was tainted. She examined it carefully.

"Oh. You're Detective Inspector Sommers. The one who's trying to find Josh. I'm sorry, but you can hardly blame me for being a bit worried. You never know these days."

Colin smiled. "Quite right," he said, putting the ID back in his pocket. "Do you know Josh Hardman?"

"He's in my son's class. He comes to play. " There was an awkward pause. The words "You mean *came* to play" hung in the air, unspoken, yet Colin heard them as clear as if they had emerged from her mouth. The woman blushed furiously at her own thoughts. Colin nodded ever so slightly, just to let her know he understood.

"Which one is your son?"

"He's that one over there." She pointed at a small skinny boy on a red bike, who seemed to be leading a couple of kids around the block. He was shouting orders at them, and they were happy to comply. "Do you want to talk to him?"

"Maybe later, if that's all right. I need to talk to Moishie Brandt first."

"Oh, yes. Moishie is Josh's best friend. They tell each other everything."

Colin nodded. "That's what I'm hoping. See you soon."

He walked off down the road toward the Brandts' house. Passing the boy on the red bike, he ruffled his hair, causing him to look up sharply with a puzzled look.

"Don't worry, son. I'm only a copper. Talk to you soon."

"A policeman?" the boy said, impressed. "Wow! You gonna arrest me?"

"Whatcha done then?" grinned Colin. The boy grinned back and zoomed off on his bike. "I'll 'ave yer for resisting arrest!" Colin called after him before walking on, smiling to himself. Then he realized why he was smiling. The idea of having to arrest this boy was, in this neighborhood, a joke.

Moishie Brandt was playing football outside his house, kicking the ball into the street. The street was quiet, and when a car did happen by, the boys quickly scattered until it passed. Colin stopped to watch for a moment, hands deep in the pockets of his light beige raincoat.

"You wanna be careful, lads," he said at last. "You might not always hear the cars coming."

The boys stopped their game and looked at him.

"You're that policeman," said one.

"That's right, and I'll 'ave yer for endangering life and limb if you don't watch out," Colin said with a straight face. The boys looked uncertain.

"You." He pointed at Moishie. "C'mere."

Moishie looked terrified. "Why me? It wasn't only me!"

He came over, nevertheless, and when close enough, Colin whispered in his ear, "Play along, will yer? I only want to ask you some more questions about Josh, but let's pretend you're in trouble, shall we?" He winked, and the boy, caught up with the game, winked back conspiratorially.

"I'm taking this young man in for questioning," he told the others. "You lot, watch your backs."

In the house, man and boy grinned at each other. Colin felt he had broken the ice well on this occasion. Last time the boy had been inhibited and unwilling to talk to him.

Moishie Brandt had dark and curly hair, upon which his yarmulke rested precariously, and startling green eyes. His lightly freckled nose and cheeks and infectious grin endeared him to Colin, who had thought he didn't like kids much.

Man and boy sat side by side on the sofa. Colin brought out a kosher candy bar and handed it to Moishie, impressed when the boy closely inspected the kosher symbol. "I do know what's kosher," Colin said with a wry smile.

"Yeah, but..." Can't trust a goy to know what's kosher were the unsaid words. Or a lapsed Jew, Colin added to himself, and a sense of shame briefly flooded him.

Satisfied with the credentials of the candy bar, the boy made a *berachah* and ate. While he munched contentedly, Colin said, "I was wondering if you used to play round Josh's place after school."

"Yeah, sure, loads of times."

"Out in the street? Football?"

"Sometimes, yes."

"You know that man you said talked to Josh out in the street at home? Did you ever see him yourself?"

Moishie thought for a moment. "Well, I might have done."

Colin tried not to react. "Go on, lad."

"Well, there was one time we were outside playing football, and this man passed by. I can't remember if he passed by specially or was just passing by anyway. But he stopped and talked to Josh. I wasn't close 'cause I was running after the ball. I couldn't hear what they were saying. They were too far away."

"How long did they talk for, d'you reckon?"

"Not long. Couple minutes, tops."

"And when the man left, did he walk toward you or away from you?"

"Away."

Oh, bother, thought Colin. "Okay. And what was Josh like when the man had gone?"

"Dunno. Okay, I suppose. But he kept missing easy shots. As if he was upset."

Colin nodded. "When the man he was talking to Josh, were you able to get a good look at him?"

"Not really. He was right down the street. I couldn't see much."

"Can you tell me his height? Was he white or black? What kind of clothes was he wearing?"

Moishie looked at Colin. "Stand up."

Colin stood obediently.

"Stand over there," Moishie ordered, pointing to the farthest corner of the room. Colin walked over to the farthest point.

"Hm. He's a bit shorter than you." Moishie made a space between thumb and forefinger, measuring about an inch and a half. "He was white. And he was wearing a checked shirt. Couldn't tell the color. And dark trousers. Maybe black jeans. And trainers. I could see he was wearing black and white trainers. They glowed, so I could see them easily."

Not bad, thought Colin. "Did you see the color of his hair or was he wearing a hat?"

Moishie thought hard. "Can't remember. His head looked dark. It might have been his hair or a small hat."

"Could you see his face? Did he have a beard or a mustache?"

Silence. Then, "I don't remember if he had a beard or not. Lots of people around here have beards. I don't notice anymore." The boy was getting stressed. Tears were welling up in his eyes, and his hands were clenched into fists.

Colin came over, sat down, and fished another candy bar out of his pocket. "Here, it's the same as the other one. Same *hechsher.*"

Moishie looked at him sharply. "How do you know the word *hechsher*?"

Colin coughed. "I used to live next door to some Jews. Played a lot with them. Learned their ways."

"Oh," said Moishie, convinced, and he ate the second candy bar. Colin lifted the boy's yarmulke for a moment, ruffled his curly dark hair, and plopped the yarmulke back on. He took a card out of his pocket and scribbled his home number on the back of it.

"Now, son, this is a very special thing I am doing for you here. This is my policeman's business card, but I am also giving you my very own home phone number."

"Wow," Moishie said dutifully, but the lack of enthusiasm in his voice led Colin to believe the boy had never made phone calls to policemen and didn't intend to start now.

"You've got to promise me you won't tell anyone else this number, okay? It's a secret between you and me."

"Right," Moishie said, still sounding dubious.

"So keep this to yourself. And have a good think about that man who was talking to Josh. If you can try and cast your mind back to that day and you remember anymore details, it would be very helpful. Maybe he had a logo on his jacket. Maybe he had some writing on his hat. Can you think about it and let me know if anything comes to mind?"

The boy nodded and pocketed the card carefully. "I'll

have a think tonight when it's quiet," he assured the policeman. "I've got a really good memory."

Colin smiled and patted the boy again. "Good lad." He got up. "I'll see you later." He walked out, smiling to himself as the boy ran past him to rejoin the football game.

Walking out again into the warm spring evening, Colin breathed in the scent of the lilac bushes that bordered the Brandt house. Spring this year was full of hope. What a conundrum. In the midst of so much burgeoning beauty and new life was a tragedy in the making.

He walked slowly back down the road until he came to the boy with the red bike, who was still zooming around like a wild animal in a circus ring.

"Hiya!" Colin called in a friendly fashion.

The boy stopped and looked at him. "Hi!" He waved and made another circuit.

Colin waited until he came close again, then said, "Son, can I ask you something a mo', please?"

The boy skidded to an abrupt halt in front of him, barely missing Colin's toes. "Yeah?"

"Careful, lad, careful. Don't want you hauled in on a GBH, do we now?"

"What's a GBH?"

"Grievous bodily harm, son. Like you taking me toes off, for instance."

The boy looked down at the juxtaposition of his front wheel tire and Colin's foot and grinned. "Whoops, sorry."

"Well, can we have a chat?"

"About Josh? Yeah, sure." The boy looked around. The street was emptying out. "Here?"

"Wherever you say. You're the boss. What's your name, by the way? I never asked."

The kid flashed another grin at Colin. "It's Mikey Mendelsohn. I know a good place. Follow me."

Chaining his bike to the front gate of his house, he led Colin round the back into a narrow passageway that led between his house and next door's. The alley, overgrown with weeds and vicious nettles, led to a small copse at the apex of the point where the two houses joined at the back.

"I made a secret house here," said Mikey. "No one knows about it 'cept me and Josh Hardman and Moishie Brandt."

Colin's heart thumped. "Show me."

Mikey ran ahead through dense undergrowth awash with wildflowers and brambles, apparently impervious to scratches and stings. Colin followed more cautiously, glad of his thick twill suiting and stout shoes. When he got to the spot, he stopped and stared.

If it hadn't been for Mikey leading him there, he would never have found it, so perfectly was it hidden among the brambles and shrubs: a tiny house, scarcely larger than a playhouse, constructed painstakingly out of old wooden pallets split up into their original planks and reformed. No glass in the two windows, but some ragged curtains fluttered. A door consisting of half a pallet closed with a hook-and-eye arrangement. Colin walked around the structure wonderingly.

"This is incredible. Did you build this?"

"Yes, me and Josh and Moishie. We all helped. Oh, and Daddy did, too. They're his pallets. Daddy has a business," he added importantly.

Colin peered in through one of the windows, pushing the torn curtain aside.

Inside was a battered, old cushioned chair, a small table, and two wooden boxes, one face up, full of bits and pieces, the other on its side, divided in two to form a crude bookcase.

Some storybooks and a plastic-covered siddur stood in the bookcase. Colin recognized the siddur though it was no longer a part of his life. He looked around the tiny room to see if there was anything that might point to the abductor having held Josh here at any stage — a mug and a cup, a packet of cookies, a candy bar wrapper.

"Those mugs and cups yours?" Colin said, pointing.

Mikey went in through the door, while Colin stayed where he was, peering in through the window. The boy picked up the items. "Yes, we bring drinks down here sometimes."

"So there is nothing here you don't recognize? Anything that isn't yours?"

Mikey looked around again. "No, nothing. All ours." He picked up the candy bar wrapper, stuffed it into his pocket, and left the little house.

Colin took out a card and scribbled his home phone number on the back. As he handed it to the child, he said, "Can I ask you to do some police work for me?"

Mikey positively glowed at the idea. "Sure!"

"Here's my home number and that's my office number on the front. I'd like you to come back here when you can but quietly and secretly and take a very careful look around. If you see anything you don't recognize, anything that might have been put there by someone else other than you and your friend Moishie, phone me at once. Okay?"

"Okay!" The boy winked. "You can rely on me. I'll sneak in real quietly and look around."

"Good lad! I'm off now. Keep in touch. And remember," Colin tapped the side of his nose, "mum's the word!"

Mikey looked puzzled for the first time in their exchange, and Colin realized, with a start, the extent of the culture gap between them. Mikey had never heard that phrase before. "It means keep it a secret," Colin explained, and the boy's face cleared instantly.

"Right! Don't worry!"

As Colin walked back to his car, his mobile phone rang. It was the desk sergeant back at the station.

"Better get back here sharpish, sir," the desk sergeant said. "The Hardmans have received another e-mail."

CHAPTER NINE

Colin arrived back at the station to find Don and Ilana waiting for him. Ilana was sobbing uncontrollably, and Colin's heart went out to her. Fearing the worst, Colin wordlessly took the printout Don was clutching and scanned it quickly.

You call me misbeliever, cutthroat dog
And spit upon my Jewish gaberdine.
Revenge is a dish best eaten cold,
Says the Internet Fox.

"A poet yet," Colin said grimly.

"I didn't want to call. I didn't want to come here!" Ilana wailed. "I'd rather take a chance and have my son back safely than risk him knowing I've contacted you."

Don and Colin locked eyes for an instant.

"I know how she feels, but you've done the right thing," Colin said. "We'll sit down together and think about this e-mail. It may contain clues." He signaled to a woman police constable. He needed to ask Don some questions, and Ilana's distress was distracting.

"Come along and have a nice cuppa." The kindly WPC took Ilana away. "I'll give it to you in a polystyrene cup. I've sent someone out for some kosher milk. There's a shop just up the road." Ilana allowed herself to be led off.

"I don't think she's much use right now, to be honest," Colin explained to Don. "Needs to calm down."

Don nodded his agreement. "She's been spaced out on and off ever since it happened, sometimes alert and lucid and at others totally out of it. This second e-mail seems to have tipped her over the edge. She's done nothing but sob since it arrived."

"Do you think she'll calm down enough to think about who might have sent this e-mail?" Colin asked.

"I don't know. At the moment, my wife is not herself. But the wife I do know is strong and resourceful. She'll conquer her hysteria if she knows it will help find Josh."

"Is anyone staying with you to see her through this? Her mother or a friend?"

"Frankly, we don't want it. We find it an intrusion. They don't know what to say to us, apart from silly platitudes we find irritating. We end up having to entertain them or keep reassuring them that we aren't falling apart. To be honest with you, Detective Inspector, the only sort of people who would be tolerable in our home right now are people like yourself. People who are getting on with finding where my son is. Anyone else is a nuisance. Sorry if I sound ungrateful, but we have to cope the best way we know how, and we have no resources left to either entertain or reassure. We just support each other."

Colin nodded his understanding. He led Don into a small and cluttered office. Sweeping a pile of papers onto a small side table and clearing some space in his desk, he said, "Bachelor habits." Don shrugged a "doesn't bother me" gesture and they sat. "Do you go into work?" he asked Don.

"Yes. I have to. It would do Ilana good to come in, too. I'm trying to persuade her. Rattling around alone in that big house with no one but Maria for company is driving her nuts. She needs the distraction of work and company. But she's constantly worried that she might miss a vital phone call or e-mail."

"Surely you can arrange to have your home calls diverted to your office during the day?"

"Of course we can. But she's lost all trust in the system. The system which allowed her precious baby to be abducted might let her down if she isn't there to constantly monitor the phone, fax, and e-mail, too. That's how she's thinking at the moment, but it's early days and I'm hoping I can persuade her to come into work soon, even for a few hours a day. Maria loved that boy almost as much as we and would guard the phone and computer like a centurion."

"It would help her if she could be persuaded to carry on as normal a life as possible," Colin said gently.

Don nodded. "I'll try my best. Now, about this e-mail."

"Yes. The e-mail. Let's take another look at it." Colin spread the printout on his desk. "Hm. Let me make a copy of this. It will be easier."

Once they each had a copy, they sat and studied it for a while.

"Well," Don began, "sounds like someone with a problem about being Jewish. Accusing *us* of antisemitism, for heaven's sake."

"Bit weird, isn't it?"

"Definitely weird."

They looked at it again.

"The last bit. The bit about revenge being a 'dish best eaten cold.' This is the clue to the motive."

"Revenge? Not money, then?"

"It certainly isn't following any of the normal patterns of kidnaping for ransom, no. There has been no ransom demand, and there nearly always is one by this stage. Anyway, if they wanted to kidnap for money, with all due respect to your good selves, you wouldn't have been the target. I've seen the way you live, and unless you are a miserly billionaire, you are not the typical target of a kidnapper for ransom."

Don managed a smile. "You're right. We don't have that much money. We get by, but there are many more wealthy families in Golders Green."

"Not only wealthy, Mr. Hardman, but overtly wealthy. Stupidly so, if you ask me."

Don said, "But who would want to take revenge on us? What have we done? I don't understand."

"That's for you to tell me, Mr. Hardman."

"Nothing as far as I know. I don't think I've made any enemies." Don sat, thinking, a puzzled frown creasing his forehead.

"Usually it's the rich ones who make the enemies," agreed Colin. "Jealousy, resentment, you name it, the rich come in for it. But in your case...?"

"I'm not rich. No one is jealous of me. I only have one son. Most people around here have large families, so they're certainly not jealous of me for that."

"What about in your work? A disgruntled ex-employee?"

"Hm. I thought I had a very good relationship with my employees."

"Have all your present employees been with you for some time?"

"You asked me this once before."

"So humor me. Tell me again. I need to get a clearer picture."

"We are four partners. We built the business up from scratch. My partners are all Jewish, all Orthodox, and I trust them implicitly."

Colin nodded his understanding at this.

"My wife is a kind of sub-partner. There are five guys on tech support. Shift workers, eight hours at a time, round the clock. We get phone calls at all times of the day and night. The two secretaries are middle-aged. They've been with us for years. One is due to retire soon. Neither of them knows a thing about computers except how to save and print. They're always calling in the tech support guys to help them if they get a problem with the word processor. The older of the two likes to type on an electric typewriter rather than a computer. Neither of them use the Internet; they wouldn't have the faintest idea how. They type letters and reports. That's it."

"Isn't that a bit of a disadvantage for you, being an Internet company?" Colin asked, mildly amused by this account of the two secretaries.

"Yeah, but to be honest with you, they're loyal and efficient in their own way, and they don't waste time. When one of them was off sick for a while, we took a young girl as a temp. She knew all about the Internet, could type like a rocket — and was absolutely useless."

"Oh?"

"Within seconds she had telnetted into an IRC server and was using the chat rooms to talk to her friends instead of working. She cost the company a fortune in work not done. Lucky our permanent connection meant no extra phone bills, too. We got rid of her as soon as we could and were glad to get our old, computer-illiterate secretary back again."

Colin grinned. "Heh. I see. So newer isn't always better."

"By no means."

"Okay. Now your tech-support people. Tell me about them."

"Three have been with us for over a year. They're slightly older than the usual techie types. Harry, Ewan, and Dave are in their early forties, graying, and very good at what they do. The other two, Ben and Kev, are young. Early twenties, fresh out of college with computer science degrees. They know everything there is to know about building and maintaining a computer from the bottom up and absolutely nothing about customer relations. Their telephone manner leaves a lot to be desired, but they know their job so well that we turn a blind eye. Ilana has been trying to teach them how to be polite and helpful on the phone and not laugh when a newbie phones in with some query the two guys perceive as ignorant. Like the lady who phoned in complaining that her coffee cup holder was broken on the front of her computer."

Colin looked puzzled for a moment.

"She had been using her CD-ROM drive to hold her coffee cups."

Colin laughed aloud.

"And the middle-aged man who complained that he couldn't get onto the Internet. The two youngsters took him through all the jargon, which went way over his head, trying to reconfigure his modem strings and making sure he had his IP address correctly entered. When Ilana took over that call, she found out the customer didn't actually have a modem. They need to learn that not everyone has a handle on computers like they do. Well, they're learning now, thanks to Ilana." Don stopped, looking stricken. "I hope she'll get over this.

Right now she can't do a thing in the office. She wanders around like a robot on autopilot."

"Can you give me a list of all your employees, their names and addresses?" Colin asked.

"Sure. I'll prepare it for you tonight. Can I e-mail it to you here?"

"E-mails have a strange connotation for us at the moment, don't they? But yes, of course. Go right ahead."

Ilana reappeared at that moment, carrying a cup of tea and looking calmer. "Sorry," she said, somewhat shamefacedly.

"Please don't apologize, Mrs. Hardman. Sit down and we'll explain what we have been discussing. Maybe you have some more input into this e-mail."

"Now I think I might be able to look at it without losing control," Ilana said, and she did indeed appear much calmer.

"It's this bit about revenge. Do you have any idea who might want to take revenge on you or your husband?"

"Absolutely not." There was a pause. "Well, none that I know of. One never knows for sure, does one. You can think people like you, and really they don't. People don't always say and do what they mean."

They looked at Ilana, not saying a word. She smiled enigmatically.

"Are you referring to anyone in particular, Mrs. Hardman?" Colin asked.

"Can't you see? Someone has taken my son. Someone who seems to know us. Otherwise, why would they want to take revenge on us? So I have to accept that the people I know and trust have turned on us. Someone has turned on us. I can't trust anyone until I find out who did this to us." She paused for a moment, staring into her cup of tea, then took a sip.

"Suddenly I am seeing shadows where there were none before. I am suspicious of people I consider my friends. Maybe one of them took my baby. Maybe the person I smiled at in the street, maybe the shopkeeper I visit regularly. Maybe, maybe, maybe. I suspect everyone, trust no one. It's a horrid thing to feel."

"It's hardly likely that someone still around has Josh," Don pointed out gently. "The abductor is obviously with him."

"Not necessarily. Maybe they've got him hidden somewhere while they conduct an outwardly blameless life here in Golders Green. Maybe they have an accomplice to look after him while they smile at me as if butter wouldn't melt in their mouth. I'd rather he did have an accomplice. I hate the thought of my baby being left on his own while someone is pretending to be perfectly normal and smiling at me in the street."

"That's not likely," Colin said again. "It would take a huge amount of brazenness for an abductor to live a normal life while having a child hidden somewhere."

"Then it's easy," Ilana said brightly. "All we do is look around the community and see who's missing." She smiled brilliantly. "Case solved!"

☼ ☼ ☼

Sha'arei Chessed. A unique area of Jerusalem, totally singular. One of the oldest neighborhoods in the new city, it had been originally built in 1910, a ramshackle hotchpotch of tumbledown shacks and houses, some with corrugated iron roofs and doors, some solidly built in the Arab style with thick stone walls and arched windows. It had become home to many great sages. Over the years, particularly in the last decade, Sha'arei Chessed's location, a mere ten minutes' walk from the center of town, had made it an attractive chunk of real estate for development. Slowly the ramshackle shacks were being replaced by elegant new townhouses and apartments, and now the area had a half-and-half look. Some of the streets had the look of a dormitory town — empty most of the year, full of life for the summer and Jewish holidays such as Pesach and Sukkos. Some locals were thinking of moving on.

In an apartment building on Ibn Shaprut Street, Avi Pincus sat, furiously working on his computer. He and his wife and four children had made aliyah recently and had their combined eye on a house a bit nearer to the shul called the Gra, but until Pincus earned enough money, it was way beyond their reach.

Avi was a skilled programmer and had nabbed himself a good job with a software company in Jerusalem, but despite working extra hours and taking work home, he was struggling to meet his everyday family commitments, never mind putting away some savings. The house in Sha'arei Chessed was looking as far away as ever.

Avi finished the program and sent it into the office via e-mail. He blessed the cheap Bezek rates that compared so favorably with British Telecom, and he blessed the fast service from his Net provider. It saved time and money, both of which were in short supply right now.

He sent off his work and downloaded whatever e-mail was waiting for him on the server. Among the work-related mail was one from the U.K. with an unfamiliar address. He scanned the work e-mail quickly to see if there was anything that urgently required his attention, then disconnected from the service and opened up the e-mail from England.

"Avi, we need your help here," it began.

As he read, his sense of shock and horror increased with each word. The Hardman kid missing? Abducted? Untraceable e-mails? His mind started to race. Quickly he typed a reply.

Please forward me the originals of the two e-mails exactly as the Hardmans received them, and any other they get, immediately. I think I know how this was accomplished, but I will need to study the letters.

He clicked Send and the letter vanished. Sitting in front of the computer, still logged in, his brain was whirring at warp speed. Then his fingers whizzed over the keyboard in a blur of movement, and he clicked Send again and the screen cleared. He disconnected and sat back, cracking his knuckles loudly. He sat there a few moments more, apparently inert, but everything inside was buzzing, circuits alight with thought. Then, with a sigh, he returned to his bread-and-butter work, the next piece of programming.

The e-mail he sent back to England was picked up, but not by who it was intended for. It was intercepted, read on the server, and deleted. The Fox absorbed the knowledge that somewhere out there was someone who was, brain for brain, a match for him.

Well, almost.

I have the kid. And as long as I have the kid, I have the upper hand.

Using a hacking program he had downloaded, he reentered the server he had used to read the mail. He forged a similar e-mail, using the same headers and return address. Then, leaving the mail on the server, he kicked over his traces. First he deleted the log files which registered his entry. Then he installed special programs that made him appear invisible. Satisfied, he logged out and left the system as if he had never been there.

The Internet Fox was gone.

DAY FOUR

CHAPTER TEN

"A Mr. Baruch Weiss is on the phone, sir," Potter said on the intercom. Colin growled.

"I'm being driven mad about that search they want to do," he grumbled. "Can't you get rid of him?"

"Why don't you just let them do the search? Can't hurt, can it?" Potter said puzzled.

"Because, Potter, I'd be daft to allow amateurs to do a job for professionals. You know what I'm most worried about here, Potter? With bumbling Orthodox amateurs fiffing and faffing about Golders Green, mucking things up, they might even flush him out of where he was and put him on the run to somewhere we really can't catch him. Make things much worse, in other words."

"Hmm. I see," Potter said and clicked off the intercom to speak to Baruch Weiss. He came on again in a minute.

"He said you told him you would authorize the search," Potter said ruefully after getting an earful from Weiss.

"Tell him I never said I would authorize it. I said I'd look into it. And I have. And at the moment the answer is no. I'll let him know if we decide to authorize a search."

☼ ☼ ☼

Baruch Weiss hung up despondently. He had managed to drum up such enthusiasm among his colleagues on this authorization, and, if he was entirely honest with himself, he was quite enjoying the feeling of importance being the organizer had engendered. Mind you, he still held the "card" of Avi Pincus. Which reminded him. He hadn't checked if Avi had sent a reply to their e-mail. He phoned Pinny Bloch.

"I just wondered if you've had a reply to that e-mail you sent Avi," Baruch asked.

"Yes, I have as a matter of fact."

"Well? Why didn't you call me and tell me what he said?" Baruch was annoyed.

Pinny sighed. "Because I didn't think you'd like it. To be honest, it's a weird reply. It doesn't sound like the Avi I know. I've been puzzling over it for ages, ever since it arrived."

"Read it."

There were a few clicks. Pinny was bringing it up on his computer screen.

"Here it is. It goes like this: 'Sorry I can't help you. This is not my area of expertise. Avraham.' "

There was a pause while Baruch digested this.

"Not his area of expertise? It's exactly his area of expertise."

"That's what I thought. Maybe we overestimated how much he can do."

Baruch shook his head violently. "No. I know this guy. He loves a challenge. Nothing he likes better than to do at least three impossible things before breakfast. The Avi Pincus I know would be tearing his brain apart working out a solution."

There was another pause.

"Darn it," Baruch said suddenly.

"What?" Pinny asked.

"Avi never signs his name Avraham. Never. Ever."

"What are you saying?"

"I'm saying this is totally weird. Maybe someone got hold of his computer and replied to the mail before he found it, then erased it."

"Then that person would be in Jerusalem."

"Yeah. Or maybe...," said Baruch thoughtfully.

"What? Maybe what?"

"It was intercepted."

"Intercepted? How?"

"Heaven knows. I don't. I don't know diddly squat about the Internet, never mind all this techie stuff."

"Well, whoever intercepted it is very shortsighted. All we gotta do is phone Avi and ask what he wrote in the mail."

"True. It bought whoever it is a bit of time, that's all."

"Maybe time is what he needed."

"I'll call Avi now and call you right back," Baruch said and hung up.

He dialed the number he had for Avi Pincus in Jerusalem.

"Avi's gone to the office, Baruch," his wife, Hannah, said. "I can give you his number there."

Baruch dialed the office and finally tracked Avi down. When Baruch read out the reply they had received, Avi sucked in his breath between his teeth.

"I didn't send that letter. Are you sure it says it comes from me?"

Baruch read out the header and return address.

"Hmmm," Avi said very slowly. "I think we are up against one very smart cookie. Someone who really knows his way around the Internet. I have to stand back and admire this guy's ingenuity."

"Would you know how he did all these ingenious things?" Baruch asked.

"Not offhand, but I'll work on it. The e-mail I sent asked you to send me the e-mails exactly as you received them so I can see them for myself and work out how to trace them."

"You think you can?"

"I'll do my best. I can't promise more than that."

"So should I send you those e-mails?"

"If you e-mail them to me, no doubt whoever intercepted the last one will intercept these, too. He's on guard now."

"So what do you suggest?"

"Print them out and fax them to me. I'll tell you when and where, and I'll be waiting for it by the fax machine. I think that should be pretty fail-safe."

"Okay, I'll do that."

They disconnected after Baruch wrote down the number and time he should fax the e-mails over. He called Pinny right away and relayed the news. Pinny was amazed, to say the least.

"Seems like it's quite an opponent we're up against," he said. "Someone who can send untraceable e-mails and who can intercept and change them. I had no idea such things were possible."

"We need some *siyatta diShamaya*," Baruch said.

"And a good hacker as His tool," said Pinny. Even over the phone Baruch could hear he was smiling.

"What about the search, then?" Pinny went on.

Baruch coughed. "Seems it's been temporarily suspended," he said, hoping that didn't show too much loss of face.

"That copper's changed his mind, then?" Pinny asked astutely.

"Seems so. For now, anyway. I'm sure he'll soon see how much help we can be. Now I have to go send this fax to Avi. Talk to you later."

☼ ☼ ☼

The fax safely received, Avi sat looking at it for a long time. His heart thumping, he sat at his computer. A half-hour later, he phoned Baruch Weiss.

"Have you got a spare bed?" Avi said without preamble.

"Sure, why?"

"Make it ready. I'm coming back to England. On my own."

☼ ☼ ☼

Ilana and Don were talking about their missing son.

"When we are sick," Don said to her gently, "we go to a specialist."

"Yes, Don," she said.

"And when we need anything in our home, or for any purpose, we always look for the top man."

"True," she agreed.

"Now our most precious commodity, our only son, is missing," he went on.

"But the police are on it. Detective Inspector Sommers seems very good." Ilana's voice rose in panic.

"I'm sure he knows his job, and he is doing the best he can under the circumstances, Ilana. But it's not his child who's missing. Maybe we should call in a specialist of our own."

"I don't know of any specialists in finding lost sons."

"I might just know someone, though," he said. "Let me make a call to New York and speak to a specialist I just happen to know."

CHAPTER ELEVEN

A young woman emerged from the subway and blinked in the bright afternoon sun. She reached in her bag and put on sunglasses. She was carrying a briefcase; she had been at work in Manhattan. Quickly she crossed the street and started walking up Avenue J toward home. Her shoulder-length auburn hair glinted like burnished copper in the sun, and she wore an obviously modest but smart city suit. She was Leora Jakober, twenty-five years old, the youngest criminologist the New York Police Department employed.

Leora Jakober was observant, but she had not always been so. Brought up in midtown Manhattan, only daughter to highflying professional parents, she had not known a life other than the lonely latchkey existence of a child whose parents were never home. At school, too, all her friends' parents worked full-time. They never knew what it was like to have a mommy at home baking brownies when they returned from school or someone to listen to their moaning against the unfair teacher. Girls like Leora Jakober and her peers had their own house keys and knew where the microwave dinners were kept in the freezer, because Mom and Dad weren't going to be home much before nine-thirty, often much later.

Leora had always been fascinated by anything to do with the police. Her peers had read novels and magazines. Leora had read police manuals and lengthy tracts on crime and forensic science. She had hung around police departments, keeping a low profile, but impressing even the hardest-nosed city cop with her brain and determination to learn. She managed to always be around when there was action without being under everyone's feet.

Her parents were not surprised when she told them she wanted to study criminology. Though they did not think it an appropriate occupation for a woman, they were too politically correct to say so to their highly motivated daughter. Since they were wealthy and had no other children, they sent her to the University of South Florida at Tampa, where she graduated *magna cum laude* in criminology in two years. Once she qualified, she got a position with the NYPD and quickly became indispensable, making detective in the minimum possible time. Her insight into the criminal mind and her sharp observation of evidence soon won her a place as a criminologist for the department. Official or unofficial, she was the one they sought out when trace evidence needed analyzing. With the aid of the latest technology she was able to spot things others missed.

Working with all ethnic groups and cultures, Leora found herself drawn to her Jewish roots despite her parents' ignorance and cynicism. She began attending a *ba'al teshuvah* program and found the answers to many doubts and questions. She never quite reached *chareidi* level, but she was strongly religious, observed Shabbos and kashrus, and traded her jeans and combat pants for elegant city suits or soft skirts and sweaters. The crossroad was reached when her career came into question. Could an observant Jewess still continue to be a police detective? What about Shabbos and festivals?

By this time Leora Jakober was indispensable to her employers, and they were willing to have her on almost any terms. And so, reluctantly, the *rav* in charge of the *ba'al teshuvah* program agreed to her continuing in her chosen vocation.

Her parents were distraught at first by what they thought of as their daughter's defection, but she kept a close bond with them, so they were soon reassured that they were not to be cast off along with her previous lifestyle. Living with them was another matter. She took an apartment of her own in Flatbush, though it meant commuting to work. She chose not to take a roommate as she couldn't have borne sharing with giggly young women. When she visited her parents, the occasions were often still and unnatural. She would sit at their highly polished elegant dining-room table, eating her own food and using plastic cutlery on a plastic mat, chatting about her work and carefully avoiding talking about her personal life. Lesser mortals than Leora would have slowly cut down on these painful visits, but she kept on going.

She reached a newsstand and picked up a copy of the *New York Times*. With it tucked under her arm she arrived at her small apartment and let herself in.

Leora went to the refrigerator, opened the door, and peered in. She found a bowl of withered salad, a packet of cheese slices, two tomatoes, and a quart of milk. Three eggs. A stick of butter. She sighed and opened the freezer compartment. A loaf of sliced bread and some vegetarian sausages. Do I call for takeout or make something out of this? she thought.

She weighed the options. If I make a meal out of this, then I have to go grocery shopping tomorrow. If I call for takeout, then I can save this food. On the other hand, this food needs to be used up and I should go grocery shopping...

Sighing, she took three slices of the bread and put them into the toaster. Then she took two eggs and the butter and some milk and made herself scrambled eggs with one of the tomatoes. Piling the mixture on top of the buttered toast, she took her simple meal to the kitchen table, washed her hands, and sat down with a cup of coffee and the *Times*.

She ate, reading her newspaper contentedly and sipping coffee, until the phone rang. It was a call from London.

☼ ☼ ☼

Colin Sommers sat at his desk, head in hands, polystyrene cup of coffee at his side. He looked at his watch. Ten-thirty. He needed sleep. It was nearly the end of the fourth day, he was no nearer finding Josh, and his whole body was screaming for rest. He lay his head down on the desk for just a moment. Just a moment.

A hand shaking his shoulder awakened him. Groggily he shook it off. "What is it?"

"Sir, it's Potter. You have a call. From America."

"Tell them to go away." Colin's mind sought sleep desperately.

"She says she'll only take a minute. She says she's a criminologist."

The fog cleared in Colin's head as if someone had blown some icy air through his ears. "Criminologist? Gimme, gimme."

Potter grinned, went back to his desk, and put the call through.

"Hi. I'm Leora Jakober." The strong New York accent made Colin wince. "I'm a criminologist attached to NYPD. I also happen to be Jewish. A special request has been received through department channels that my services might be needed to help you with the case of Josh Hardman."

"Have I just died and gone to heaven?" Colin sighed blissfully.

" 'Scuse me?"

"Don't mind me. I'm talking to myself. You're a criminologist with the NYPD."

"That's what I just said."

"I could certainly use some help. We seem to have ground to a halt. We have some trace evidence, but I'm sure there is more that we are missing."

"That's what I do," Leora said. "How long has the kid been missing?"

"This is the end of day four. We are frankly very concerned for the lad's safety."

"If you want me, I can be on the next plane. I just finished a case here in New York, and I have some time off due to me. The source who requested me has assured me that my expenses would be paid."

"I'd have to okay it with my superiors, of course. They may not be willing to allow an outsider to come in on a British case. But if you give me the number of your superiors, I'll call them for confirmation, and then get back to you."

He passed on the information and numbers to his superiors and sat back to wait. Drinking a cup of coffee, he thought about the phone call from Leora Jakober. Colin wasn't a fool and quickly made the connection between the American Don Hardman and the NYPD. It was pretty obvious to him who had requested that she join the investigative team.

Who cares who requested her? If she brings results, who cares?

Within twenty minutes his super was on the line, having made the call to the NYPD.

"Well, Colin, lad, it's most irregular, of course, but since her ladyship is being bought and paid for by person or persons unknown, and she has a reputation any one of us here would envy, it would be churlish of us to refuse, really, wouldn't it. No point in cutting off our noses to spite our faces, and if she produces no results, well, we haven't lost any money, have we?"

"No, sir," Colin said, then added curiously, "So the NYPD are impressed by her, are they?"

"They certainly put on a good show of reluctance to let her go, but since she has just finished a case and has some holiday time owing, they could hardly say no. They said she was the best criminologist they've ever had, and could we please hurry up and solve the case so they could have her back. She'll be on a flight arriving tomorrow evening."

Colin grinned. "Well, as you say, sir, we can't lose if someone else is paying. Worse comes to worse, she's useless and we jettison her ASAP."

Just knowing she was on her way made Colin feel better about the whole thing. He made a note to phone the Hardmans in the morning and inform them about the new development, left himself instructions on a yellow message slip to go and talk to Don Hardman's employees, and went home. After a quick shower, he fell into the first real sleep he had enjoyed since Josh went missing.

DAY FIVE

CHAPTER TWELVE

Ilana slept deeply. One would have expected sleep to be hard to come by, but for her it was an escape to a place where she was still with her son.

In her dream, she was running through a field of poppies, holding his hand. He was keeping up with her long-legged strides, two paces to each of hers and laughing up into her face. They collapsed together into a heap in the crushed flowers, giggling and rolling, the opiate scent filling their nostrils, making their heads swim. She cuddled her son, ruffled his dark hair, and looked into his vivid blue eyes. Her heart was so full of maternal happiness and fulfillment that she thought it might burst through her skin. They played together in the poppy field, heads dizzy with happiness and crushed flowers.

Her dream ended. She struggled to clutch onto it, but it slipped from her unwilling grasp. She could feel herself beginning to waken, and like a fish being dragged from the water by an angler, she fought against the hook and line and dove under for one last breath of life-giving fluid.

Reluctantly, so reluctantly, Ilana was dragged, internally

kicking and screaming, from the dream into the vacuity of reality. Her empty arms ached. She could still feel the warmth of her small son's body within them, and now they hurt with the pain of absence.

"Leave me alone," she moaned, fresh tears already flowing, watering the last of the poppies as they dissolved from her consciousness. No, no, no. Don't drag me from this wonderful place where I play with my son. Please, don't make me leave...

The fish lay gasping on the riverbank.

Ilana opened her eyes to a world without Josh in it. Then Don came into the room, carrying the cordless telephone.

"Ilana? Oh, good, you're awake. Colin Sommers is on the phone."

"I don't want to talk to anyone," Ilana wept, turning her back on him and pulling the covers over her head.

"Ilana, come. You won't mind this phone call. Remember that specialist I said we should call in? It seems she's coming over! Let's not tell anyone how we got her to come. It's our secret." Don handed her the cordless phone.

Struggling, she sat up in bed and took it. She looked at her watch. It was nine o'clock. If she had not been disturbed, she would have slept the day away. There seemed so little point in being awake.

"Hello?"

"Good morning, Mrs. Hardman. It's Detective Inspector Sommers. I have some news for you."

Her heart leaped. "You have found Josh?"

"No, not yet."

Her heart sank a little, even though she knew the purpose of the phone call. "So, Inspector Sommers, what news could you possibly have which would be of interest to me?"

"An expert criminologist from New York has been assigned to this case. Is coming over even as we speak, in fact."

"Oh? And how did he hear about us? We hardly rate the same giddying heights of fame as the Lindbergh baby, do we?"

Don, listening to this one-sided conversation from across the room, could not help but grin at Ilana and give her the thumbs up for her acting ability.

"The criminologist is a she, Mrs. Hardman. Her name is Leora Jakober. I am not sure how or why she has been assigned to us, but I must say I am most pleased to have the assistance."

"Leora Jakober? That's a very Jewish-sounding name, Detective Inspector."

"Lots of Jews in New York," Colin said uncomfortably.

"Yes, I suppose there are," Ilana admitted, feeling silly.

"Well, Leora Jakober has graduated *magna cum laude* from the University of South Florida in criminology. She now works for the New York Police Department and is treasured by them for her expertise in detection. Her specialty is the analysis of trace evidence. She can find out a lot from the flimsiest of clues. Which is what we have here," he added.

"And she is interested in this case?"

"She certainly is. So much so that she is on her way over to give us her expertise."

"Is she Mrs. or Miss Jakober?" Ilana couldn't help asking.

"Miss, apparently."

"Iron-haired, iron-willed spinster type," Ilana surmised.

Colin smiled to himself. "It's hard to say over the telephone, Mrs. Hardman, but she certainly didn't give the impression of being very old."

"We'll see anyway. So she's coming today?"

"I think so. I am sending a car to meet her at the airport this evening."

"Where will she stay?"

Colin hadn't thought that far ahead. "I have no idea."

"She can stay here," Ilana said firmly. "After all, I have plenty of room. Especially now."

"Makes sense, I suppose," the policeman agreed. "She will have more opportunity to study the situation. Thank you very much, Mrs. Hardman. Now, I have spoken to your husband, and he has agreed to let me and my colleague interview the staff at his office. Try to get a handle on them, if you get my meaning. I will spend today doing that until Miss Jakober arrives."

"All right, Detective Inspector."

The connection broken, Ilana sank back on her pillows. "This woman. You know her?"

"Actually, my mother told me about her. Her aunt is a friend of my mother's. She told me about Leora because she thought it was unusual that a criminologist would become religious."

"Oh, so she's a *ba'alas teshuvah*? How far has she come?"

"I would say modern Orthodox."

"Is she really as good as she sounds?"

"Her reputation as a criminologist definitely precedes her," Don said.

"We're paying for her to come?"

"Yes."

"She'd better be worth it."

"Will you get up and maybe try a little bit of work today?" Don coaxed. Since the discovery of the second e-mail, Ilana had refused to go anywhere near her computer, almost as if she were afraid it might jump out and bite her. "I have to go into the office to be present when Detective Inspector Sommers interviews my staff," he went on. "Maybe you'd like to be there? A woman's intuition can sometimes pick up things we poor, simple-minded men might miss. A look, an intonation in someone's voice. A glance between two people that speaks more eloquently than words. You've always been good at noticing things like that; I'm the unobservant one. Will you be there? Please, Ilana?"

"The detective said the lady in New York will be arriving tonight," she said, sitting up straighter in bed.

"That's right. So we might as well do something productive in the meantime to help find Josh."

"All right. I think I will come with you to the office," Ilana said.

Don was stunned and pleased. During the past five days she had shown little interest in anything. It seemed the impending arrival of Leora Jakober had infused Ilana with new life for the first time. He sent up a silent prayer that her arrival would not be a let-down. If that were to happen, he said to Hashem, it will destroy my wife. Please don't let that happen.

"I shall get dressed and put on makeup," she announced suddenly. "I haven't worn makeup for days now." She peered at her face in the mirror. "Oh, dear. My skin looks all flaky and dry." She washed her hands and face, then applied a liberal layer of moisturizer. Don watched his wife come to life again and prayed anew that this rebirth was not a temporary blip in her general downward spiral.

"You haven't been doing much of anything lately," he said gently. "I'm glad to see you taking care of yourself again."

"This moisturizer just sank right in. My skin is so dry. Why didn't you tell me, Don, how horrendous I have been looking?" She reached into the tub and pulled out a large glob of cream and applied it, feeling her skin drink thirstily.

"It would have fallen on deaf ears," he said, and she nodded her acceptance of this truth. "I'll wait for you downstairs, okay? How about some breakfast?"

"I would love some scrambled eggs on toast," Ilana said brightly, "and gallons of hot coffee."

Don saluted. "Coming up, ma'am." Feeling lighthearted for the first time in days, he went downstairs.

She dressed smartly in a light suit and a newly done *sheitel* that had been sitting in her closet for weeks. She had been wearing an old ratty one, not caring how she looked.

"I'm still alive," she said to her reflection in the mirror as she applied makeup. "I am me and I am alive, and I am going to help find my son." Smiling, she went downstairs.

After the most nutritious meal she had managed to eat (and enjoy) since it happened, Ilana was ready to accompany Don into the office. She had even put perfume on, Don noted as he helped her into the car. Ilana left instructions for Maria and they drove off.

Colin Sommers was waiting for them in his car when they arrived at the offices of Intergraph in Camden Town, with Sergeant White sitting next to him. When the Hardmans pulled up and parked, Colin and Peter got out of their car and stood waiting for the Hardmans to unload whatever they needed to take in with them.

It was a cool but bright spring morning. The sun dazzled as it bounced off small puddles left by overnight rain, puddles which residues of gasoline turned into shimmering rainbows. The leaves on overhead trees were rustling as crisply as new currency. Ilana breathed in deeply. "Mm. What a simply gorgeous day!"

They all walked into the offices together. The secretaries were the front line of defense. One, white-haired and bespectacled, was sitting at a reception desk manning a switchboard while she typed letters on an old-fashioned electric typewriter.

It had been so long since Colin had seen anything other than a computer for typing that he couldn't resist the urge to go around the edge of the desk and take a peek at this historic machine.

"Luvaducks, it's been yonks since I've seen one of these," he commented, half-sitting on the edge of the desk. The secretary looked at him curiously until Don explained who he and Sergeant White were and why they were there.

"I'm afraid I belong to a bygone age," the secretary, who introduced herself as Mary Nolan, said. "An age where even this machine, aided by electricity, is an innovation. In my day we typed on manual Remingtons and had to use considerable force to get the keys to type."

"But don't you think that maybe typing on a computer might be useful? If you make mistakes, you don't have to use correction fluid."

Mary Nolan shot Colin a supercilious look. "Inspector, I don't make mistakes. The very few occasions I have been forced by circumstance to use the office computer to type on, it has behaved in a most unpredictable manner. Giving me blue screens and error messages, crashing so that I lose all my work."

"You're meant to save it, Mrs. N.," Don said kindly.

"Save," Mary said scornfully. "I type on this typewriter, I don't need to save. It's just there."

"Mary," Colin said, "have you known all the employees in this company for some time?"

"Well, now, let's see. The partners themselves, of course. They were all here when I was employed, and they're still here now."

"How long ago was that?"

"Five years."

"That's about how long this business has been running, Detective Inspector," Don explained. "The Internet itself has scarcely been user-friendly for that long. Before 1994, the Net was under the control of a bunch of nerdy propeller-head academics who were absolutely horrified at the idea of the Internet being anything other than a tool for university lecturers to exchange information. Once our dear friend Bill Gates started making user-friendly software and the World Wide Web was introduced, more and more 'ordinary' people started using it, too."

"I know," Colin said, feeling patronized. "I do recall in my dim and distant past when the Internet belonged to a few university people who tried their best to pretend it was difficult to use so no one would encroach on their territory."

"Bill Gates became the most hated man in history at one time," Ilana put in with a grin. "Of course, there are still plenty of Unix snobs out there who think anyone using Microsoft products is a sad loser."

"So you started Intergraph when the Net started becoming user-friendly," Colin summed up.

"Yes, we were in at the beginning when hardly anyone else was designing Web sites, and we had the lion's share of the market for a while. At least, here in London. Later on the pie grew. Our slice shrank, and we had to work harder to win clients. Every man and his dog could design his own Web site. We had to show them how a corporate Web site should look."

Mary Nolan had very little to contribute to this conversation except to say that she knew all the present staff fairly well and the technical staff, too. The latter she regarded rather maternally as they all seemed to be scarcely out of school.

"Myself and Alicia have been the only two secretaries from the year dot. Mr. Hardman, he doesn't hold with getting these flibbertigibbet young typists. He knows quality when he sees it, even if we don't know much about computers. The world got along quite nicely before computers came along, and it can continue on its merry way after computers are dead and gone, too." She paused. "When Alicia was ill, they took on a flibbertigibbet for a while, and they never did it again, I can tell you!"

"Troublesome, was she?" asked Colin.

"Not exactly troublesome as much as lazy, I think. She knew her way around computers too well. Used them to play rather than work. She went on-line and chatted to people and played games," said Mary Nolan disapprovingly.

"It's lucky we have a permanent connection, or she'd have ended up costing us money in phone bills as well as wasted time and lost work," Don said grimly.

"Well, that episode certainly taught the partners the value of us older secretaries," said another voice. A smiling, gray-haired lady entered the room with a tray of mugs. "Tea's up. I'm Alicia Morgan by the way. How do you do, Detective Inspector?"

Alicia Morgan was a tall, slender reed of a woman, supremely elegant, with perfectly coiffed hair and manicured nails. A total contrast to Mary Nolan, who was everyone's favorite granny, no one could imagine Alicia ever wanting to deal with grandchildren. She was like a duchess, and Mary was like the downstairs maid. She served tea and coffee to everyone like it was being served in the finest china cups instead of chipped and ill-assorted mugs, asking if anyone wanted milk and sugar with the most elegant of manners.

"Thank you," Colin said, sipping from his pottery mug and wondering if he ought to extend his little finger in the manner of well-bred English gentlemen.

"How long have you been working here? As long as Mary?" Sergeant White asked.

"No, no," Alicia Morgan hastened to point out. "I am not as old as Mary Nolan." She smiled sweetly.

Don and Ilana had a sudden fit of coughing, and Mary looked miffed.

"I've been here four and a half years, actually," Alicia added. "I'm a very experienced shorthand typist. I trained in the top girls' college in London." (She pronounced it "gels.") "I also have a good telephone manner so Mr. Hardman likes me to be the first to respond."

"And computers? Are you familiar with them?"

"Well, they weren't around when I went to college. But Mr. Hardman taught me the basics, how to type and how to save and print. What else does one need? And anyway, we have technical support on tap if things go wrong. As they frequently do, unfortunately." A well-timed sniff showed her real feelings about computers.

It was clear to Colin that these two secretaries had both a common bond and a divisive streak that forged them together as a unit and divided in mutual but mostly good-natured sniping. Both secretaries exhibited a maternal affection for the Hardmans and expressed their deep concern for Josh's safety.

"I hope you find the wee laddie safe and sound," Mary said, traces of her Scottish ancestry peeping out.

"Indeed, yes. We were all terribly fond of him. When he used to come to the office in his holiday times to 'help,' he was so sweet..."

There was an awkward silence at Alicia's use of the past tense. She coughed.

"He really is a delightful little boy," Alicia said with emphasis into the silence. Everyone shuffled around a little, then relaxed, as if talking about the boy in the present tense made it so.

"Sorry," Alicia said.

Imperceptible nodding of heads showed that forgiveness was granted.

Colin went on to interview the other partners. They were three Orthodox men in their thirties who spoke supportively of the Hardmans.

All of them had small Gemaras or Mishnahs on their desks for study during the quiet times, when they weren't busy working on Web sites. Colin looked at them and remembered a time when he, too, would gain spiritual pleasure from the study of the Talmud and its commentaries. He remembered learning with his *chavrusa* regularly, arguing heatedly and discussing the finer points of some *gemara*. He recalled the buzz, the intensity of it, and could not, at this moment, recall anything that came close to that feeling. Sighing, he turned his attention to the matter at hand.

The partners were close friends of Don, and none, as far as he could see, had any ax to grind. They all seemed genuinely distressed at Josh's disappearance, and Colin reckoned he'd have an almost impossible task to prove they were being hypocritical. However, he'd been a cop too long to take things at face value, so he made a point of taking all their names and addresses to check them out later.

Then came the technical staff who were on duty at that time. Harry and Ewan seemed loyal and committed to the business. They both vaguely recalled the "flibbertigibbet."

"Name was Cindy, I think," said Harry. "A whiz on the keyboard. Surprised us all, to be honest. Looked as if she had nothing but air between her ears, but she could find her way around a computer."

"Sounds like she should have been useful, then."

"Should have been, but wasn't. Too young, too lazy, too interested in playing rather than working."

"So she was sacked?" Colin asked.

"Yup. Given her marching orders. Didn't like it, of course. She thought she had a meal ticket, free access to the Net to chat to her friends, only do a bit of work when the bosses were looking over her shoulder, keeping the chat rooms hidden behind a work screen. Only the bosses knew the work they had given her wasn't getting done in a reasonable time frame and started looking harder at her screen, did a few Alt-Tabs to bring up what was hidden..."

"I suppose she could have gotten another similar job fast enough?" White said.

"Maybe, but she'd have had to forge references, 'cause we certainly didn't supply any."

The rest of the staff didn't have much more to add. The two policemen left Ilana and Don in their workplace and went back to their car. Sitting inside it, windows rolled down to let in the warm spring sunshine, Colin said, "Disgruntled employee?"

"The flibbertigibbet is the Internet Fox? Do you really think so? Bit hard to imagine it being a girl, but then again, we do tend to typecast villains, don't we?"

"Playing on-line games and chatting on IRC doesn't add up to the skills the Fox possesses," Colin said. "It adds up to a pretty good computer know-how, agreed, but, Peter, the Fox knows how to do things that even propeller heads we have consulted don't know. This person has to be a seriously good hacker."

"Hacker? How so?"

"Before we came in this morning I had a phone call from

that annoying pest of a man who keeps driving me mad about doing the search."

"Mr. Baruch Weiss," said Peter with a smile, pronouncing the Baruch as "Baruk."

"That's the one. I usually tell Potter to tell him I'm out. But this time he was most insistent that I come to the phone. Apparently he and his little group of expert searchers for lost children had sent an e-mail to someone in Israel who they reckon can find out who this Internet Fox is."

"Get to the point, man," Peter said.

"The point is, White, that the reply came, but it wasn't from their friend. It had been intercepted en route."

"Intercepted? How? It's not like grabbing a letter from a postbox and replacing it with a different one, surely. E-mail is digital signaling transmitted over the telephone lines. How can it be intercepted?"

"White, I don't need you telling me what e-mail is. I, too, have read *The Internet for Total Cretins* or whatever the book is called."

"Sorry." Peter grinned.

"The point is, your average chat room enthusiast and on-line games player wouldn't know how to intercept an e-mail either."

"So you don't think the flibbertigibbet could have done it?"

"Not sure. Let's try to find out a bit more about her."

The two policemen walked back into the Intergraph offices.

"Oh!" gushed Alicia, who was at the front desk manning the telephones. "We thought you had left."

"That was just our dastardly evil plan to catch you unawares," Colin told her. "We pretend we're leaving, but really we're hiding in the bushes out back. Then we sneak back in and catch you in the act."

Alicia opened her blue eyes wide. "We don't have any bushes out back," she said innocently.

Colin sighed. "Is the Big White Chief around?"

"How!" said Don, coming out of an inner office and raising his right hand in a mock Native American greeting.

"Might we talk in your office?" Colin asked.

"Sure, come in."

Don's office was small and cluttered with computers and cables. He cleared some space on two chairs and they sat.

"We were wondering if you had an address for that temporary secretary you sacked."

"And a surname," White added.

"Sure, I have the one she gave me. Don't know if it's current, of course." Don opened a file drawer and rifled through it. He handed them a piece of paper.

"Cindy Wallis," Colin read aloud.

"Mightn't have been her real name, of course," mused White.

Colin looked Don straight in the eye. "Would you say, sir, that she was capable of sending untraceable e-mails and hacking? I know you said she was good, but was she that good?"

Don stared at him. "You think Cindy is the Fox?"

"We don't think anything. We are trying to find out."

"To be honest, my knowledge of Cindy is limited. She was only here a couple of weeks before we sacked her, but from what I know, I would say it was doubtful she was capable of such sophisticated techniques. Yes, she knew how to use a computer, and she knew her way around the Internet. She even knew Unix. But none of this is vastly unusual today. Most computer-literate kids study it in school and university.

Doesn't turn them into sophisticated hackers."

"Had Cindy gone to university?"

"No, she was fresh out of high school, eighteen or nineteen years old when she worked for us. She said she had studied computing to A level and graduated with honors. I found that surprising, to be honest. She seemed like a social stereotype. Essex accent, sort of cockney, you know."

"And she drove a Ford Escort XR3i?" Colin asked, completing the stereotype.

Don grinned. "Didn't have a license, as far as I know. She came in by train. We're very close to the Camden Town station."

"Did she ever meet Josh?"

"Once, I think. Ilana would bring him into the office when he had school holidays and hadn't arranged any play dates. He was an only child and got bored at home on his own, but he loved playing with computers and pretending to help out, so we'd bring him in from time to time. Playing on the computer at home wasn't the same for him as being here, with all the staff. They all adored him; he was never a nuisance or a nag." Don stopped and grimaced. "It's got me doing it, too. Talking about Josh in the past tense."

"Try not to let it upset you. It's natural. Doesn't mean anything."

"I hope not."

"Well, we'll be off now. We'll investigate Cindy and see what we can find out." He shook hands with Don, partly as a human gesture of comfort. He turned to his sergeant. "Come on, Peter, stop slacking, man. There's work to be done."

CHAPTER THIRTEEN

Back in the car again, Colin and Peter looked at their watches. "It's almost eleven. I want to be around when Miss Cleverlogs from Noo Yawk City arrives this evening. Until then, we have some time to kill."

Stung by guilt for a second, Colin remembered a *shiur* he had attended long, long ago, when the speaker had talked about the RSPCT, the Royal Society for the Prevention of Cruelty to Time, and how precious time was, how we mustn't waste a second of it.

"We have some time to fill usefully," he corrected himself, and Peter shot him a look.

"What are you looking at me like that for, White?"

"I think you're going soft in the head, Colin. Ever since you started on this case you've been acting weird."

"Have I?" Colin looked thoughtful.

"Yeah. It's as if I don't know you any longer. You've changed. You used to avoid Orthodox Jews like the plague. Now you're gazing at 'em all misty-eyed and soppy like. What happened to the hard-nosed cop we all know and love, that's what I'd like to know."

"I'm still hard-nosed. And I never avoided them," Colin lied. He felt disoriented.

"Did, too. Always used to send me into Goldbergs Green to do your dirty work, you did. I always thought you were antisemitic. Didn't like to say much about it 'cause, well, each to their own and all that. But this is a real change of heart, or something's happened and I don't understand it."

"You don't understand anything, Peter," Colin replied in a harsh undertone. "And to be honest, right now, neither do I. Now let's go check out Miss Wallis."

☼ ☼ ☼

Baruch stood at the arrivals at Heathrow watching the passengers from the El Al flight LY315 come in through the doors. Would he recognize Avi Pincus if he saw him? It had been quite some time since they'd last met. Anxiously he scanned the crowds. Many similar-looking bearded men came out, but they looked blankly at Baruch. Surely Avi would remember him, even if he didn't really remember Avi? Baruch shifted from one foot to the other and worried that he had missed him altogether.

Suddenly there he was, walking swiftly toward him, waving and smiling broadly, so familiar, how could he possibly have worried that he wouldn't know him? The two men embraced warmly.

"Baruch, my friend! It's good to see you!"

"*Shalom aleichem*, Avi! Welcome back to London."

Avi looked around the arrivals lounge. "Seems like I've never left this place," he said.

Baruch led the way to his car, parked on the third floor of the multistory parking lot. Avi carried only a small suitcase on wheels, which Baruch eyed curiously.

"Not planning on staying long, then?"

"I hope not. Without wishing to cast aspersions on your generous hospitality, I have a wife and kids out there, and I can't leave them for too long. Also, I am hoping to achieve results quite fast."

"Yeah? You think you have a way to trace the Fox?"

"If it was just tracing him through the Internet, I could have stayed where I was. But we have to find him physically. That's why I am here."

"So," continued Avi as Baruch pulled out into the busy traffic on the M4 motorway toward London, "what else is being done to catch the Fox? You can't all just be relying on me."

"No. I don't even think the police know you are here, to be honest. In my opinion, they are being incredibly devil-may-care about this whole business. Here I am with my troop of ready-to-go searchers, just waiting for authorization, and the cops keep putting me off."

"Searchers?"

"Yes. Do you remember the time I got a band of guys together and we searched for that teenage girl in Stamford Hill and found her with an Indian family?"

Avi frowned. "Yes, vaguely." Baruch shot him a disapproving glance. He expected his moment of glory to be indelibly etched on everyone's brain, and it seemed, instead, that everyone had forgotten.

"Well," Baruch went on, trying to stifle his disappointment, "I thought we could do something similar here. But the cops seem to be messing about over the authorization."

"Hmm," Avi said, and after a moment added, "Maybe they aren't messing about. Maybe they're stalling because they don't think it's a good idea for you to go blundering about."

"Blundering about? Me?" Baruch suddenly felt annoyed. He had been hoping for unconditional support, and Avi seemed to be taking the opposition stance.

"I don't mean to offend, but I don't think this case is the same at all as the one of the recalcitrant teenager who hid herself away in a family of Muslims to try out an alien culture and religion. From the little I know of the Fox, he is extremely intelligent and resourceful. What his motives are I cannot imagine, but the last thing we want to do is flush him out of his lair and drive him further afield where he will be much harder to catch. And a fox who knows that the hounds are on his tail will flee. You and your troop of searchers, however well intentioned, are little more than a pack of baying hounds snapping at his heels, sending him streaking across the fields and out of our reach. A much more sophisticated and devious approach must be made if we are to catch this fox."

Baruch retreated into offended silence at this. After a few moments, Avi said lightly, "Hey, friend! Don't be *broiges* with me, please. I'm gonna need all the help I can get, and I need you on my side."

Baruch shot him a slightly mollified look. "You do? What can I, poor, blundering, useless I, do to help?"

"Do you have a computer with the Internet?"

"My kids have a PC at home for work and play, but we don't have the Internet."

"No worries. I brought a modem and some software with me just in case. I'll configure the modem to your PC and load the software. Then I can connect to my e-mail account and we're in business."

"Do whatever you have to do," Baruch said.

☼ ☼ ☼

Colin and Peter went to the address given as Cindy

Wallis's. It was an apartment in a low-rise estate, where the original developers had obviously attempted to landscape pleasant surroundings. Grassy borders, flowerbeds, and small trees had been planted and were now strewn with litter and Coke cans.

"Shame, innit," White remarked, kicking a pile of old newspapers out of the way to access the main entrance. "I bet this place was the pride of the neighborhood when it was new."

The inner courtyard, from where several blue-painted front doors opened, was cemented over, and more litter blew around in the breeze. It smelled of unpleasant things, and both policemen wrinkled their noses.

"Poo," said White expressively.

"Disgusting place," agreed Colin. They rang the bell at number 18. A loud barking immediately could be heard from inside, reminiscent of a large Rottweiler. The two cops exchanged glances.

"Gulp," said Peter.

They were just about ready to change their minds and leave when the door opened and a harmless-looking little old woman peered out. The frenzied barking continued in the background.

"Madam, we have called about a..."

"EH?" yelled the old woman.

"I SAID, WE HAVE COME ABOUT..." But it was hopeless over the terrible din.

"Just a minute," she said, and she disappeared into the bowels of the house. Seconds later, the barking stopped abruptly. Smiling, the old woman returned to the door. "You was saying?"

The two policemen stared at her, astonished. "How did

you stop the dog from barking?" Colin couldn't help but ask.

"Come inside. I'll show you." She shuffled off inside the house again. Bemused, the men followed her, looking anxiously left and right for the huge dog that was the source of all the racket. The old woman went straight toward a small box, a tiny red light glowing from it, on the hall table.

"Here's your dog," she said. To illustrate, she threw a small switch, and immediately a deafening and aggressive barking filled the house. She switched it off, and blessed silence reigned.

"It helps protect an old woman who lives alone," she explained with a toothless smile.

"That'd scare off the most persistent burglar or mugger, that would," White agreed.

"You are policemen, aren't you? I guessed at once."

"How? We're not in uniform."

She gave them a shrewd look. "You have the look. Unmissable. Come in and have a cuppa tea. At least with two coppers in the house, I feel safe."

The two men grinned and followed her into a dingy living room attached to an even dingier kitchen. "Sit down, sit down. I'll put the kettle on. Won't be a minute."

The old woman didn't have an electric kettle, only an old whistling one she set on the gas stove, while she bustled around with old blue-striped pottery cups and saucers and a packet of chocolate digestive biscuits. "Me favorite," she said, bringing it all to the table. Sugar was dispensed from a dirty and encrusted blue-striped sugar bowl with a grimy chrome teaspoon.

"Now," she said when they were all sipping at the strong hot tea, surprisingly good tea despite the lack of hygiene in its preparation, "if you've come about me TV license, I'll pay it in stamps. I promise I will."

Colin raised his hand in dismissal. "We haven't come about your TV license. We're looking for someone. Cindy Wallis. Apparently she lives here."

"Nah. Doesn't."

The old woman took another digestive biscuit as if the subject was closed.

"Did she ever? How long have you been here?"

"I been here going on three years. Before that I was in a home, but the money ran out."

"So how do you afford this place, then?" White asked.

"This is me own place. Me husband, George, bought it afore the war. I didn't like it then, and I like it even less now. But it's somewhere to live, better'n a park bench."

"So Cindy Wallis never lived here?"

"Did I say that? She might have lived here before I came back. We had tenants. Flat-sharing girls, office workers. She might have been one of them."

"Do you have any records of your tenants?"

"Yes, somewhere. Who knows where, though. Could be anywhere." She made a vague gesture.

"Look, we need to trace her. Did you have an agent who handled the leases?" Colin said with increasing exasperation.

"An agent? Too posh for the likes of us. Nah, we did it oursel'. George was real methodical. It's me what has let things go to pot. But if you need to find her, I'll look for the tenants' records."

"Thank you," said Colin, and waited for her to get up and start looking. She made no move.

"Not now, " she said when she realized they were waiting. "Later."

"Now," Colin said forcefully. "White here will make us all

another cuppa, won't you, White, and while he's doing that, you're going to look for those records."

"Slavedriver," muttered the old woman, but she got up and shuffled over to a wall of cupboards, which she started opening and closing.

"What's your name, then?" White asked.

"Gladys. Gladys Jones."

"Nice to meet you, Gladys."

"Slavedriver," she muttered again, continuing to open and shut drawer after drawer, closet after closet. "Oh, here it is. In this red tin box. I remember now. He kept all the records in red tin biscuit boxes." She pulled it out and brought it over to the table. Inside was a neat index card system.

Thumbing through the cards, Colin quickly found that Cindy Wallis had indeed been a tenant there three years before. She had been the last tenant before Gladys had moved back in.

"If she was the last tenant, maybe you met her when you moved in and she moved out," suggested Colin.

Gladys thought hard. "Oh, yeah," she said, and the two men could almost see the lightbulb going on over her head. "Blonde, wasn't she?"

"Yes. Blonde, blue-eyed."

"I remember her. She paid the last of her rent and said she was moving on. Said she had better places to stay in than this dump. Can't say I blame her."

"Did she say where she was going? Leave a forwarding address for her post, maybe?"

"If she'd left one, it would be in here. George was very methodical. Oh, look here. 'Moving to Edgware.' Said it was more countrified out there. I've never been to Edgware, so I wouldn't know."

Edgware was a suburb of London only two stops further north on the subway lines, but the way Gladys described it, she made it sound like some exotic foreign resort. She handed Colin a card on which George had inscribed a forwarding address.

"Thanks a lot," Colin said, pocketing the card. "And thanks for the tea. It was delicious." He reached into his other pocket. "Here's a tenner for expenses. Help you pay for your TV license, too."

Gladys stuffed the ten-pound note into her apron before the two men could blink. Outside they looked at each other.

"Edgware?" said White.

"Edgware," confirmed Colin.

☼ ☼ ☼

"Here's your room," said Baruch, opening the guest room door with a flourish. He expected some comment about the comfortable facilities, since he and his wife had gone to some considerable trouble to prepare the room.

Avi casually flung his overnight bag onto the bed and looked around the room. Baruch waited.

"Where's the computer?" he asked.

Baruch sighed inwardly. "It's in the study. Follow me."

Avi took a quick look at the PC. "Pentium III with sixty-four megabytes RAM. Hmm, not bad," he said to himself. He spent the next few moments attaching and configuring his modem to the machine, then loading the free month's trial Internet account. As the amazed and computer illiterate Baruch watched, Avi had logged onto the Net within ten minutes of encountering the computer.

Avi then looked at the printout of the e-mail apparently sent from himself. "Whose computer did this land on?" he asked.

"Don's. We arranged it so that all mail in connection with the case would be written from and to one machine. Pinny thought it would make things easier to control."

"Yes, it makes it easier, but it also made it easier for the Fox to monitor and intercept the mail. If it had been randomly sent, it would have been almost impossible for the Fox to know where an e-mail was coming from and to whom it was destined. Oh, well. I need more than a printout, because I think there are hidden headers his e-mail reader isn't displaying or printing."

Baruch frowned. "I don't like bothering Don Hardman," he said worriedly. "He has quite enough on his plate."

"I can ask him to send it on to me here," Avi said. "It will still have all the original hidden headers on it."

A phone call to Don proved fruitful, and a few moments later the e-mail landed in Baruch Weiss's PC. Baruch was impressed.

"How about some coffee and a piece of cake?" Baruch offered hopefully. He was hungry and tired after his trip to the airport.

"Yes, thanks," Avi said distractedly. It was obvious he was the sort of man who would forget to eat unless someone put the food in front of him. Not a syndrome the ample Baruch had ever suffered from.

Baruch went downstairs to prepare himself and Avi a much-needed cup of coffee and an extra large slice of yeast cake.

Avi munched and drank without paying the food and drink much attention, unlike Baruch himself, who was relishing every mouthful.

He brought up the e-mail and studied it carefully. Then he went into the e-mail reader and studied that. Baruch was sitting very still and quiet, as if to disturb him would be to ruin all chances of success. Avi sat thinking for a while, then he started typing furiously. His fingers flew over the keys so fast that Baruch couldn't even see what was being typed. Avi saved what he had done and rebooted the computer. While they waited, Baruch dared to ask what Avi was looking for.

"Shh. Just wait. "

Baruch, suitably chastised, waited. Once the computer had rebooted, Avi went back into the e-mail program and brought up the relevant e-mail.

"Bingo!" he shouted.

"What? What? What?"

"Look." Avi pointed. At the top of the e-mail there was now a line of figures.

192.168.100.1

"*Yesss,*" Avi hissed.

Baruch stared at the line of figures. "What on earth are those?"

"That's the IP address of the Internet provider through which this e-mail came."

"IP?"

"Internet protocol. It's dynamite. It means we can at least find out which provider..."

"The Fox uses!" said Baruch, clapping his hands.

"Yes!"

"Or used. How do we know it wasn't just to send the e-mail and then he changed accounts?"

"It's possible," Avi agreed, "but, I'm willing to bet, unlikely. If our foxy friend went to all the trouble of making his e-mail untraceable, what would be the point for him of changing ISPs? He is arrogant. Thinks himself invincible. This is when mistakes are made." Avi tapped the screen. "Like this." He looked up at his host. "I am going to go on-line with this to do a DNS lookup on this IP. That will tell us who the Internet provider is."

Within seconds he was on-line again, and Avi switched to black-screened DOS mode, typing rapidly. The black screen suddenly filled with data.

"I just did a DNS lookup on the IP, and it's come back with a reply. This is SmallNet."

"SmallNet? You're kidding me. There is an Internet service provider called SmallNet?"

"I think they pride themselves on the 'we are small and the service is personal' angle. The bigger providers do get a bit impersonal. On the other hand, the small ones don't have the resources."

He brought up a Web browser and looked for the Web site of SmallNet. Their site was, predictably, Avi thought, alive with dizzying animations, all recognizable from free download sites. Even the company logo was made up of individually rotating letters in glaring, three-dimensional gold. Avi winced. He clicked on one of the links and was rewarded with another animated page, this time showing a construction worker with the message "This page is under construction. Come back later."

"Bit dazzling, isn't it?" commented Baruch, pretending to shield his eyes from the glare.

"It's deserving of the Appalling Web Site of the Year Award," Avi said with conviction. "Look. It has far too many animations, none of which are original. It is extremely hard to find your way around, and when you do click on something, it gives you an 'under construction' animation. There is very little useful information on the site. Basically it's a waste of space. And it's exactly how I would have expected SmallNet's site to look." He clicked on a few more links, some of which led nowhere, some more of which were under construction, but finally hit pay dirt. A page with their "snail mail" address, or postal address details, and phone and fax numbers.

As the computer wasn't connected to a printer, Avi scribbled down the details and logged off. "This place is not too far I think. I can get there in less than an hour." He looked at Baruch and grinned. "If somebody takes me, that is. Or lends me a car."

"My second car is insured for all drivers," Baruch said thoughtfully, "and to be honest, I don't think I would be of any help. Besides, I do have to get back to work. Do you actually need a second person there or is it just a driver?"

Avi thought. "I'd rather do this on my own. I can think more clearly. So if it's okay with you, I'll take you up on that offer of the car with thanks, Baruch."

"Sure, I'll go get the keys. Do you have a cellular phone? I'd appreciate being kept in touch."

"No. My Israeli one doesn't work here."

"Okay, I'll lend you mine. But then, how will you keep in touch with me?"

"I'll phone you at home or in the office," Avi promised Baruch.

"You'd better! And look after the phone with your life!"

Avi grinned and hugged it to his chest. "I will. Is it charged?"

"Fully. Should last at least a day on standby and a couple of hours talk."

Keys and phone in possession, Avi left in a small blue Ford, street map on the passenger seat.

Baruch stood looking after him. "I wish I was going along," he said aloud. "I'd love to see what he intends to do."

CHAPTER FOURTEEN

The address in Edgware was a small detached house on a green leafy street, quite different from the rundown estate they had just left.

"She's come up in the world," White remarked.

"If she's still living here. Come on, let's investigate."

They walked up the neatly groomed front path bordered with flowerbeds on both sides and a small lawn beyond. Colin rang the bell, and they heard it echo inside the house.

"At least no dog this time," Peter remarked.

They waited a good while, rang again a couple of times, more insistently. Someone had to be home. There was a small car in the driveway, and the house was too far from the local shops to be easily walkable. Colin kept his finger pressed on the bell for a good minute.

"Do you mind?" came a haughty feminine voice. A thirty-something elegant woman wearing gardening gloves and an annoyed expression came around the side of the house. In her hand was a small earthy trowel. "You don't have to ring my doorbell like a total maniac," the woman said crossly. "I was in the garden, as you can see."

Colin flipped open his ID. "Can we talk, please, madam?"

The woman took the ID and examined it carefully, then handed it back. "Detective Inspector," she acknowledged.

"And this is Sergeant White," Colin introduced his partner, and the lady nodded to Peter.

"Your name please, madam?"

"It's Karen Whitestone. Mrs. Karen Whitestone."

Colin felt a stab of disappointment that her surname wasn't Wallis.

"You'd better come round the back. There's a garden table and chairs, and I'll bring out some cool drinks." Her voice had undergone the usual alteration from haughty to respectful. Colin and Peter grinned at each other behind her back as they followed her to the garden.

"This is very nice," Colin commented. And it was. The garden was beautifully tended and lush with spring and early summer flora. Under a bright umbrella was a white table and chairs set on a small patio.

"Sit down, gentlemen. I'll be right out with some drinks."

They sat in the shade, caressed by the warm breezes, and looked around the garden.

"I could get used to this," Colin said, stretching out his long legs.

"This is the life," agreed Peter.

The woman came out presently bearing a tray of cool sodas clinking with ice cubes.

"A gorgeous day, isn't it?" she asked the two men.

"Thank you. Yes, it is lovely. Been a while since I've been able to enjoy it," replied Colin.

"Oh?" she inquired, taking a tall glass and sitting next to them. "Why is that? Busy on an exciting case? A murder, maybe?"

"I sincerely hope not," Colin said. The tone of his voice dispelled any mockery in her voice.

"Oh?" she said seriously.

"We're investigating the disappearance and probable abduction of eight-year-old Josh Hardman from his parents' home in Golders Green earlier this week."

"Abduction? How terrible! But how do I come into this exactly?" Her clear green eyes showed concern.

"We have had information to the effect that a Miss Cindy Wallis lives here," Peter said pompously.

"Cindy worked for a brief time for the Hardmans as a temp while their secretary was ill. We wondered if you knew her."

"Of course I know Cindy. I'm her landlady. Or used to be."

"Doesn't she live here now?"

"Well, she does and she doesn't. She occasionally comes back. Bit of a drifter. But she pays her rent, so I keep her room available. She hasn't been here now for several weeks."

"Does she leave her things in her room when she isn't here?"

"Some bits and pieces, yes. Do you want to see?"

"Yes, we would, madam."

She hesitated. "I don't know. They're not mine. Don't you need some kind of authorization?"

"We could get a search warrant. It would take a bit of time, but we'd get it. It's up to you."

"Well, I suppose it's all right. There's nothing much anyway, and I can always tell her you coerced me into it." A sly smile.

"Might as well finish our drinks, eh, Colin?" Peter said with a contented sigh.

A blue-colored bird swooped down from a nearby tree and hopped across the perfect lawn. "Looks like someone's budgie has escaped," remarked Colin dreamily, sipping his drink. He was aware that he had a missing child and an abductor to catch, but this was a moment to be savored. Just a moment.

"Oh, that's Georgie. He's mine. I let him out for a fly about every day. He always comes back." Karen gestured lazily to a cage with an open door sitting in a corner of the patio.

"You'll be sorry if one day he doesn't," Peter said.

"Georgie likes his home comforts far too much to fly away and not come back," Karen said.

"I wasn't thinking of it being exactly voluntary," Peter said, pointing to a rather large ginger tomcat who had suddenly appeared on the neighbor's fence.

"Marmalade wouldn't hurt my Georgie, would you, Marmalade?" cooed Karen Whitestone. In reply the cat yawned, exhibiting a fine set of far-from-innocent-looking teeth.

"Just the right size for a snack or small lunch," murmured Peter half to himself, eyeing the budgerigar.

"Cindy loves Georgie," Karen commented, ignoring the cat comments. "She's always playing with him and teaching him to talk when she's home."

"Does she come home on a regular basis or just any old time?" Colin asked, finishing his drink.

"As I said, she hasn't been home now for several weeks. But that doesn't mean I can expect her any minute. It doesn't work like that with Cindy. She's her own boss and does as she pleases. Bit of an independent missie, she is."

"Okay, let's see her room."

The small room was uncluttered. There were few possessions in it of any interest. The two men looked through the clothes and pockets. Cindy had a garish dress sense, veering toward the short and gaudy. A couple of pairs of high-heeled boots were all the shoes in the wardrobe, probably because of the season. Colin looked through the bedside cabinet. A couple of novels and a box of tissues. He picked up one of the novels. It was a science fiction adventure.

"Looky here, Pete, she's got the very one I'm missing in the series. I've ordered it and ordered it, and they keep telling me it's out of print and they can't get it." He looked up at Karen. "I've been wanting to read this for years. I don't suppose..."

"You can't expect me to give you permission to take that book away." She sniffed disapprovingly.

Colin made his mind up. "Sergeant White?"

White stood to mock attention. "Yes, sir?"

Colin held out his hand like a surgeon waiting for a scalpel to be slapped into it.

"Evidence bag. Large."

Peter produced a clear plastic bag with a Ziploc top and slapped it into Colin's hand. Straight-faced, Colin picked up the novel with a tissue and dropped it into the plastic bag.

"Essential evidence," he said to Karen. "Here's my card. If Cindy should get in touch, or if you think of anything which might help, please phone at once."

Leaving her openmouthed, the two policemen walked out of the house. In the car, Peter said to Colin, "Well, whatcha reckon?"

Colin grinned. "I reckon I've got the missing book in the series. Can't wait to read it tonight."

☼ ☼ ☼

Avi found the address for SmallNet Ltd. It was situated on a small industrial estate in the western fringes of London. He could have told which it was without looking up the exact address. Its concrete block, looking like a matchbox lying down, was positively bristling with cables, antennae, and wiring. The other identical concrete blocks on the estate seemed to be mainly manufacturing outfits or warehouses. Avi parked the car and strolled into the building.

There was no reception area. The whole outfit seemed to be in the one horizontal matchbox room, mostly taken up by two banks of monitors and several PCs at which sat a few bored-looking technicians playing games. The modems flashed red and green. No phones rang. The room was silent.

"Er, who is the boss here?" Avi called.

A tall man stood up from behind a computer. "You're talking to him. I'm Renard Lukavac. Who are you?"

"Hey." Avi came forward with an outstretched hand. "I'm the guy you've been looking for."

"You are? I didn't know I was looking for anyone."

"The guy who will sort out all your technical problems, the guy who will get your networks and firewalls working just so. You are looking at the answer to your prayers!"

Renard Lukavac came forward and peered at Avi as if he were an interesting specimen under a microscope. "Hm. Well, it just so happens that I could do with a good network and Internet man. Just seems funny that, to paraphrase a famous saying, out of all the Internet providers in all the towns, you had to drift into mine."

"You run yourself down, Renard!" Avi said with a broad smile. "Why would I want to work for a large, impersonal provider when I could work in this lovely, cozy office with all you friendly people?"

Lukavac, chewing on a cigarette, seemed unconvinced. "Got a CV?"

Avi produced one out of his inner pocket. He'd brought it with him from Israel, hoping for just such a situation. Lukavac studied it for a while.

"Impressive working history. Well. I could give you a trial run. Pay isn't brilliant. We're small and can't afford much. Can you do the night shift? We're short-staffed at night."

"That's perfect," said Avi. "I just love working nights, and I love working on networks. It's quiet then and my needs are simple. Can I start right away?"

"Yes. Marty will show you the ropes before he goes off his shift."

"I'm a fast learner," Avi assured him. Secretly he was astounded that Lukavac was willing to take him on without references or looking into him too much. But looking around at this cowboy outfit, maybe he shouldn't have been so surprised. And it was the perfect provider for the Fox to use. Nice and sloppy and one where they wouldn't bother checking around too much. Well, he intended to do some checking just as soon as he was left alone.

"There's a café around the corner if you want to go out and get some dinner," Marty told him as he showed him around later, when the others had left. A male cleaner worked grumpily behind them, sweeping and mopping.

"Nah, that's okay. I brought some sandwiches for supper," Avi said, silently blessing his forethought to bring food with him from home. That morning seemed an awfully long way away now.

Marty peered at him. "You're Jewish, aren't you?"

"Yup, I am. Why?"

"That's why Mr. Lukavac took you on so quick. He trusts Jews. I think he has Jewish blood somewhere in his genes."

"Ah, I see. I did wonder."

"Specially when it's one of them religious Jews. He really trusts them."

"And so he should," Avi assured him firmly.

Marty finished showing Avi all the relevant parts of the network and machines. "There, that about wraps it up," he said.

"I feel right at home here already," Avi said, wishing the young man would leave. He started work on a machine and waited.

Marty stood around watching him for a while, testing his competence, no doubt. Avi wasn't worried. He had studied long and hard and worked for several computer companies. There was little he didn't know about computers. Besides being a superb software engineer, he could build a computer from the ground up in any configuration one could want and had studied firewalls and networks in his last place of employment. After ten minutes or so of listening to Avi's purposely tuneless whistling designed to drive even the calmest man to beg the men in white coats to come and take him away, Marty succumbed. It was either that or the funny farm.

"Well, if you're sure you'll be okay, I'll be off. You've got your worksheet, so you know what your jobs are for tonight."

"Yep. Plenty to keep me busy till the shift ends," Avi assured him. "In fact, there's enough here to keep me busy for three shifts. Bit of a slavedriver, Renard is."

"A bit," Marty agreed, relaxing into the "slagging off the boss" role, which instantly gave them a peer-group camaraderie. "He can be a real pain, especially when he gives us extra work and goes home early himself."

The two of them spent a few minutes in a general moan about the boss which Avi decided was time very well spent. Marty relaxed even more and decided the new employee was a good sort.

"I'll be off, then," Marty said for the third time, and this time he meant it.

Once he had gone, Avi was left alone in the premises except for the cleaner. His tasks were to answer all overnight calls from customers (which, they assured him, were rare), fix the firewall and networking which wasn't working properly, and attend to some minor software bugs.

Avi worked fast and efficiently. He had a purpose in mind, and it wasn't the salary or the ambience. But he wanted to be fair to his employer, too, so before he got down to the real business at hand, he did all the jobs listed on the worksheet. And did them well. He also answered two support calls from regular complainers who were amazed at how sensibly he sorted their problems. "Hey, you must be new. The usual guy on the phones has zilch idea how to answer my questions," one of the regulars said, impressed. Avi glowed with the praise despite himself.

At eleven, the cleaner knocked off for the night, having mopped and dusted all around Avi and practically over him, too. Grumbling to himself about night staff getting under his feet, he packed up his cleaning materials and let himself out of the locked offices.

Avi was alone at last.

☼ ☼ ☼

Colin and Peter waited at arrivals for Leora Jakober to arrive.

"We could have sent a constable or someone else to pick her up," Peter grumbled. "I'm tired and I wanted to go home early tonight."

"Stop whining, man," Colin chided him. "This is a VIP, and we can't just send any old copper to go meet her. Anyway, I want to see her arrive, first impressions and all that."

Peter grunted. He didn't see why he couldn't have been let off this particular duty, but Colin wanted him along.

"I hate airports," Peter grumbled. "Too many people coming back from too many exotic holidays for my liking. When's the last time I had one? A week in Bognor, that's what I got last summer."

"Nothing wrong with Bognor if you like freezing cold English seaside resorts with low-class hotels," Colin said. "Myself, I prefer Tenerife."

Peter glared at him. "The furthest abroad I've been is to Calais on the shuttle to buy duty-free liquor."

Peter, who had been holding up a small placard which read "Leora Jakober," was approached by a tall woman with auburn shoulder-length hair and slightly slanted green eyes.

"Hi," she said with a broad American accent. "I'm Leora Jakober."

They both stared. Whatever they had envisioned a criminologist to look like, it wasn't this.

"My suitcase is there. I only brought one small one. Can one of you carry it for me?" She smiled broadly.

Peter picked up her bag. She carried a small knapsack on her back and a neat shoulder purse.

"Any news on the kid?" she asked as they loaded her baggage into the car.

"Not had any more e-mails, but we might have a lead. We'll explain more on the journey home."

"You've got trace evidence for me to look at, right?"

"Yes, from the kid's room. Puzzles us, to be honest, so we could do with an outside opinion."

She grinned as they drove onto the motorway. "That's what I'm here for."

CHAPTER FIFTEEN

"I've taken the liberty," Leora said from the back seat as the car neared North West London, "of renting some equipment."

"What kind of equipment?" asked Colin.

"A computer, compound microscope, comparison 'scope, fuming frames, a polarized light microscope. And I bought some other stuff — latex gloves, goggles, tweezers, that sort of thing."

"We do have computers in Golders Green," Peter said. "We aren't still in the Dark Ages here."

She shot him an arch look. "I'm sure you have, but this computer is specialized. It hooks up to the microscope and gives me an instant on-screen image of what the slides show in whatever magnification I need."

"Oh, right," Peter said. He retreated into embarrassed silence.

Leora laughed at the anxious look on Colin's face. "Don't worry, Detective Inspector Sommers. I've okayed the expenses with your CID. They're having the stuff sent over to your offices first thing tomorrow morning. I presume I'll have an office to myself there?"

Peter said no and Colin said yes simultaneously. Colin shot Peter a dark look and said, "It's okay. Peter will doss down in my office and you can have his. Can't she, Peter?"

"Sure, any time," Peter said in response to a sharp sideways elbow in the ribs from Colin.

Leora beamed at Peter. "You British are just too kind. Thanks so much."

Peter leaned over to Colin. "You could have asked me first," he hissed.

Colin grinned. "We'll both be squashed, so we'll suffer together for the little lady."

"Such cute houses!" Leora exclaimed as she gazed out of the window at the city. "I hope I'm staying in one just as cute."

"The Hardmans are putting you up," said Peter. "They have plenty of room to spare, and you'll be on the spot for surveying the crime scene. I thought maybe they wouldn't have the head for visitors, but Mrs. Hardman seemed very keen to have you stay. I think it will be a comfort to her to have someone involved in finding her son under her roof. And Mr. Hardman is American, so you'll feel more at home. But please, remember her fragile state."

"What do you take me for?" Leora said, miffed. "I know how to behave, Sergeant White."

"Have you not been to England before, Miss Jakober?" Colin asked.

"Never. Always wanted to come visit. So when I heard about poor little Josh it was just too good a chance to miss."

The two men exchanged a glance.

"If you will permit me, miss, this isn't a tourist trip, and I do hope you won't regard it as such. This child has been missing for over five days now, and we are no nearer solving the crime."

"You are nearer," Leora assured him. "You just don't know it yet. You have lots of clues, lots of evidence, lots of pointers. You just have to be able to read them. You just have to have the right reading glasses on to make everything come clear as day."

"And you're the ophthalmologist?"

Leora laughed. "No, I'm the reading glasses."

☼ ☼ ☼

Avi worked fast, silent as mist, through the computer systems he was being paid to fix. Partly software, partly wiring, he had done what he was paid to do before 2 A.M. He took a brief rest, washed, and ate his sandwiches and drank some strong black coffee. His whole body shrieked for sleep, but he couldn't stop now.

Once he had eaten and drunk, he sat back at a terminal and started to look for the Fox. As yet he wasn't sure how he was going to find him, but he had a hunch that in SloppyNet's offices, things hadn't been too tidy and things could have been left visible.

He did several searches for log files, which record conversations either by phone or Internet, on each machine. Nothing. He moved from machine to machine, looking at the overhead clock. His sight was beginning to go. He could see red and green stars dancing in front of his eyes, and he kept having to blink to clear his vision. He actually fell asleep sitting up twice, waking up after two minutes groggy and disoriented.

When he found it, he almost missed it. He was swaying in his seat, dangerously close to falling onto the floor and passing out. The whole world was shimmering in and out of focus.

And there it was. A hundred megabytes of log files. He was instantly awake and alert, all sleep banished from his body, every cell vigilant and attentive. Now all he had to do was scroll through them until he found what he was looking for. And he had all night.

He would need it.

☼ ☼ ☼

Leora Jakober entered the Hardman home. Ilana and Don were there to greet her together, standing close, like a buffer against the world. Leora thought them a very good-looking couple, and despite the stress they were under they both looked well groomed and tidy. Ilana's skin was smooth and clear, her eyes liquid and soft, her smile genuine.

"Welcome to our home," she told Leora, holding out her hand in greeting. "We are so grateful that you came all the way from New York to help us find our son."

The innocent gratitude in her eyes was so moving, so touching, that for the first time since she'd heard about Josh in New York, Leora felt the real tragedy of this mission. Before it had been just a job. Suddenly it had become more personal. Without knowing why she did it, Leora held out her arms to the other woman. Instinctively Ilana went into her arms, and the two women hugged like old friends and wept. Ilana felt a kinship with this stranger that she had not felt in a long time. It was as if all her old friends were of no relevance at this time of stress and worry, but this woman alone could share her torment.

"Come on, I'll show you to your room," Ilana said. "And when you've freshened up, maybe you'd like something to eat and drink?"

"Thank you, I ate on the plane, but I'd love a hot chocolate and some toast, please," said Leora with typical candor.

She followed the older woman upstairs and noticed how she skirted widely past a closed room on the right at the top of the stairs.

"Josh's?"

Ilana nodded. "We keep it locked because of the evidence. We've been told not to touch anything."

"Good. I'll want to look at it in the morning if that's okay. Hopefully the stuff I rented will have arrived by then."

Leora was shown into a comfortable double guest room with a bathroom en suite.

"This is great! My own facilities," she exclaimed.

"We aren't as short of space as most Golders Green families," Ilana replied smoothly.

"Well, thank you very much." Leora put her stuff on the bed. "I think I'll take a shower, then I'll come down for that hot chocolate and toast."

"Certainly," Ilana said and left her.

☼ ☼ ☼

"Home time, please," Peter begged. "I can't see straight."

"Yes, I think we deserve it," agreed Colin. "I have some thinking to do anyhow. You and I have been on the go since about eight this morning, haven't we? Starting with the Hardmans' workplace, ending with picking up Miss Cleverclogs from New York. Quite a day, eh, Peter?" He looked at his watch. It was midnight. "Let's go home."

Colin shut the door of his apartment by leaning on it and groaned with the pain of his aching limbs. He stretched, hearing some satisfying cracks, kicked off his shoes, and walked into the kitchen to make himself something to eat and drink. He made a toasted cheese sandwich and a large mug of tea, carried it to the small living room, and sat in his favorite armchair. Placing his sandwich and tea on the coffee table, he leaned back in the chair and closed his eyes. A minute later, he was asleep.

He awoke with a start an hour later. His sandwich was stone cold, the toasted cheese like a slice of rubber, and there was a layer of gray scum floating in his tea. Bleary-eyed, he went back into the kitchen, trashed the sandwich, poured the tea down the sink, and made a fresh batch of both. Carrying his new meal back into the living room, he sat down again, this time feeling slightly refreshed, and ate and drank.

He thought about the Hardman case. He got out his notebook and started writing. What did he have?

Possible motive: revenge.

For what? Could it be Cindy Wallis? Unlikely but possible, if she was better than he thought. Certainly Cindy had been mysteriously missing for quite a while now.

The trace evidence pointed to the abductor having been somewhere else other than the Hardman front yard before the kidnaping. That was up to Cleverclogs to work out. He'd be interested in what she came up with.

Then there was the Internet side of things. That pesky Baruch Weiss had something up his sleeve, some supergeek or other. If he couldn't do a search to really mess things up, he was going to do it with the geek instead. Colin started to worry. He had been so busy brushing off Weiss like an annoying fly that he hadn't given any thought to what he might get up to behind his back. He made a note in capitals: *CHECK OUT WEISS.*

As he lifted himself out of his armchair, he noticed the red light blinking on his answering machine. He had been so tired before he had disregarded it. He got up and went over to it to play the messages.

Beep. A young voice. "Hello, this is Mikey Mendelsohn checking in. I might have something for ya, Chief. Call me back after school tomorrow." And a number.

Beep. Another young voice, slower, more hesitant than Mikey's. "This is Moishie Brandt. I remembered something else about the man, but I don't want to tell you over the phone. Mum says maybe you could meet me outside school tomorrow?"

Beep. "End of messages."

Colin stood there grinning. Both boys on the same day. Amazing. Maybe he would get some breaks after all.

Then the room started swaying, and he walked unsteadily to the bedroom, where he crashed into oblivion.

☼ ☼ ☼

Somewhere in the dead of night, Baruch Weiss's phone rang. Like most Jews, his first thought was, Oh, no, something has happened to someone! He sat up in bed with a start, reached for the phone and peered at the clock at the same time. Four twenty-two in the morning.

"Hello, who is this?" Baruch snapped into the phone.

The voice came back in a whisper. "Shhhh, it's me. Avi."

Baruch instantly dropped his voice to a corresponding whisper. "Avi! Where are you?"

"Where do you think? I'm in the offices of SloppyNet Ltd. Been here since about six last night."

"How did you pull that one?" Baruch hissed.

"I...er...I'm working here," Avi hissed back.

"Wow, how did you manage to swing that?"

"Never mind. That's not important. The thing is, I think I have something. SloppyNet keeps logs of all calls. And they have caller ID enabled."

Baruch was instantly wide awake. "Caller ID? You mean you can find out who the Fox is from that?"

"It's a start. He could be giving a false name, of course, and moved from the address he was calling from. But somehow I don't think he imagined he'd be caught out like this."

"So what's the name? Give, give, give."

"The name I have here is Bill Venice. And he's calling from a local exchange by the sound of it."

"Local? As in Golders Green?"

"Well, it's one of those newer exchanges that could be anywhere in a few districts in North West London. Trouble is, it covers a pretty wide area."

"Surely the phone number can be traced to an address?"

"Yup. It will need a bit more of my hacking skills, but I'm not leaving until I have an address for this guy. I'll talk to you later. Go back to sleep."

"Right. Uh, do me a favor. Keep the rest of the news till morning. Once a night I can take being woken up, but twice? No way."

Avi chuckled. "When did you last have a small baby in the house, Baruch?"

Baruch managed a chuckle, too.

"I'm coming home soon, pal. How will I get into the house if I'm not allowed to wake you up?"

"Didn't I give you a key? Oh, bother. Er..." Another look at the clock. It was amazing how seeing it was four-thirty in the morning could get the mind focused. "I'll go down and put the door on the digital Shabbos lock. Got a pen? Write down this combination..."

When he hung up, Baruch sank back against the pillows, and it took all his strength to get out of bed and go downstairs to put on the digital Shabbos lock. Once back in bed, he thought about Avi working alone in the deserted offices of SmallNet, doing his heroic bit to find Josh's abductor, and felt guilty for not being there, too.

For about fifteen seconds. After which he was deeply asleep again.

DAY SIX

CHAPTER SIXTEEN

Friday. Was it really only six days since the morning Ilana had gone into Josh's bedroom to wake him for school and found him missing? Shabbos was coming. Shabbos, with its promises of rest and tranquility. Shabbos, which had been described as one-sixtieth of the World to Come; one could glimpse the wonders if one experienced Shabbos in the right spirit. What kind of Shabbos would Josh be experiencing?

I just hope he is alive to experience it at all, Ilana thought as she wearily got herself out of bed and readied herself to begin preparations. She had a guest, too — the illustrious Miss Jakober, who, even now at this early hour, she could hear moving about in the guest bedroom. No thoughts of sleeping in, then. This young woman was motivated and eager to make a start. That gave Ilana hope. Something positive to hold on to. Ilana was glad Leora was staying in the house. She could really keep on top of events with the criminologist under her roof.

☼ ☼ ☼

In Baruch Weiss's house a few streets away, Baruch, Malka, and the children were all up. Baruch had taken the kids to shul and was back having breakfast. There was the usual panic about lost schoolbags and recriminations against Malka for having run out of the kids' favorite carton drinks, all of which Malka bore with the stoic patience of one long used to such behavior.

"No Five Alive? Fine, so take Ribena for today. I'll try and get Five Alive later if I have time before Shabbos.

"Your schoolbag is where you dumped it last night: on the chair in the living room. Maybe if you put it where it is supposed to be put, you wouldn't lose it.

"You didn't do your maths homework? Your problem. No, I won't write you a note claiming we were too busy trying to find Josh Hardman. That excuse does not wash with me, and it certainly won't wash with your teachers. You are not looking for Josh Hardman; only Daddy is. Now go to school and suffer the consequences or do your maths homework now. You still have ten minutes before you have to leave.

"No, I will not open a new packet of Frosted Flakes until you have finished the old one. I don't particularly care if you get a few crumbs in your bowl, that's life. Someone has to get the crumbs at the bottom of the packet."

Eventually, with an expressive banging of the front door meant to be indicative of her small son's disgust with his mother's parenting skills, Baruch and Malka were alone. Sighing, Malka made herself a strong cup of tea and joined Baruch at the breakfast table. She reached for the unopened box of cereal and noticed her husband's raised eyebrows.

"Hey, I don't like the crumbs either," she said, grinning at her husband. "I like opening the new packet of cereal!"

Baruch grinned back. "You're a cruel mother, Malka

Weiss. Can I have the free gift?"

The couple ate companionably for a few minutes until Malka broke the silence.

"Do you have any idea what time Avi Pincus got in?"

"No, I was asleep. But he did phone at four-twenty-something to say he had found a way of tracing the Fox. After that I put the door on the digital so he could get in and went back to sleep."

"Digital? You mean you didn't give the poor man a key before he went? What would have happened if he had come back without phoning first?"

Baruch looked suitably ashamed. "I suppose he would have rung the bell and woken me."

"Well, I did hear him come back in, as a matter of fact. Yossi was crying, and I went to make him a bottle, so I was up."

Once again, Baruch marveled at the maternal instinct. A mother could sleep through a medium-size earthquake but would wake like a shot as soon as a baby whimpered in another room.

"So what time was it, then?"

"Six-fifteen. I heard the lock being coded while I was downstairs making the bottle. Avi stumbled into the kitchen and asked for a cup of hot chocolate. I had the kettle on for the bottle, so I made it quickly. When I asked him if he wanted anything to eat, he said, 'You gotta be kidding. I need sleep,' and stumbled upstairs with the cup of chocolate. And that was that."

"You didn't even ask him what he had found out!" Baruch exclaimed.

Malka stared at him. "The guy was literally falling over from exhaustion. He had flown in from Israel yesterday, which you know is exhausting, and he had barely eaten and hadn't slept a wink the whole night working on the Hardman case, and you expect me to quiz him on his findings?"

"Heaven knows how long he'll sleep. Another whole day wasted, and then it's Shabbos," grumbled Baruch, unwilling to back down.

"Don't be ridiculous. Avi will sleep as long as he needs to, and anyway, he isn't the only person on the case. From what I hear on the grapevine, the Hardmans have a very interesting house guest at the moment."

"Yeah? Who?"

"A lady criminologist from New York. Leora Jakober. From what I hear, she's religious. Can you imagine?"

"A *frum* lady criminologist? Never heard of such a thing."

"Well, I have Shabbos to prepare," Malka said, making it perfectly obvious that her husband was underfoot.

"And I have work to do," Baruch said importantly, and they parted company for the day, despite the prickly top layer of conversation, deeply contented with each other.

☼ ☼ ☼

Ilana welcomed her guest for breakfast. Don had left early for the office since he came home early on Fridays. Ilana was putting the finishing touches to the cholent in the Crock-Pot, which would now simmer away until Shabbos lunch.

"That cholent smells good!" Leora exclaimed, coming over and taking an unladylike sniff at the fragrant steam. "You're a good cook. Scrambled eggs on toast is about my limit. My parents never cooked."

Ilana, who had learned to cook at her mother's knee and had been able to prepare a full Shabbos menu by the time she was fourteen, shrugged. "I suppose you don't have to cook in New York. You have so many places to eat out and take out from if you need to."

"Yeah, but there's nothing like home-cooked food," Leora said, taking another sniff. "Don't tell me you bake your own challos, too. That would be just too much for me to take in."

"Yes, I do normally, but to be honest, with all this business I really haven't had the head. Luckily I have some in the freezer from before..." Tears welled up.

"Hey, hey," Leora said, distressed. She gave Ilana a hug. "I'm here now and we're all going to do our best to find your son. I wouldn't have come all the way from New York if I wasn't determined to find him."

Ilana allowed herself to be comforted and after a few moments composed herself enough to make breakfast for them both. Leora ate heartily and drank a good deal of herbal tea, then asked to use the phone to call Colin's office and see if her equipment had arrived.

"There's a flipping great heap of boxes here taking up all the space," Potter grumbled. "Be ever so grateful if you'd come and take it away, miss, really we would."

"I'll be right there, but not to take it away," Leora informed him. "To set it up. Sergeant White said he would share offices with Colin Sommers and let me have his. I hope that's been arranged."

An audible gulp. "Peter said that? Never known him to be so generous. Well, he's in his own office at the moment, but no doubt if he said that he'll move just as soon as you arrive."

Leora hung up and turned to Ilana. "My stuff has arrived at the police station. I need to get there as soon as I can. How far is it? Can I walk?"

"You can. It's not that far. About ten minutes' walk. Or I could run you there in the car."

Leora looked out the window. Another glorious spring

morning. What was all that she had heard about the terrible British weather?

"I wouldn't dream of troubling you. The walk will do me good, and I need the exercise and fresh air to clear my head. I'm still jet-lagged. Just give me the address and a street map. I'm very good at finding things."

"Of course. I think we have a map in the study," Ilana said.

"Thanks." Leora smiled gratefully.

"By the way, the police station is very close to a kosher food store, so you can pick up something to eat later on if you want."

"Perfect," Leora beamed. "If only I had some English money. Could you change some dollars, by any chance?"

☼ ☼ ☼

Colin woke to find himself lying on top of his blanket. Apparently he had not moved a centimeter since he fell onto it the previous night. He got up painfully. Every muscle seemed to ache, and his head was one huge ball of fuzz. After a shower and shave, he dressed and sat down at his little desk. He opened a drawer he hadn't opened for a long time and drew out of it, from right at the back, a velvet pouch. His fingers brushed the fabric, felt the old familiar bulk of his tefillin, so long abandoned and forgotten. He took them out and held them in his hand, feeling the weight, turning them over and over in his hands, thinking. Then, with a sigh, he put them back in their velvet pouch and into the drawer, closing it out of his life for now. It was the first time he had looked at his tefillin for seven years.

He made himself some breakfast and went to phone back the two boys, hopefully before they left for school.

Moishie Brandt first.

"I remembered something about that man, the one who talked to Josh while he was playing football."

"Go on," Colin prompted.

"I saw him twice, that's all. Once at the school, once on Josh's road. And when he was on Josh's road, he had someone else with him. In the car."

Colin's senses went on red alert. "He was in a car?" Colin hadn't thought to ask if the man had come by car. In retrospect it made sense. How else would he have gotten there?

"Not in a car," Moishie said patiently, as if talking to an idiot. "There was a car parked and he had come in that. He kept looking back at it as if to see if the lady was still in the car. It was a black car. I think it looked like a Toyota Landcruiser or a Jeep. I couldn't tell the number plate, sorry."

"Just a minute. You said a woman was in the car?"

"Yes, a lady. He kept turning to look at her."

"Did you manage to see what she looked like at all?"

"The car was even further away than the man," Moishie said, and his voice was regretful. "I could see it was a lady, that's all. Sorry."

Colin pressed on. "Did you see what color hair she had, at least? Blonde or dark or red? And did you see if her hair was long or short? Or was she wearing a hat? For heaven's sake, boy, think! Think!"

Moishie Brandt's voice sounded distinctly distressed and on the verge of tears as the frustrated policeman's voice grew more forceful.

"I don't know! I don't know! I have to go to school now. My ride has come."

Colin sighed and backed off. Not having any kids of his own didn't help his skills with other peoples'. Adults might respond well to being leaned on a little, but kids just fell apart.

Make a note, Sommers.

"I'm sorry, lad. I didn't mean to make you upset. You've done a sterling job. Just have a think about it again and call me back if you remember anything else, okay?"

"Okay" came the small, sniffy voice. " 'Bye." The child hung up.

If I'm not careful, I'll alienate him completely and he won't ever cooperate again, Colin chided himself. He spent a couple of minutes psyching himself into being the kindly uncle every kid wished he had before he made the second phone call.

Mikey Mendelsohn reminded him of the Artful Dodger in Dickens's *Oliver Twist*. He was smart, streetwise, and very cheeky. Unlike Moishie Brandt, who had seemed overwhelmed by being in the presence of an Important Policeman, Mikey was more of the "nudge, nudge, wink, wink," slap-on-the-back, male-bonding kind of kid. Colin wasn't sure which he preferred — to be the subject of awe and intimidation or to be the "pal" of an eight-year-old with an overworked imagination.

"Hullo, mate. It's Detective Mendelsohn checking in," Mikey began without preamble. "Gotta move fast. Have to be in school in five minutes."

"Report in, Detective Mendelsohn," Colin said, getting into character.

"Person or persons unknown has been in the secret house, sir," Mikey said in an overbearing, self-important voice which made Colin want to crack up. "I have checked every day as instructed, and yesterday I noticed there were crisp packets and other food wrappings which were not there previously, sir."

"Did you, by George," Colin said. "Good work, Detective. Anything else?"

"Yes, sir. A crushed-up plastic cup, sir. I took the liberty of analyzing the contents. Tea. Definitely tea with milk."

Colin had an image of Mikey standing at attention and grinned. "Good work. Keep up the surveillance."

"I will, indeed, sir. Oops, there's my ride honking outside. Gotta dash. 'Bye!" The last part was a total remission into kidspeak. The connection was broken.

Colin sat back, drinking his cooled-down coffee, munching on a piece of soggy toast, and thinking. Both boys had given him something to chew over. A woman in a car, and the garden playhouse had been utilized. He had to investigate. He would go into the office, pick up White, and get a look at the playhouse, preferably with Cleverclogs if she was willing. He'd give her a call at the Hardmans and arrange it.

When he did, Ilana told him that Leora Jakober had left for the police station half an hour ago.

"Keen," Colin said. "How are you, Mrs. Hardman? How is it with Ms. Jakober? Not being too much of a bother, I hope?"

Ilana laughed. "On the contrary, Detective Inspector. She's delightful company and most comforting to have around. It's been a while since I had a woman friend to stay who I could relate to. She and I really seem to click, and it's a real bonus knowing she's here to help us find Josh, too."

"That's good," Colin said. "We're pulling out all the stops now. I had some more leads from school friends of his which I intend to follow up today. I'll call you tonight and let you know what I have found out."

"Oh, don't call me tonight, please," Ilana said with a little embarrassed laugh. "It's our Sabbath."

Colin was glad of the anonymity of the phone as he blushed to the roots of his hair. "Oh, right. Of course it is. Sorry."

"Don't be sorry, Detective Inspector. In fact, if it isn't asking too much, could you, or someone from your office, pop by sometime over our Sabbath to update me on any developments? I know it sounds a bit of a cheek, but I don't think I could wait twenty-five hours to hear any news."

"Of course. In fact, I think I might pop over myself in the afternoon, if that's okay."

"That would be wonderful, thank you. I know our Sabbath must sound strange to you..."

Colin almost snapped, "I know about Shabbos. Once, I was like you, *frum* and smug about it. So don't act patronizing with me, madam!" But he bit his lip and stopped himself. I never used to be so defensive. What's the matter with me? Get a grip, Sommers, get a grip.

Instead, he said politely, "No, I understand. After dark," and hung up. Get a grip. This is about Josh Hardman, not about you.

He rinsed his plate and mug and left them on the draining board. His twice-weekly cleaning lady was due today, and, along with various undertone mutterings and grumblings about bachelors and their attendant messes, she would clean up very satisfactorily and change his bedding, too. He always liked coming into the house when she had just been. It smelled of lemony polish and fresh linen. Even when he made an attempt at cleaning up himself, the place didn't have the same look, feel, or smell. He decided he would leave that modern quirk to Peter White. White not only cleaned up at home, he even did the cooking for himself and his wife, Marie, on alternate evenings, when he wasn't working late shift, and picked up the supermarket shopping on his way home from work from the twenty-four-hour place. Though Marie worked, albeit part-time because of the children, Colin still secretly thought Peter was a bit of a softie. Mind you, these modern women were all the same. Lucy was, too, hating every minute she spent doing household chores.

As if a mental signal had been sent with his thoughts, the phone rang and it was Lucy.

"How are ya, Chief?" she asked him cheerfully. "Haven't seen or heard from you in days! Can I assume it's all over between us?"

"Don't be daft, woman," Colin said. "I've just been busy on this Hardman case."

"Anything newsworthy?" asked Lucy, ever the newshound.

"You keep your nose out of this. It's highly sensitive stuff, and at this stage the last thing we want is to flush the Fox out of his lair by having the story plastered all over some local rag and all the peasants out on a witch hunt. Once the Fox is caught and young Josh is safe, you can have an exclusive interview with the amazing detective inspector who caught him."

"Very funny. I'll hold you to it, mind. And I want an exclusive with that criminologist from New York, too. I hear she's quite something."

"How did you hear about her? News travels fast."

"I'm a newshound, remember? When do I get to meet her?"

"You will soon enough. Right now we all have work to do. I'll make it up to you, Lucy."

The call over, Colin prepared to leave for the station at last. He found Leora Jakober there, unpacking boxes. Peter White, with a rather disgruntled expression on his face, was moving his stuff into Colin's office, freeing up space for Leora to take over his own room. Leora, with the delicacy and tact of an invading army, was shifting armfuls of Peter's paperwork and equipment off his desk and shelves onto the floor in the corridor "to make things easier for you," as she put it.

"There's not enough room in your office for both of us and all our stuff," Peter grumbled to Colin as he stood there, surveying the mayhem in progress.

"We'll just have to downsize the amount of stuff, then, won't we?" Colin said with a forced smile. "We do tend to have far too much anyway. Most of it is never needed. Let's have an efficiency drive this morning and put the stuff we never use into those boxes Miss Cleverclogs is unpacking, only leaving out that which we really need."

"Oh, you can't do that, sorry!" Leora called from the next room, ignoring the Cleverclogs reference. "Those boxes are from the company I rented the equipment from, and they're going to need everything packed back into them after I'm through with it."

"Better keep our voices down in future, mate," Peter whispered to Colin.

"Yup, you sure had better!" Leora called. There was a smile in her voice.

"You got bionic ears or something?" Colin said at normal voice pitch.

"Just young, fit, and healthy," she said, popping her head round the door and grinning at them. "Don't worry. I have skin like a rhinoceros, but that shouldn't stop you from at least trying to be polite to a lady."

"I think we're just not used to having ladies around," Colin apologized, blushing.

"Oh, really!" came the indignant protest from a young female police officer who worked mainly in the family division.

"Whoops," said Peter and Colin together, and they all laughed.

Somehow they managed to squeeze Peter and his accouterments into Colin's office. It would mean the two men almost climbing over the desk in order to get out the door, but they'd manage. Leora, meanwhile, had spread out her equipment very comfortably in Peter's office and was busy setting up the microscopes, concentrating mainly on the polarized light microscope. The two policemen, and several others, peered in to see what was going on. Leora felt obliged to give an explanation.

"The polarized light microscope allows the analyst to actually see and manipulate the samples, even though they consist of particles only a few micrometers in diameter. In many cases, an experienced microscopist, like myself, can identify particles based on their appearance alone. Measurement of optical properties of the sample can provide a unique identification for thousands of compounds. Samples can be poked and prodded and submitted to the entire battery of qualitative tests available to the analytical chemist, but at the microscale."

They all gawped at the young woman.

"Impressive," Colin said at last.

"Yeah, very impressive," managed Peter.

"In a recent case I worked on," Leora continued unabashed, "I was asked to determine whether soil samples found on the floorboard of a suspect's car could be used to place him at the scene of a murder. The soil in the car was superficially similar to the soil at the murder scene, but under detailed scrutiny by polarized light microscopy, the soils were not the same. Specifically, the soil from the scene contained mica, a mineral not found in the suspect soil, which in turn contained a clay not found in the soil from the murder scene."

"Soil is one of the things we will want you to analyze," Colin said. "We found soil on the windowsill of Josh

Hardman's bedroom, and, as you say, superficially it looks like the soil from his front garden below the window. But something is different. We wonder if you'd be able to pinpoint more closely where it comes from."

"Most soil investigations consist of comparing two or more samples by their mineral content, color, and density," Leora said. "Plus, of course, animal and vegetable matter, glass, paint chips, asphalt, brick fragments, and stuff like that. I hope you have some samples of the soil from the Hardmans' front garden for comparison."

"We certainly do. Joe, our forensic guy, bagged all of that. Plus he got some fabric threads from the window catch. It may just be from Josh's pajamas as he was dragged over the sill, but then again, maybe the abductor also caught some of his clothing."

"What can a few fibers tell us?" Peter wanted to know.

Leora explained. "Every time an individual comes in contact with a place or another individual, something of that individual is left behind and something of that place is taken away with the individual. If your aunt Bertha gives you a big hug and walks away, fibers from her clothes will be on your clothes and fibers from your clothes will be on hers. Your hair is constantly falling out. You leave it all over the place. Just look around your house. You pick up carpet fibers on your shoes, dirt from the ground. Your skin flakes off. Look at the Wayne Williams case in Atlanta. He was convicted because fibers found on the body of one of his victims matched fibers from the carpet in his house. Might not sound like much, but it's great physical evidence."

"I see," Peter said.

"I hope the crime scene, the kid's bedroom, hasn't been touched at all since he was taken through that window?"

"Not as far as we know. You're in the house. I presume you asked Mrs. Hardman?"

"Yes, sure I did, but you know how these overzealous cleaning ladies can be sometimes. I just hope someone has kept Maria under control. I intend to look at the stuff you have here first once everything is set up and working, then go on back to the house and see what I can pick up."

"Joe was pretty thorough," Colin said.

"I'm sure he was," Leora replied soothingly. "But sometimes two heads are better than one. Was any shoe print picked up, for example? If the abductor climbed over the windowsill, he must have left a shoe print."

"Joe did recover a partial print of a pair of trainers. Pretty standard print — thousands of trainers all have the same tread — but we're working on it," Colin said doubtfully.

"I really need to see that. Was it a print, a lift, or a cast?"

"No idea. I can ask. What will you look for in the shoe tread?" Peter asked.

"Most physical evidence concerns itself with class characteristics and individual characteristics. Class characteristics are those characteristics that are common to a group of similar objects. For example, you buy a pair of Air Jordan sneakers. All Air Jordan sneakers have the same shape and tread design on the bottom. These are class characteristics. Individual characteristics are those characteristics that are unique to a given object and set it apart from similar objects. You wear your Air Jordans around for a while and they get worn. The treads wear down. You put more pressure on the left heel. They get little pits and gouges in them. These little pits and gouges are individual to your shoes and no others, since no one has walked over the exact same surfaces in the exact same way in their Air Jordans. So it is possible to trace someone from a footprint, or find another pair of shoes similarly worn down, to prove they belong to the same person."

While she was talking, Leora was screwing together the various pieces of machinery that made up her forensic tool kit. They watched her deftly moving and securing, fixing and fastening. They also noticed how orderly she was. The boxes were neatly stored one inside the other in a closet full of Peter's belongings which she had tidied up to create space he had never believed existed there. Peter admitted shamefully to himself that he had always been meaning to tidy up that particular cupboard.

The rented equipment itself was put neatly in place on various surfaces, and boxes of latex gloves, tweezers, and other such things neatly stored away. Once the room was tidy, she set about with a cleaning cloth and spray until all the dusty surfaces revealed by the evacuation of Peter's belongings had been banished and the place sparkled. Then she scrubbed her hands in the washroom and put on the first pair of thin latex gloves. A grin and "Okay, guys, where's Joe with the evidence?"

Colin clapped his hands, maitre d' style.

"Joe! The evidence!"

CHAPTER SEVENTEEN

Malka shaped the challos and set them aside to rise for the second time. She looked at the Shabbos table, already laid, just the way she liked it. Even though Shabbos had started coming in later and she had plenty of time, she still felt nervous until everything was ready. She was listening for her visitor, but he seemed to be sleeping the "sleep of the just." She hoped he had found something that would help bring back little Josh.

Malka thought of her lively, healthy family, driving her totally bananas at times, yes, making her heart ache with pain and frustration, yes, all the time wishing kids came with instruction manuals or had backup service, but...

But at least she had her children around her. At least they were alive and kicking and well enough to drive her to distraction. She thought of her friend, Ilana Hardman, cutting herself off from her friends and supporters because, understandably, she just couldn't cope with everyone's well-meaning sympathy. Malka thought that even though the sympathy and well-meaning support were from the heart, she felt it was tinged by just a little touch of self-righteousness and ever so marginally a touch of smugness as Golders Green's mother hens gathered their nestlings safe around them. People were human, after all, and however much they wanted to feel selfless empathy and pity, it was not always possible when the haves and the have-nots were so starkly divided. Now that Ilana had joined the unfortunate ranks of the childless (hopefully temporarily, but who knew?), she became a nonmember of the exclusive sisterhood — the sisterhood every woman joined when she gave birth to her first child. It was impossible to belong to it without having gone through that initiation and it was unfortunately possible to be un-joined from it if one no longer had the requisite specifications.

So rapt was she in her musings that Malka started with surprise as Avi Pincus stumbled into the kitchen, gazing around him bleary-eyed.

"Good morning," she said brightly. "I think you might just have time to daven *shacharis* if you really put your skates on."

Avi gave the kitchen clock a blurry glance. "Actually, I davened *vasikin* before I came in. I hope I didn't disturb you."

"No, I was up anyway. My youngest, Yossi, wanted a bottle. Normally I would sleep through a middle-sized earthquake. So my husband tells me, anyway."

"Well, it was a missed night's sleep well spent, if you get my meaning."

Malka placed a pile of hot toast and some packets of cereal and milk in front of him. "I suppose one could just about call it breakfast time." She grinned. "Tea or coffee?"

"It's brunch, and I'll stick to toast and coffee, maybe a little cheese, if you have any?"

"Sure." Malka brought out a selection of hard and soft

cheeses that would do any top restaurant's cheese board selection proud.

"Wow, such choice! Which shall I go for?"

"If you like hard cheese, these baby Goudas in the red netting are wonderful. I have some fresh baby plum tomatoes to go with them," said Malka with all the aplomb of a top chef.

"Sounds wonderful! I don't suppose you have a strawberry yogurt as well, by any chance?"

"Surely do," and Malka brought out a selection of various fruity yogurts at which Avi gasped appreciatively. Malka glowed. It was nice to have a grateful guest who was so enthusiastic about everything she put in front of him. Unfortunate but true, as a marriage proceeded and lengthened over the years, a wife tended to get taken for granted more and more. Malka was lucky if Baruch grunted her a "thank you" when she made his meals these days.

Avi washed and ate some toast. "I have a name and an address for the Fox," he said without preamble.

"You do? Well, then, let's go get him!" Malka clapped her hands excitedly like a little girl.

Avi took a big bite of toast, cheese, and tomato, munching loudly, and slurped some yogurt. His table manners made Malka suddenly realize that Baruch wasn't so bad after all. She found herself edging away from her house guest.

"It's not that simple," Avi said around a mouthful of breakfast, spraying crumbs in all directions. "The name and address could easily be an old one. I went past it on my way home this morning, and it looked as if it was inhabited by a family with at least two kids. I saw a baby carriage, a stroller, and some toddler toys out front. I could be wrong, of course. I'll go check out the address right after breakfast."

"Don't you think maybe you should leave this to the police now?" Malka suggested.

"Hm. Well. Maybe I'll speak to that cop who's handling the case. Sommers, is that his name?"

"Yes, Detective Inspector Colin Sommers. And I would. You don't want to tread on anyone's toes and mess up the case."

"He'll probably be really annoyed with me for going as far as I have done," Avi worried.

Malka had worried about the same thing. Even though she had been swept along by Baruch's enthusiasm for the cloak-and-dagger act the other night, she had voiced her concern for obstructing the course of justice or whatever the police would throw at them for taking the law into their own hands.

"It's probably okay because you did such a great job, Avi," she said. "But I really wouldn't do any more on your own. I'd hand over what you know to the cops now."

"Yup. I think you're right," Avi said with conviction. He had a sudden image of himself in prison while his wife and children suffered alone in Israel without him. "Where is that cop anyway?"

"No idea. Call the station. Here's the number." Malka pushed a piece of paper and a cordless phone at him. He made the call, only to be told that Detective Inspector Sommers had just left but could be reached on his mobile.

☼ ☼ ☼

Leora had examined the soil and fiber samples, comparing them to the samples taken from the garden outside the Hardman home and the clothing Joe had taken from the boy's bedroom. She showed him the results on the computer screen, which displayed the magnification of the polarized light microscope. A jumble of lumps of soil, vegetable matter, and other undiscernables (to Colin anyway) filled the monitor.

"Look," said Leora, manipulating the sample on the slide. "This is soil taken from the Hardmans' garden. You can see decayed plant matter, entomological corpses — that's dead bugs to you guys — paint chips which are consistent with the paint on the outside of the Hardman house, some broken glass from a window Josh might have broken once, and the soil itself, which is consistent with all the soil in that flowerbed. I think the Hardmans had a delivery of topsoil at some stage to help with the landscaping, because there is a very high humus content in the soil which does not occur naturally in that area."

"I see, yeah," Colin said, peering at the mess on the screen and trying to look scientific. Leora removed the slide and replaced it with another, which looked identical. Another jumble.

"This is a sample of soil taken from the windowsill of the boy's room. Some of it, as you can see, is exactly the same. But look at this and this and this." She pointed. Colin peered, trying to look intelligent, giving wise nods and suitable "hmms." Leora looked at him and laughed.

"You really don't have the faintest idea what I'm talking about, do you? I'm sorry. I'm always doing this, assuming expertise where none exists."

Everything in Colin rose up in rebellion at remarks like this, and yet Leora was so likeable that somehow it was almost impossible to stay angry at her.

"The second soil sample shows some much rougher, more uncultivated soil than the one from the Hardman garden," Leora went on. "More like from a wasteland or untended garden. There is a much higher clay content and less humus, certainly not the commercial humus the Hardmans would have had delivered by a gardener. The dead bug fossils, too, are different. There are wood lice fragments and other bug fossils more consistent with country than city environment. If not country, then certainly some totally uncultivated land somewhere in town. Does London have such places? It all seems so built up to me."

"There are such places," Colin replied, thinking of Mikey Mendelsohn's playhouse in the wild land between the houses. Mikey had reported activity in that playhouse.

"If I brought you a soil sample from a place like that, one I am thinking of, could you match it?"

"Sure. You think you know where this soil came from?" Her expression was alert.

"Could be. A kid from Josh's class in school showed me a playhouse he and his friends had. It was in a triangle of wild land between the houses."

"Wow, you think maybe Josh is being kept there?"

"Well, he wasn't when I was there, and that same kid has been monitoring it. He isn't there all the time, but he did see some changes. Cups and some food wrappers, I think."

"Food wrappers and cups. Great! Think DNA. Think saliva. Let's look at the fiber samples. I want to show you something."

She put another slide into the microscope and manipulated it until she got a clear, focused picture on the computer screen.

"This is a fiber from Josh's pajamas." She pointed to the left where something that looked as thick as a rope appeared on the screen. "And on the right is a fiber from the red thread on the windowsill."

"They look the same to me," Colin commented.

"Yes, almost the same. Josh has two pairs of the same pajamas, so we can safely assume Josh was wearing those pajamas when he was abducted, and they are, after all, missing. But now we have some other fibers. Most likely from clothing belonging to the abductor. Take a look at this." She pointed at some other, dark fibers, like black rope. "I would say these are from cords. Look at the vertical ridge running down here and here. The kidnapper was wearing black cords."

"Black cords. Well, that's not usual gear. Jeans are more common. It might be easier to find someone with black cords."

"So long as he's still wearing them," Leora said. She went back to the soil sample and took a closer look.

"There's something here. I need to increase the magnification. Give me a sec..." She twisted some knobs and the image on the screen grew blurry. She focused it, and sharpened yet again the soil sample took on a very different aspect, with each particle filling the screen. Between the huge boulder-like particles of soil were round balls with spikes coming out of them, pale yellow or green in color.

"They look like mines, the old-fashioned kind with spikes coming out of them from all directions," Colin said with a grin. "What on earth are they?"

"These, believe it or not, are pollen spores. And they might help us place the abductor both in time and location even more accurately than the soil. Forensic palynology is a new science and obviously only useful at certain times of the year."

"Spring and early summer," Colin said.

"Yup. Right now."

"I've never heard of that study. How does it work?"

"It is the science of using both modern and fossil palynomorphs, primarily spores and pollen. It's not precisely known where and when it was first used, but the early 1950s is probably a good guess. The first well-documented case was in Austria in 1959 involving a criminal case where a man traveling down the Danube River disappeared near Vienna. His body was never found. A suspect, with a known motive for killing him, was later arrested and charged with the man's murder. With no body or confession, the case was in jeopardy of default. The only real clue seemed to be a locally uncharacteristic mud found on the defendant's shoes. Identification of the palynomorphs within the mud consisted of tree pollen — spruce, willow, and alder — as well as an extinct fossil, hickory pollen. Only one small area along the Danube Valley had soils with the precise modern pollens in association with the rocks containing the fossil pollen. When confronted with this information, the defendant confessed and showed authorities precisely where he had buried the body."

"Interesting," said Colin, feeling even more inadequate in the face of this paragon.

"I must confess I haven't studied forensic palynology at any great depth," Leora said. "But I have done some study days on it, and I'll try to remember what we learned and what to look for. I'm not a botanist, but I do know how to compare. This is the soil sample taken from the windowsill, not the garden. Let's get the one from the Hardman garden back up."

With the garden sample in and magnification increased, Leora drew in a sharp breath as she focused on something between the boulders.

"I may not be a botanist," she hissed, "but this does not look like the same kind of pollen as the one from the windowsill. I'll try to zoom in on just one of those spores." She twisted the knobs on the polarized light microscope. "C'mon, zoom in close for me... Yes! It is a totally different spore. I suggest we try your playhouse land and see what kind of spores we can pick up there."

"All right," Colin said, stunned by what he was seeing on the screen.

"C'mon then! Let's go! I have to get back in time for sunset."

She covered the microscopes and put the samples away safely. Sommers and White were waiting for her in the unmarked squad car, and she hopped in the back. While Colin sat, brooding, Leora looked around the unfamiliar streets of Golders Green with interest, exclaiming at the narrow roads and small cars.

"The boys are in school now," Colin said at last, "although they do finish early, it being Friday. But I know where the playhouse is. It's behind the Mendelsohn place. Between it and the house next door. The kid showed me a sort of secret passageway."

"Great. Let's find it," Leora said with a grin. Colin couldn't help but admire her enthusiasm and good humor, despite the fact that she was obviously jet-lagged and exhausted. He knew himself well enough to be aware how difficult he became when he was overtired. Lucy had told him often enough.

They reached the Mendelsohn house and parked.

"Do you think the kid might actually be here?" Peter asked.

"Don't know. Let's go see. And be quiet, White. Your great clodhoppers make far too much noise. Get them rubber-soled."

"Yes, boss," White said with a mock pout.

The three of them padded as silently as they knew how along the street as Colin looked furtively for the secret passageway.

"I feel a bit like the Pink Panther," Peter whispered, "and more than slightly ridiculous."

"Shh. Ah, here it is. Come on, down here," hissed Colin, and they all crept down the passage in tandem, all three of them making humorous Pink Panther movements and trying very hard not to crack up.

Leora brought up the rear of the trio, and as she walked, she picked up samples of the flora and bagged them. The passageway opened into the triangle of ground that held the playhouse.

The three stood there for a moment, looking at it. Leora took out her Leica and took several photographs in quick succession. There was no immediate evidence of anyone being in residence. They inched forward in case anyone was hiding, then the two men stormed the playhouse, one on each side, peering through the windows.

"No one home," Colin called out.

"Don't touch anything," Leora ordered, slipping on some latex gloves and taking out some tweezers. Squatting carefully, she manipulated her slender body through the narrow frame of the doorway and into the playhouse without sitting or touching the walls. She shot off several pictures with her Leica, then handed it carefully out through the window to Colin and started a vocal inventory as she bagged items.

"Paper cups, four, used. Traces of unknown liquids in the bottom." She handed the bags through the window, one bag for each cup.

"Plastic teaspoons, three, stained. Candy-bar wrappers, six, various." Again, each in a separate bag. "Used tissues. I'll bag these together, Colin." She looked around. "Okay, that's the obvious bits. Now the trace. Footwear."

"Footwear?" Colin repeated, feeling stupid.

Leora switched to her explaining scientific stuff to the uninitiated voice. "Since criminals must enter and exit crime scene areas it should, therefore, be reasonably assumed that they may leave traces of their footwear. Criminals have become smarter and wiser. They wear protection over their hands to avoid leaving fingerprints and masks over their faces to avoid eyewitness identification. However, they make little attempt to conceal footwear. It's common to see an individual wearing gloves, but people don't normally protect their shoes."

"How on earth can you pick up anything in here?"

"First," Leora said, "we darken the area as much as possible. I'll get out in a minute. It will make it easier to see." She bagged a few more items with tweezers, then carefully eased herself out of the playhouse. Colin noticed she tried to place her feet in the same prints as her incoming steps had made. Once outside, she did a three-hundred-sixty-degree swivel, placed her feet carefully apart, and took from her backpack a large black cloth, which she slung over the top of the playhouse, obscuring the windows. Then, again without moving from her stance, she took out something from her backpack.

"At a time like this she gets her hair drier out," grumbled Colin. "Typical woman."

"The Polyray is a tunable, hand-held light source designed specifically for forensic crime scene investigation," Leora said. "But the crime scene needs to be dark first. It's a portable version of a forensic light source, which would be too big for me to carry around." She switched it on and directed it through one of the windows, having first thrown the blackout cloth over her head so she was underneath.

"Can I peek?" Colin asked curiously.

"Uh, yeah, but try not to make too many new footprints.

Just use the ones you already used." Colin obligingly stepped in his own footprints until he reached another window, threw the blackout cloth over his head, and peered in. Leora was struggling to get the light at a low angle. Eventually she moved to the door of the playhouse and shone it from there, over the dark floor.

"Look at that," she whispered. "Lights up like those illuminated walkways on airplanes. Those are my footprints, but there are at least two others. And one, I would guess, is definitely a kid's."

Colin coughed. "Only one is a kid's? You sure?"

"Why?"

"Mikey Mendelsohn's been in here. He's in Josh's class. He's been my chief investigator."

"Oh, I see," Leora said, crestfallen. "Well, one kid at least and one adult at least. I'll have to photograph and analyze these a bit more to see if there are any more than that."

Colin peered and waited, then let Peter have a go at peering and waiting, while Leora painstakingly shone the light at a low angle across the floor of the playhouse, turning what had looked like a boring brown wooden floor into a fluorescent light show of patterns and textures.

"What does that forensic light source show up besides footprints?" asked Pete.

"Mostly blood, urea, saliva, powdered and DFO-treated fingerprints, and ninhydrin-treated prints. Stuff like that."

"Oh, right," Peter said.

Leora took several photographs. "Shame there's nothing to take a raised impression from," she sighed. "But I think I'll have something to work on with these." She got up gracefully and took the blackout cloth from on top of the playhouse, folded it neatly, and put it back in her backpack.

"So do you think they were here?" Colin asked.

"Well, somebody was here, that's for sure," Leora replied. She looked at her watch. "I think if I can get access to a darkroom now and get back to the station to compare these samples, that will be enough. It's after two o'clock. Maybe I can get something to eat? Ilana said there was a kosher grocery near the station."

"Yes, of course. You can pick up a sandwich or a danish."

"And the darkroom?" Leora asked as they got into the car.

"There is one at the station. We keep it for just such a purpose. It's small but you are welcome to use it."

"Great!"

Back at the station, the three walked in to find an agitated desk clerk. "You turned your mobile off," he accused.

"Did I?" Colin replied, unruffled.

"I've been trying to call you ever since you left the station. Your mobile is definitely switched off!"

Colin pulled his phone out of his pocket, looked at it, pressed a few buttons. "Bother. It's not switched off. It's dead."

"Don't you ever recharge it?" Peter snorted derisively.

"I do recharge it. Every single night before I go to bed I put it in the charger..." Colin stopped and thought. Last night was a total blur, but he vaguely remembered being so exhausted that his usual pre-bed ritual had gone right out the window to be replaced by an all-encompassing collapse and oblivion.

"Flip," he said, stopping.

"Yeah, flip," Potter said.

"Sorry. Last night...well. What did you want?" Colin asked, looking suitably chastised. Keeping the lines of communication open was one of the basics of police work.

"Someone called Abraham Pincus has been ringing and

ringing. Said he had some news relevant to the Hardman case."

"Oh. The supergeek. I wonder what he's been up to. Where was he ringing from? Somewhere nice and far away, I trust?"

"Local call," Potter said.

"Uh-oh. He's in England, is he? I thought that pesky Baruch Weiss said he lived in Israel or Australia."

Colin suddenly got even more worried about what Baruch had been up to behind his back. He hated it when Joe Public got up to all kinds of crime-solving messes and took the law into his own hands. Joe Public should be sitting nicely and quietly at home, waiting for people like he, Detective Inspector Colin Sommers, to solve crimes for them.

"He's left a number. Said it was urgent." Potter pushed a piece of paper across the desk. He assumed the bored expression he had been practicing whenever Colin started on the "pesky Baruch Weiss" tack, which was beginning to get rather tedious.

"Um, a darkroom?" said Leora, who had been standing there patiently during this exchange. "I'd like to get these films developing, and then I'll look at this trace evidence that we picked up at the playhouse."

"Oh, yes. Potter, show Miss Jakober the darkroom while I call Mr. Pincus back, will you please?" Colin said, going into his office and closing the door. He was irritated. Irritated because he felt increasingly that the case was being taken out of his hands, by pesky interfering civilians on the one hand and by Super Cleverclogs on the other. And if that wasn't enough, his office was cluttered with Peter's stuff and he could barely move. He liked to have space. It helped him to think clearly.

He climbed over the extraneous furniture and equipment

and managed with a bit of contortion to sit down at his desk where he attempted to stretch out his legs without kicking over Peter's stuff. He heard something crunch. "Whoops, what was that?" Colin muttered. "Oh, well, too late now. Later. Now, I know I have a phone here somewhere..."

He phoned the number Potter had given him, and the connection was made almost at once, as if Pincus was sitting by the phone, which he probably was.

"Oh, at last!" Avi said with a deep breath. "I've left so many messages I was beginning to think it was my deodorant."

Colin couldn't suppress a bark of laughter. "I'm really sorry. I forgot to recharge my mobile. It won't happen again. I'm likely to be officially reprimanded for it because it's a heinous crime around here to be out of touch."

"Oh, I see. Well, what I wanted to tell you was that I think I might have an address for the Fox."

Colin's legs flew out from under the desk, and he heard another crunch. "Whoops. An address, you say? As in a postal address?"

"Yup. Right here in Golders Green."

"And how, may I ask, did you find that out?"

"Ah. Yes. Well. I was afraid you might ask that."

Colin sat up very straight in his chair, and whatever it was that had crunched underfoot was dragged forward, crunching a bit more. "Yes, Mr. Pincus. I am asking you. What have you been up to? You'd better tell me the whole story, and this had better be good."

When Avi had finished telling his story, he said, "At this stage I thought I had better hand it over to the professionals. I've done the preliminary legwork, but now it's up to you."

"Nice of you to see it that way," Colin said with heavy sarcasm.

Avi sighed. "I know, but would you have been able to achieve what I achieved, legit? Be honest. I had to find SmallNet's log files, and they were unlikely to have given them up voluntarily, certainly not without alerting the subscriber involved."

"But you got a job there under false pretenses in order to search through their confidential files. Hardly ethical."

"It's called going undercover, Detective," Avi said.

Colin sighed. "Yeah, well, I can't deny you did a good job. Did you leave the workplace tidy and neat and in a state where they could not have guessed you'd been snooping around?"

"Oh, don't worry. They couldn't have found out what I'd done. As far as they were concerned, I was just one more annoying employee on probation who skipped bail on the first night at work."

"I bet they're none too thrilled about that. I bet you've put them off ever taking on a casual employee without checking out references really carefully."

Avi gave a little whine to show remorse as it was a bit difficult hanging his head in shame over the phone.

"Well, we'll forgive you for now, if you in turn forgive us for not handing you the medal for wonderful police work."

"Deal." Avi grinned.

"Okay, now what do you have for us?"

Avi gave him the address. "But I have to tell you, I've done a cursory look-see of that place, and it doesn't look like the sort of place the Fox might be now."

"Leave that to the professionals," Colin said with more confidence than he felt.

The connection broken, he got up, heard some more crunching underfoot, and looked around for Leora.

"She's gone, sir," Potter said. "Something about having to

go home for her Sabbath. Left everything neat and tidy and asked if she could come back tomorrow night."

Colin looked at his watch. Shabbos. It was almost Shabbos. The sun was sinking in the west, a light breeze was lifting the soft leaves, and he suddenly felt he wanted to go home. He struggled for a second, regained control.

"Come on, White. We have to visit this address. Abraham Pincus thinks the Fox might have been there or might still be there."

"If it's Orthodox Jews, though, they won't appreciate it if we barge in on their Sabbath preparations," Peter pointed out.

Colin felt the pull of the setting sun again, calling him from his past.

"Okay, let's leave it. I want to go home. I'm tired."

☼ ☼ ☼

"Last Shabbos Josh was here with us," Ilana said to Leora after lighting the candles and sitting down with a siddur.

"Hardly seems possible that almost a week has gone by since he went missing," Leora replied with a sympathetic sigh.

"Having Josh around seems like a whole other life now," Ilana said, and began to cry. She had managed to hold herself in reasonably well until now, but the flood tide was coming and she could no longer stop it. Distressed, Leora sat down next to her on the sofa and held her while she sobbed on her shoulder, wetting the smart city suit she had put on for Shabbos.

"I'm sorry. I'm ruining your suit!"

Leora just patted her and made soothing noises until the storm had passed. When Ilana felt calm enough, she got up to splash some cold water on her face and dabbed it with tissues. When she returned, she looked much more composed. Without another word she opened her siddur and started to daven

Kabbalas Shabbos and *ma'ariv*. Leora joined her, a little awkwardly because she was not yet completely comfortable with davening, and for a while the sitting room was quiet and peaceful. When Ilana closed her siddur and put it away, and Leora did the same, the two women sat down and looked at each other.

Ilana sighed. "I don't know how I am supposed to behave, Leora. I know you're not supposed to fret and be anxious on Shabbos, but how can I not?"

"I don't know how you can stop yourself worrying, Ilana. I know I probably couldn't. All I can say is, try to get as much spiritual input from Shabbos as you can and let it carry you over."

Ilana looked curiously at Leora. "If you don't mind me asking you something personal..."

Leora grinned and spread out her arms. "Feel free to probe. I'm an open book."

Ilana blushed. "Well, it's just that you don't seem to fit into any stereotypical pigeonhole of a Jewish woman. I know you are American and I am English, but I am married to an American and have been to the States lots of times, and you are not the typical American Orthodox Jew."

"I know. I'm an original. I guess some people would call people like me deprived. I was one of those latchkey kids whose parents barely knew we existed except to show us off as cute little accessories to their friends at dinner parties. Trophy kids. I was never read a bedtime story, never tucked in and kissed good night, and if I woke up screaming after a nightmare, or cried when I was sick or in pain, my parents would come in and yell at me for disturbing them, and didn't I know they had to go to work tomorrow?"

"How dreadful," Ilana said, thinking of Josh and the

many times she had held him through night terrors, how she had comforted him through childhood illnesses, of the stories they had read together and talked about afterward.

"I'm painting it blacker than it was. Actually, since I didn't know any different, I thought that was how it had to be. I grew up tough and streetwise and very independent, so it wasn't all so bad. By the age of seven I knew how to order in a pizza, get myself across town on the subway, and call the cops if I thought an intruder was around. And I could sweet-talk myself into almost any place I wanted to be. By the age of fourteen there was only one place I wanted to be, and that was the police department. I hung around there the way other girls hung around the movies and pizza shops."

"It doesn't sound like much of a Jewish upbringing," Ilana commented, fascinated by all this.

"It was totally secular. My parents ate treif. Saturdays were for dinner parties or helicopter trips to the Hamptons to visit their wealthy friends in their fancy shorefront properties. The only way I knew I was Jewish was when I got called 'Jew-girl' at school. It wasn't even that offensive when the guys called me that. It was just a statement of fact, and I didn't feel threatened by it. I was popular and pretty, so my being Jewish didn't matter so much. It was just like being a redhead or having green eyes. Being a bit hard-nosed didn't harm my popularity either; I got a name as having leadership qualities. Well, there were some extremely softly reared American princes and princesses in that school, Jewish or otherwise, so anyone with a bit of oomph was automatically the leader."

"I'm one of those softly reared Jewish princesses," Ilana confessed.

Leora looked at her. "You aren't nearly as soft as you make yourself out to be."

"No? Look at me. I'm in pieces."

"You are going through an experience that would topple far stronger people than you, my dear," Leora told her. "But I don't see any pieces in front of me. I see a woman in trauma who is coping pretty well on the whole."

"So what made you want to become religious?" Ilana asked, choosing not to respond to Leora's assessment.

"When I was working in the NYPD, inevitably I was involved with the Orthodox community from time to time. Burglaries, petty assaults, muggings, some worse crimes, unfortunately. The Orthodox aren't immune from those. I got talking to some of the victims. It wasn't as if I had had any resistance to being religious. I was just ignorant of my roots. One of them invited me to attend a *ba'al teshuvah* program where an extremely charismatic rabbi got me hooked."

"It wouldn't be a *ba'al teshuvah* program without a charismatic rabbi," Ilana remarked. "I sometimes wonder if they clone them for the purpose."

Leora was the Hardmans' only Shabbos guest. Usually they filled their house with relatives and friends or needy souls who required a good meal, or else they were invited out to Ilana's mother or friends. But the community, whether out of respect or out of discomfort, had left the Hardmans alone. Ilana got a few phone calls during the week from some very close friends asking if she wanted them to come around, be there, do anything. She had thanked them all warmly, begged their tolerance and understanding, but said she just couldn't face socializing at the moment. She promised to throw a party when, please God, Josh was returned safe and sound. In the meantime, she found Leora Jakober a perfect foil; being single and childless, there was no immediate competition, and yet being the powerfully professional criminologist that she was made Ilana feel cosseted and pampered, like a small child does when she feels total confidence that her mommy has taken over and will make everything better. That was how Leora made her feel, and it was a good, safe feeling that no one else could give her at the moment, not even Don. For the present, Leora was all she needed.

DAY SEVEN

CHAPTER EIGHTEEN

On Shabbos morning Leora and Ilana went to shul, though Ilana wasn't sure she wanted to. She felt the eyes of every woman in shul on her, smiling sympathetically or looking at her to seek signs of the ravages of her torment. She held her head high, remained calm and serene, and davened harder than she had in her life outside of Yom Kippur. She prayed for the safety of her absent son. She prayed that whoever was holding him captive was caring for him well and that he was not hurt, frightened, or distressed. And she prayed that if God had decreed that he would not survive this ordeal his death be without suffering and his immaculate soul returned totally cleansed and pure to its Maker. As she prayed, she rocked and swayed, her eyes closed, and she was totally unaware of her surroundings. Tears rolled down her cheeks, and it was only when Leora wiped them away gently with a tissue from Ilana's box that she came back to reality with a snap.

"I'm sorry," she whispered, suddenly acutely aware of many female eyes upon her. "I've made a spectacle of myself."

The female eyes were all soft and full of sympathy; she saw no judgment within their depths, but she felt ashamed of their pity.

After the service, women came up to her to wish her good Shabbos, and all looked curiously at Leora Jakober.

"My cousin from New York," Ilana said smoothly, praying for forgiveness for this smallest of white lies. It was easier than explaining the truth. She didn't want to deal with the inevitable intrusive questions.

On the way home, Leora said, "Maybe you shouldn't have done that."

"Maybe not. But for now it's easier for me than having everyone come round wanting to see Sherlock Holmes in action," Ilana said. "Right now I don't think I could bear that."

Leora nodded her understanding. "Well, it's not such a terrible lie. We're all related somehow." She grinned at Ilana, who grinned back. Leora felt relieved. Despite her caring attitude, she found it hard to cope with the other woman's acute distress. But it seemed to come in ebbs and floods, and there were many periods when she was calm and serene, even content.

After lunch they all went to lie down for a while. Leora, alone in the comfortable guest room, went over to the window and looked down upon the sunny garden and further onto the street full of children running about and shrieking in defiance of scolding parents ordering them to keep quiet. The Hardman garden was picture perfect, all flowers brightly upright and in place, the grass as smooth and untouched as green glass. Leora knew Ilana loved to garden, but even so, she was surprised at how beautiful it was. It looked like the kind of garden where you had to pay to get in, not the kind of place where children played and messed around, trampling on the flowerbeds and churning up the perfect lawn with their boots. It was an immaculate garden and as sad a place as Leora had ever seen. As she gazed upon its flawless lushness, she thought she could see superimposed the image of a small boy playing happily on the lawn, his ephemeral feet leaving no imprint on the upturned grass blades. She heard, inside her head, a tinkling child's laughter as he ran and kicked a ball, tossing his dark curly head in the sunshine. He looked up at her window and waved, smiling, and she waved back.

She blinked, cleared some involuntary tears from her eyes, and when she looked down again, the image had vanished.

"Goodbye, little Josh," Leora whispered. "I hope somewhere, wherever you are, alive or dead, that you are happy. Whether you are on this world or playing with the angels."

She turned from the window, closed the curtains, lay down on the bed in a light robe, and slept.

Leora awoke in the late afternoon. The sun cast long, slender shadows across her bed from the big old apple tree in the garden. She felt cool and comfortable and rested. Then she became aware of a very gentle knocking on her door and Ilana's voice calling, not wanting to wake her if she was deeply asleep.

"Yes?"

"Are you awake? We have a visitor. I think you should come down."

"I'll be right there," Leora said, and Ilana's footsteps retreated. Leora dressed hurriedly, ran a hand through her hair to smooth it, and went downstairs, wondering.

In the sitting room, looking extremely uncomfortable, was Colin Sommers.

"I'm really sorry to trouble you on your Sabbath," he was saying. The detective was sitting on an armchair nursing a long cool drink. Don was sitting at the table with a Gemara open before him.

"Do you have some news?" Ilana asked breathlessly.

"No. Sorry. I was just passing and thought I would drop in and see how you all were. I hope I'm not intruding."

Colin didn't say that he had, for some reason he couldn't even fathom himself, decided to walk over to the Hardmans' today rather than take the car. He rationalized that it was a beautiful day, a shame to take the car.

"Well, that's very kind of you," Ilana said, feeling vaguely uncomfortable that this non-Jew was visiting her on Shabbos. But he seemed comfortable in their presence so they relaxed. After a while, Don closed his Gemara, joined them in the lounge area, stretched his long legs out, and became expansive. He chatted about his youth in Iowa, about being in a Jewish family in a small middle American town where the Jewish community of some twenty families was like the token blacks in a company. They had a very small shul in someone's house, a mikveh shared between four small towns in the region, and a day school, also shared between them.

"We went to non-Jewish high schools," Don said, in a reminiscing mood. "It was tough. No one really understood our ways, particularly the secular Jewish kids; they were the most antisemitic of the lot. The non-Jewish kids were willing to be tolerant; the secular Jewish kids just thought we were weirdos or worse, tried to talk us out of being religious. And since they had at least a marginal knowledge of their faith, they were better able to hit us below the belt or sting us with fragments of half-known knowledge twisted out of all existence. There was one boy, made my life a total misery. He had a fair knowledge of the Bible and Talmud, enough to put doubts into the heads of the most staunch believers among us. Luckily, speaking for myself, that pain in the neck had the effect of making me build huge invisible fences around myself, fences through which no one could touch me." He paused, drifting. "I heard he came to live in England when his father's company redeployed him. I often wonder what became of him. Anyway, as soon as I possibly could, I left Iowa and came to yeshivah in Lakewood — that's in New Jersey — and later on in Jerusalem."

Ilana smiled. "I was in seminary there at the time and not really interested in getting married. But then we both went to the same wedding, and a mutual friend pointed him out to me as I stood watching the men's dancing at the edge of the *mechitzah* — that's a dividing screen to separate the men and women. My friend said, 'Do you want to go out with him?' I just blushed and made some inane comment, but she got the hint and put a few words in the right ears. The rest, as they say, is history."

"Did you get married in Israel, then?" Colin asked casually, as if this kind of lifestyle was totally alien to him. Admittedly he had not gone to yeshivah before his sliding away from tradition, but he knew what it was to sit and study a page of Gemara and enjoy it, too. In another lifetime...

"No, he followed me back here to meet my parents. We got engaged and married over here. His parents didn't mind that he wanted to live in London."

"All my computer studies and training were done after marriage," Don explained, "although I learned the basics in high school, of course."

"I see," Colin said. "So you haven't met up with your Iowa small-town tormentor over here?"

"Nope. Always wondered if I would. Somehow, when you're grown-up, your nightmares don't seem so bad and you don't mind confronting them again just to exorcize them."

"Was he really such a nightmare?"

Don leaned back and closed his eyes, remembering.

"He had the dangerous combination of arrogance and just enough knowledge to cover up the fact that he was, in fact, incredibly ignorant about Judaism. With the little he did know, embellished to the *n*th degree, he managed to really screw my head up. He made me doubt and worry about things that were not my concern. He had a way with words, a way of looking right through me."

There was a short silence, then Ilana laughed, a little embarrassed. "Don often talks about this guy. He obviously had a devastating, if short-lived, effect on his teenage years. Can I get you a tea and some cake, Detective Inspector?"

"I don't know about short-lived," Don said thoughtfully. "Whenever I have any doubts, he creeps into my head like a demon and niggles and niggles at me until I want to crush him like an annoying insect."

"Thank you, I would love it," Colin answered.

"I'll help," Leora offered, jumping up.

The two women left the room together.

"So your association with this boy ended when you went to yeshivah, I presume?" Just the right amount of faltering over the word *yeshivah*, just the right amount of mistake in the accentuation to show I am not really familiar with the word.

"Well, before really," Don said. "Things...things happened, and the family moved out of town. Next thing I knew his father had been transferred to England. I never heard from him again."

"Things?" Colin prompted. He didn't really understand

Don's need to talk about his past, but if he wanted to talk, he was willing to listen, and, after all, this Shabbos visit was a social call, not official police business. He had wanted to see how the family was holding up under the stress.

"Things. His father. I don't really want to talk about it. Not necessary now. Ah, here's the tea."

Colin left soon after, the images of the Hardmans' tranquil Shabbos lingering in his mind.

CHAPTER NINETEEN

Shabbos finished late, around nine-thirty. As soon as Havdalah was over, Leora went upstairs and changed out of her Shabbos clothes into her "work" clothes — a long loose skirt, a three-quarter-length-sleeved T-shirt, and black and purple Reeboks. She tied her hair up on top of her head with an interesting purple velvet scrunchy and came downstairs again, announcing she was going back to her office at the police station to look at the trace evidence she had prepared before Shabbos.

"Oh, are you going out without *melaveh malkah*? Wouldn't you like a coffee at least and a piece of toast?" Ilana, ever the Jewish mother and hostess, asked her.

"Umm, there's a coffee machine at the station. I can take it black, and I have sachets of Sweet'n'Low in my pocketbook. I'll make myself a sandwich, maybe. I think it's going to be a long night."

"I'll make it while you get ready," Ilana offered. "Tuna, egg, or cheese?"

"One of each." Leora grinned with her usual disarming lack of guile.

Ilana liked her for it; nothing more irritating for a generous hostess than a guest constantly protesting that he or she didn't want anything, that it was quite all right, that she was fine really, when it was patently obvious that she was hungry or thirsty or, if she wasn't, that she should be. Grinning back, Ilana set to her sandwich-making with goodwill, while Leora finished packing her small knapsack. Adding some fruit and a container of yogurt with a plastic spoon, Ilana bagged the lot and handed it to Leora, who stuffed the package on top of the knapsack.

Leora kissed the older woman's cheek and left with a cheery wave. "Off to look at all this evidence and finish developing the films!"

☼ ☼ ☼

After Colin's visit with the Hardmans, he had walked back home. He had left his mobile phone at home, too. Technically he was off duty and didn't have to have his pager or mobile with him, but he normally was able to be contacted at all times. Why am I walking about on Shabbos? he asked himself. Shabbos doesn't mean diddly squat to me. He got back to his flat and turned on the lights and the television with a note of defiance. Yes. I am in control.

He still hadn't been to investigate the address from that supergeek friend of pesky Baruch Weiss yet. It was growing dark now, hardly worth it. He might as well wait until tomorrow. Anyway, Cleverclogs was going to be at the station tonight, going through that trace evidence, and he would really like to be there to watch her at work. He made himself a note on his personal organizer to go to the address Pincus had found first thing the next morning.

After Shabbos, Colin waited a decent amount to allow for Havdalah, then drove to the station. Peter had declined to join him as it was his night off and he didn't share quite the same fascination with the analysis as Colin seemed to.

Potter was on duty tonight, and a couple of constables worked steadily on computers in a back room, entering data. They glanced up and grinned at Colin as he passed their open door, and one of them hooked a thumb toward Peter's office.

"She's in there, sir," she said. "Doing things, she is."

"Ah. Doing things. I'd better go and see what it is, exactly, that she's doing, hadn't I?"

He walked through to the office and knocked.

"Come in," called a muffled voice, and Colin entered the inner sanctum. Leora Jakober smiled at him from her microscope. A pile of neatly organized slides stood at the side.

"This is fascinating stuff," she told him eagerly. "Come and look."

Colin went over, and Leora pointed to the computer screen where images were shifting and changing as she focused on them.

"Look, this is the earth taken from the windowsill in Josh's bedroom. We already looked at it, with the pollen spores in the middle. The sample, as you recall, was totally different from the sample we took from a random area in the Hardmans' garden where an abductor could not have trodden to get up a ladder to the kid's bedroom. Right?"

Colin nodded.

Leora replaced the slide with another, and the computer image changed. "Now this is a sample taken from the ground around the playhouse."

Colin stared at the lumps of soil granules and pollen spores and other, unidentifiable things.

"And?" he said at last, baffled.

Leora sighed. "Oh, well, I suppose I shouldn't expect too

much. I'll explain it in words of one syllable, all right?"

Colin tried to look offended and failed as she shot him a white American grin.

"Okay. Basically it's like this. The sample taken from the windowsill of Josh's bedroom was not anything remotely like the sample we took from the area around the playhouse. Ergo, the abductor was *not* in the playhouse. Not as far as I can tell anyway."

Colin felt his heart plummet to the approximate vicinity of his shoes. He had, despite trying desperately to remain professionally aloof about it, become hopeful that the playhouse would house the secrets to Josh and his abductors.

"What about the saliva and stuff on the paper cups?"

"Not having anything to compare it with makes it a bit difficult to pin it on anyone," Leora said. "But I've documented all the DNA in the saliva and any hair and skin cells I have found. Now all we need to do is find a match for it."

"I see," Colin said, hardly able to contain his disappointment. "So I wonder who it is who is using that playhouse if not the Fox?"

"I have no idea. Maybe your pint-sized investigator who has been keeping an eye on it till now can continue doing so and catch the person in the act."

"Good idea. What about the footprints?"

"Oh, yes, the footprints. I developed the photos I took with the Polyray. I'll put them up for you to look at." She pinned up some ten-by-eights on the wall, sharp black and white prints of shoe treads.

"These are the treads I photographed at the playhouse."

"They are very clear. Amazing," Colin said.

"I could have lifted them if the ground had been softer and made a cast, but it was just the wooden floor and some dust to work with, and not even enough dust. But I think these are pretty sharp."

"They look amazing, as if they were dipped in paint and pressed onto paper. But what do they tell us?"

"Well, I have a photograph here that your forensic man Joe took of the partial footprint lifted on the windowsill. In this case he did a lift rather than a photo or a cast, because it was pretty deep in the earth left on the sill, but not quite deep enough for a cast. A photograph or lift differs from a cast in that it is a two-dimensional reproduction of a print, like a fingerprint lift. A cast is a three-dimensional structure that can provide a positive reproduction of the footwear.

"Remember," Leora continued, "that some impressions may only lift in partial and others do not lift at all, so I always attempt to photograph the prints first. If the footwear leaves a visible print on an item that can be retrieved from the scene to the laboratory, then this should be the method of choice. It is much easier to work on the evidence under controlled conditions than to try collecting the footwear at the crime scene, but in some cases this is not possible."

"Right. And how do you actually get the impression out of that fine dust?"

"This lifting method works by placing adhesive paper or contact paper, adhesive side down, over the impression in the dust and smoothing it over," Leora explained as she put up the second batch of photographs. "This allows the impressions to be transferred to the adhesive side of the paper. Once this is done, the paper is peeled off the impression and photographed. The paper can be treated with a mixture of crystal violet and distilled water, which stains the footwear impression but produces a reversed image when collected. Once this is completed, a piece of clear acetate is placed over the print to preserve it for impounding and later examination purposes."

"I think I'll stick to simple investigation," Colin said dryly. "This all sounds horribly complicated. I'm more of a Mr. Plod type of copper than a Hercule Poirot. I plod along, noticing things and talking to people. I wouldn't know what to do with a piece of trace evidence if it jumped up and bit me."

Leora laughed. "Both kinds of police work are needed, the Mr. Plod kind and my kind. We complement each other. I'm not nearly so good at talking to people as you are."

Colin glowed at this small praise.

"Anyhow," Leora went on, "looking at these two sets of prints from the footwear, even you can see what they show us." She grinned to soften her words.

He studied the two sets of photographs she had pinned up. "I'm no expert, but these two treads don't look the same."

"Not even remotely," Leora added. "Look at the pattern of the tread here and here. Never mind that they're not from the same shoe, they're not even the same make of sneaker. From my knowledge of footwear, I would say that the one on the windowsill was lifted from a Nike, and the one in the playhouse was a Puma."

"Is it possible that it was still from the same guy, but he was wearing two different pairs of trainers on these two occasions?" Colin asked.

"Nearly impossible, I'd say," Leora replied. "First of all, the two prints are from shoes of different sizes. The first one, from the windowsill, I estimate is a size nine, even though we only have a partial lift, and the one from the playhouse a size ten. Even if we assume that the Fox wanted to fool us by wearing two different pairs of shoes for two occasions, in two different sizes, there is no way he could hide the way he wears his shoes. The tread on these two pairs, if worn by the same person, would be worn down in the same place, and it isn't. Look. In this shoe, the wearer tends to lean inward. In this shoe, the wearer leans on the outside. See how the tread is worn down there and there?" She pointed.

"So the bottom line is, whoever was using the playhouse isn't the Fox," Colin summed up, hardly able to contain his disappointment.

"Sure looks like it," Leora said sympathetically.

"Oh, bother. I'll get some of my men to watch the playhouse on their beat, see who it is. Now I know it isn't the Fox, we don't have to be quite so surreptitious. I was sort of worried to scare him off before. My biggest fear is to drive the Fox even further away from us than he is now. I have a gut feeling that, at the moment at least, he is very close by. "

"Well, I'd still be cautious, if I were you. Just in case I'm wrong," she replied.

"My men will be discreet. Don't you worry." Colin sighed. "So your analysis is conclusive?"

"Sorry," she replied. "The playhouse mystery man is not the Fox."

"Oh, well. Back to the drawing board. Tomorrow first thing we go check out that address. Do you want to come with?"

"Sure thing. Tell me what time and I'll be ready."

"I'll drive by at nine," Colin said.

That night Colin found sleep elusive. Eventually he surrendered to the insomnia that had gripped him, got up, and padded barefoot to the kitchen to get a cold drink from the refrigerator. The apartment was cool. A breeze blew in from a high window, sending the net curtains dancing like brides. He stood in the center of his living room, eyes closed, taking long swallows of his cool drink.

I'm never going to get to sleep like this, he told himself. I need to read something. He was reminded of that crucial chapter in Megillas Esther when the king couldn't sleep and called for the Book of Chronicles to be read to him.

Colin wasn't a great reader of Books of Chronicles, or of anything much, still retaining some of his schoolboyish antipathy to reading which was so common among young males. He remembered his sisters at home with their noses always buried in some novel or other, while he and his brothers lumbered around the house, protesting "I'm so boooorrrreeed!" When his mother suggested, "So go read a book — there's plenty around!" the boys would stare at her as if she had suggested they amuse themselves by learning a lengthy poem by heart (another hated occupation).

However, at the age of twelve, Colin discovered science fiction. Even though it was not encouraged in their household to read non-Jewish books, Moshe and Rifka Sommers had vetted the sci-fi series Colin increasingly began piling up around the house and could find nothing averse in it other than a nonspecific "filling your head full of *shtusim.*"

"At least the boy is reading at last," Rifka had said to her husband, "and he is sure to know that this is pure fantasy and not mix it up with reality, so I'd let him get on with it."

Moshe thought his son would be better occupied learning Gemara than filling his mind with distant planets and alien civilizations, but he did understand his need for escapism, so he relented. Colin was finally hooked on reading; he joined his sisters with their "nose in a book" position, slouching around the living room in various unhealthy-looking postures, and his school grades improved with his knowledge of language, grammar, and spelling.

He thought of it all now as he stood in his quiet, dark living room, allowing the spring breezes to cool him. He had never outgrown his love of science fiction, never moved on to anything more "adult," never taken to reading worthy biographies or political thrillers or classic novels. His reading was as stuck in a time warp as some of the characters in the books he loved. His face turned red as he thought about the two sci-fi conventions he had attended "just to see what went on there," although he had left them before the end, feeling foolish among middle-aged men and women dressed in alien costumes and spouting the language of their favorite characters in their books.

Now he needed to read a bit, to just allow himself to drift into another galaxy somewhere many thousands of light-years away, so that sleep might eventually take him prisoner. He looked around his flat. And then he remembered the book he had taken as "evidence" from Karen Whitestone's house.

Grinning, he went to retrieve it from his briefcase where it still sat, forlorn and forgotten, in its plastic evidence bag. Colin gave a deep sigh of satisfaction and, returning to bed with his prize, prepared to dive in and enjoy.

He opened the book, and as he did so a piece of paper fell out. He took it and unfolded it.

These violent delights have violent ends,
And in their triumph die like fire and powder.

It was signed, "Will."

Hmm, thought Colin. He wondered about it for a few moments, decided that Cindy probably had a shunned boyfriend somewhere in the wings, and then thought little more about it as he got involved in the plot.

As he reached a natural break in the story and his eyes began to close at last, he turned his light off and, as he drifted, thought a bit more about the slip of paper inside the book. Something about it...he couldn't quite remember what. So familiar... What was it?

Colin Sommers slept.

DAY EIGHT

CHAPTER TWENTY

Ilana woke early on Sunday morning, the habit ingrained from having to get Josh ready for school. Don had managed to persuade her to go to work during the past few awful days for at least a couple of hours. Even though, with Leora Jakober now firmly ensconced in her guest bedroom, Ilana clung to home, needing to be around the woman who brought her hope, she also needed to focus on something other than her son for a short period each day. Work provided this; the intense concentration needed when programming Web sites took her far away from her personal anguish and into a world where binary and digital overcame reality.

But it was Sunday, and on Sundays the office was closed. This was not Israel, where Sundays were the first day of the workweek. In England, most offices ran a strict Monday through Friday schedule. Non-Jewish schools, too, were closed, as were most of the Jewish girls' schools. It was only the boys who attended morning school on Sunday so their requirement of daily Torah learning was filled.

So Ilana was used to never sleeping in. On Shabbos and

holidays she would get up and go to shul, and on Sundays she rose diligently to get Josh up in time for his morning classes. Last Sunday she had arisen and gone into the vacuum which was her son's room, and this Sunday she tried to recapture, just for an instant, the feeling she had first felt when she saw he was not in his bed, the feeling that Don must have gotten him up early and taken him to shul with him. A comforting, everything-is-going-to-be-fine sort of feeling. A sensation, like the long-lost scent and taste of a wondrous vacation, as fleeting as it was elusive.

Josh's bedroom door remained firmly locked. It was no longer the room of a much loved and lively child; it was evidence and as untouched and untouchable as a buried treasure. Only the outer surface of its door remained available to her, and this Ilana caressed, thinking ironically of the Kotel HaMa'aravi, the Western Wall in Jerusalem, the holiest shrine in the Jewish world, which was only an outer wall of the Temple but was, to present-day Jews, the nearest they could get to the inner sanctum now hidden to them by centuries of history and devastation.

She had found herself writing Josh little notes and leaving them around the house, loving notes from a lonely mother. This Sunday, this day marking a full week since Josh had been taken from her, she sat down and wrote him a poem.

Where are you hiding, Josh?
Where do you keep those charms?
I recall the baby boy
Who nestled in my arms
You grew into a flowering shrub
With scented blossoms sweet
Now my arms are outstretched toward you
To make my life complete

Who do you talk to now?
Where will you sleep tonight?
I get through my life somehow
Waiting for the morning light
To lose a child, a son
Is more than human flesh can bear
I hope he cares for you
One day I'll find you there

Reading the poem again and again through her tears, as the page blurred and the ink smudged, gave her comfort. She wanted desperately to put the poem on his pillow, but she knew she could not, so she taped it to the outside of his bedroom door.

As she stood there, sniveling and wiping her tears with the back of her hand, Leora emerged from the guest bedroom fully dressed and made up, auburn hair brushed and glossy, bouncing on her shoulders. Her bright smile faded at once when she saw Ilana crying at Josh's closed bedroom door.

"Oh, honey," Leora said, coming up to read the poem. Then, without a single word, she took Ilana into her arms for an embrace.

Once Ilana had composed herself, the two women went companionably downstairs for breakfast. Don usually spent Sunday mornings in the local *kollel* catching up with his learning. He tried to have a regular evening *chavrusa*, but he often ended up working too late for it to be practical, so this Sunday morning's study had become sacrosanct.

Over toast, cereal, and coffee, Leora told Ilana that she would be going to the address Avi Pincus had found to see if there was any trace of the Fox or Josh there. Ilana became very excited at the thought that there was actually an address where her son might be staying.

"Don't get your hopes up," Leora told her, "but it might be a steppingstone. According to Avi Pincus, the e-mails came from that address or, at the very least, a person living at that address had the account from which those e-mails were sent."

"He only sent two. No more," Ilana mused. "I wonder why. Maybe he has no more messages to send us. Maybe he knew we were on his trail and decided to take drastic steps." Her voice rose in panic.

"No, no. Don't think like that," Leora soothed.

"But if he's the Internet Fox, as he says he is, then he should use the Net, shouldn't he?"

"It's only a few days since the last e-mail. Maybe he's on the run with Josh and has no access to a computer," Leora said reassuringly, though she herself had wondered at the lack of e-mails. Since the Fox had showed himself to be comfortable with a computer, it didn't make sense that he had stopped using this medium. Unless...

Unless he knew he was being tracked. Which would achieve exactly what Colin didn't want to achieve — to drive him underground, to scare him away. Scare him to where no one would be able to find him. Leora closed her eyes for a moment and sent up a silent prayer that the Fox was still somewhere close by.

After breakfast, Ilana went into Don's study while Leora cleared up the breakfast dishes. She let out a cry, which brought Leora running.

"I don't believe it!" She was pointing at the screen with a shaking finger. Leora looked.

"It's from him! The Fox! I don't believe it! What a coincidence!"

"Sure is," Leora said, breathing an inward sigh of relief and sending up a prayer of thanks. Wow, I must be better than

I thought if You answered my prayers so fast!

The e-mail read:

When devils will the blackest sins put on,
They do suggest at first with heavenly shows.
The Internet Fox

"What does it mean?" Ilana said, her voice rising dangerously out of control.

Leora read it again. "To me it sounds as if the Fox feels threatened. Print it out, Ilana. I'd better call Colin."

Within ten minutes Colin was staring at the screen alongside Ilana and Leora. "There's something very familiar about the style of the writing," he said, rubbing his chin. "I can't place it. Hang on a second." From his inside jacket pocket he withdrew a copy of the book he'd been reading last night.

"A paperback novel? Oh, come on," Ilana said derisively.

"No, not the novel. Look. I found this slip of paper inside it." He held out the sheet with the poem.

There was a brief silence while they all read it.

"It's not that similar," Leora said at last.

"No," Ilana agreed, "but there is something..."

Colin said, "The book belongs to Cindy Wallis. It's just too much of a coincidence."

"You think the person who wrote the letter to Cindy and the person who wrote this e-mail are one and the same?" Ilana asked.

"I think so. I'm not sure. I'd have to find an expert. Someone literary."

"Well, at least one thing's for sure. He's still sending e-mails, which is a good sign," Leora interjected.

"It means he still feels confident that no one can trace them," agreed Colin, "though the content of this one seems to hint that he feels threatened."

"We don't want him to feel threatened. Then he'll be much harder to trace," Leora said worriedly.

Colin looked at the two lines of text. "I think this isn't composed by him. I don't think he is a writer. He is using someone else's work. Does anyone recognize it?"

They all shook their heads. "It sounds very classic, but I must confess, the classics never interested me that much; I always found them boring," Ilana said.

Leora nodded her agreement. "I've always preferred modern writers," she said. "In any case, you know what this could mean, don't you?" Leora said slowly, and they both looked at her. "It means Cindy and the Fox may know each other, could even be working together on this kidnaping."

"Are you seriously suggesting that Cindy's grievance against Don for sacking her was enough to make her commit this crime?" Ilana said incredulously. "For heaven's sake, she must be twisted if firing her for using chat rooms and playing games on-line during working hours would make her angry enough to kidnap a child."

"And use an accomplice like the Fox to carry it out," agreed Leora. "You're right. It doesn't make sense. It's taking a sledgehammer to crack a peanut."

"I suppose if she's got a screw loose she could be capable of anything for the slightest provocation," Colin said, mostly to himself.

"I knew Cindy," Ilana said. "She was an intelligent girl, computer literate. She was just lazy and wanted to have fun, not work. I can't imagine her being provoked enough to want to do this. She'd more likely just find some other job where she wasn't watched too closely and have fun there instead."

"Hmm. Maybe we can find out from Karen Whitestone if

Cindy had a boyfriend, and if so who. Come on, gang, we have work to do! First to the Fox's address, then back to Edgware to speak to Karen Whitestone. We could speak to her from the cell phone on the way. Maybe she has more news about Cindy's whereabouts."

"I want to come with you," Ilana said suddenly. "Don't leave me here alone, please."

They looked at her with compassion.

"We're doing police work, Ilana," Leora said at last, putting her arm round the older woman. "Couldn't you get your mother or a friend to come and be with you?"

Ilana visibly sagged, like a rag doll from which someone had removed half the stuffing. "No, it's okay." She looked at the wall clock. "Don will be home from the *kollel* soon. Maybe we'll go out for a while. It's a lovely spring day."

Her words were positive and upbeat, but her tone and body language gave a whole different message. Leora felt terrible, but taking Ilana along on today's trip would set a very worrying and impractical precedent.

"I'll tell you what," Colin said. "We'll pass the *kollel* on our way out and drop in and tell Don to come home a bit earlier. How's that?"

Another glance at the wall clock. "I don't want to cut his learning short. He doesn't get much chance during the week. Work is always in the way. I'll walk to the *kollel* and pick up some groceries on the way. By the time I finish my food shopping, he'll be ready to leave." She beamed at them both. "There! See? I'm sorted! Off you go!"

"We'll go if you go, too," Leora said firmly. Ilana went and got her shoulder bag and sunglasses. She wouldn't need a jacket; the weather was warm. She joined them outside the house and locked up carefully.

"Want a lift?" Colin asked politely. He didn't actually want her to accept, as once she was in the car, he had a feeling she'd be a job and a half to get out again. Anyhow, he had to pick up Peter on the way.

"No, no, I want to walk," Ilana replied on cue. "It's a glorious morning, the flowers in my neighbors' gardens need my inspection as I walk up the road, and there's plenty of time to get my shopping done before I pick up Don."

They parted company. Leora looked back at Ilana as she walked slowly up the street, pausing to examine each flowerbed and blossoming shrub. She reminded the younger woman of a small child taken on her first walk by a patient mother who allows the child free rein to pause at every insect, every piece of chewed-up gum and dried leaf along the path. An invisible hand led Ilana slowly up the pavement and waited calmly while she stopped to inspect and admire. She seemed to be turned inward, to be living her life from the inside outward, focusing on small flowering things that stayed where they were planted and did not vanish with the dawn as her son had done.

"Leave her be," Colin said softly. "She'll be okay. I promise you, she'll be okay."

Leora shot him a scathing look. "Don't ever promise something like that," she snapped. "How can you possibly know?"

Colin was taken aback at her vehemence. "I'm sorry," he mumbled.

"I know you aren't a religious man, and maybe you don't believe in anything, but I firmly believe there is only One Who can know," Leora went on, slightly softer now in the face of his humility.

Suddenly it all seemed so horribly ridiculous, this charade. Like a clown with his makeup applied wrongly. Why did he have to pretend? "Look, it's not all as simple as you make out," he began.

"Oh, I know," she interrupted. "I'm sorry. I shouldn't make assumptions about other faiths."

They reached Peter's place and Colin honked his horn. The moment for truths had passed. I think I might tell her, he thought. I think she might understand. It was a mind-blowing thought. He had known Lucy for years, and telling her his background had never occurred to him. And yet to this stranger, this woman who had come on a big silver bird across the ocean into his life only three days ago, he felt he had to let her know he was not so different from her. He felt she would understand and not judge him for his divergence. Their eyes met briefly, and she flashed him a reassuring smile. The reassurance, misplaced as it was, comforted him nonetheless.

Peter came lolloping out to the car like an overgrown rabbit, all legs and flapping raincoat in place of floppy ears. He was one of the so-called safe ones — married, with two small children. Peter had no long lonely evenings staring at the TV on his own; instead he spent his evenings trying to placate his wife and give quality time to his kids. Being a cop's wife didn't have many compensations and required much patience and calmness of spirit. Marie White had neither.

When she had married Peter as a young rookie, she had a stereotypical image of a policeman, all glamor and status. She never got used to his long working hours and interrupted free time when he would be called away in the middle of a dinner party or family outing. When he was actually at home, she found it hard not to harp on him for leaving her on her own so much. At one time, their marriage had almost failed. Then Peter had suggested she might like to get a part-time job now that the kids were in primary schooling. The job she found as a supermarket checkout girl was Marie's salvation; besides getting her out of the house, it enabled her to network with her peers and learn that her own marriage was not nearly as bad as some others she heard about. At least Peter was honest, hard-working, devoted, and loyal and brought home a reasonable pay packet that he didn't gamble away when her back was turned.

The two policemen, Colin and Peter, often exchanged confidences when they were working together. Peter had often asked him why he didn't marry Lucy, and that question Colin could not answer honestly. Was it the fact that she wasn't Jewish that really bothered him? Was it Peter's often negative complaints about married life that made Colin glad of his independence? If so, he would never tell Peter and possibly add fuel to the domestic battle fires. He would just mutter something about "not being the marrying kind, hate kids, though yours aren't too bad, I suppose" and leave it at that. Even if Marie wasn't the absolute perfect policeman's wife, his two children were the most perfect ever born to any man. He knew Colin tried his best to play the genial uncle when he came over for one of Marie's delicious home-cooked meals and appreciated his efforts to entertain Simon and Jenny with highly embellished "true crime" tales of cops and robbers.

"If you ever do get married and have your own, you'll see, they'll be the bees knees in your eyes," Peter had told him wisely, but Colin had merely shuddered at the idea of small beings taking over his life.

In the car now, Peter greeted Leora, who had moved to the back, and then said to Colin, "So what's the score?"

Leora took this to mean the British equivalent of "What's up?" and it probably was, but Colin decided to deliberately misinterpret.

"Manchester United totally decimated Tottenham last night," and soon the two men were totally immersed in soccer talk, arguing the finer points of the referee's handing out a red card to a favored player and if a goal should have been disallowed. Leora, whose knowledge of soccer was only marginally less than her knowledge of obscure Croatian dialects, tuned out and occupied herself with a tourist's eye view of glamorous Golders Green.

The journey took only five minutes or so. Colin drew the car up outside a semidetached house on a quiet street, the hum of the traffic on the main road safely a few streets away.

They all got out and stood, looking at the house. As Avi Pincus had described it, it had small bikes and toys littering the front garden and a general look of being lived in and in use. After rechecking the address and exchanging "this can't be right" glances with the other two, Colin marched up to the front door and rang the bell.

A harassed-looking young woman opened it shortly afterward. She was pretty, wore an extremely elegant wig in a hair band, and was fully made up even at this early hour on a Sunday morning, but there was no disguising the dark circles under her big blue eyes and a sour pout to her mouth. She carried a large baby on one hip, and from the bowels of the house a toddler in full tantrum mode could be heard screaming and crashing about.

"Yes?" she asked impatiently. Colin could see that from her perspective the three of them looked rather like missionaries trying to sell her an alternative religion. And from their perspective, she looked just about ready to buy it.

"We're police officers, madam," Peter explained. "Might we ask you some questions, please?"

The young woman's expression changed from closed to defensive.

"Oh, gosh. Things are a bit hectic, as you can hear. You'll have to excuse Goldie; she's having a temper tantrum, and I don't want to give in just for the sake of peace."

"No problem," Leora said firmly, striding into the house, the two men following bemusedly after. Colin wasn't at all sure he wanted to excuse Goldie. They passed her lying on the living-room floor, toys littered around her, thrashing her small legs furiously, each kick threatening to disembowel yet another favorite plaything. The young woman seemed oblivious and took them into the kitchen, closing the door.

"Will she be all right out there?" Colin asked, more out of curiosity for this woman's parenting methods than any real concern.

"Yeah," Peter answered for her with a world-weary father's dismissive wave. "Leave her to get on with it. Best thing."

The woman bade them all to sit around a large kitchen table and put the baby in his highchair where a pretzel kept him amused.

They soon elicited that her name was Shoshanah Segal, married to Jacob Segal, and that this wasn't their own home.

"We've only just returned from Israel. We lived there for the first few years after we got married," Shoshanah explained. "We rented out there, and we are renting here. For the time being anyway. We are in the process of doing up a house not far from here. Our own home at last! I can't wait."

"I see," Colin said. "And how long have you been in this house?"

"We've only been here a few days. End of last week. We arrived from Israel on Thursday and moved in here Friday. Luckily it's fully furnished, so we didn't need to do anything. It even has crockery and cutlery and pots and pans, although from what I heard from the agent, he wouldn't let the last tenant use them."

"Oh? Why is that?" Colin was aware that Leora had slipped out during this conversation, leaving the kitchen door ajar. The screaming from the living room seemed to have ceased to be replaced by the occasional hiccup.

"The agent specializes in kosher lettings, well, that's what goes around here. He told me the last tenant wasn't Jewish or wasn't *frum* — he didn't seem sure which — and either way it didn't matter. He locked away all the household utensils and told the last tenant he'd have to use his own."

Colin felt a nub of excitement. "He? A man alone? Or was he with a family?"

"I don't think he had a family. Well, he certainly didn't have a wife from what I know. You'd have to ask the agent. I'll give you his number."

As she turned to get it, Mrs. Segal saw Leora busily bagging bits of fluff from the hall carpet.

"I know I should vacuum more often," she said, embarrassed.

"Oh, no. It's fine," reassured Leora, who was on her knees, collecting samples. "I'll take some samples from your garden on my way out. Just a little soil."

"Oh, I never vacuum the garden," Shoshanah said and grinned at the three startled faces.

CHAPTER TWENTY-ONE

Shoshanah followed them outside, carrying the baby. Goldie's tantrum had completely dissipated, and the toddler followed curiously.

"This garden looks as if it was recently cultivated," Leora remarked casually, bagging some soil samples.

"Yes, it was," Shoshanah replied. "I think when the last tenant left they did a bit of a rush job, laid some turf, put some 'instant garden' down — you know, plants from the nursery already in flower."

"Did you see what it looked like before?" Colin asked.

"Er, no. But I heard that the owner told the agent in no uncertain terms to get the garden done double quick because they'd never get the place let with it looking like a wilderness. They only had a day or two to do it, I think."

"Wonderful," Leora muttered sarcastically. "I would have liked to have seen the garden as it was before they put down all this instant garbage."

Peter squatted down in a corner and began worrying at the edges of the turf with his fingers.

"What are you doing, Peter?"

"I'm just seeing if this turf might possibly not have taken root." He pulled and tugged at a corner. "Gotcha." Peter lifted a corner of the turf up completely, exposing the raw uncultivated earth underneath.

"I do hope they didn't put down compost or topsoil before they laid the turf," Leora worried, coming over to look. She bent down to examine the soil. "Bingo. I think we have liftoff," she said, opening an evidence bag.

"By the way," Colin said casually as they prepared to leave, evidence bags securely fastened, "did the previous tenant have a girlfriend, do you know?"

Shoshanah shrugged. "No idea. Ask the agent."

Leora had a question. "Is the back garden cultivated, too, or is it still a jungle?"

"Same thing," Shoshanah said. "There's one of those Anderson shelters still from the war, I think, ugly things they were, so the gardener turfed over it and they planted daffodils. It looks lovely now."

They all thanked her and walked off down the path. As Shoshanah Segal turned to go into the house, Colin said casually, "Does this house have a computer?"

She stopped dead. "No, why? I think there was one, though. There is a desk with a space for one upstairs."

"Phone line nearby?"

"Yes, I think so. Why?"

"Nothing. Thanks, Mrs. Segal."

Back in the car, they all looked at each other.

"I think the Fox was there," Leora said.

They all nodded.

"Let's see what we can find out from the agent, and then it's back to Karen Whitestone," Colin said, revving the engine.

"Oh, bother, it's Sunday. The agents will be closed," Peter said suddenly, slapping his thigh.

"Vee heff our veys," Colin said with an evil snicker. They drove up to the agent's offices, ascertained that they were indeed closed, and then Colin made a quick call to the station, which elicited the agent's home address and number. He then phoned the agent's home and told him not to go out, that they were on their way over.

"Good move," Leora said, sitting upright and looking pleased.

Mike Younger was, like his name, young, eager, and overendowed with an extra helping of the purple prose necessary to sell undesirable residences. He had black, slicked-back hair and smooth tanned skin (no doubt as a result of expensive foreign holidays paid for by unsuspecting purchasers) and wore a pinky ring.

"Sorry for disturbing you on a Sunday," Colin began.

"That's all right. Police officers, you say. Always delighted to help the law. Please, come in, sit down. Can I get you anything? Coffee, tea, something long and cool, maybe? With a cherry and an umbrella?"

"You're not renting us one of your poky little flats now," Colin said with a grin, "so just relax. We don't need anything except information."

"Officer, I don't lease poky little flats. Only highly spacious and luxurious residences."

Colin had an almost unrestrainable urge to go on the attack about estate agent–speak, but managed to hold back. He named the address at which Shoshanah Segal was now living.

"Oh, yes," Mike Younger said. "Lovely property, mid-wars construction, recently refurbished and extended, now a spacious family home comprising —"

"We need to know who was the tenant before the Segals," Peter interrupted him in mid–purple prose flow.

"Before the Segals. Now let me think. I have all the details at the office, of course, not here."

"Try to remember. It can't be that difficult, even for you. It was only a few days ago."

If the barb hit home, Mike displayed no sign of it.

"Oh, yes, it was a gentleman. I recall exactly because we don't usually do short-term lets. Six months is the minimum, and this gentleman wanted it for only a week or two, he said. At first I refused, but he offered to pay twice the rental, and I checked with the homeowner. Since we had this little gap between two long-term tenants anyhow, I said okay."

"Do you recall the name of the gentleman?" Peter asked.

"Bill something or other, I believe. Valence?"

"Could it have been Venice?"

"Oh, I don't think so. I'd have remembered an unusual name like that."

Doubtful, Colin thought, but pressed on.

"Can you describe him to us?"

Mike's face showed the strain of effort. "Well, he was tall and sort of thin and had longish hair, sort of down to here."

"How old would you say he was?"

"Hard to tell. Mid- to late thirties, maybe?"

"Did he say the letting was for him alone or did he have anyone with him? A wife and child, one or the other?"

"When I showed him the property, he was on his own. He didn't mention anyone but..."

"But?"

"I noticed something. He was carrying a Toys R Us bag. And there was definitely a toy inside."

"He could have just been buying a present for a nephew

or friend's kid," Leora pointed out.

"Yes, of course he could. Silly me," Mike said.

"Did you see what kind of toy was in the bag?"

"Well, the only reason I did was because it was brightly colored, and the bags are so thin these days. And it was a toy I fancied buying for myself. Silly, I know. It was one of those new color Gameboys. I've been addicted to Gameboys for ages, and the color ones promise much better graphics —"

"But he made no specific mention of a child or wife?"

"None. And since he was only in the property a short while, I never went there to speak with him, so I have no idea if he brought anyone else to live there with him."

"I'd be very grateful if you could find out the exact name of the tenant and any previous or forwarding addresses he gave to you," Colin said firmly.

"I'll do that first thing in the morning when the office opens," Mike said.

"Are you a key holder of your office?"

Mike looked affronted at last.

"Key holder? I own the company." He puffed out his skinny chest so that he looked like a concave pigeon.

"Ah, you own the company," Colin mused. "Well, in that case, sir, we'd greatly appreciate it if you would go into your offices today and get me out the relevant information. Phone me on my mobile, okay?"

"Today? Go into the office?"

"Yes, please, and pronto," Colin said firmly. "There is a child's life at stake here and waiting till your offices open tomorrow does not sit very well with me. Call me impatient, but that's how it is, sunshine."

Mike swallowed. "All right. I'll go straightaway."

"What a good idea. In fact, if you like, we can drive you

there, wait while you retrieve the relevant files, and drop you back here. All part of the service, sir. How's that?"

Ten minutes later, they were standing in his office and waiting for his computer to boot.

Mike tapped some keys. "Ah, here we are. Gosh, I was right. It was Bill Valence. Here are the addresses he gave for his previous and forwarding."

They dropped him back home and sat despondently in the car.

"Of course he wouldn't use his own name. Why should he? He's far too smart," Leora said, looking at the scribbled names and addresses. "So I guess the addresses are false, too."

"Very often when people change their names they keep the initials the same," Colin said. "Bill Valence, Bill Venice."

"So you think this is the Fox," Peter said.

"I'm sure of it," Colin answered. "Now we have a name or two, all we have to do is find him. Simple." He pulled away from the curb with a screech of rubber. "First Karen Whitestone. Get her on the phone."

Peter punched in the number. "Karen Whitestone" came the voice over the speaker.

"Detective Inspector Colin Sommers here."

"Oh, yes. How can I help you, Inspector?"

"We just wondered if you'd heard from Cindy."

"No. I would have phoned you. I do keep my word, you know." An edge to her voice, like a serrated blade.

"I'm sure you would, I'm sure you would. One more question I wanted to ask you. You remember that sci-fi book I requisitioned as evidence?"

"Of course I do. Enjoy it, did you?"

"Heh. Well, I didn't read it, actually. Not yet anyway. A slip of paper fell out as I opened it. A note from someone who calls himself Will. A literary couplet. Do you know anyone called Will associated with Cindy?"

"Will is Cindy's boyfriend. Of course I know him," Karen said impatiently. The voice, coming as it did over the tinny speaker in the car, drew sharp intakes of breath from the three passengers.

Leora called out from the back seat, "Mrs. White, you don't know me. I'm Leora Jakober, a criminologist working on this case. Could I ask you, how long has Cindy known this man and have you ever met him?"

"I have no idea how long they have known each other. I have met him once or twice. To be honest, I think he is far too old for her. She's only a slip of a girl, and he's almost old enough to be her father. They're into completely different things, different music, different social scenes. I've had a few words with her about him. As her landlady I sort of feel responsible, a bit like a mother figure, but of course she resents me interfering. If you ask me, I think he has some kind of hold over her."

"Hold? What kind of hold?"

"It's as if he's mesmerized her. Well, I suppose he must have some charismatic charm to do that, although I can't see it. He seems a bit unpleasant to me. But he has obviously charmed this girl."

"Can you describe him to us, please?" Colin asked.

"Tall, gangly, long-haired, sort of sixties-looking, if you know what I mean. Today's youth would wear a ponytail, but he seems proud to have it just hanging. Penetrating blue eyes. I think at one stage or other he had a beard, but he might have shaved it off; it wasn't a long-term growth."

"Do you have any idea at all where Cindy might be found? Any places she used to hang out when she wasn't at home?"

"I can only presume she is with Will, Inspector. And from the little I know of him, he's a bit of a nomadic type, so heaven alone knows where they are."

Colin sighed as loudly as he could.

"I'm sorry," Karen said. "I am telling you everything I know."

"Not your fault. You've been most helpful," he assured her. "I'm just voicing my frustration at not being able to trace her. Please, Mrs. Whitestone, if you hear anything, anything at all..."

"I'll phone you at once, don't worry."

Colin disconnected and muttered something under his breath.

"Back to the station, please," Leora said. "I want to examine the evidence I took from that house and garden."

"Might as well," Peter sighed. "We seem to have hit bedrock in this case, and there's nowhere else to dig."

☼ ☼ ☼

Avi brought down his small suitcase. Baruch and Malka were battling with their children; not all of them had school on Sundays.

"Oh, are you leaving?" Malka said with genuine disappointment.

"I have a wife and family of my own," Avi said, "and I think my task here is complete. I managed to find an address from which the Fox was sending mail. It could be useless, or it could be a trail that would lead to finding him. If the Fox sends any more e-mails, phone me — don't forward them by e-mail — and we'll arrange a time you can fax them to me. I want to see every word this clown has to say."

"I still think we should do a search," Baruch said. "I'm convinced we'll find him hiding out in our neighborhood.

Probably right under our noses, only we can't see it right now. That girl was hiding with a Muslim family right in the middle —"

Malka sighed loudly. "Your moment of glory has been and gone, Baruch, my dear."

"This case is completely different," Avi reinforced. "The Fox would only be right under our noses if he was pretty sure he was untraceable there. As soon as search parties started beating the bushes, as it were, he'd be off like a shot. I just spoke to the police. At least my theories were partly correct. The Fox was in that house I traced him to, only he didn't stay long enough to be found. There was a computer in that house. He took it with him, I suspect. Where he is now is anyone's guess. Maybe he even fled the country with Josh."

"Fled the country? Oh, no! How will they ever find him?" Malka cried, distressed.

"I did put that suggestion to D.I. Sommers, and he assured me that he had alerted the proper authorities at all points of entry and exit from the country to be on the lookout. But, as we all know, someone who is determined enough can slip past most checkpoints. However, I must say one thing."

"What?" asked Baruch, clutching at straws.

"The Fox seems bent on revenge for something we don't know about yet. He wants to torture the Hardmans, dangling their son just out of their grasp. It wouldn't make much sense if he disappeared totally. He needs to be where he can torment them the best. That's just my theory, anyhow. It's one I am clinging to, because the alternative is just too dreadful to contemplate."

"Yes," Baruch said quietly. "And if he is close by, at least we have a chance."

Avi nodded and looked at his watch. "I should go to the airport now."

"I'll drive you."

"No, it's okay. I can go by tube. Thanks anyhow. I'll keep in touch. Oh, listen. I decided to leave that external modem on your computer, so it's all set up to receive and send e-mails. I know of a good provider you can sign up with if you want. You can get the first month free. I hope by the time that runs out, Josh will be found. I know you've decided to send and receive all mail through Don Hardman's PC, but I don't think that's a good idea. Only makes the Fox's job easier; he would not have been able to monitor e-mails if they were coming from any which way. It will be easier for me to communicate directly with you by e-mail than through Don's machine all the time. You can pay me back for the modem any time."

"Thanks," Baruch said. A short pause, then, in a panicked tone, "But I have no idea how to work e-mail."

Avi smiled. "Get that ten-year-old son of yours to show you how."

The two men shook hands. Avi thanked Malka for her hospitality and left.

☼ ☼ ☼

Leora ran the tests on the new forensic evidence. Even while they waited, they knew what the tests would show. This time they were sure. Before it was mere wishful thinking that made them sure the Fox had been at the playhouse. When the results of those tests had come back negative, though Colin had been bitterly disappointed, he hadn't been unduly surprised. It had all seemed too predictable, too expected. It would have been too easy to trace the Fox if he had used the playhouse. He was too clever for that.

"Results positive," Leora said. "The samples match. The Fox has definitely been in the Segals' house. The soil samples match, the carpet samples match fibers taken from the windowsill, and the forensic palynology matches, too."

She sat down, looking at the two policemen. "Does it help us, though?" she asked. "What about those addresses Mr. Smoothy from the real estate agency gave us?"

"I've had them checked out. As expected, none of them exist. All invented addresses. Blind alley."

"Sheesh," Leora said, throwing up her hands.

"You know what I think?" Peter said after a minute's frustrated silence.

Colin said, "Okay, I'll take the bait. Tell me what you think."

"I think," Peter replied, "that if the Fox has fled his lair, there may be no harm at all in allowing Mr. Weiss to do that search."

They both looked at him.

"Peter," Leora said at last, "I think your reason has finally departed. If the Fox has fled his lair, a search of Golders Green will be fruitless. If he hasn't fled, a search will flush him out and scare him off. Either way, I can't see the point."

"Well, think of something better to do now. Anything is better than doing nothing," Peter said sulkily, seeing that Colin agreed with Leora.

"Sometimes doing nothing is the best option," Colin said. "If you just sit tight and wait it out, things happen."

There was a pause where all three were still. Statues. Frozen moments in time.

"You mean," Peter said slowly, enunciating each syllable, "that you are putting this case on the back burner?"

"Not exactly putting it on the back burner," Colin said uncomfortably. "More like sitting back and waiting to see what happens next."

There was another incredulous pause.

"There's a kid's life at stake!" Peter, the only parent among them, burst out. "You can't just sit tight! And just imagine what Mrs. Hardman would say if she knew the police had given up on her son."

He walked to the door, opened it, and turned around.

"Who is going to be the one to tell the Hardmans?" He glared at Colin. "You? Are you going to tell them we don't have any more ideas?"

Colin looked back, shocked and silent.

"Or you?" he demanded of Leora. "You've come all the way from New York to help us. Well, maybe now that we have all given up you can do what you really came here for. When is the guided tour of Buckingham Palace and the Houses of Parliament scheduled for? And don't forget Madame Toussaud's and the planetarium. An unmissable tourist attraction for anyone visiting London, wouldn't you say?"

Leora stared, openmouthed.

"I'm not that much off beam, am I, Ms. Jakober? You wanted to find Josh because the case fascinated you and it would look good on your CV. 'International criminologist' sounds so much better than 'New York criminologist,' doesn't it? So you came over, all enthusiastic and keen to help and hoping for some free time to see the sights. Thought finding Josh would be easy, just like one of your high-profile cases in America that made your name for you. But it wasn't a walk-over, was it? Met your match in the Fox, and you don't like the feeling one bit, do you? So everyone is giving up, and the Hardmans don't count anymore. Well, I leave the telling to you, because I am not going to be the one to tell them that we are dropping the case for lack of effort."

He stopped for a moment, and an incredulous sneer came over his face.

"I don't believe what I am seeing and hearing from you guys, I really don't. You make me sick. I just hope you can live with yourselves after this, that's all."

With that, Peter walked out and slammed the door.

CHAPTER TWENTY-TWO

Her cry of anguish was like the death pangs of a whole people. The sound echoed through the world like glass shattering in a tall building, domino after domino crashing against each other, building into an unbearable crescendo of agonized pain and abandonment. The people she had trusted had turned blank, featureless faces toward her, blind masks willingly assumed to face her, nightmarish countenances which only a short time ago had been friendly, warm, human, real. She had clung to hope because those faces had given her hope. She had depended on Colin Sommers, because he was the investigating officer, and thus, like a doctor, he had the power to bring her cure, her solution, her closure. She had clung to Leora Jakober because she had perceived her as the conduit through which her son would be returned to her. She had seen her as the only friend worth having, the only friend who would understand and not judge. She had gently but firmly pushed all her other friends away; even her family had been discouraged and now did not know how to help her.

The shock of the doctor telling the patient that there was nothing more to be done, that the disease was terminal and she had no hope, that the kindly man in a white coat was in fact the Angel of Death, not the bringer of life, sent Ilana reeling. And Leora Jakober's apologetic hugs, saying that for now they had met a brick wall and would be just awaiting new developments, was the knockout blow as she staggered, disoriented, to her feet again. They had both looked acutely embarrassed, shuffling their feet and trying not to meet her eyes, but their faceless masks of abandonment carried their messages without pity.

"I...er...I guess I'll be moving out," Leora had said. "I wouldn't want to impose on your kind hospitality any longer."

Ilana had metabolized this remark somewhere deep in her psyche, her distress too acute for surface-level absorption. Subconsciously she assumed this meant Leora would be flying back to the United States, her mission a failure. Somehow this would have been more comforting than the truth had Ilana known it.

Leora was staying in London a while longer, in a hotel in the West End, and true to Peter's accusations was seeing the sights. The accusation was not entirely justified; part of the reason she did not fly back immediately was that she was hoping something would turn up in the Josh Hardman case, some new evidence or development. But in the meantime, the other reason remained; while she was waiting for developments, why waste the gorgeous late-spring weather just hanging around when she could be seeing London?

Leora Jakober was not a devious young woman. She had her heart in the right place and was genuinely distressed at the Hardmans' tragedy. But it was exactly because she was not hypocritical about her feelings that she could not look Ilana in the eye and say her missing son had been her only motive for wanting to come to London. Besides a natural interest in a great city unvisited, her torment at not being able to help at this time was tempered with the slightest feeling of relief that she had a small oasis of time to spend alone.

In her mid-twenties and living alone in New York, Leora had become slightly intolerant of crowded living spaces. She loved people and interacted with them well, but at the end of her workday she liked to close her own front door on the world and keep it at bay.

With the Hardman case, she had been living, breathing, eating, and sleeping Josh Hardman. Staying in the same house as the distraught parents had been useful, perhaps even necessary, but it had been extremely claustrophobic. Even in her luxuriously appointed guest room with its own shower, she could not escape the tragedy that had befallen this family. It seeped under the door, through cracks in the floor, through the very fabric of the walls, to engulf her. During the first few days in London, she had embraced the overwhelming aura because she had needed it to investigate the crime, but now that there was a hiatus, she needed her space again.

"We promise to contact you the minute there are any new developments," Colin had told Ilana before departing. He left on her kitchen table a contact number for bereavement counselors. The piece of paper promised, in tasteful purple script decorated with flowers and scrolls, to support, help, and advise people who had recently suffered loss of any kind. It reached out to her with insincere, disingenuous hands.

Alone, Ilana sat in her kitchen, hugging herself and rocking back and forth, back and forth, a strange keening sound coming from her mouth.

She was the last woman on earth.

Abandoned, deserted, alone.

Those she had trusted had turned their backs on her and went back to their safe, happy lives.

Don could not reach her. Though he, too, shared her acute anguish, he understood that there had been no new developments and that it might be better to sit tight for a while and see. In business, sometimes chasing after the elusive butterfly only drove it away forever. Sit still and wait, and it may yet alight on your hand.

Don had never understood why Ilana had felt the need to cut herself off from everyone in the community and cling to Leora and the police. To his way of thinking, there was nothing like family and friends to support a person in times of need, whether they had a zillion kids or none at all. He went to shul every day, and people there felt able to approach him, to lay a kindly hand on his shoulder and ask him how things were going. And he felt able to respond to them, to draw on their combined strengths, to open his heart a little. They all asked him how Ilana was and if she felt ready for their wives to contact her, and he always shook his head sadly and said she felt unable to cope with the sympathy and pity of the community.

Ilana's mother was the only exception. Sarah Grossberg had refused to be held at arm's length. Despite the force field Ilana had built up around herself, repelling all boarders, Sarah had continued to telephone and come around whenever she could, even if her daughter just told her to leave; she kept on coming, like the tide. Surging at the shield around her daughter, the sea of her unending love and support was there, even if Ilana did not want it. Dimly Ilana was aware of it and would have felt its loss if it were withdrawn, but she did not want it.

"Ilana," Don said, "please. Don't do this to yourself. There are people around you who care, who want to help. Don't shut them out."

She rocked and keened, and mewled and rocked, but in the midst of her pain the words came out, like a kitten crying.

"I trusted them. I believed in them, and they let me down so badly, Don, so badly."

Don sat down next to her. "Listen to me, Ilana. Listen to me!"

Ilana stopped rocking and keening, but remained with her head bowed, not looking at him, arms wrapped around herself.

"Detective Inspector Colin Sommers, Leora Jakober, Sergeant Peter White, none of them have let you down. They are only tools. God has plans for us, and at the moment He is showing us only the dark side of the tapestry, the side made up of twisted, gnarled strings in an apparently meaningless pattern. We have to trust in Him. When He is ready to show us the right side so that we can see the whole picture, then He will. But until then we must continue to have faith and to pray and to draw on the strength of our friends. Don't be too quick to condemn those you perceive as letting you down. They are mere puppets. How can you blame them when they have no choice as to how their strings are pulled?"

She raised red, ravaged eyes to his, looking like a hurt puppy wanting to understand. He held her gaze.

Finally she nodded. Something left her eyes. Something like despair. Hope crept back in, like a punished kitten anticipating forgiveness and acceptance.

Don continued to look at her, watching the transformation creep across her face, like a sudden shadow across the moon. He waited, trapped in a microsecond.

Ilana unwrapped her arms and got up from her chair. She looked at the telephone, long abandoned on the worktop.

"You're right. I've turned all my friends and family away. I thought, foolishly, that only Leora and the police could help me. My friends must have felt dreadfully helpless and useless. Donald, I will phone them all. But first I will phone my mother."

☼ ☼ ☼

Lucy stood in the middle of Colin's living room, staring at him angrily. She had spent the best part of two hours trying to calm his ruffled male feathers, but her patience was wearing thin.

"What's the matter with you, Colin Sommers? You've been like a bear with two sore heads all evening, and both of them snapping mine right off my shoulders. If you won't calm down enough to at least tell me what's wrong, then I'm going. And you'll be lucky if you see me again!"

Colin was pacing around the room. Her innocent suggestion to order takeout for dinner suddenly had him ranting about several past misdemeanors on her part — such as considering Chinese takeout cooking him a meal and other, similar evidences of her nondomesticity. Lucy was shocked. She knew she lacked homemaking skills, but Colin had never seemed to mind before. Now he was throwing his book of hidden resentments at her.

He stopped pacing and looked at her. He seemed to sag a little at her retaliatory outburst, like a doll with some of the stuffing removed.

"Sorry, Lucy. I know I've been wretched company tonight. You deserve an explanation. Sit down and I'll give you one."

By the time he had finished explaining the lack of progress in the Hardman case, the decision to adopt a wait-and-see policy, and the resultant devastation this seemed to have caused all around, Lucy was nodding, full of empathy.

"I might as well leave the force," Colin said. "A high-profile, sensitive case like this lands on my desk, and I've managed diddly squat to solve it. I'm useless." He put his head in his hands.

"Oh, balderdash," Lucy replied. "You've hit a blockage, that's all. Wait for it to clear, and the road ahead will be smooth. Anyhow, I think it's high time I was called in to help."

"You? I don't want the press making a meal of this case. It will drive the Fox underground where we can't reach him."

"Not the press. Me. Remember me? Lucy? Your girlfriend? I do have a life outside the paper, you know. And I intend to use my insider knowledge, coupled with my writer's experience, to clear your blockage for you. There. I sound like a rather good plumber, don't I?"

Colin managed a wan smile.

"I want only one thing from you," Lucy said. "Copies of all those e-mails the Fox sent. I intend to find out a lot more about him from those e-mails."

☼ ☼ ☼

Peter White sat at home, staring at the television unseeingly. Marie tried to lighten him up by jokingly passing her hand between his eyes and the television. Concerned when he didn't even blink, she sat down, looked at him, waited for him to say something. He flicked off the TV with the remote control and swiveled his head toward her like a ventriloquist's dummy, without his body changing position.

"They've given up on Josh Hardman," he said in a dead voice.

It took a beat till it sunk in.

"They did what?" Marie gasped.

Peter sighed. "You heard right. Colin and Leora have given up. For now at least. They say they have nowhere else to go."

"So what happens to Josh?" Marie was aghast.

"Colin says that a wait-and-see policy sometimes gets results."

"Oh, yeah, right, and Colin is the Sherlock Holmes of local policing, of course. How much really serious crime has he actually tackled in the past few years? Most of the stuff around here that you get is petty crime — burglary, car theft, breaking and entering, the occasional mugging or street brawling outside the pubs. You haven't had a case like this in all the years I've been your wife, that's for sure. And you have been Colin's partner as long as I have known you."

"I know, I know," Peter said, head in hands.

"So his experience of abduction, and yours, too, for that matter, can presumably be written on the head of a pin."

"Yes, probably."

There was a long pause.

"I protested," Peter said, not without some pride mixed in with the distress. "I'll probably get suspended."

" 'Course you won't," said the ever practical Marie. "I bet you shook 'em up some, though."

"You should have seen their faces," Peter said with a hint of a smile.

"I can't believe you are all going to just sit back and let the Fox win," Marie burst out angrily.

"Those two may be going to do that," Peter said slowly, "but I am not sitting back and doing nothing. I just can't do that to the Hardmans, or to Josh."

"Ooh," Marie exclaimed. "You going to do one of those 'I'm taking the law into my own hands' stunts?"

Peter grinned. "Sort of, only not so dramatic. I intend to have a long hard think about the best move to make, and then I'll make it, with or without Colin's approval."

Marie hmmed. "Be careful, Peter. Doing things on your own might be risky, both to yourself and to Josh and his parents."

"I think overcautiousness hasn't helped much, either," Peter replied. "I'm convinced we might have found Josh by now if we had allowed Baruch Weiss to do that search."

"Peter. You aren't."

He looked at her. "I might."

"Please don't do anything rash," Marie pleaded. She knew that look in his eyes. It came up rarely, when reason seemed to desert him and instinct took over. It seldom led to anything sensible being achieved; on the contrary, more often than not she ended up bailing him out of trouble. On the other hand, it was the part of him that salvaged his personality and lifted it out of dullness, polished it and made it sparkle, like new silver.

"Sometimes," Peter said slowly, rolling each word around his mouth like hard candy, "you just have to flush foxes out of their lairs in order to resume the chase. In his lair a fox is safe. Out in the open country he is vulnerable."

"But there are infinite numbers of lairs for him to hole up in," Marie said.

"Yes, but this fox is different. He uses the Internet. And thus, as Abraham Pincus demonstrated, he is traceable, even if he thinks he isn't."

"You're going to get Abraham Pincus back?"

"No, I don't need to get him back. I just need to get him to keep watch in case anymore e-mails come. In the meantime, Mr. Baruch Weiss is finally going to have his day."

DAY NINE

CHAPTER TWENTY-THREE

Until now, Ilana Hardman had been reasonably content to leave matters to the experts. There were policemen and investigators and criminologists all out looking for her son, and she placed her trust in them. Foolish, foolish woman, placing her trust in a human being, she thought now. She had placed her trust in them, and they had let her down badly. They had tried, halfheartedly in her opinion, to find Josh, and now they had given up and abandoned her. Not case closed, exactly, but case on the back burner until something happened.

Ilana had gone to pieces and put herself back together again with Scotch tape. Fragile now, held together only by her faith in God, she walked through life like a paper doll, its body parts stuck together precariously. Any light breeze could blow her asunder.

Ilana had reestablished diplomatic relations with her friends and family, who, forgiving and understanding, drew around her like a shield, protecting her against the unprotectable. Even those who had no idea what to say to her were like trees of the forest safeguarding against the storm. They made her feel safe and loved and warm.

But no one brought back her son. No one had any ideas how to find him.

They davened with her, said *tehillim* with her, told her to be patient and brave, that God had His plan, that the dark side of the tapestry was indecipherable and eventually she would glimpse the right side and understand. She nodded and prayed and accepted all everyone said to her with a gentle smile.

But Josh did not come home.

Now she was restless. She felt that if the experts were as useless as dust, and her friends and family were supportive but helpless, then someone had to do something. Ilana resolved to take action. She'd start walking the streets of Golders Green looking for her son.

And so, like a lonely, lost soul in search of its Maker, she walked alone, calling his name. People thought it was odd, this tortured woman walking the spring streets calling for her child.

The weather had turned; the long, unseasonably warm sunny spell had ended, and the day was cool, blustery, and rainy. More typical British May weather than the heat wave of the week before. Ilana wore a long, pale trench coat, PVC boots, and a scarf tied over her wig, and she walked, calling for her lost child. People moved aside to let her pass. Like a scythe through a field of wheat she moved through her people on the streets. Everyone pitied her; no one had the least idea how to help her.

When Don heard how she was spending her morning, he secretly feared for her sanity. He was not alone in this. Well-meaning friends called him at work and suggested in hushed tones that maybe she should be admitted to a clinic for psychiatric assessment. Sedated and drugged to the eyeballs, she would not embarrass the community any longer. Out of sight, out of mind. Josh was gone, and there was no use in pretending he would ever return. If Ilana couldn't cope with this, she should be "helped." People in the community had heard of other cases like this, women who had gone mad when intolerable tragedy had struck and had been institutionalized. The husband had been obliged to divorce her eventually and had remarried.

Don was angry when he heard these insidious ideas. He shook them off like a puppy shakes off the rain. He had to go on supporting Ilana, no matter what.

Meanwhile, Ilana walked the streets of Golders Green like a bag lady, searching.

☼ ☼ ☼

Lucy sat at her desk in the offices of the North West London *Echo*, studying the e-mails Colin had copied for her. There was no doubt in her mind that they were the work of one man, however different they seemed in places. The question was, which man?

Was the Fox a poet or a literary writer?

She looked at one again. It was the first one received.

The devil can cite Scripture for his purpose,
An evil soul producing holy witness.

There was something about it, something familiar and yet just out of reach, like a dream one tries to remember upon waking.

"Hey, James," she called to a passing colleague of hers, "come and look at this a sec."

"No time," James said, making a big show of being in a rush.

"James," Lucy said with deathly intent, "I need you to look at this. I'm sure you wouldn't want that little matter of the plagiarized biography mentioned to the editor, now would you?"

James stopped fluttering and stood at her desk, eyeing her through narrowed lids. "You wouldn't."

Lucy grinned up at him. "Just watch me."

James shook his head, muttering, "Blackmailer," under his breath and then, "So what is it you want me to see?"

"These couplets. Do they mean anything to you?"

James flicked through the pages of couplets like a card shark doing a fast deal. "Sure. Quotations from Shakespeare. Where did you get them?"

Lucy stared at James, openmouthed.

"Shakespeare as in *William* Shakespeare?"

"Sure, didn't you recognize them? I'm a bit of a Shakespeare expert, actually." He pronounced it "acksherlly." "That first quote — 'The devil can cite Scripture for his purpose, an evil soul producing holy witness' — that's from *The Merchant of Venice*. Act one."

Lucy blushed. "I only know the better known Shakespeare quotations, and even then I'm not sure where they come from. I found Shakespeare boring at school."

"Shakespeare has such a wealth of beautiful imagery in his plays and sonnets. It's timeless, as you can see; you had some vague idea the writer was highbrow and literary, but you weren't sure if he was current or not. You should make more of a study of it. Like me." He preened.

"You're sure? All of these quotes are from Shakespeare?"

James scanned them again. "Yes, I recognize all of these."

Lucy was on the phone to Colin in an instant.

"I have something. Something big. I don't think we should talk on the phone. Meet me at the coffee shop downstairs ASAP."

Colin had been tapping pens against his desk, feeling as useless as a screen door on a submarine. He heard the lift in Lucy's voice and felt hope. It was rare for her to be this excited. He jumped up, told Peter he was going out, and left the office with no further word.

Peter, who was used to accompanying Colin everywhere, was miffed at this sudden departure. Revenge crossed his mind for an instant. The revenge of the pesky Baruch Weiss. He grinned, but caution slowed him down. I'll just wait until Colin lets me know what this is all about, he told himself, and went back to his laborious paperwork.

Lucy was waiting in the coffee shop, although waiting hardly described her behavior at that moment. It was more leaping up and down like a child on a pogo stick, running to the door to see if Colin was approaching. When she saw him, she waved like mad until he entered the shop.

"Lucy, calm down. What on earth is the matter with you?" Colin was still feeling disgruntled with failure.

"Sit! Sit! I might have cracked your case for you."

When he had heard what she had to say, his brain spun like a ball on a roulette wheel.

"Shakespeare. Lucy, why didn't we see it?"

"See what?"

"Bill Venice. He used the name Bill Venice to access the Net from SmallNet. Criminals like the Fox love to drop clues; they love to play games. He was using Shakespeare quotations and his name was Bill Venice and we just didn't see it. How stupid could we possibly have been?"

Lucy looked at him. "Okay, call me stupid. I still don't see it."

"Bill equals Will equals William. Venice equals *The Merchant of Venice*, where the first quote was from. He was pointing to Shakespeare from the first."

"Yes, but are we any closer to knowing who he actually is?" Lucy asked, suddenly deflating like a punctured balloon.

Something was niggling at the back of Colin's mind. Something from long ago, in his past, when he was still Chaim Sommers, not Colin. When he wore *payos* and a yarmulke and was still battling with his inner conflicts about religion. Something...

Lucy was talking, but he tuned her out as effectively as if he had been wearing headphones. He waved a hand at her to indicate that she should be quiet. And he journeyed into his head, into his past.

As Colin made the journey through his memory, Lucy saw him frown, his brow creasing like folded paper, his eyes misting with concentration. From Colin's perspective he was battling against the fog that had built up over ten years, trying to pierce its gray woolly depths, to see beyond.

"There was a party," he said slowly. "I was sixteen and rebellious. I wanted to taste a different lifestyle from the one I had been brought up to. My friend Ben brought me to the party..." He was in a kind of self-induced hypnotic trance now, exploring the dark chasms of his youth, allowing the full rush of his thoughts to flow freely, without resisting. So deep was he that he was unaware that he was telling Lucy things about himself he had never told her before.

He struggled with elusive memories.

Someone slid down the wall next to him. A long-haired young man, older than himself by at least four years, with a straggly beard, looking rather like a young William Shakespeare. Piercing blue eyes observed him curiously for a moment.

"I even called him Shakespeare," Colin said, "and he didn't correct me."

"You can call me Shake," he told Chaim seriously, then, after a pause he added, "Maybe I'm a reincarnation of William Shakespeare. I really dig his plays, man. They speak to me, y'know? At school, all my friends thought them mega-boring, but I found them deep, you know?"

"This guy was instrumental in turning me off being religious," he said. "Ben wasn't the real cause, Shake was. Well, I suppose I only have myself to blame. I was ready to be turned off, but Shake was the one who did it. He had the smoothest, most sneaky arguments, and they seemed to make sense."

"Colin, what are you talking about?"

The sentence was like the snapping of fingers at the end of a session of hypnosis. Colin snapped to awareness and stared at Lucy. Her concerned face was that of a stranger.

"I never told you this before, Lucy. I've been terribly unfair to you. I've lied about who I really am."

"Who you really are? Why? Who are you really? An ax murderer? An evil psychopath?" Her words were jocular; her tone was not. Lucy was badly frightened by the Colin she now saw in front of her.

Colin did not smile. "None of those things. But I led you to believe I was a non-Jew, whereas the reality is I am Jewish. And I come from an Orthodox background like the Hardmans, the Weisses, and Avi Pincus. All the people in this case, they are part of my culture, part of my past, part of me, Lucy. It's a part of me I sought to escape ten years ago; the party was the catalyst. No, not the party. Shake. I sought to escape it, but look what's happened. It's come back and grabbed me by the throat, dragged me back inside. I have become involved with the very culture I have tried so hard to avoid, and all of a sudden, it doesn't feel so wrong anymore.

"Peter noticed. He noticed that I seemed to be for the people I had been so against. When I first took this case on, Lucy, the most terrifying aspect of it was not the fact that a kid had been abducted, nor the fear of failure. No, my greatest fear was being sucked back in to all this stuff I had tried so hard to escape from. But you know what, Lucy? I don't seem to mind the idea so much."

"You're Jewish and were Orthodox." Lucy grappled to assimilate this.

"Yes. I ignored my past for so long, I almost managed to persuade myself that the story I told you, the invented past that suited me better than the genuine one, was real. You do come to believe lies if you tell them often enough, don't you. Well, I believed mine. My parents live right here in Golders Green, but they don't know me. I never go to see them or telephone them. I broke their hearts when I left my home and my faith behind, along with all my religious clothes — the white shirts and dark suits, the black hats, the yarmulkes and tzitzis, the tefillin I used to put on every morning since I became bar mitzvah. At the end, I was wearing Native American headbands to keep my long hair out of my eyes so I could put my tefillin on in the mornings; it must have broken Dad's heart, but I did it anyway. He was so afraid of losing me altogether if he made a stand. Well, he did in the end. I haven't seen or spoken to my parents in the best part of ten years. Well, that's not strictly true. I sometimes caught glimpses of them in the street, but I made sure to avoid a meeting. It's amazing how you can do that, work in a community and avoid meeting someone who lives in it."

"You wore black hats and those fringey things that stick out of trouser waistbands," Lucy said, incredulous.

"The more I got to know the Hardmans and the people around them — the kids in Josh's class, their mothers, Leora Jakober — the more comfortable I felt being around religious people again. But being comfortable around a different culture one tried to alienate oneself from isn't the same at all as wanting to be back in it, Lucy."

Lucy looked at the stranger before her. "No, but it's a good way along the line," she said, "especially if it's your own culture in the first place."

"Perhaps. I don't know," Colin said.

"Nor do I," Lucy agreed. "I don't know you. I thought I knew you, but I don't."

"I don't know me either right now," Colin replied.

"Well, I don't like being lied to, and I hate the idea of having spent several years of my life with someone I thought was someone else entirely. But for now, let's put that aside. The immediate issue is Josh Hardman and how this Shake of your past fits in with him. That I don't get. I mean, I don't understand why the Fox would want to attack you, as he seems to have achieved his purpose in putting you off your religion. But if he did still want to attack you, why go for someone else's kid, for heaven's sake? It doesn't make the least amount of sense to me."

"Nor me," Colin admitted miserably. Despite Lucy's willingness to put the issue of his lies to one side for the present, he felt immensely uncomfortable knowing that important and probably unpleasant discussions were on the cards for them both.

"You said," Lucy said after a moment's unhappy silence,

both deeply aware that their relationship was at a crossroad, "that you were taken to the party by a friend called Ben. Is there any way you can contact him?"

"I suppose I have the number I last knew him to be at, the one I moved into after I left home."

Again the shame flushed through him, like water through a newly opened manhole. Thinking of the Hardmans made him realize for the first time the anguish he had put his parents through. But there was one difference: Ilana had the small comfort of knowing her son had not deserted her willingly.

"Well, get on with it!" Lucy said with a false attempt at brightness. Her earlier mood, full of excitement and pride at being the source of the big break, had dissipated. She looked ahead at her relationship with Colin and saw only dust.

She couldn't believe she had been with Colin for so long and it had all been a lie. The carefree policeman with an uncomplicated past (well, except for "my parents died in a car crash when I was six; I was brought up in children's homes...didn't do me any harm, though") turned out to be a lapsed Orthodox Jew with a past as twisted as gnarled tree roots.

Lucy had nothing against Jews. She was of the "some of my best friends are Jewish" school of racial tolerance. Living as she did in a community where Jews were not a rarity, she had grown accustomed to seeing them around and was tolerant of the differences in the way the Orthodox Jews lived and dressed. But tolerance of a different culture was very different from accepting that one's boyfriend was from that culture. Whether or not he was "reformed" now, he had been like them once and seemed to be showing a marked degree of sympathy for them now.

"Yeah, let's get to it!" said Colin equally brightly and equally falsely. His confession to her had been terminal, and they both knew it. All the time they had been together he had known that if she ever found out his true past it would be over between them. The difference was that once he would have minded very much. Now... Now it seemed to fit. He was saddened because he was genuinely fond of Lucy, but he no longer felt things were right between them. He knew she was not overfond of Jews; even though she pretended not to mind, he knew she did. It was almost as if he had revealed himself as a scaly-skinned alien monster with only a superficial outer skin of a human being, a skin which might burst open at any moment, revealing the horror of the reptilian creature beneath. For reptilian, read white shirt, dark pants, black hat, and tzitzis, thought Colin bitterly. Same difference.

For the moment, an uneasy truce reigned between Lucy and Colin. They were joined in a common goal — to trace the Shake of the party ten years before.

"I have Ben's number at home, I think," Colin said.

"I'll come with you, if you like," Lucy offered.

"If you like," Colin said stiffly. It was all so difficult, like dismissing an employee but having to be polite to him while he worked out his notice, when all you wanted was for him to go.

At Colin's apartment, some considerable time was spent looking for Ben's phone number. He hadn't needed it for ten years. Had he destroyed it with the rest of his past? He rummaged around for ages without success. Finally he sat down and tried to remember it, but he couldn't even recall the address.

"If I had the address, I could phone Information and get the phone number. Why can't I remember where he lived?"

Lucy took a deep breath. "You could always go and ask your parents."

He looked at her.

"If Ben was your friend, then surely they would know where he is."

"I haven't been to see my parents for ten years, Lucy."

"Well, until today I didn't know you had any parents, so this is all news to me, too."

They exchanged a long look.

"I'm sorry, Lucy, I really am. I knew that if I told you the truth it would be over between us. And until now I wasn't ready to admit it, even to myself."

"Yes, I know," Lucy said, studying her shoes. She cast around desperately for something to say to make things better between them, but the right words wouldn't come. Part of her was curious to see the parents she had not known existed, but the other part, the stronger part, knew this would be impossible now. What would his parents, delighted to see their son again after so long, make of this non-Jewish woman at his side?

"Well," she said at last, "I'll be off. Glad to be of service, Colin."

She started to walk away.

"Lucy..."

She turned on her heel and their eyes met.

They stood there a few more moments, looking at each other, never having imagined it would end like this, wordlessly, hopelessly, without closure, without saying goodbye, without saying thanks for the good times.

It was like dying suddenly.

CHAPTER TWENTY-FOUR

Before going to see his parents, Colin went back to his office. Besides putting off the inevitable, he needed time and space to assimilate what had just happened to him. It seemed that in the past hour his life had turned inside out. He had known Lucy for four years. A long time. A chunk of his life that was now a Lucy-shaped hole in the universe.

Colin sat at his desk and put his head in his hands. Peter came in, concerned.

"Colin? Mate? Colin, what's up? Colin, speak to me."

Colin raised his head. "Lucy and me. We just split up."

Peter drew up a chair, twisted it around, and sat on it cowboy- style, back to front. "I don't believe it. I thought you two were set up for life. What on earth happened?"

Colin sighed. "Life happened. Truth happened. The inevitable happened."

"Truth? Life? Inevitable? Talk sense, man."

"In for a penny, in for a pound, I suppose," Colin said, mostly to himself. He looked at his partner. "Peter, I told Lucy the truth about myself. That's why we split. I told her I was not the gentile orphan she had thought I was, but I am, in fact, a failed Orthodox Jew with parents living right here in Golders Green."

Peter stared at him. "You're Jewish? You have to be kidding me, Colin. You look like the biggest gentile I've ever seen."

Colin couldn't help laughing. "Yeah, it's a look I cultivated over the last ten years. I never had a Jewish nose anyway. I just grew my hair, and the rest kind of followed."

"You Jewish. I just can't believe it. It takes some getting used to. Mind you, it explains quite a few things. It explains why you were so set against going back into Golders Green and kept shoving all the Orthodox cases onto me. It also explains why recently you've started behaving differently about Jews. I even commented on it."

"Yes, you did."

There was a pause. "I'm sorry about Lucy, though," Peter said at last.

Colin looked at him. "I'm upset, too. But you know what? If I hadn't been ready for things to change between us, I wouldn't have done the big confession bit. I knew, by telling her, what would happen. So I was crafting my own destiny, really, wasn't I. I was ready to make that step, knowing the chain of events it would inevitably set in motion. So I reckon, whatever I am feeling now, things will sort themselves and I did the right thing by telling her."

"So what's happening now?" Peter asked, trying to imagine life without Marie. He couldn't.

"Well, as it turns out, the last thing Lucy and I did together was find a lead in the Hardman case. She found out that all the poems were clips from Shakespeare. And it all made sense. The Fox often used the name Bill Venice, which is a combination of William and *The Merchant of Venice*. And I remembered a guy in my youth who called himself Shake who was instrumental in turning me off being Orthodox. He used twisted arguments to augment my own doubts. From what I recall, he fits the description of the Fox. Tall, gangly, bearded, piercing blue eyes, American accent."

"But why on earth would the Fox take Josh Hardman to get at you?" Peter said. "It doesn't fit at all, Colin."

"No, it doesn't. Unless..."

"Unless what?"

"Unless my connection with Shake has absolutely nothing to do with why Josh Hardman was taken. It was merely a coincidence, and Shake has absolutely no idea that he and the policeman he is trying to outwit ever met under very different circumstances."

"In which case," Peter said excitedly, "you could have an immense advantage. You know the Fox, and he doesn't know you know him."

"If it is the same person, of course," Colin mused. "And if I recognize him after all these years."

"All these years? It's only ten, for heaven's sake, not half a lifetime. People don't change that much in ten years."

"Maybe. Anyhow, I have to find Ben. Ben is the mate I used to escape from religion with. He took me to parties. He took me to the party where I met Shake. Shake was at another party at Ben's place, too. That was the finish of me, really. I owe my total destruction to that guy, helped along by liberal doses of my own stupidity, of course."

"So let's find Ben."

"That's the problem. I can't remember where he lived, what his number is, even what his surname is. The only people who might remember it are my parents, whom I haven't contacted for almost ten years. They used to come to Ben's house to try and get me to come home after I moved in there, so they should remember where it is."

"Good time to start, then," Peter said, smiling.

"It's hard, Peter. It's been so long. They've given up. When they heard I was seeing Lucy, a non-Jew, they just cut me out of their lives altogether. They didn't go as far as to mourn my death, which is done sometimes if a child marries out of the faith. I hadn't married her. But I imagine they were devastated. I've hurt them so badly, what will they say when I go to see them again?"

Non-Jews seldom understand the depth of pain caused to parents by Jewish children forming interfaith relationships, and Peter was no exception. To him it was no big deal. Jewish, non-Jewish, who cared? But he saw that his partner was genuinely wrought up about it and tried to empathize.

"I'll come with you to see them if you like," he offered. "Maybe it will be easier if there are two of us."

"No," Colin said firmly. "I have to do this on my own. Thanks anyway, Peter."

☼ ☼ ☼

Peter called Marie once Colin had left.

"Marie. Forget pesky Baruch Weiss and his search, at least for now. Something big is going down."

"It is? Like what?"

"Like I can't tell you right now, but listen to this. Colin is Jewish. And he used to be one of those black hatty types. The full bit."

"No way."

☼ ☼ ☼

The house where he grew up. How strenuously he had avoided it these past ten years and how tremulously he stood before it now. Looking up at the whitewashed exterior, the double-fronted bay windows on the ground and first floors with their neat white net curtains fluttering in the breeze, he felt such a tug of belonging that it took his breath away. The front garden hadn't changed, either. The yellow forsythia hedges already past blooming and in full leaf, the neat flowerbeds with azaleas and roses, the oblong patch of lawn appliquéd with daisies. He was trembling with fear and yearning.

I'm scared. Me. The great Detective Inspector Sommers is shaking in his shoes, afraid to ring this doorbell and open up the last ten years. He felt it was like opening a long-forgotten crypt, not knowing what demons or angels he might release as a result.

Detective Inspector Colin Sommers of the Golders Green Police stepped forward and rang the doorbell of his past.

It echoed in the hallway like a thousand voices unheard striving to speak. It reverberated down the corridors of long ago with all the other things he had shut out of his mind, pounding there, trying to enter once more. It sounded like music from a million Jewish songs unsung in his non-Jewish world.

Rifka Sommers opened the door. She stared at the tall, handsome policeman in plainclothes and she knew him. The shock drained the blood from her face, and her fingers fluttered by her side like fern fronds. But her first thought was that someone had died and he had been deputized to come and tell her. She could not believe her son had come back to see her for any other reason.

"Hello, Mum," Colin said, smiling tremulously.

"Chaim?" She put a hand to her throat, as if fearing her heart would burst forth if she didn't.

They stood on the doorstep, looking at each other.

"Please, can I come in?"

"Oh. Yes, come in. Of course."

Colin walked into the familiar house, smelling remembered aromas of vegetable soup his mother cooked almost every day from good stock and fresh garden vegetables, some undefined but delicious meat roasting in the oven, and a faint but noticeable lemony furniture polish in the background. He walked past her laundry room, where a basket of freshly washed and dried washing lay folded, smelling of meadows as it always had. Some things never changed.

In the living room, his mother sat down on her favorite chair, a recliner. It had been reupholstered, he noticed. It was now a soft peach instead of brown. It looked good. He sat opposite, on the gray leather sofa, and looked at his mother.

Rifka Sommers had aged. Her pretty slim face had fallen a bit, like a wax statue beginning to melt. Her wide blue eyes were the same, although the skin around them was more papery and there were fine lines spidering out from them. There were deep lines furrowing vertically on either side of her mouth, which in its turn seemed to have taken a downward curve, as if it could never smile again.

Chaim had broken her heart, and she had never fully recovered.

"What are you doing here, Chaim? I never thought to see you again."

He smiled at her, encouraging her to smile back, but she was wary.

"Mum, I never thought I'd be here again, either. Coming here today has been one of the hardest things I have ever done, believe me, so please, don't turn me away."

"I invited you in. You are sitting here. I haven't turned you away. I am waiting to hear what you want."

"Ten years ago, about the time I went off, there was a friend of mine called Ben."

"Ah, yes, Ben. I recall him well. He was a very bad influence on you."

"Mum, I had a bad influence on me. Ben and the other guy, they just helped. Isn't there a saying? 'Where man wants to go God will lead him.' If I hadn't wanted to be influenced, I wouldn't have chosen a friend like Ben."

"You always were a rebellious boy," Rifka said.

"I felt there was something out there better than what I had. I was determined to find it, to taste it, to live it."

"And now you have. You've done it all, haven't you, Chaim? Been a complete goy these past ten years, even had a shiksa as a girlfriend. Thank God you never brought that girl home to me. At least you had respect enough for us to stay away."

"Lucy and I have split up. I no longer have a non-Jewish girlfriend. And it wasn't really respect that kept me away. Although, of course, I respect you hugely. It was fear, Mum. I was terrified to face you. But not only that, I was terrified of what facing you would mean."

"Why? What would it mean?"

"Getting sucked back into all this religion stuff."

"Ah." She said nothing more for a few moments and then, "And now?"

Colin put his hands out, palms up. "I don't know yet. I...at the moment I am here because I need your help to find Josh Hardman."

"Me? How can I help?"

"I need to find Ben. Do you have a number for him?"

"I should have. I contacted him often enough when you were staying there, trying to get you to come home. I don't even have to look it up. It's engraved on my heart."

She wrote down the address and number on a piece of paper and handed it to him wordlessly. They stood facing each other, awkward now.

"Mum," Colin said at last, "I'm not just using you, believe me."

"Aren't you?"

"If I wasn't ready to make this step, I'd have moved heaven and earth to find another way to locate Ben."

She nodded her acceptance of this.

"It's a step, Mum."

"A step," she acknowledged. "Make sure you don't trip over it."

"I've missed you," he said softly.

She nodded again. "Go find Josh. I know how his mother feels."

He left without saying he would come back. He didn't need to. Nor did she need to hear it.

CHAPTER TWENTY-FIVE

Colin stood in the doorway, looking at Ben.

"Long time, Chaim," Ben said, stunned. "Come in."

Ben had changed. He had grown heavier, jowlier. Though he was the same age as Colin he looked middle-aged, like years of soft living had bloated him. He looked like a heart attack on two legs.

"You need a gym," Colin said bluntly.

Ben colored. "I know I've turned into a bit of a couch potato," he admitted as they entered the sunny living room. "I work in a bank. The most exercise I get these days is jumping to conclusions. Look at you, though. Tall and trim and fit as a fiddle. Police work keeps you slim, does it?"

"Often I don't have time to eat," Colin agreed. "And I work out at the gym four times a week. How can I be a competent policeman if I don't stay in shape?"

"Thought you had a cushy desk job now," Ben replied. "You don't need to move around anymore. You can get your lackeys to do it."

"I like to be where the action is, to find out things myself."

"And what have you come to investigate me for? I haven't done anything, except turn you into a complete goy, by the look of you. I feel a bit ashamed, to be honest. You were *frum* in those days."

"Don't blame yourself," Colin reassured him. "I was only too willing to be turned into a goy. All I needed was a bit of a push. In fact, it was that guy I met at the party you brought me to I need to find."

"I don't remember any guy."

" 'Course you do. You took me to that party. Try to remember. It's very important."

They sat down in armchairs opposite each other, sunlight streaming onto their faces.

"I took you to that party," Ben repeated blankly.

"Yes, it was my first non-*frum* party. All kinds of bad things going on there. I was being a real pain at first. I wouldn't relax."

Ben's face cleared. "Ah..."

"Then you came over to me a bit later and found me sitting on the floor with this guy. Do you remember? Tall guy, long curly hair, sort of American accent..."

"Oh, yes, I remember him. Bit of a weirdo? Pretentious about the classics. He was the only one among us who not only read them, but also spouted them verbatim at every opportunity."

"That's him."

"Type of guy who knows everything about everything or pretends to. Whatever it is, he knows just enough about it to outwit you. Sound familiar?"

"Yup. Sort of looks the way you imagine Shakespeare looked, too."

"He cultivated that look. It was all part of his pseudo-classical nonsense."

"Are you still in touch with him?"

"Nah. I haven't seen or spoken to him in years. No idea where he is now, sorry. He was part of my misspent youth, and to be honest I was glad to be shot of him. He was just normal enough to escape being classified as peculiar, but just weird enough to be a little scary. Know what I mean?"

"I do," Colin said thoughtfully. "Do you have a name for him?"

"Yeah. George. George Foley."

"I only ever knew him as Shake. For Shakespeare."

"That sounds like George, giving himself airs and graces and fancy names."

"Name doesn't ring a bell," Colin mused, "but I'll ask around and see if it rings with anyone. It's a shame he didn't call himself by his real name when he wrote to Cindy Wallis."

"Cindy Wallis?"

"His girlfriend, as I understand it. Young and blonde, streetwise and computer literate enough to get herself sacked for chatting on-line instead of working. I don't suppose you have the address where you last saw Foley?"

"I doubt he's still there. He was a bit of a gypsy, but here it is." He grabbed the address book lying on the coffee table and opened it to the right page.

Colin took out a pen and his notebook and scribbled down the information. "I'll get one of my men to check it out. I also don't hold out much hope that he's still there, but it's worth a try."

Ben and Colin looked at each other. Colin saw an overweight saggy guy with a sad, lost look in his eyes. Had Ben ever been religious? he wondered. Did he care about anything other than his own physical gratification? Was that sad, lost look any indication of the state of his soul or merely an exterior facade of his lackluster life? If there was ever a classic model for "is this all there is?" Ben was it.

Is this all there is? Colin thought. He knew that his parents and the Hardmans and all that lot believed in something higher and more enduring. He felt sure that it was the Hardmans' faith alone that enabled them to cope with this terrible agony of loss they were going through. Wouldn't it be comforting if he could feel the same amount of faith? Had he ever done so, or had it always been a problem for him?

Now was not the time to think back.

He said goodbye to Ben with a halfhearted promise on both sides to keep in touch. Neither really meant it. They had grown apart, become too different even as they had become the same as secular Jews. Their paths had diverged. The soft banker and the hard-nosed policeman.

He went back to the station and asked one of the constables on duty to check out the address Ben had given him. Then he sat at his desk and put his feet up. He rocked his chair back and forth, wondering about the Fox.

Another name to conjure with. George Foley. Who on earth was George Foley when he was at home? And how on earth was he to find out? He didn't expect any miracles from his men checking out the last-known address. The Fox wouldn't still be there or have left any clues; he was much too smart. A classics fanatic. Hmm. Colin wondered.

"Clark!" he called out to one of his detectives. "Come here a minute."

When the young detective stood before him, Colin said, "I want you to check out all the classics literary societies in London. See if a George Foley belongs to any of them."

"Gotcha," Clark said and left.

Peter White wandered in to his office. "So what's doing?

Got any new leads?"

"Can you help me on this?" Colin said. "We need to ask everyone associated with this case if they have heard of the name George Foley or if they have any idea how we can get any closer to the identity of the Fox. And when I say everyone, I mean absolutely everyone."

"Let's make a list and split it," Peter suggested.

"All right. You can take Baruch Weiss."

"Baruch Weiss can be a conduit to a lot of people. There was a whole crowd round his place last week for a meeting about the Search that Never Was. One of them might have some ideas."

"Okay, let's go for it."

The two men spent the next half-hour listing everyone they could think of associated with the case, from the children in Josh's class at school to Karen Whitestone. Then they split the list by a "one for you, one for me" method, making sure Peter got Baruch Weiss.

The task of phoning around was mind-numbingly methodical and took forever, but when they had finally gone through the entire list, not a single person had heard of George Foley.

Pinny Bloch, one of the last on the list, said, "Have you contacted Avi Pincus in Jerusalem?"

"No, I forgot about him," Colin admitted shamefacedly. "Got a number for him?"

Pinny gave him a number. Colin was just about to dial Israel when the desk clerk, Sergeant Potter, put his head around the door.

"Sir, there's been an incident at that playhouse you investigated. Palmer, who's been watching it, has stopped a man. Maybe you'd better come and see."

"Cleverclogs said the forensics didn't match. The Fox had never been in the playhouse," Colin mused.

"So the person who abducted Josh had never been in the playhouse," Potter said. "But who's to say that the person who abducted Josh and the Fox are the same person?"

Colin looked at him strangely. "Potter, the man has been signing the e-mails 'Internet Fox.' "

"Maybe he has an accomplice."

"Maybe, if Cindy Wallis is a man who wears size nine shoes, yes."

"Might be worth checking out, though."

Colin sighed. "I'll pop along quickly after I make this phone call to Israel."

Avi Pincus was out, so Colin left a message with his wife to call him back, then drove quickly to the playhouse site. He found Palmer sitting in the squad car with a dirty-looking man in filthy clothes who smelled most unsavory. He got in and sat next to him, trying to ignore the stench. It wasn't easy.

"This is Greg Phelps," Palmer said.

"Ain't done nuffing wrong," Phelps mumbled. "Just used the 'ouse for somewhere dry to sit and 'ave me a cuppa. Didn't know there was a law against it."

"There isn't, mate," Colin reassured him, slipping into the vernacular of this vagrant. "We just need to know 'o's been using the playhouse, that's all."

Greg Phelps looked at Colin through rheumy eyes in a grimy face. "Me."

"Where do you sleep at night?" Palmer asked him.

"Sometimes I sleeps in the playhouse. Sometimes I doss down in the park on a bench. The playhouse is best coz the floor is wood and it's warm."

Colin looked at Greg's feet. A pair of grubby running

shoes resided there. "Don't get rid of these trainers, mate," he told Phelps. "We might need forensics to run 'em over."

"I don't 'ave no other shoes," Phelps told him. "These are all I 'ave."

Colin thought for a moment. He put his hand into his pocket and pulled out a twenty-pound note.

"Palmer," he said, "run this gentleman over to the discount shoe shop and buy him some new trainers. Maybe get them to throw in a pair or two of socks if you smile real pretty at them."

"New shoes. Thanks, guv," Phelps said reaching down to untie his laces. "I'll just get these orf so I can give them to yer."

Colin got out of the car hastily. "I'll wait out here if you don't mind. Palmer, got a large evidence bag handy? And give it to me sealed, will you please?"

Greg Phelps wanted to shake Colin's hand and thank him for the shoes, but Colin declined and waved the grimy proffered hand away.

"Oh, it's all right. Be off with you. Palmer, give him a couple of quid to get a bed in a hostel tonight, will you?"

He drove back to the station, his precious, albeit ripe, evidence bag on the seat next to him, thinking.

Cleverclogs.

He needed Leora Jakober to come back and analyze these trainers. Where was she? Had she left a contact number? She must have. He would check with Peter.

Back at the station, he reported to Peter about Greg Phelps, and Peter laughed aloud at the story of the trainers.

"We do need Ms. Jakober to analyze them," he agreed. "I have a contact number for her. I'll give her a buzz."

"Has Avi Pincus phoned back yet?" Colin asked, comfortable with using the shortened forename instead of the formal Abraham he was using before he confessed to being Jewish.

"Nope, not yet. And I had at least four phone calls from associates of Baruch Weiss who said they didn't know who George Foley was. Why they bothered phoning in the first place, I'll never know. Waste of police time, that is."

"Well, it looks like we have conclusive proof that the user of the playhouse is a vagrant. We'll need to analyze the trainers, but it certainly looks final."

The phone rang on Colin's desk. The switchboard WPC said, "It's Ms. Jakober for you, sir."

"Wow, talk about telepathy." Peter winked at him and sat on the edge of Colin's desk to listen.

Colin glared at him and took the call. Her cheerful American accent lifted his spirits.

"Hi, there, guys. How's it going? I'm having a wonderful time here in downtown London seeing all the sights. It's certainly different from Golders Green."

"Um, yes, I suppose it is," Colin said.

"Any news on the Hardman case? I thought I oughta touch base and see how things are."

Colin filled her in on all the latest news, talking about Shake without mentioning that he was Jewish, just that he was someone he had known in his youth. Leora was quiet until he had finished, not interrupting or offering any comments. He almost thought she had gone off-line, until she spoke again.

"I don't know who George Foley is, but I am really pleased you have made progress. I just don't see what his motive is in taking Josh, though."

"No, that's the mystery part. He seems to be a part of my past, not the Hardmans'. Unless, as I am surmising, he has no idea that he ever knew me, and our connection is a pure fluke and the Hardmans were his target. But for what reason?"

"Beats me," Leora said. "Has Don Hardman heard of George Foley?"

"No, but I am sure the Fox has changed his name again and again. The estate agent had the name Bill Valence listed at the address Avi Pincus found. But Bill Venice was the name Pincus picked up at that address from the offices of SmallNet. The name the Fox was using to send those e-mails."

"Well, what about Bill Venice?"

"I always wondered why he used that name, but now of course it's obvious. Bill equals William or Will, as he has used before, and Venice from *The Merchant of Venice,* the Shakespeare play first quoted in the e-mails sent to the Hardmans. It's definitely Shake."

"Seems quite a character, your Shake," Leora commented. What she did not, however, comment on, although she wondered about it, was his use of "Avi" rather than "Abraham" as he had used in the past. She filed it away in a corner of her mind to be dealt with later. Leora Jakober seldom missed a trick. It was the key to her success.

"Well, anyway, the estate agent, whatsisname, Mike Younger, said he had given the name Bill Valence. Not so different from Venice. Same initials, same overall look, but just different enough to confuse."

"I don't know how he will ever be found, in that case," Leora said.

"We do need you at some time to eliminate this vagrant Greg Phelps from the equation," Colin said. "He was found in the playhouse, stinking the place out and wearing ancient smelly trainers. I got well out of the way when he took them off."

Leora laughed. "Well, I guess I've seen a lot of the sights I want to see, so I'll come back to Golders Green soon, okay?"

"That would be great," Colin said, smiling into the phone.

"I don't think I'll stay with Ilana again," Leora said. "Useful though it was to get a feel for the case, I found it a bit stifling. I'm used to living alone. Are there any apartments in the area I can rent?"

"Flats? I have no idea. I am not an estate agent. But I do happen to know one," he added with a grin.

"Mike Younger?"

"Yeah. I bet he'll pull out all the stops to find you one now he knows we're cops."

"Might as well use the *protektzia* where we can, huh?" Leora grinned.

"That's right," Colin said easily.

Leora frowned. *Protektzia* was a very Jewish word, and Colin hadn't batted an eyelid. Maybe just living in the community had familiarized him with the expressions.

No, there was more to it than that. She knew enough about her non-Jewish colleagues in New York to confirm that. Despite living in a city with one of the largest Jewish populations in the world, they remained unfamiliar with the grass-roots idioms of Jewish streetspeak. Could a simple London *goyishe* copper not so ingrained with Jewish culture as the New Yorkers have learned the language from walking his beat?

No. There was something going on.

As if by telepathy, Colin said, "When I next see you, Leora, I have something rather big to tell you."

I bet you do, Leora thought. "Okay."

They said their goodbyes, and the connection was broken. Colin sat for a while, looking at the phone, wondering what her reaction would be to his bombshell.

Then the switchboard put another call through to him. It was from Avi Pincus in Jerusalem.

CHAPTER TWENTY-SIX

Avi listened carefully to everything Colin was telling him about the Fox. The policeman had called Avi back so he wouldn't have to pay for the international call. At the end of it, he said, "Well, the name George Foley doesn't ring any bells, but..."

"But?" Colin asked hopefully.

"Leave it with me. There's been something biting at me ever since that night I spent at SloppyNet. I haven't yet pinned it down, but I shall."

"You found the name and address of Bill Venice a.k.a. Shake a.k.a. Shakespeare a.k.a Bill Valence a.k.a. George Foley," Colin filled in. "Not that it got us anywhere because he had already moved on when we went to visit that house. He had left only a few days before we showed up. We were that close."

"And the real estate agent was of no help?"

"Well, his description of the guy he let the house to matched all the other descriptions we've had for the Fox. He didn't see any woman or kid with him, yet the guy had a Toys

R Us bag with him containing a color Gameboy, which, according to the Hardmans, was Josh's favorite toy or one he really wanted."

"All meaningless on its own, but adding up to a whole picture," Avi mused. "Look, as I said, let me have a think about this for a while. I'll call you back ASAP."

"Okay," Colin said and hung up. Avi Pincus was a decent sort of a bloke. Seemed very bright, too. He'd make a good detective.

Colin shook the thought off. Avi Pincus was living in Israel, busy with his own life. How many more cases like Josh Hardman was he likely to encounter? Not too many, he hoped. Meanwhile, Leora Jakober was on her way back to Golders Green.

Colin realized with a start that he hadn't thought about Lucy at all in the past few hours.

☼ ☼ ☼

Avi Pincus sat at his home computer and thought about SmallNet Ltd. and his brief stint there as an employee. He tried to order in his mind the sequence of events of that night. He remembered the boss, Renard Lukavac, and Marty who showed him the ropes. He remembered fixing the computers and then spending the dark, quiet hours looking for log files and eventually finding the caller log of a Mr. Bill Venice and the address from which he was calling. He remembered the cleaner, mopping silently around him until it was time for him to leave, too. He remembered calling Baruch in the wee small hours and telling him of his exciting find.

What was it that was niggling him? Something... Something just out of reach, tantalizing him like a carrot on a stick in front of a trotting donkey, keeping him moving ever forward.

Let's work this out. Methodically. Person by person, event by event.

Avi's brain hurt as he tried to remember.

☼ ☼ ☼

Colin found Leora Jakober a flat through a nervous Mike Younger, who thought it prudent to cooperate rather than make problems. The flat was small but nicely furnished and sunny, and Leora said this would do very nicely, thank you, and she would be fine. She moved around the apartment, arranging her personal things. Within a few moments, it looked homey, as if she had always lived there. Colin was impressed. She had her own electric kettle, which she had bought when she left the Hardmans, and offered him and Peter a cup of tea or coffee. They declined, saying they had to get back. Leora looked at Colin questioningly. She was very curious as to the "big thing" he was going to tell her about.

Colin remembered from his Orthodox roots that it was improper for him to be alone with Leora; he thought it might be a problem even if Peter was present, too, but he wasn't sure. Something was telling him, Keep your distance. Leave the door ajar. (He had.) Don't have coffee in her apartment.

He, who had spent time alone with Lucy, now would not spend time alone with Leora Jakober. Interesting, he said to himself. He felt himself drifting more toward his roots, but he was far, far from ready to take up the full gauntlet of his faith. And yet...

And yet.

Something was making him keep his distance from Leora Jakober.

All these thoughts happened in an instant, while she was looking at him expectantly.

"I do have things I need to talk to you about, Ms.

Jakober," he said, shocking even himself with the use of the proper form of address, "but maybe I can do so either at the station or over a cup of coffee and something to eat at a restaurant?"

Leora colored a touch. "Detective Inspector Sommers, are you inviting me out to dinner?"

Peter's mouth dropped as he witnessed this exchange.

She doesn't even know I am Jewish yet, Colin thought, bemused. Or maybe she does. Women are clever like that.

He coughed. "I'm just suggesting we might go somewhere and talk," he said. "And since we both have to eat, and since young Peter here has a wife and kids to go home to..." He stumbled. What was the matter with him? He wasn't a gauche young yeshivah student out on a *shidduch* for the first time. He was a man of the world. He had just broken up with a long-term girlfriend.

But he did not know how to talk to Leora Jakober. He was shuffling and coughing like a stupid schoolboy.

Leora helped him out of his misery. "Detective, as you say, we both have to eat, and I have nothing in this new apartment yet, so I would be delighted to join you for dinner at a kosher restaurant of your choice."

He grinned and named a local dairy restaurant. In truth, he had not bothered with eating kosher for so long — he barely knew the names of the local kosher establishments — but he passed this one almost every day, and it seemed bright and clean. It mattered a lot to him to take her to a nice place.

"I'll meet you there," Leora said. "It's only up the street, and I don't like being picked up from home. I'll see you there at seven."

"Why don't you like being fetched from home?" Colin asked, curious.

She smiled at him, her head on one side, like a bird. "Let's just say I value my independence too much."

Colin looked a bit crestfallen. "Okay, seven o'clock."

Outside, on their own, Peter turned to him. "Now, what the blazes was that all about exactly?"

"I've got to tell her I'm Jewish, so I am trying to find the right time and place to do it, that's all. She thinks I'm a nice gentile policeman."

Peter looked at him. "The heck she does, mate."

Colin felt extremely uncomfortable going into the kosher dairy restaurant with an uncovered head, so he compromised and put on a baseball cap. It made him look casual and cool, albeit not very dressed up.

He searched the crowded place for Leora. She was sitting at a corner table. He approached, feeling faintly ridiculous and exposed. In the Orthodox community of Golders Green, most people knew each other, and he was under considerable inquisitive scrutiny. He walked across the room to her table feeling as if he was on a catwalk and being examined minutely by everyone seated.

They ordered coffee, baked potatoes with toppings, and salad. After the potato, they drank their coffee and chatted easily, avoiding the subject of Josh Hardman. Finally, Colin realized the time had come.

"Okay, confession time, I guess," he said, flushing.

"I can hardly wait," she replied dryly.

"You aren't making this very easy for me, Leora," he complained irritably.

She put her hands up in a gesture of surrender. "Sorry. Go ahead. I'm listening."

"Well, I wanted to tell you that I am not quite the person

you think I am." He stopped.

She smiled. "How do you know what I think you are?"

He looked confused. "Well, I presume you think I am a nice, simple..."

"Okay, I'll make this easier for you. I guessed you must be Jewish a little while back. All righty? So now that we have that neatly out of the way, can we get on with our coffee?"

"How did you guess?"

"Oh, the way you used certain words so easily. It wasn't difficult."

"Ah. Right. Yes. Of course not."

She smiled again. "It takes a bit of getting used to. I had always imagined you a Godless creature."

"I was for a while," he confessed. "For ten years."

"So what happened to change your mind?"

"Josh Hardman."

"You mean the whole *frum* thing has its attraction for you again?"

"I thought it was the last thing on earth I'd want to get sucked back into. But it seems my soul had other ideas." He gave her a small, shamefaced smile. "And in fact, it was Shake who turned me off religion in the first place. Well, not exactly, but he was instrumental in giving me a push along the way."

"Ah, I did wonder what your connection with him was."

"I'll be honest with you, Leora. I'm not *frum* again yet. But I think I'm on the right train now."

"Colin, I know where you're coming from. I've ridden that train myself."

CHAPTER TWENTY-SEVEN

Sarah Grossberg opened her daughter's front door with her own key. She was extremely worried about her daughter. Since the disappearance, she had taken to coming around every day to do a sanity check on her, and so far the score was getting lower and lower. In Sarah's opinion anyway. She liked to find her daughter at home, working on her computer or cooking supper. Ilana knew this and so she returned from her search in the afternoon and made a supreme effort to wait it out until her mother had paid her daily visit, reassured herself that Ilana was okay for the moment, and left again. Soon after her departure, Ilana put on her pale trench coat, scarf, and PVC boots, the uniform she had adopted for her search, and left the house. She also added a pair of dark glasses, incongruous in the gray drizzle, but they served as a shield, protecting her (or so she thought) against the prying, pitying eyes of her community. The way a child playing peekaboo thinks herself invisible when her eyes are covered, so did Ilana feel invisible wearing her dark glasses. It made her feel safe on her safari to find her lost baby.

Sarah had heard about Ilana's search that morning. She was not a fool. Ilana would be out again this evening, calling her son's name on the streets of Golders Green. So she pretended to leave, parked her car out of sight, and waited to see her daughter exit the house wearing her bag lady outfit and dark glasses. She waited until Ilana was up the street, then, sighing deeply, she returned to her car and used her cell phone to call Don, who was still at the office.

"Don, you have to do something about Ilana," his mother-in-law began without preamble. "She is my daughter, and I love her dearly, but she is seriously in need of psychiatric help."

Don, who had this suggestion prodded at him at least half a dozen times that day from various sources, was not receptive.

"And what do you suggest I do exactly? Have her committed? Have her straitjacketed and sedated and declared insane for wanting to find her son?"

"After her search this morning, everyone is looking at me and feeling sorry for me for having a crazy daughter who wanders the streets."

Don lost his temper. "How about you stop feeling sorry for yourself and start thinking about how Ilana might be feeling right now?" he snapped. "She feels abandoned by the police and that woman from America who came over to supposedly help but who now seems to be gallivanting all over London enjoying the sights. She feels no one gives a hoot where her son is. Everyone has given up and assumed he's gone forever. Now tell me. How would you feel under such circumstances?"

There was a hurt silence. "There's no need to shout at me, Don."

"You're her mother and you love her, right? You want to do the best for her, right? Then for pity's sake, have pity. For compassion's sake, have a little compassion. You have many children; my wife and I only have Josh. Try to understand."

"I'm sorry," Sarah said. "You're right. But having a large family doesn't take away from the pain of losing one of them."

"No, but it sure does compensate a little," Don replied harshly. He was in no mood to be kind to his mother-in-law at this moment.

"I hate seeing her like this," Sarah went on, "and if Ilana is sick, then she needs help."

"She may not be sick. She may just be genuinely grieving and searching. And if she does need help, I for one will not deny her. But seeing that she has help and sending her to the funny farm are two very different propositions. For the present, at least, I will not entertain the idea."

"Well, I hope you know what you are doing, Don Hardman," Sarah sniffed, and she hung up, feeling aggrieved. When she repeated the conversation to her husband, Yaakov, he was horrified.

"I will not see my daughter put under the care of shrinks. If you aren't crazy when you go to see them, you are by the time you come out."

"That's an old-fashioned idea, Yaakov," Sarah scolded. "Nowadays psychiatric care is a much more exact science."

"I'm as worried about her as you are," Yaakov confessed, "but it's too soon to brand her a crazy woman."

Ilana, meanwhile, in her trench coat, scarf, dark glasses, and PVC boots, walked the streets of Golders Green, calling for her son. She walked up everyone's garden path, into the back gardens, turned every eight-year-old boy around so she could look at his face.

The faces she saw were never that of her son.

The Jewish residents were trying to be tolerant of her behavior, but it was difficult. The children had come in, frightened, saying that "a mad woman grabbed me and turned me around to look at me. It was scary!"

Once, one of the mothers, with a lower tolerance than most, had lost her cool and screamed, "Ilana Hardman! Leave my children alone! You're behaving like a *meshuganeh*! Go to the doctor and get some help!"

Ilana had stood there, looking at this mother. She had removed her dark glasses so the woman could not avoid direct eye contact. She gazed at her with a clear, level look.

"I just pray, Penina Rosenberg," Ilana said coolly, "that you never have to go through what I am going through. Remember the saying: 'Don't judge a person until you have walked a mile in his shoes.' How many miles have you walked in my shoes, Penina Rosenberg? How many inches?"

Penina looked away, ashamed.

Ilana gave her one more contemptuous glance and put back on her dark glasses, walking away without another word.

☼ ☼ ☼

Avi Pincus was busy on his computer. His wife, Hannah, had tried in vain to get him to help her bathe the kids. He was oblivious. She needed him to go down to the supermarket deep in the bowels of the Wolfson buildings just down the street from her Jerusalem house; he waved her away like a man in a swamp brushes off a fly.

Hannah was annoyed. "You and that computer might as well be married to each other for all the attention you give me and the kids," she snapped. "You have a wife and four children in case you had forgotten. I don't have live-in help. And I certainly don't have anyone old enough or strong enough to shlep our week's supply of groceries back from Wolfson."

"Fgmhh," Avi said, gazing intently at the screen, his fingers flying across the keyboard.

Hannah placed herself firmly in front of the monitor, blocking his view. She stood, hands on hips, waiting.

Avi looked up at his wife and sighed.

"Hannah, please, cut me some slack, just for now. I'm working on a way to find out who the Fox is."

"You have four children. You have responsibilities. My back hurts, and I cannot go down to the supermarket and carry all the stuff back."

"We have four children. At the moment, Hannah, Ilana and Don Hardman have none."

"I feel very very sorry for Ilana Hardman, but feeling sorry for her won't get my kids bathed or my groceries bought."

Their seven-year-old daughter, their firstborn, spoke up. "Ima, the supermarket delivers for an extra ten shekels."

Hannah glared at her.

Avi beamed at his daughter and held out a ten-shekel coin.

"Why, so they do. How clever of you to remember. Here's the money. Go."

"And I'm big enough to bathe the kids," said the worldly wise seven-year-old, even as she was aware that her mother was not pleased.

"Of course she is big enough! Seven-year-olds can run the household. Now go and let me get on with this."

Hannah shot her daughter and husband one last glare and stomped out. Avi waved the child out, too, much to her consternation.

Outside Avi's study, Hannah pounced.

"Shira, you should not interrupt when Daddy and I are

discussing something," she said disapprovingly.

The little girl was without guile. "I only told the truth, Ima. The supermarket does deliver, and I am big enough to bathe the little ones."

Hannah was taken aback by the clear logical argument.

"And, Ima," the child added, "I remember Josh. We played together sometimes when we were in kindergarten. I don't want him to be gone forever. I really hope Abba finds him."

Her mother gave her daughter a sad smile. "Shira, you have a good heart. Come, let's go to the supermarket. You can push the baby in his stroller."

Left alone, Avi concentrated on what he was doing. He was running words, names, and events through various programs to see if anything came up. So far, nothing had. He was still itching with the bite of that something he couldn't reach, that something that was connected to his night at SmallNet.

He stopped using the computer for a while; his head was spinning. He leaned back in his imitation-leather swivel chair and let it rock, closing his eyes.

And he remembered.

He arrived at the offices of SmallNet.

"Er, who is the boss here?"Avi called.

A tall man showed himself from behind a computer. "You're talking to him. I'm Renard Lukavac. Who are you?"

Avi thought about Renard Lukavac.

He spoke English with a strange accent. Not English. Foreign, but not continental. The name didn't match the accent. Renard Lukavac was an odd name for an Englishman.

Avi wondered what it meant.

He opened his eyes and logged on to his Internet service provider. Once on-line, he used Alta Vista, a free search engine on the Internet and typed "on-line translator." He hit the Enter key and waited. The search engine found 268 Web sites that contained these words, most of them irrelevant. He snorted in impatience and tried typing "on-line English language translator" to narrow down the search.

This time fifty-nine Web sites were found. With a bit of extra trawling, he found one that translated anything he keyed in into a number of different languages from and to English. This was it. Soon he would know what that name meant.

☼ ☼ ☼

Leora examined the sneakers taken from Greg Phelps with a clothespin over her nose. Some saliva swabs had also been taken from the vagrant, and now she could compare them with the DNA taken from the paper cups and other trace evidence from the playhouse. It didn't take her long to establish that Phelps had been in the playhouse; the prints matched, and so did the treads of the sneakers. The saliva matched the samples she had taken from the food containers.

"Phelps was the guy in the playhouse," she told Colin conclusively.

"Well, if the Fox is Shake, then Phelps certainly isn't Shake. He is at least twenty years older than Shake must be, and I imagine his knowledge of the classics could be written on the head of a pin. Besides, under all that grime he doesn't even look remotely like Shake."

"With your scientific method of identification and my way of analyzing things, we make a great team," Leora said. "Although I kind of prefer my own. Greg could have easily made himself look older with makeup and pretended to be brainless. And it doesn't take a great deal of time and effort to smell disgusting."

Colin looked at her. "You mean you think Greg Phelps could be Shake?"

Leora smiled indulgently. "No, I don't. But my reasons are scientific, not circumstantial. Through forensics, I have proven beyond a doubt that Phelps didn't abduct Josh and really was the wino in the playhouse."

"Unless he put on different feet, different shoes, and genetically modified his saliva," Colin deadpanned.

"Yeah, unless that," Leora said without even a twitch of a smile. Colin was impressed. Somehow, though it was patently obvious that she was brighter than he, it didn't matter. Even when she patronized him, as she often did, he didn't mind, because she did it in such a charming way. It would probably be difficult to find someone who could match Leora Jakober's intellect.

Why am I thinking like this? She would never consider me. I'm a boor, nonreligious, a plodding, deliberate, methodical worker with none of the fire and flash of her criminologist's brain about me. I would bore her inside of our first year of marriage. Even if I did become as religious as she wanted me to be, which I am unlikely to. So just forget about it.

"Now, of course, the question is, where is Shake now?" Leora voiced both their thoughts. "I'm good at analyzing evidence when I get it, but I'm lousy at seeking it out in the first place."

"That's my job," Colin asserted. "Right now I feel pretty useless."

"Not every case is solvable," Leora consoled him. "It's only in the movies and detective novels that the cops always find the bad guys. In real life, a lot of cases never get solved."

"Tell me about it," Colin said gloomily. "I'd just rather it wasn't this particular case that remained unsolved, that's all."

"Don't give up hope yet," Leora said. "There are still avenues open."

"I'm putting too much hope in Avi Pincus," Colin told her.

"Hey, he's a smart guy, and don't forget — we have God on our side, too."

"Good," said Colin grimly. "We need all the help we can get."

DAY TEN

CHAPTER TWENTY-EIGHT

It was eight in the morning in Israel. Avi had given up the night before and had gone back to his computer as soon as he had returned from shul. It was impossible to figure out what *Renard Lukavac* meant translated into English. He needed to figure out what language to ask the on-line translator to translate it from. He hoped he could do it before he had to leave for the office.

Avi spent another half-hour trying to figure it out, when the cleaning lady showed up and started bustling around his study, sloshing water on the floor and mopping it around. After a while, Avi looked up pointedly.

"Do you mind," he said loudly. "I am really busy here."

Devora, the cleaning lady, a Moroccan Jewess of a loud and typically Israeli uninhibited nature, smiled at him and peered at the computer screen.

"What you doing on there? I no understand nothing about computers. What's this you writing about?"

"I'm trying to find out what the name Renard Lukavac might mean," Avi replied, wishing she would leave.

"Oh, sure. *Renard* is French for 'fox.' But I don't know what *Lukavac* means."

"What?" He stared at her, openmouthed.

"*Renard* is 'fox' in French. Anyone who knows French knows that."

"How do you know French?"

She shrugged. "I'm Moroccan. Moroccans speak French."

"My gosh," Avi said. "I do believe you have solved a crime."

"Me?" Devora was preening, but Avi was already hard at work trying to figure out what *Lukavac* meant. Once he knew that *Renard* meant "fox," it took him the best part of five minutes to figure out that *Lukavac* was Croatian for "fox."

He sat back, staring at the on-line translator as if it would jump out and bite him.

The Fox had been his boss for a night. The Fox was Renard Lukavac, otherwise known as George Foley, playing mind games. He wouldn't have guessed in a million years that Avi Pincus would come to his offices and work for him for a night. He called himself Renard Lukavac just to see who would figure out who he really was.

Avi sat for a moment, relishing the feeling of victory.

George Foley, I have tracked you down like the sly fox you are. I have sniffed you out and hunted you, and I will bring you to your knees yet.

He picked up the telephone and put a call through to Colin Sommers.

"I've found him," Avi said, trying hard, and failing, to keep the note of exultation out of his voice. "I've found George Foley for you. I've found the Fox."

☼ ☼ ☼

"Come on, Peter, let's go see the Fox," Colin announced,

sliding into his bomber jacket. It was drizzling again. He had been running high on adrenaline ever since Avi Pincus's call, but he had forced himself to wait until office hours, when Foley was most likely to be there. Shake actually had an address, and Avi had seen him there only a few days ago. He could hardly wait to go and confront him himself.

"Shouldn't we inform Mrs. Hardman of developments first?"

Colin considered it for a moment. "No, I'd rather not get the woman all excited about something that might turn out to be a non-starter. From what I hear, she's in an extremely fragile emotional state at the moment, and we don't want to do anything precipitous."

Peter looked at him. "Fragile emotional state?"

Colin sighed. "The word going around the grapevine is that she's losing her marbles."

"Poor lady."

"If she thinks we are close to catching the Fox, and then nothing happens, it could tip her over the edge."

"Tell her husband then?"

"Not yet. Let's go see first."

Leora, who had just shown up and came in when she heard them talking about Ilana, said, "Ilana going bananas? No way. She's the most together person I know."

"Well, that's what I hear. The whole neighborhood is talking about her wandering the streets like a crazy person."

"I'm going to see her right now," Leora said firmly. "You go chase your foxes."

The two men left for West London and SmallNet. Leora set out at a brisk clip for the Hardman house. On the way, she thought about Colin and his revelation.

He had always struck her as a nice guy, and there had

been something there that hadn't added up; now it all made sense. The man was a lapsed Jew and just beginning to claw his way back. She herself was a *ba'alas teshuvah* and knew Colin faced a long, difficult journey ahead. He was coming at it from a different angle, having been religious, then abandoned it. Was he to be admired more than those who had never known how hard it was to be Orthodox? Colin knew the life. He had lived it and had thrown it away and was now searching in the garbage cans of his past for the remnants of what he had been to try and piece it back together again. She knew Colin was nowhere near ready to adopt the full mantle of Orthodox life again. But his earlier antithesis to all things *frum* had melted like snow in the face of the spring sun, and he was at least sympathetic to the people he had previously scorned.

Leora shook off her thoughts of Colin as she walked up the Hardmans' front path and rang their doorbell. Ilana answered. She looked like she had been expecting someone else. Leora, sharp as needles, perceived a "ready to receive mother" look on the older woman's face.

"Oh. It's you." Ilana did not look pleased to see her. She turned abruptly on her heel and walked into the kitchen, as if she didn't care whether Leora followed or not. Leora, crushed, followed meekly, not knowing how to reach out to her. She had not expected this reception.

In the kitchen, Ilana turned on her, eyes blazing.

"You came to England to find my son, tried for a few days, failed, and just went off sightseeing?"

Leora absorbed the attack like a punchball, hanging her head.

"How do you think that made me feel, Leora Jakober? Everyone giving up on me, just giving up, saying, 'Oh, well, we tried, it's too bad,' and just closing the case?"

"Absolutely awful," Leora acknowledged. "But they haven't closed the case, and I'm back. I only stayed away for a day, and now I'm back and I won't go away again till we find Josh."

"Yeah, right. Don't give me platitudes like that, please. I can't cope with it anymore, and I don't believe it either. You aren't going away until you find Josh? What rubbish are you talking? What if you never find him? Are you planning on staying here forever?"

Leora stared at her, not knowing how to answer.

"Exactly. I rest my case. Now do me a real kindness and get out of my life."

"Look, Ilana, please believe me. Things are happening. There have been developments in the case. Yes, things were stalemate, but the logjam has started moving again and we are very hopeful of a breakthrough."

"You sound like a politician," Ilana scorned. But the fire in her eyes flickered, and she looked willing to listen.

Leora tried to take the other woman's hands in her own. Ilana crossed her arms and tucked her hands protectively under her armpits. But she looked expectant.

"Okay. Colin wasn't going to tell you anything yet, because he felt that to do so might set you up for a fall. Also, well, the word has been going around that you aren't...too well."

"Crazy. Why don't you say it? I know what people have been saying. 'Poor Don Hardman, saddled with a crazy woman for a wife, gone demented because of her lost baby.' "

"Well, yeah," Leora said candidly. "That's what they've been saying more or less."

Ilana suddenly grinned. "At last. Someone willing to tell me the truth. Thank you, Leora Jakober, thank you very much." She unfolded her hands and took the other woman's.

"So long as you promise me always to be honest, I'll forgive you for abandoning me."

"Deal."

"Do *you* think I'm crazy?" Ilana held her gaze intently.

"The woman I am looking at right now isn't crazy."

Ilana almost sagged in relief. "But I walk the streets looking for my son," she pushed.

"Maybe that way you'll find him."

"I'm not crazy, I'm not," Ilana said, almost to herself.

The two women hugged.

"I have to pretend to my mother that I don't go out looking," Ilana told Leora.

"Most young women spend their adult lives hiding certain things from their mothers," Leora said with a grin.

"It sure is good to hear you say things like that," Ilana said. "I've been feeling like such a pariah. No one seems to understand how I feel. They daven and say *tehillim*, but if I want to do something practical, like look for Josh, I'm branded a madwoman."

"Maybe today I'll come walking with you," Leora suggested. "That will scotch the rumors."

Ilana looked at her delightedly. "Would you really come walking with me?"

"Just watch me," Leora said, teeth flashing. "Let's go."

Ilana made to put on her raincoat, boots, scarf, and sunglasses.

"Won't you dare go out without them?" Leora asked gently. She had heard about Ilana's "search uniform."

"It's raining."

Leora opened the front door. "No, see, it's stopped. The sun has come out."

And it had. Weakly, wetly, the sun gleamed on the rain

puddles, making them steam.

"It's turning into a lovely day again," Leora told her. "The rain seems over for now."

The rain clouds were moving swiftly away, as if swept by an unseen broom, revealing a freshly washed and polished pale blue sky behind.

It was a day of hope.

Ilana put away her raincoat, scarf, and boots, but clung to her sunglasses like a blanky.

"I still need these," she said shamefacedly.

"Okay," Leora smiled. "Let's go."

Together they walked off up the street, sisters in arms against a hostile and uncomprehending world.

☼ ☼ ☼

Colin and Peter drove up to the offices of SmallNet. Like Avi Pincus, they noticed the building at once, bristling as it was with antennae and cabling.

"See any foxes lurking about, Pete?" Colin asked.

They parked the car out of sight around the corner and went into the courtyard. The building looked silent.

"Well, I suppose Internet offices don't have too many reasons for having staff out of doors," Peter said lamely.

Colin, his face grim, went up to the doors and pushed. They were closed fast. He rang a small green bell situated on the wall at the side of the door. It echoed emptily inside.

"Give them a minute or two to answer," Peter said. "Maybe they need time to get off the dodgy chat rooms and come to the door."

"They should have a front-line receptionist or something," Colin said harshly.

"Dodgy Internet Providers R Us? You have to be kidding," Peter replied. "Probably two and a half staff members, an answering machine, and a dog. Actually, scratch the dog. It's too up-market."

They rang the bell a few more times and waited a good seven minutes. Then Peter walked round the side of the building, leaving Colin looking up and down to see if he could see anyone to ask.

"Forget it, Colin," Peter sighed, coming back.

"Why?"

"Come have a look-see."

Colin followed Peter round the side of the building where a small notice was affixed to a wall.

> SmallNet Ltd. has ceased trading. All its financial affairs are in the hands of Smith, Wilson & Co, Official Receivers. For further information, please phone Smith, Wilson & Co at...

They both stared at the notice, as if willing it to say something else. It remained stubbornly the same.

"I don't believe this," Colin spat. He pulled his cell phone out of his pocket and dialed the number on the notice.

"Hello? Ah, can I speak to one of the partners, please? It's Detective Inspector Colin Sommers of Golders Green CID regarding SmallNet. I understand you are the official receivers for that company."

He was put through to Mr. Smith.

"The managing director of SmallNet, a Mr. Renard Lukavac, I believe? I need to find him. Do you have an address for him?"

"Will you excuse me, Detective Inspector, if I sound pedantic, but I have to verify that you are, in fact, the police before I can drop confidentiality."

Colin flushed. In his anger and frustration he had acted precipitously.

"Call the Golders Green police station and ask them to give you Detective Inspector Sommers's cell phone number," he told Smith. "Will that confirm who I am?"

"That will be fine, thank you."

In a moment they were reconnected, and Mr. Smith was willing to divulge information.

"Now, where were we? Ah, right. Renard Lukavac. Yes, he is the registered managing director. However, as you have no doubt discovered, the company is in receivership and we are handling all the company books, trading having ceased."

"They can't have been trading for very long," Colin suggested.

"Not long. You know how these new Internet providers are. Easy come, easy go. Rise and fall like yo-yos. They think all they have to do is buy two dozen modems and a leased line and they're in business. They forget about all the maintenance and service they have to consider, too. When that hits, they cave in and go under. Happens a lot. The big fish will swallow the little fish and become even bigger. That's the cruel facts about commerce, especially with Internet companies, where smaller doesn't seem to be better."

Colin bore this lecture patiently, then asked if Mr. Smith had an address for Renard Lukavac. The address he received was the one they had visited, the one Avi Pincus had traced him to. The one now inhabited by Shoshanah and Jacob Segal.

"That's the only address you have?" Colin asked, heart sinking.

It was.

"Well, I presume you have a phone number, then? You

must be in touch with your client."

"Yes. I have a number, but he never answers. He does have a cell phone, though. Usually I leave a message on it, and he calls me right back. Here's the number."

Colin made note of the number.

"Mr. Smith," he said, "Mr. Lukavac is wanted in connection with a very serious crime. It is imperative that we contact him. If you do not have a better way of giving us a contact number than this, we will station a man in your offices until such time as he calls in. We will also monitor all your phone calls in and out of your office."

"What kind of serious crime?"

"Abduction of an eight-year-old boy."

Mr. Smith was suitably upset. "How tragic. I hate it when kids are involved. So messy, so unnecessary."

"All crime is messy and unnecessary. But child abduction really sticks in my craw, Mr. Smith, and I don't intend to let it lie until I find Josh Hardman. Your Mr. Lukavac has led us a merry dance for too long now, and I intend to run him to ground like the sly fox he is and have my hounds tear him to pieces. And I will do anything in my power to achieve that end. Is that clear?"

Peter stared at his partner as he spoke on his cell phone.

"Very clear, Detective Inspector. You may have your men do whatever they need to do in my offices, tap my phones, have someone monitoring all calls. I will cooperate fully with you on this investigation. I had no idea we were dealing with a child abductor, only a bankrupt Internet businessman."

"He probably set up the ISP specifically so he could send untraceable e-mails," Colin told him, "then closed down once the purpose had been served."

"I cannot imagine his motives," Mr. Smith told Colin.

"As yet we have no clear idea either. Anyway, thank you for cooperating. I will get things moving as fast as I can."

Colin took down the receivers' address and hung up. The connection broken, the two policemen looked at each other.

"I can't imagine any motive strong enough to want to abduct someone's only child," Peter said. "No matter how badly hurt I am by someone else, I wouldn't exact that kind of revenge."

"Nor can I imagine it," Colin said, "but we are dealing with a criminal mind here, not a mind like yours and mine. In Shake's warped, twisted brain, he thinks he is behaving perfectly logically. Criminals always justify their crimes to themselves; that's how they live with it. Whatever grievance, real or imagined, was done to Shake, he has worked it out that it deserves the kid being taken. He will never understand why it is wrong."

"Is this the Shake you remembered?"

"I hardly knew the bloke, but he certainly was odd," Colin replied. "Who can tell. I was a kid. I was only sixteen when I knew Shake." He sighed. "Well, not much point in hanging around here. Let's get that monitoring team set up at Smith and Wilson and a phone tap. Hopefully Shake will dial in and then we'll catch him. Or at least get a handle on him."

The two men disconsolately returned to their car. The Fox seemed always one step ahead. He seemed to have thought of every move they were going to make just before they made it. Fox by name and fox by nature, Colin thought as they drove despondently back to Golders Green.

Would they ever catch him? Would they ever find Josh Hardman?

CHAPTER TWENTY-NINE

Don Hardman sat in his office, unable to work. His face had grown thinner, more gaunt and haggard in the past ten days since Josh had been missing, and the strain was taking its toll. His hair, formerly so thick and dark and lustrous, was dull, lifeless, and dry, and he had found some gray hairs amid the dark. He was only in his early thirties, and right now he looked like an old man.

He had possibly lost his son forever. He had to come to terms with that now. The police seemed to be coming up against one brick wall after another. The Fox, whoever that was, was just too smart for them.

But whatever the anguish of losing his only child was, it was exacerbated by the double anguish of possibly losing his wife.

Ilana was a stranger to him these days. She seemed to live in a world of her own, in a plastic bubble where he couldn't reach her. Maybe this was her way of coping — turning into an ice queen and living on a frozen island where no one could touch her.

Don still felt pain. Don still cried. Don wanted his son back, but, even more, he wanted his wife back.

Mary Nolan brought him a cup of tea. "Please, Mr. Hardman, don't be like this. We all hate to see you like this."

He accepted the tea and tried to smile. "Sorry, Mary, I'll try not to be too despondent. How about doing some dictation?"

"Gladly," the faithful secretary said with a smile. "I'll get my book."

Before he could start dictating, the phone rang. Mary picked it up. From her expression as she listened, Don could tell that something was wrong. He sat up, heart pounding.

"Josh?"

She covered the mouthpiece. "No, not Josh. But I think you should listen to this man."

Don grabbed the phone. "Don Hardman here. Who is this?"

"Hi, there, Don." A soft, smooth, mid-Atlantic accent. "Remember me?"

"Should I?" But even as he said the words, doors were unlocking, memories beginning to trickle, the trickle becoming a flood.

"Well, I am flattered. After all the good times we had back home in Iowa, you've forgotten all about me. How charming."

"I haven't forgotten you, Gabriel. How could I?"

The voice on the other end laughed delightedly. "Your childhood tormentor, huh? Well, you sure got your revenge on me, didn't you?"

"Did I?"

"Yeah. Sure you did. You had a rich and powerful daddy, and you were religious. I was bothering you, making you doubt what you believed in. Why? Because my arguments made sense. So you told Daddy all about it, and Daddy saw to it that my father lost his job and all he had, including his name, and had to leave the country in disgrace."

"It wasn't like that, Gabriel, and you know it."

"Oh, wasn't it? I think it was, Don Hardman."

"No, I told my father about it because I needed his spiritual guidance to help me when you kept messing around with my head. It wasn't his fault or mine that your father was embezzling company funds. Your father was a crook, and what I told my dad had nothing to do with it. Dad found out about the missing funds totally independently from what I told him about you messing with my head."

Gabriel snorted. "Your daddy Big Boss, my daddy little man. The little man always loses, doesn't he, Don?"

"If he's a crook, sure he does. And rightly so."

Gabriel didn't seem to be listening. "What you told your father ended up with us having to leave the country in disgrace and coming to England like paupers, looking for anonymity and a new start. I vowed then that I would get my revenge on you, and I kept my word."

Don stopped. "What?"

Gabriel laughed. "Missing Josh, are you?" A snicker.

Don gasped. "You're the Fox?"

"But of course. I always said I'd get my revenge for the way you ruined my family. I've waited a long time for this. And I can tell you now, it's very, very satisfying."

"Gabriel. I didn't ruin your family. Your father did it all by himself by embezzling company funds over a long period. I didn't know he was doing that. How could I? I was only a child. I only knew that you were making my life a misery by tormenting me about being *frum*. So I told my dad and asked if he could do anything about it. He said he'd speak to the school principal. That was all. There is no connection between that and the fact that your dad chose to leave the country because of fraud. Please believe me." Don paused. "Where is your father now, by the way?"

"He committed suicide four years ago when he realized he would never escape his past. Jumped off a bridge in Devon."

"I'm really sorry to hear that," Don said sincerely, "but it has nothing at all to do with me and what happened between us, please believe me."

Gabriel let out a high-pitched, maniacal laugh. "What garbage you do talk, Don Hardman. Hahahahahahaha!"

At that moment, Don was certain that he was dealing with a madman. Gabriel was totally insane. But devilishly clever, too. He had to be to have escaped detection so far, to always be one step ahead of the chase.

Don decided that to plead his innocence was a waste of time. He tried another tack.

"Gabriel, please. Ilana is falling to pieces. If you don't care about me, for whatever reason, think about her. She hasn't done anything to you. She's an innocent party in all this. She only has the one child."

Another maniacal laugh. "I *know.* That's what made it all so perfect. It's not nearly as much fun if there are loads of kids. But to take the only kid, now that is seeeeeeeeeerious fun! Hahahahaha!"

"Gabriel, at least tell me. Is my son okay?"

"That's for me to know and for you to find out! Hahahahaha! It was good talking to you. I really enjoyed this little talk! 'Bye!"

And Gabriel hung up.

Don dialed 1471 immediately, which would provide him

caller ID if the caller hadn't blocked it.

Which, of course, he had.

Don phoned Colin next. The detective, who had been sitting miserably at his desk chewing a pencil and wondering what his next move might be, was shocked at what he heard.

"Gabriel who?"

"Gabriel Feiner. The bane of my whole life, so it seems. Did I say I wanted to confront my ghosts? Well, I just have, and my ghosts seem to be alive, kicking, and still intent on haunting me into an early grave."

"Gabriel Feiner. George Foley. The man plays mind games. Whatever name he chooses he has a dozen variations on it. If it's Shakespeare, he uses Bill Venice, Bill Valence..."

"Shakespeare, did you say?"

"Yes."

"Gabriel was a real classics fanatic. He used all kinds of weird quotes to prove his points. Particularly Shakespeare."

"Yeah, that's how he seemed to me, too. And how he signed his e-mails." Don didn't pick up on the fact that Gabriel was a part of Colin's past, too. He was far too troubled by the recent event. "If he calls again, try to keep him talking as long as you can. I'll get someone to set a tap on your line. And if Gabriel Feiner is his real name, I can have the Iowa PD do some checks on him locally."

"At least we have a motive," Don said, mostly to himself. "Twisted as it may be, to him it makes sense."

"His father was had up for fraud you say?"

"Not had up, if you mean arrested. My father found out, and the guy fled the country before the police could get to him. Apparently he committed suicide four years ago, so Gabriel just told me. He blames me for the whole thing. I was a kid, for heaven's sake. How can I have even known about the embezzlement, never mind done anything about it? All I wanted him to do was stop messing with my head because I was Orthodox."

Colin realized, by Don's use of the word *orthodox* that he didn't know yet.

"Mr. Hardman, there's something you should know. Everyone else does by now. I am Jewish and was very *frum* once, but went off."

"Gee," Don exhaled. "Wow."

"And when I said about how Gabriel had shown his classics side to me, too, I meant that I, too, had my head screwed around with by him in my youth. Only in my case his technique worked. He managed to plant just enough seeds of doubt in my admittedly fertile soil of a messed-up brain to grow into a complete turnoff from religion."

"I find this hard to take in," Don said.

"I never even knew his name," Colin went on. "To me he was just Shake. I told him he reminded me of Shakespeare, and he laughed and told me I could call him Shake. Did he ever call himself Shake to you?"

"No. I only ever knew him as Gabriel. Hey, does Leora Jakober know you're Jewish?"

"Yup."

"What'd she say?"

"She didn't say much actually. She knew already. Women's intuition or something."

The two men were silent for a while.

"Well," Colin said finally, "I'm going to get a phone tap set up on your line in case he calls again. That's two phone taps. One for you, one for the official receivers. Apparently he has recently gone bankrupt."

"What should I tell Ilana?" Don asked.

"You know her state of mind better than I do," Colin told him.

"I wish I could get through to her."

"Maybe this news will help."

Don went straight home after the phone call to Colin. Work could wait; he needed to see Ilana. But when he got home, only Maria, the Filipino cleaner, was there. He found her in the kitchen, scrubbing the sink.

"Ilana, she go out with that American lady," Maria told him with a cheery smile. "She look happy."

"American lady? You mean Leora Jakober?"

"Yes, that's the lady."

"She's back?" Don was aware that he was grinning like an idiot.

"Yes, she back, and she seem to make Ilana very happy. I am so glad to see her smile."

"Well, that's great news!" Don exclaimed, still smiling broadly. And when the door opened soon after and a laughing pair of young women came into the house arm in arm, he felt a sense of relief that had nothing to do with his lost son, but everything to do with his lost wife.

"Leora! *Shalom aleichem*! It's good to see you," Don said warmly. "You seem to be the tonic my wife needed."

"I wanted to show the world that Ilana's walks were not the actions of a *meshugeneh*," Leora explained, "but that of a mother with a natural maternal desire to look for her child. And I think we achieved that aim today. People stopped looking at her sideways because I was with her. With us both calling out Josh's name, it gave the whole exercise more credibility. I drew the line at walking into people's backyards, though."

Ilana blushed. "Yes, I guess that was a bit over the top. No wonder people thought I was crazy. I don't think I will do that again."

"Way I look at it, Don," said Leora, throwing herself onto the nearest sofa, "this lady here can't sit at home all day waiting for the phone to ring. She'd definitely go crazy then. So these little walks, looking for Josh, however pointless you may think them, do have a point. They give her a purpose to her day. So why deny her?"

Ilana nodded and grinned. "We didn't find Josh, of course, but we had fun. I am so glad Leora is back."

Don worried about the "of course," as if she had come to accept Josh's disappearance.

"I have some news, as it happens," he said, and sat down to tell her about Gabriel Feiner. At the end of it, Ilana looked at him calmly, her eyes clear as pools.

"It all makes sense now. And even if it doesn't, at least we have a real person to think about."

"You don't think I caused Gabriel's father to commit suicide, do you?" Don asked. This aspect obviously was worrying him a great deal.

"No. You have nothing to blame yourself for. It just makes sense from Gabriel's point of view, however warped that might be."

"You never actually met him yourself, did you?" Leora asked Ilana.

"No. By the time I came to Iowa, Gabriel and his family had long gone. I almost feel as though I have met him, because Don talked about him so often. He obviously left his mark."

"And is still leaving it," Don said bitterly. "If that moron hurts my son even a little bit, I'll..." He clenched his fists angrily.

"Cool it, Don. It won't help anyhow. We're almost there

now, almost at his lair."

"Almost isn't good enough," Don said. "We could be almost there and never catch him, never find Josh. He might have..." He stopped. He couldn't say the words, couldn't even allow himself to think them, not with Ilana suddenly looking so happy and hopeful again. Later, when he was alone, he would allow himself to think about the possibility that Josh was no longer alive, that he had been dead almost from the beginning. To Don it seemed almost impossible that the world still held his son alive somewhere in it and he could not reach him. The ultimate revenge Gabriel had wanted, and had taken, was to deprive the family permanently of their child and then set them on a cruel wild goose chase, giving them hope that he was still alive. These thoughts had often chased around inside Don's head when he was alone, but he had never voiced them to anyone, except in prayer.

"They're setting up phone taps in your office and the receivers' offices," Leora told him. "All he has to do is call in and they'll trace him."

"If he stays on the phone long enough," Ilana said. "He probably knows exactly how long until they get a trace." She got up and began to pace. "At least things are happening again."

Don looked at her. She looked bright-eyed and alive, almost like the old Ilana. How could he deprive her of hope now? Soon enough it would be taken from her forever. Let her be happy a while longer, while she still had it.

Don found himself wondering if there was any way they could have another child. It had eluded them for the past eight years, but sometimes things just happened. God gives, God takes away, God gives again.

Where are you, Gabriel Feiner, you and your black, black soul? Where are you and what have you done with my son?

DAY ELEVEN

CHAPTER THIRTY

Colin had arranged for the monitoring of the two phone taps. This was not as simple as it seemed and required the approval of the Home Secretary, Jack Straw. With a bit of pull in the right places, this was achieved with the minimum of delay. He had a surveillance van with sophisticated equipment positioned between the two locations, monitoring all calls going in and out. A rookie called Mitch monitored the calls and sat in the van with a continuous supply of burgers, fries, and polystyrene cups of coffee and some paperback novels to help stave off the extreme boredom while nothing was happening.

"This has got to be the most boring job in the world," Mitch grumbled to Colin.

Colin glared at him. "You're a pain in the neck, but I have put in your complaint for you, and your grumbles were heard in high places."

"And what happened?" Mitch asked.

"You've got double pay for the time you do surveillance in the van. And since I, as your detective inspector, don't get double pay for any of this job, no matter how perfunctory or boring or routine it may be, you'd better not whine again, my friend, or you'll be complaining about something worse than boredom."

Mitch grinned at his superior officer. "Yeah, but for you this case has become kind of personal, hasn't it, guv?"

Colin looked down at Mitch as he sat surrounded by wires and machines in the van.

"Allow me to let you in on a little secret, Mitch," he said softly, leaning over. "To be a good copper, a really good copper, you have to allow your cases to become a little personal. You have to get involved, to care. Don't believe all that garbage they tell you at Police Academy about not taking your work home with you at the end of the day. About staying detached. You have to care about the people you are trying to help or you will never make a good copper, Mitch. Me, I've never met that kid in my life. I never knew the Hardmans before I went to see them the day their boy went missing. But to me, for a while at least, for the duration of this case, no matter how it turns out, for good or for bad, they're my family. They're more than just any old family; they're my kids, parents, sisters, brothers, everyone who ever mattered to me or ever will. Can you understand that?"

"Doesn't sound like the stuff they pushed at us in the academy," Mitch said, but nodded his comprehension all the same.

"It never is the same as when you're learning it. When you're actually doing the job, it's as different as you can imagine. You can't stay detached and be a good investigative copper. You have to care."

"From the goss in the canteen," Mitch ventured daringly, "they're saying there's more to it even than that. They're saying it's not like you to be so involved with the Jewish community. You used to avoid them like the plague."

"Never listen to canteen gossip, my lad. It will lead you into trouble with your superior officers. Now back to work."

Colin stepped off the van, leaving Mitch gazing after him with a grin.

☼ ☼ ☼

Since Leora's return to Golders Green two things had happened. First, she had taken to going with Ilana on her walks. Don approved of this highly. He felt that Leora kept his wife calm and prevented the walks from becoming too much like the meanderings of a crazy woman. Ilana no longer wore her "searching uniform," although she still clung to the sunglasses like a baby's comforter. She wore ordinary clothes according to the weather, but the trench coat, PVC boots, and head scarf were relegated to the back of the closet. This had the effect of lessening people's sense of wariness around her, of lowering their guard, making them accepting of her once more. Leora's presence helped even more to achieve this end. Her friendly, open approach chased away dark spidery shadows from the corners and let the sunshine in. Her bouncy auburn hair, gleaming in the sunlight, her broad smile with its perfect American dentistry, and her guileless green eyes invited trust and confidence from all who saw her. If that girl is with Ilana Hardman, she can't be as crazy as she looks.

That was the thought flowing freely around Golders Green when the two young women went out walking, searching for Josh. Leora Jakober was the perfect foil for Ilana; she set her off like a beautiful frame and reflected her inner turmoil as calm, like standing next to a shimmering pool of water might make one feel relaxed even if one wasn't.

The second thing that happened to Leora Jakober since

her return to Golders Green was that she had come to regard Colin Sommers with more than just academic or professional interest.

She did not understand this herself. Colin was, on paper at least, a combination of all the things she didn't like in a man. First, he was her intellectual inferior. Second, he wasn't nearly as far along the track toward Orthodoxy as she was. Indeed, he had been living as a virtual agnostic for the past ten years and was only now just beginning to reclaim some kind of acceptance of his religion and cultural heritage to the extent that Orthodox Jews were no longer objects of derision for him. Third, he was slow and methodical, plodding and deliberate, while she was quick, fleet in thought and movement, and tending toward harebrained, impulsive actions. And yet...

And yet.

There was something about Colin that she found unnervingly endearing. She knew that even with his first tentative steps toward returning to observance, he wasn't, at this point at least, someone suitable for a religious girl. But should he return, should he become a *ba'al teshuvah* — a real *ba'al teshuvah* in the classic sense of the word, not one who came from a secular background, but one who had erred, strayed, and repented — then perhaps...

With a slightly rueful grin she thought of her parents' reaction to someone like Colin with his background and profession. She knew they would disapprove. But then again, her parents disapproved of most things she was doing these days, except for her work. They were very proud of her being a leading criminologist. Her struggles to discover her roots, and her moving to "Black Hat Belt" Flatbush were a source of bemusement to them. They found it embarrassing that when she came to visit them, as she often did, she wouldn't drink so much as a cup of coffee made in their home, but brought her own food and drink. In recent conversations, they had intimated that they hoped she would soon "come to her senses." They regarded her religiosity as a sort of belated teenage phase to be outgrown and forgotten as soon as possible. Leora didn't even think they would approve of Colin in his nonreligious state. He wasn't high-flying enough for them, not a doctor or a lawyer.

Laughing at the thought of Colin meeting her parents, and laughing even more at her own imaginings, Leora put the idea out of her head.

Ilana, meanwhile, was preparing herself. She was getting ready for today's walk with Leora Jakober and the continued search for her lost child.

When Leora arrived that morning, Ilana was already waiting outside, impatient to begin. The morning was bright, but the sun was covered with high clouds.

"Come, I want to go out already. It's such a beautiful morning!"

Leora shot Ilana a glance, trying to assess her mood, but it was impossible to do so. She decided to take her at face value and looped an arm through Ilana's. They set off together up the street, as they always did, with maybe an extra dose of sisterhood this morning for some reason Leora couldn't fathom.

They walked up Golders Green Road as they had become used to doing, looking into shops and windows, walking into cafés and pizza parlors, looking for people who might have a small boy in tow. When they went down the side streets that led off Golders Green Road, where it was quieter and there were no stores or restaurants, only residential houses, they felt less inhibited and started calling his name.

People here were used to the two women calling out the

name of the child by now and no longer regarded it as strange or noise pollution, nor did they come out of their houses and tell them to be quiet. But, on the flip side, because they did not take much notice of it, the calling out for Josh had little or no impact anymore.

As they walked, Leora wondered about going back to New York. Ten days had passed since Josh had gone missing. She found it hard to believe he would be found alive. There would come a time, and it must come soon, when she would have to return home. Her leave of absence was almost over, and pressing cases awaited her. Josh Hardman would join the ranks of other vanished children who were never found, whose casebooks were left open but marked "unsolved." Leora wondered how she could break this to Ilana, who had come to rely on her so much. Leora wondered, too, if Ilana's very sanity depended on these walks with her and if the fragile thread that held the older woman to her sanity would snap if she said she had to go back to New York. This frightened her immensely; she had never experienced another person depending on her so much before.

Leora glanced at Ilana as these thoughts went through her head, and Ilana, on cue, smiled back and gave her arm a little squeeze. Leora's heart sank. How on earth will I do it? How on earth will I tell her the time has come to let go? To let *me* go?

They were halfway down one of the side streets, each lost in her own thoughts, when a young woman dashed past them, almost crashing into them, and vanished down an alley. Leora made as if to move on, but Ilana was frozen to the spot.

"That was Cindy, Leora. That was Cindy Wallis!"

CHAPTER THIRTY-ONE

"Are you sure?" Leora asked, gripping her friend's shoulders.

"As sure as I can be. I recognize her hair, and the jeans and training shoes she always wore. I'm pretty sure that's her."

Leora whipped out her cell phone and called Colin, even as she began walking very fast in the direction Cindy had taken.

"I think Cindy has been sighted," she said simply. "Running into an alleyway right in front of us."

"Follow her!" Colin yelled.

"I'm trying, but our reactions might have been a bit slow," Leora panted. The two women dashed into the alley. It had no turnings left or right. Cindy could only have gone straight onward. Luckily they were both wearing comfortable running shoes, so they ran swiftly and silently on rubber soles after their elusive quarry.

The alley emerged into another side street off Golders Green Road. They stood there, looking left and right. No sign of Cindy.

"Lost her." Leora sighed.

"She looked terrified," Ilana commented.

"Yes, she did, didn't she? As if a pack of wolves were after her."

"A pack of wolves, or a fox."

"I've an idea. It's a long shot, but it might just work." Leora began to walk swiftly up the side road into the main Golders Green Road. There she entered a hardware shop and spoke to the salesmen. She described the young woman they had just seen and asked if she had ever frequented the shop. No one seemed to remember her.

Leora repeated this in several more shops along the main street. It was not such a long shot as she had made out; Cindy's appearance set her apart from the usual shoppers.

In the Jewish-owned toyshop, they remembered her.

"Yes, a blonde young woman came in just the other day dressed like you say. Most of our customers are Jewish so I noticed her; she stood out."

"What did she buy?"

"She bought some Jewish storybooks and a flashlight. She asked me what would be suitable reading material for her nephew. Eight years old, she said. I must say, I did wonder how she managed to have a *frum* nephew when she didn't even look Jewish, never mind *frum*, but these things do happen."

"She didn't give any indication of where this nephew lived, did she?"

"No, but I noticed her for another reason besides her looks. Her demeanor. She kept looking over her shoulder as if someone were after her."

"We're getting somewhere," Leora said firmly, outside on the sidewalk again. "Not sure what. It's pretty clear that Cindy is in on this, in up to her neck and scared for her life."

They tried a few more stores. A kosher grocery salesgirl also recalled Cindy having been in and buying some candy bars, pot noodle meals, and snack foods.

"I asked her if she was an au pair," the Israeli salesgirl recalled, "because I told her she didn't need to pay so much money if she wasn't Jewish; kosher food costs much more. I remember her laughing and saying the food was for a little Jewish boy, a son of her friend. She seemed insulted at the idea that I thought she was an au pair."

"No indication of where this little Jewish boy lived?" Leora asked without much hope.

"No, but I don't think around here. I think maybe in town somewhere. She said that where they lived there were no kosher stores, so she had to come into Golders Green to shop. She was on foot, no car. We offered to help carry her bags to the car, and she said no thanks, she would be going back by tube. She carried a few bags and ran down that road to the tube station."

More luck in a local children's wear shop.

"Yes, I remember a blonde girl coming in a couple of days ago. She bought underwear, a pair of trousers, a sweater, and socks. All for age eight. I asked if she could bring the boy in to try them on, and she said she couldn't because he was sick. I did wonder at the time why, if he was sick, he needed clothes, but things are so busy in here that the thought just went clean out of my head. I get all kinds of strange requests every day."

They left the shop and stood forlornly on the pavement again.

"He was taken in his pajamas," Ilana recalled sorrowfully. "He needed clothes."

"Well, give Cindy her due. She got him clothes. She was trying to help him by the sound of it. I just wonder why she bought the clothes here rather than in town, where she would have been more anonymous. Probably since she was here anyhow, buying the kosher food, it made sense to get everything in one trip."

"I wonder if this was with or without the approval of the Fox," Ilana mused.

Leora related all this to Colin by cell phone. "No doubt Cindy is in on it. She's been in the Jewish area, buying things for the kid. She told the grocery store that there were no kosher stores where this so-called son of a friend was. Trouble is, this means he's out of the area. He could be absolutely anywhere in London or even the country." Leora sounded panicky at the thought.

"No, he's in London somewhere, almost certainly. You said Cindy went off with the bags to the tube station. But where? Where?"

"Ilana and I will keep on looking and asking," Leora said.

"I'll get some of my best men to have a look round Golders Green to see if they can pick up any clues about Cindy," Colin said, "but I think Josh, and the Fox, are somewhere else entirely."

"She was here this morning, that's for sure," Ilana said as they resumed their walking.

They walked around the area several times. No more shops remembered seeing the young blonde woman. They asked everyone they met in the street if they had come across her. One or two vaguely remembered seeing someone in the area who answered her description, but they would have probably said yes to anything.

They walked around the back streets again and down the alley they had last seen Cindy. The alley, thick with nettles and bushes, made it hard to pass through. It was the kind of place parents warned their children about.

"Horrid place," Ilana said with a shudder. "I hear there have been attacks in this alley. No one I know lets her kids use it as a shortcut."

They walked on. They no longer called out for Josh. They were looking for Cindy Wallis.

☼ ☼ ☼

Mitch sat in his van reading his paperback novels, eating vast quantities of junk food, and slowly turning into Jell-O from boredom. He wanted nothing more than to get out of this stuffy, airless van and go for a run. He felt cramped, listless, and stiff. The calls in and out of the official receivers and Intergraph's offices had been routine.

"I should get triple pay for this," he grumbled as he turned the pages of his paperback. What trash this was. Guaranteed to fry the brain.

"Hi, there. Could I please speak to Don Hardman," said the smooth, insidious mid-Atlantic voice that brought Mitch bolt upright and sharply focused. It was Gabriel. He was sure of it. The secretary put him through. Mitch could hear Don's labored breathing. He was nervous and afraid.

"Don! How are you? It's Gabriel."

"Gabriel...where's my son? What have you done with him? Please, I'll give you anything you want..."

"Oh, you're no fun at all," whined Gabriel. "You're like a mouse who refuses to run away from the cat, but just sits there waiting to be eaten. The cat likes to play with her victim before finally delivering the *coup de grâce*. Honestly, I thought you guys would be more clever than you have been at figuring out where Josh and I are. I have obviously overestimated your intelligence. Even that American criminologist hasn't managed to figure it out, huh?" Gabriel laughed insanely.

"How do you know about her?"

Only a few more seconds and I can get a trace, Mitch thought desperately.

"Never mind. I have to go now or they'll trace my call. Tell your detective friends to think a bit harder about me and what I represent, huh? " Another maniacal laugh and the connection was severed.

Mitch, unable to get the trace, pounded his fists helplessly against the desk in front of him and let out a shout.

Colin listened to the tape a few minutes later.

"He's playing mind games with us," he growled. "Maybe I've been thinking about this all the wrong way. Maybe I need to try and think like him. Obliquely. Laterally."

Colin's cell phone rang. He snapped it on and listened, barked a "thank you," and hung up. His face was grim.

"Feiner had told Hardman that his father committed suicide jumping off a bridge in Devon. I ran some checks with the local department there. Apparently there was no proof at all, but locals in the pub said a young man answering Gabriel Feiner's description was in the pub the evening following the suicide and got very drunk. Started boasting about having pushed his old man off the bridge. No one believed him, of course. They just thought it was the drink talking. Quiet sort of country village, you know the sort of place. No one pushes his old man off bridges down there. But a local bobby was drinking there, too, and he remembers the incident, and he remembers Gabriel Feiner. And the look in his eyes."

"Sheesh," Mitch said.

"Yeah. Seems we're looking for a murderer as well as an abductor. Not good news for the Hardmans."

"You going to tell 'em?"

Colin looked at him. "Would you?"

☼ ☼ ☼

An hour later, the local bobby Colin had dispatched to take another look round the local area was in that same alleyway, when he noticed a niche in the wall running along the side of it. The niche, only a few feet deep and about five feet along, was heavily overgrown with bushes and weeds. Its purpose was unclear. Probably there had originally been a back door to one of the houses leading off it and it had later been bricked up.

The bobby noticed it because a shoe was sticking out of the bushes. And the shoes had a foot attached to it. And a leg attached to the foot.

The bobby was very young and rather inexperienced. He had never found a dead body before, but he certainly knew one when he saw one. As he radioed for help, Ilana and Leora came back into the alley and saw the shoe. It was a white running shoe, and the leg was denim-clad.

Leora clutched Ilana. "Don't look. I think it's Cindy."

"Oh, no!" Ilana was compelled to look.

"Stand back, ladies, please. This is a crime scene," the young bobby said, full of self-importance. "The area will be cordoned off soon."

"I am working with Detective Inspector Sommers," Leora informed him, showing him her ID. "I'm a forensic criminologist. Please stand back, Constable."

The young policeman flushed, but he knew his place, his moment of glory over.

Leora crouched by the body of the young woman.

"Is it Cindy? Is it?" Ilana sobbed.

Leora looked up with a grim expression.

"Yes. Cindy is dead. And at first examination anyway, it looks like murder."

Ilana began to scream. She had suddenly realized what the implications were for her son.

CHAPTER THIRTY-TWO

The post-mortem examination had borne out Leora's preliminary findings. Cindy had been murdered by persons unknown. Ilana was under sedation again now that she realized she was dealing with a murderer.

Leora and Colin sat in his office.

"That poor, poor girl," Leora sighed. "She was only trying to help Josh a bit, to make his captivity a little easier. Buying him clothes and kosher food. Obviously she overstepped some unwritten boundary in Gabriel's eyes. We had better find Josh fast, Colin. With Cindy gone, things are going to get much harder for him."

"If it isn't already too late," Colin added grimly. They both sat in silence for a while, then he spoke again. "He said to Hardman, 'Tell your detective friends to think a bit harder about me and what I represent.' I think we had better work on that a little, you and me."

He got out a piece of paper for each of them. They both started doodling.

"Brainstorm. Write down everything Gabriel Feiner represents to you," he suggested to Leora.

"Okay."

She wrote: *Kidnapper, abductor, killer, patricide.*

He wrote: *Antireligious, mind-twisted, bigoted, warped, insane, criminal, dangerous.*

They looked at each other's papers.

"Hmm. Not much help there. Let's try writing other things about him, not just the negative."

"I can't think of anything but negative right now," Leora said.

"We have to. Remember, we are thinking of it from his viewpoint, not ours. He thinks he has right on his side, for whatever twisted reasoning. Try to put yourself into the mind of the Fox and imagine how you would regard yourself then."

"Okay."

This time she wrote: *Computer geek, Internet whiz, supernerd, hacker.*

He wrote: *Classics aficionado, Shakespeare expert, poet.*

They exchanged papers.

"There's a link here somewhere. There has to be. I can't see it right now, but somewhere, inside all this, there's a link."

"A link between computers and Shakespeare?"

"Somewhere."

"Hardly. Computers weren't invented when Shakespeare had his day."

"I know. But...something..."

They sat staring at the two pieces of paper. Outside it was growing dark. Leora was afraid that Josh, if not already dead, had little chance of survival without Cindy's help. She stared hard at the pieces of paper, willing them to speak to her.

Colin went to the computer on his desk and sat looking at it. It had a number of icons for all the different programs he could access. His computer in the office was on a permanent link to the Internet; he had no need to dial in to a provider. Sitting there for a moment, he brought up a browser. Netscape Navigator. He looked at it. Its icon both on his desktop and on the browser itself was a ship's wheel. He closed Netscape and brought up Microsoft Internet Explorer. Its icon was a blue *e* with a swirl around it. But when it was open, in the top right-hand corner of the browser, just for a moment, he saw it. Then it was gone and replaced with the Microsoft Windows icon.

The icon for the Internet was always a planet. A spinning earth, sometimes interlaced by a web, to show the intricacies of the World Wide Web.

"Leora," he said, "the Internet, it's always shown as a spinning globe, isn't it?"

"Yes. Why?"

He swiveled on his chair to look at her. "I think I know where he is holding Josh."

"What? How? Where?"

Without another word, Colin used the browser to open a search engine and typed a few quick keystrokes.

"Here we are. Look."

She looked. "Oh, my gosh."

The page was entitled, "Shakespeare's Globe."

"The Globe Theater," she breathed.

They read on, breathless.

The original Globe opened in 1599, burned down in 1613, was immediately rebuilt. It was closed in 1642 and torn down in 1644. Now, two hundred yards from its original site, after almost four hundred years, Shakespeare's Globe has been opened to the public again: the rebuilt playhouse was officially inaugurated by Her Majesty the Queen on Thursday, 12 June 1997. Its opening season ran from 29 June to 21 September 1997, and every summer it now offers performances of plays by Shakespeare and his contemporaries on the type of stage they were written for, many in authentic costumes.

"He has him there. I know it."

"There's a map," Leora said. And there was. "The wonders of the Internet," she commented.

"Okay. I'm going to get a squad ready. Snipers. The lot. We aren't taking any chances with this joker. Come on."

Colin told Peter to inform the Hardmans of developments. Don wanted to come along, even though Ilana was too sedated to be coherent, but he was firmly told to stay away.

"The man is dangerous, Mr. Hardman," Colin told him. "We'll be in constant touch. I will let you know by cell phone what is happening. But it would be foolhardy for you to come along. He has already murdered at least once, probably twice."

"Twice? Who? I mean besides Cindy Wallis."

"Seems his father's death might not have been a suicide."

"*Oy vey.*"

"You stay home and look after Mrs. Hardman."

"Yes, okay. But please keep us informed."

"I will," Colin promised. He broke the connection and began making preparations to sneak into the Globe Theater. He had never been there in his life, despite being a born-and-bred Londoner. This was not unusual; many locals hadn't even seen the most popular London sights, being too wrapped up in their own lives.

The Globe looks, feels, and sounds different from other London theaters. The theater is a circular, open-air structure. The three covered galleries seat a thousand people, and six or seven hundred people stand in the yard around the stage. This makes it the third largest theater auditorium in London, yet it comes over primarily as intimate. The stage is roofed.

Performances used to take place in daylight. There is little or no scenery; drapes, hangings, and furniture adorn the stage and set the scene. Music and sound effects (a cannon can be fired or bells sounded in the attic) are live and part of the performance.

Since the last performance began at 7:30 P.M., Colin knew that by ten-thirty the theater would be empty and dark. That's when he chose to make his stealthy appearance there and look for Josh.

"I'm coming with you," Leora said firmly. "Wild horses couldn't keep me away."

"And I always avoid clichés like the plague," Colin deadpanned.

Leora laughed aloud. It was good to find things to laugh about, even at moments of high tension like these. It made them feel that they were still alive, that normal red blood coursed through their veins and there was life despite Josh. Or was that after Josh? Leora sent up a small, shivery prayer.

Then there was the matter of Colin's chosen outfit for the night's activities. He was wearing dark sweats, black sneakers, and a black baseball cap.

"Colin, you look like a cat burglar," Leora remarked.

"Very amusing, I'm sure," Colin said, but a corner of his mouth twitched.

"If you're hoping to look inconspicuous..." Leora was suddenly seized by giggles and couldn't stop.

"You'll have to dress in dark clothes, too," he said. "We'll stop at your flat on the way. I'll wait in the car while you change."

"What about my hair? It's far too bright, and I don't own any hats." Colin rummaged in a drawer and brought out a balaclava helmet knitted in black wool.

"You have to be kidding," she said, holding the knitted hat with its face piece revealing only her eyes and mouth. "I'll look like an IRA terrorist."

"That's an order," Colin bossed. "Like you said, your red hair will stand out a mile in the dimmest lamplight."

She laughed and pulled the knitted helmet over her head and face. "Stand out a mile? I've heard about big hair, but this is ridiculous!"

Colin grinned and left her to go brief the squad.

☼ ☼ ☼

At the Hardmans', Ilana came out of her drug-induced stupor and became very restless. She questioned Don over and over about what would happen that night, but Don could not answer, for he did not know himself. He began to pace, his palms clammy, his heart pounding uncomfortably. Ilana, in turn, was pale and trembling.

"Come into the garden with me for a little walk, Ilana," Don suggested. "It's cool and fresh out there."

Outside, it was dark and quiet, with hardly any noises from the nearby main road. Golders Green was not downtown London; there was little or no night life here, just a few pubs that closed at eleven, some kosher pizza parlors, coffee houses, and grocery stores, all of which were now closed. A few die-hards were abroad, walking. Ilana, shivering like a kitten in the rain, stood in her garden, listening to the quiet of the night. He, too, was very afraid, but dared not show it; his wife needed a rock, not a slender sapling threatening to bend and snap.

"Oh, Don," she murmured as they walked around the garden. "Oh, Don, I'm so scared."

He was longing to say, "Me too, hon," but he could not, for her sake. He just said, "Shh, have *bitachon*, have faith. Hashem is watching over us. Can't you feel it?"

She breathed in the sweetness of a thousand night flowers, lilacs and night stock and roses. She breathed in a thousand people's prayers and wishes and dreams. She breathed in all the longing of every mother for her child since Chavah in the Garden of Eden when her sons had destroyed each other. She breathed in the yearning of Sarah for a child and her joy when she had Yitzchak. She breathed in the craving of Rachel for sons when her sister gave birth to six. She breathed in the sisterhood of every woman in her holy ancestry who had longed for children, some of whom had been cruelly robbed of them before seeing them become men and women. Would she ever see Josh at his bar mitzvah, in a new suit and hat, or see Don lead him under his *chuppah* to some young, pale girl with doe-dark eyes and a ready smile? Her thoughts projected forward, floating like silver streamers, carrying her like winged angels on their backs.

"I am so restless. I can't imagine what is happening. I don't want to think..."

"You can do it. Let's sit on the patio wall and say some *tehillim* together. Then we can talk about all the nice things we remember about Josh."

Ilana visibly relaxed as first they prayed together, drawing strength from each other, and after, as they talked in low voices, remembering his babyhood, his first attempts at crawling, his first shaky steps on his first birthday...

"Do you remember when he started tearing up your books, the ones on low shelves, Don?"

"Yes, the little brat. How annoyed I was, finding him standing there, ripping my *siddurim* and other books apart. He was all of fifteen months and knew no better, but just gave me this sweet, innocent smile. How could I get angry at him when he looked at me like that? All dark curly hair and bright blue eyes with those long curly lashes women would die for."

"Don't say die for, Don," Ilana said. "Please, don't say die for."

CHAPTER THIRTY-THREE

Colin, Peter, and Leora stood in the yard of the Globe Theater, looking around. The manager had been most helpful, and snipers were situated in every tier of the gallery.

"Where could someone hide a small boy for a week or more?" Colin asked the manager.

"Well, there are lots of nooks and crannies in this theater," the manager said worriedly. He didn't like the idea of all those snipers with their night-sight rifles and goggles. The theater had not been rebuilt just to be blown apart again in a blast of gunfire.

"Do you have a new actor here, maybe?" Peter asked. "Someone called Gabriel Feiner?"

"Not to my knowledge, but then again, I'm only the manager, not the producer or director. I don't hire and fire actors."

Leora was looking at the attic above the stage. "What's up there?" she asked.

"The attic contains a huge room that is used both for storage of props and costumes and as a rehearsal and audition space."

"Nooks and crannies?"

"Well..."

"Let's go look. Come on."

They climbed the stairs to the attic and looked around. As the manager had said, it was one huge room full of props and costumes. There was also a trapdoor in the floor.

"What's that for?" Leora asked.

"It leads to the heavens ceiling on the stage. It is used for descents. And it's used for dropping various props, like flowers, drapes, leaves."

"There's no hiding place in that trap," Peter pointed out. The manager opened it, and they all peered through onto the dark stage.

Colin, meanwhile, had found a stepladder and was climbing up to the roof of the huge attic room. There was roof space above it. He looked carefully at the wooden slats that formed the ceiling.

"These slats have been moved and replaced," Colin said. "See, they are lighter than those around them. Is there anything up there?" he asked the manager.

"I don't know. Just the roof. No one goes up there."

"Until now," said a voice, and they all whirled. There, at the door to the attic room, stood a figure.

"Not so fast," said Gabriel Feiner. "Not so fast, my friends."

He wore dark corduroy pants and a bomber jacket in black leather. His long hair was scruffy; not curly and Regency, as they had been led to believe, but stringy and in bad need of a wash. It flew around his head in the night breeze that blew in suddenly like a bead curtain at an open front door. He held something long and dark under one arm. A rifle. They all stared at it, transfixed.

"Mr. Lukavac, what are you doing with that gun?" the manager asked tremulously.

"Mr. Lukavac?" asked Colin.

"This is Renard Lukavac, my new stagehand. He's been working on props and things these past ten days or so."

"Handy," Colin remarked, looking up at the roof space.

"I see I underestimated you, Detective Inspector Sommers," Gabriel said with a smirk.

"You did, indeed, Shake," Colin replied.

A puzzled look passed across Gabriel's face for an instant, like a shadow of cloud across the moon. "You the live one? The one with the *payos* and the black yarmulke?"

"The very same," Colin said.

"Wow, one of my success stories then."

"Hardly, since I am here to arrest you for murder and kidnaping."

" 'God hath given you one face, and you make yourselves another.' " He laughed at Colin's expression. "*Hamlet.*"

"I don't understand," the manager said. "Can you please explain, Detective Inspector?"

Gabriel turned to the theater manager. " 'Fair is foul, and foul is fair,' " he said, laughing. " 'Nothing is but what is not.' You should know, more than anyone. In the business of make-believe." He raised the gun and pointed it at them. "Anyway, who am I supposed to have murdered?"

"Cindy and your father, for starters. And we have yet to be convinced that Josh Hardman is alive."

" 'When our actions do not, our fears do make us traitors.' *Macbeth*, act four, scene two, line three. Hahahaha!" His eyes shone insanely.

"I'm going up there, Shake," Colin said.

Leora spoke up. "Gabriel, the Hardmans have suffered

enough. It's over and you know it. He's only a baby, Gabriel, a little kid. He has his whole future in front of him. Please don't take that from him."

" 'If you can look into the seeds of time and say which grain will grow and which will not, speak then to me.' *Macbeth*, act one, scene three," Gabriel said almost disinterestedly. Colin felt panic creeping up. The man was losing focus, sliding into a netherworld where they might not be able to reach him.

"Gabriel, listen to me," Colin said. "Whatever happened between your father and Hardman, it's all in the past now. Time has passed; it's all over. If you give back the kid, then things can be made easier for you..."

Gabriel, who was swaying slightly now, focused on Colin.

" 'Rogue, thou hast liv'd too long.... [Thou] appeareth nothing to me but a foul and pestilent congregation of vapors.' " He aimed the rifle.

"No!" Leora cried. "We have backup. You don't stand a chance! Give up your gun!"

" 'There's no more faith in thee than in a stewed prune.' *Henry V.*"

"I'm going up there, Gabriel," Colin said, and started up the stepladder.

In one movement, Gabriel leaped over and seized the theater manager, holding him as a shield in front of him. The plump little man shrieked and struggled like a stuck pig.

"Make one move up that ladder and he's dead!" Gabriel shrieked, and laughed maniacally.

"You're crazy if you think you will get away with this," Colin said. "We have two dozen snipers hidden in this theater. You'll be picked off like a monkey picks off a flea."

"What does anyone care if I get away with it or not?" Gabriel replied. "All you care about is the boy, and with that I hold the trump card and always will. Whether I walk free or rot in hell is of no interest whatever, is it? What comfort will it be to you if I die here tonight and the kid dies with me? Or is already dead?"

"Is he dead?" Leora couldn't help herself.

"Probably," Gabriel said casually. "He's been kind of neglected for a while. Cindy was good to him, but she overstepped the mark." He moved toward the door, carrying the manager in front of him. "This is my ticket to escape."

The manager shrieked again and struggled, but Gabriel had him in an iron grip. As they descended the stairs from the attic, floodlights were suddenly trained on the stage. Blinking in the light, Gabriel put one arm over his eyes and looked at the snipers in the gallery.

"Ah, the U.S. cavalry, I see," he said.

He turned his face and looked up the stairs at the policemen. "You didn't really think you'd catch me by tapping phone lines, did you?" he yelled. "Remember, I am the Internet Fox! The technological whiz who can outsmart a bunch of dumb policemen and any geek you throw at me!" He gave a sly smile. "Not bad, eh, mixing classics and the world of high technology? Most classics men wouldn't know one end of a computer from another, and most people who sit in front of a computer screen all day and night wouldn't know a quote from Shakespeare if it jumped up and bit them. But I am the Fox. Possessor of all knowledge, always able to outsmart my enemies! Hahahaha!"

"Yes, but I figured you out, didn't I, Gabriel? I caught the Fox in his lair," Colin said sardonically. "So you weren't so clever after all, were you? I figured out where you'd be, and I came after you."

Gabriel looked momentarily nonplused. Colin remembered learning somewhere that a true psychopath always believes he is more clever than his pursuers and can outsmart them. By pointing out that he hadn't, Colin managed to throw Gabriel off track.

"You don't have Josh," he said.

"Release the man now and put your hands on your head!" came a voice from a loudspeaker somewhere. Gabriel shook his head at the source of the voice.

"Sorry, mate, no can do. Gone too far to back out now, know what I mean?" He positioned himself cleverly now — behind a pillar with a thick square base so no snipers could pick him off from the galleries. He held the manager in front of him as a shield.

"Josh Hardman is *dead*!" Gabriel screamed at the policemen as they came toward him, and he laughed hysterically.

Then, from the back of the stage, a ghostly figure walked. Slow, deliberate steps. The tableau in front of him froze as he came into the floodlights. He seemed to be made of cobwebs and rotting garments. His skin seemed as pale as death. He began to quote.

" 'I am thy father's spirit, doom'd for a certain time to walk the night, and for the day confined to fast in fires, till the foul crimes done in my days of nature are burnt and purg'd away. But that I am forbid to tell the secrets of my prison house I could a tale unfold whose lightest word harrow up thy soul.' "

For a frozen moment, no one spoke. Then, "Hello, my son," said the specter.

Still holding the manager tightly, Gabriel took a step forward, peering incredulously at the apparition. His whole body shook with terror.

"Dad?"

"That's right, son. It's me," came the ghostly voice. "Your old dad. Aren't you glad to see me?"

"But...you're dead!"

"The dead come back to life when the occasion demands. To wreak vengeance."

"I saw you die!" Gabriel gibbered.

"That's because you pushed me. You pushed me off that bridge, Gabriel, into the swollen river, and you watched me being swept downstream until I died. You watched all of that."

"What are you doing here now?" Gabriel said shrilly, clutching the manager ever more tightly.

"I have come to wreak vengeance upon you. For my death, and for Josh Hardman, who never did you any harm."

"Don Hardman's father harmed you! His father snitched on you to the cops and you lost your job, and we all had to leave the country, sneaking away at night like thieves. I hated you for that, hated you for turning us into fugitives. But I hated Don Hardman's father even more for putting us there."

"He didn't put us there, son. I put us there by my stupidity and greed. Don's father just did what he had to do. He was my boss, after all."

"He could have kept quiet! He could have spoken to you or sacked you. He didn't have to report you! That's why I took Don Hardman's son. Payback time at last. I wanted him to suffer the way I suffered, being made to leave my home, my school, my country, and come to England. But you never quite made it here, did you, Dad? Fugitives we were and fugitives we remained. Always jumping at shadows, always looking over our shoulders. Well, I didn't want to live like that anymore."

"So you decided to kill me."

"Yes. And you're dead!" Gabriel screamed. He raised his rifle and pointed it.

The manager, squeaking and struggling like a pig, managed to slide down a bit so that his head wasn't in immediate line with his captor's.

It was the only moment.

The apparition pulled out a .22 automatic pistol from his pocket, aimed, and fired. A neat hole appeared right in the center of Gabriel's forehead.

" 'Et tu, Brute,' " murmured Gabriel, and he folded up, like a puppet whose puppeteer had released its strings. He collapsed on the stage and lay on his side, eyes staring, sightless forever.

The manager stood there, crying like a baby. "He seemed like such a nice man," he sobbed.

The ghost stood, looking at his smoking barrel and the dead man on the stage. Colin came forward and peered at him incredulously.

"I found this costume upstairs, thought it might come in handy," Peter White told his superior officer, struggling to rid himself of the cobwebby clothes. "With all that was going on, no one noticed that I hadn't come downstairs with everyone else. " He grinned at Colin. "Hey, aren't you impressed with my Shakespeare quotation? I crammed up on it the other night just in case."

Leora and Colin gawped in openmouthed admiration.

"Hidden talents. Mum always said I had hidden talents," Peter said modestly. Then he started to tremble from the shock of having taken another man's life, as the theater filled with police and paramedics. Sirens filled the night with sound as ambulances screeched to the front and ambulance men rushed in with stretchers. Colin patted Peter on the back and then turned to the paramedics.

"I'm going up. After all this, I want to be the one to go up."

Calmly he went back up to the attic and climbed the stepladder. He broke apart the wooden slats until there was a decent-sized opening and climbed in. Everyone waited with bated breath below.

The world waited. No one breathed.

Colin reappeared, carefully carrying a small, crumpled, silent figure. He climbed down the stepladder and laid him on the floor of the attic room. No one moved. Colin leaned closely toward the boy's still face, listening and feeling.

"He's breathing," Colin said.

Medics took over, and Josh was examined on the ground where they lay him. An oxygen mask was put over his face, and they wrapped him in a foil survival blanket.

"He's alive!" the medic said loudly so everyone could hear, and a cheer went up, a cheer that filled the whole theater. It was the standing ovation of all standing ovations. Everyone was rejoicing that Josh Hardman had been found alive.

Colin phoned the Hardmans from his cell phone.

"He's alive. I think he'll be okay," he said. "He's being attended to now." He turned to the ambulance men. "Which hospital are you taking him to?"

"Royal Free, Hampstead."

Colin repeated it to the Hardmans. "Go there. You can join your son there soon."

Leora leaned over to look at Josh. "Hi, Josh. I'm a friend of your mom's. My name is Leora Jakober."

His blue eyes fluttered, and he looked at Leora from above the oxygen mask.

"He's opened his eyes!" A joyful cry resounded in the auditorium.

Josh managed a very small smile. He held out a grubby, stained hand, and Leora gripped it tightly.

"How is he?" Leora asked the medic anxiously.

"Too early to tell. We need to examine him in hospital. At first glance, I would say he's dehydrated and malnourished, with a few bruises, but nothing time and good care and loving won't cure."

"Let's get him onto the stretcher and into hospital," said a kindly voice from above from the ambulance driver. "No bones broken, I gather?"

"None that we can ascertain at this juncture. Wiggle your arms and legs for us, young man, if you can manage it."

Josh wiggled obligingly and smiled weakly from behind the oxygen mask.

"Okay. Nothing seems broken. Let's move him carefully onto the stretcher. Do you want to come with him in the ambulance, miss?"

"If this young man doesn't mind, I'd like to very much," Leora said. "We'll meet your mom and dad at the hospital, okay?"

A nod, barely perceptible.

"We'll come and see you in hospital," Colin promised as the doors of the ambulance closed.

Once the ambulance had been driven off with Josh and Leora, Colin and Peter stood on the floodlit stage, alone.

"That poor kid," Colin said. "He looked barely alive. Do you think he'll be okay?"

"He'll pull through. I'll lay odds on it," Peter said.

Colin looked at Peter. "Are you all right?"

Peter smiled. "I'm fine. It's the first time I ever shot anyone. I suppose I'm a bit shaky. But I'll be all right."

"It had to be done. Gabriel was dangerous and about to

shoot. You do realize that you're the hero of the hour?"

"Well..." Peter spread his hands out modestly.

"If it hadn't been for your Hamlet's father act I don't know what we would have done. Our men just couldn't get a clean shot at him. Still, there'll have to be some kind of official fuss about the fact that you actually shot him dead. We aren't in New York, you know. We're supposed to arrest people, not shoot them." He looked at Peter again. "I won't be at all surprised if you make detective inspector after this."

Peter flushed, pleased. "I won't be able to order you around anymore. How shall I cope?"

They all laughed.

"Tape the whole scene," Colin ordered his men as they began putting up crime scene tape around the attic and stage. "I shall want to come back in daylight and have a good look inside that roof space. Don't want anyone touching a thing. Put someone on guard round the clock. I'll be back in the morning."

EPILOGUE

Ilana opened her eyes. She was lying on a folding cot in a hospital ward. At first, disoriented, she thought she might have had an accident. Why was she here? Was Don sick?

And then she remembered. Sitting up sharply, she saw Josh lying in a high-sided hospital bed. His eyes, with their impossibly long, dark lashes, so long they looked false, were closed. The lashes fanned his cheeks. She watched his chest rise and fall softly for a while, then reached out and touched his arm through the bars. Instantly the blue eyes opened and looked at her.

"Hello, Mummy." He smiled and the world was full of sun.

"Josh. Oh, Josh."

Don came in at that moment, dabbing his face with a towel. He had obviously been washing and shaving. He grinned broadly at his wife and son.

"How you feeling, son?"

"Wobbly." That said it all.

There was so much they were longing to ask him about

his ten days in captivity. So many thoughts had gone through their minds, so many terrifying what if's. But they had been told by the hospital psychologist on admission that he would probably need counseling for a while, and that the full story would emerge, but it must be allowed to emerge at its own pace and only when Josh was ready to tell it. In the meantime, their task was to give him unconditional love, to make sure he knew that his absence from home was not his fault and that no blame was laid at his door. How could she blame him for what happened? Ilana had protested to the psychologist, but the kindly woman had explained that this is how he might perceive it.

"Sometimes, even subconsciously, blame is apportioned to the blameless. Saying things like 'You shouldn't have played outside on your own,' 'You mustn't talk to strangers anymore' — all this sends a message to the abducted child that makes him feel he could have avoided the incident through his own actions and therefore is to blame for what occurred. All children have the right to a certain amount of safe freedom. We can't wrap our kids up in cotton wool twenty-four/seven. What happened to Josh was not his fault. He was at the mercy of a very determined psychopath, and it was unlikely any action, either yours or his, could have prevented the abduction."

It had been a long night. Josh was admitted and formalities attended to. Then he was gently bathed and examined by a pediatrician. He seemed to be, on the surface at least, suffering from no more than mild malnutrition and dehydration and a few bruises and lacerations that were probably due to struggles during his captivity rather than any deliberate act of violence. Once the examination was complete, the nasogastric tube was set up, much to Josh's consternation, and a high protein liquid feed sent down it. Another needle, in a vein in his hand, dripped glucose solution directly into his bloodstream. He was then tucked up in bed, and Ilana sat with him until almost dawn, watching his eyelids droop into sleep even as he looked at her.

"Why do I have to have all these tubes, Mummy? They hurt," he whispered.

"It's because you need feeding up and fluids," Ilana explained.

"I was always hungry and thirsty in the roof," he admitted. "They gave me things to eat and drink sometimes, but not always when I wanted. And it got so hot in there in the daytime."

Ilana could not imagine the place in which her son had been held prisoner and did not want to try.

"Did he die, Mummy?"

"Yes, he died. Now shush, darling, and go to sleep. He's dead and he won't bother you anymore."

As his eyelids closed, he murmured, "Cindy was nice sometimes. She gave me toys and kosher nosh, and Coca-Cola, even when he said I couldn't have any. Where is Cindy, Mummy?"

"Go to sleep, darling."

Now he regarded her sleepily. "I'm so glad you're here, Mummy. I missed you. I knew you must be so worried, but they wouldn't let me phone you to let you know I was okay. You always told me to phone you if I was out for longer than you said and let you know where I was. But he wouldn't let me. I'm sorry, Mummy. I didn't mean to be bad."

"Oh, Josh." Ilana's eyes filled with tears. "You weren't bad. You did nothing wrong. That bad man stopped you from phoning me, that's all. It wasn't your fault."

Josh nodded, satisfied, and drifted off again. Ilana was so tired. She thought she would never feel awake again. But her whole body was suffused with such joy and contentment that the feeling of tiredness was not negative, but a good feeling, like a manual laborer might feel after a job done well. She would face his questions about Cindy when she felt stronger.

Around her, the hospital, which never fully sleeps, was coming to life.

☼ ☼ ☼

At the theater, Leora was busy collecting evidence.

She found a small area of wasteland at the rear of the theater from which Gabriel had made his entrances and exits to the stage attic. This wasteland grew a profusion of wildflowers and entomological corpses and would prove to be, through forensic palynology, the source of the pollen spores and dead insects Leora had taken from Josh's windowsill. She had also found traces of this soil in the roof space where the Fox had kept Josh.

Colin crouched grimly at the entrance to the roof space, looking at Josh's prison. There was no window in the shelter. When the wooden slats were in place, only the spaces in-between allowed any air or daylight to come through. Artificial light was supplied by a low-voltage battery-charged lamp, which glowed dimly in a corner. Other than that, there was a stained mattress covered in a tartan blanket and a baby's potty. The darkness of the place, and the smell, was indescribable.

"Oh, here's something else," Colin said, reaching in with a gloved hand. He drew out a small oblong box. It was a color Gameboy.

"The poor kid," Leora said, bagging it. "He couldn't possibly have seen well enough in this light to play with it. And it was the only amusement he had in here."

"What a dreadful place to keep a kid," Peter said, shaking his head sadly.

"At least he had Cindy some of the time," Leora said. "From what I gather, she tried her best to be kind to him when Gabriel wasn't around. We'll have a lot more to hear about her from young Josh, no doubt, when he feels well enough to tell us about her."

"He can't know yet that she's dead," Peter pointed out.

"It doesn't bear thinking about, what it must have been like for him in here," Colin said finally, as the last pieces of evidence were bagged and taken away for analysis. "It would screw my head up for years, having to spend even a night here, never mind ten days. I hope with all my heart that Josh isn't too badly affected by the experience."

"Well, he will be getting counseling for a while, from what I understand," Leora told him. "And kids are much more resilient than adults."

Colin sighed and turned to the policemen working the scene. "Okay, men, tidy up here. We have all we need. Leora, Pete, let's go back to the station."

Peter sensed the two needed to talk, and when they were all back at the station, he made himself scarce.

Leora labeled and set up the samples ready for examination. Colin sat on the edge of the desk. "I suppose you'll have to go back to New York now," he said.

"Well, yeah, I do live there," she replied.

"Yes. I suppose you do."

There was a pause while she continued setting up the samples. Finally she sat down opposite him.

"Colin. Chaim. Whoever you are now..."

"Somewhere in-between, probably," he said with a small

smile. He was very nervous and feeling faintly ridiculous, but plowed on. "I have been thinking a lot about my religion recently, about all it meant to me and about all it means to me now. I can't go back to how I was before I lost my faith, Leora. I can only go forward."

"Yes, but *I* have to go back, Colin. I have to go back to New York. I live there. My parents live there. I have a job there."

"I know. But if I continue to go forward, would you ever consider...? I have a commitment to myself to keep kosher again, as far as I can manage it. Shabbos is difficult, but I am trying to find a way to work things out. If you give me a chance, Leora..."

"I will be very honest with you. As of this moment, you are not the type of guy I, or my family, would find suitable. For different reasons, of course. They wouldn't want me to go out with a cop. But their reasons don't bother me in the least. Mine do. You are still far from the level of *frumkeit* I'd be happy with."

"You're right. It would be ridiculous to imagine I would. I'm sorry, Leora. You go back to New York and forget I ever existed. "

"But, and I am making assumptions here," she went on as if he hadn't spoken, "I assume that now you are on the right road and that you will continue along that path and steadily become more and more *frum*."

He lifted his head and looked at her.

"Let's leave it like this," she said. "I am certain we will work on other cases together. As soon as I go back to New York, I'll put in for a transfer to London. I would like to live here and work with the Metropolitan Police. I feel I might be needed as a criminologist here; my skills are more in demand. I like the

British mentality, and I love London."

"You certainly helped solve the case." Then, tentatively, "Before you go back, would you do just one thing for me?"

"Sure, if I can."

"I'd like to go see my parents again. I've only been the once, and I only saw my mother then. I want to go back now. And I'd like you to come with me."

She smiled. "Yes, I'll do that with pleasure. I'd like to meet your parents. And maybe you'll come with me when I submit my application to work here? Put in a good word for me, maybe?"

"I might just manage to think of something nice to say," Colin agreed.